T0094851

The F**k It! List

Also by Melanie Cantor

Life & Other Happy Endings

The F**k It! List

Melanie Cantor

PENGUIN BOOKS

TRANSWORLD PUBLISHERS
Penguin Random House, One Embassy Gardens,
8 Viaduct Gardens, London SW11 7BW
www.penguin.co.uk

Transworld is part of the Penguin Random House group of companies
whose addresses can be found at global.penguinrandomhouse.com

First published in Great Britain in 2024 by Penguin Books
an imprint of Transworld Publishers

A CIP catalogue record for this book
is available from the British Library.

ISBN
9781529176797

Typeset in 10.75/14.5pt Sabon by Falcon Oast Graphic Art Ltd.
Printed and bound in Great Britain by Clays Ltd, Elcograf S.p.A.

The authorized representative in the EEA is Penguin Random House Ireland,
Morrison Chambers, 32 Nassau Street, Dublin D02 YH68.

Penguin Random House is committed to a sustainable
future for our business, our readers and our planet. This book
is made from Forest Stewardship Council® certified paper.

It takes a strong woman to stay by herself in a world where people will settle for anything just to say they have something.

The Queen's Gambit

Let there be spaces in your togetherness, And let the winds of the heavens dance between you. Love one another but make not a bond of love: let it rather be a moving sea between the shores of your souls . . . Sing and dance together and be joyous, but let each one of you be alone.

Khalil Gibran, *The Prophet*

PART ONE

PART ONE

1

October

Jack rushes out to the front porch, grabs the paper, comes back in and slams the door behind him.

There's a moment's silence. I roll onto my back, waiting, nervous.

'It's in!' he shouts. 'Massive photo. Huge spread! Bloody hell!'

'Woohoo!' I throw on my dressing-gown and hurtle down the stairs to find him standing at the bottom, waving the article at me, like a banner. 'Amazing,' I say, and we prance around the hallway doing a cross between an Irish jig and a Mexican wave.

He sits at the breakfast table, folds the paper in half, smoothing it, and props it up against the vase of lustrous dahlias he bought me last week 'just because'.

I start to rustle up scrambled eggs while he sips his espresso, deep into the read. It's way too early to be up on a Sunday morning. I'm in a semi-haze of sleep and excitement, wondering what he's said in the interview, how he's come across.

'Toast?'

'Sssh, let me finish.'

Two slices go into the toaster.

Finally, just as the eggs are coming together in soft

3

unctuous mounds, still slightly runny, exactly as he likes them, he says, 'I think I've nailed it.' He stretches out his arms and, yawning, places the newspaper on my side of the table. 'But I'd like to know what you think. How I come across. Be honest.'

'Sure,' I say, wondering if he really wants me to be honest. Does anyone in these situations? I hand him his plate and sit down opposite with mine.

'Thanks,' he says, picking up his fork. 'I'm so psyched. I might have to go for a run in a bit.'

I flip my hand, granting permission.

The first thing that strikes me is the photo. It's a great shot, his dark hair swept back from his forehead, white shirt, sleeves rolled up, tan twill trousers, brown polished brogues (I'd watched him diligently buffing them on the morning of the shoot, he was so anxious), leaning against one of the stunning grass-green-velvet chairs in the Brighton Hotel, the vintage mix of chandeliers, more jewel-coloured velvet furniture, slightly blurred, in the background.

He guzzles his eggs, butters the toast and munches, texting furiously, constantly checking his phone. 'Well?'

'It's good,' I say, taming his impatience.

It is. He sounds very impressive. An only child of long-dead parents, who left him no legacy, he dropped out of school at sixteen with no qualifications, no particular career in mind, and found himself working in hospitality. He started in hotel receptions and worked his way up through the ranks until he'd built a multi-million-pound business. Its much-discussed sale has led to this profile piece.

I look up at him. 'Wow, Jack!' I say.

'I know,' he says. 'It does feel a bit wow!'

I carry on reading, letting out a gasp of surprise. 'You

gave us a name check. That's another wow!' I reach out my hand, still reading, and he squeezes it.

'Why not? Baxter Settle's designs changed everything. You know that, baby.'

'Maybe. But it's always nice to be acknowledged in print.'

'I'll put it on a T-shirt,' he says.

The vibration of his phone resonates across the table. He picks it up and laughs with a swagger of contentment. 'Polly says we've had loads of positive response already. Amazing how quickly these things get around. And the *Telegraph* is pissed off, which is good. They messed us about. What did they expect?'

Polly is his publicist. She's done a great job. There have been quite a few news pieces about the sale of the group but this is his first major interview and getting him into the *Sunday Times* business section is a massive coup. Next weekend he's in the *Financial Times*, Lunch With. My father will be in his element. We're all in our element. This is the culmination of months of tension, highs and lows, Jack working all the hours God sends. But he's done it. He's about to sell for a crazy sum. Too many noughts for me to take in.

Yet it's not about the noughts. For me, the sale of Turner House Hotels marks an important leap forward in our relationship. If it's the culmination of Jack's dream, it's the beginning of mine.

Six years ago Marcus Baxter, my business partner, and I were invited to pitch for the redesign of a crumbling Cotswold estate. The client, a certain Jack Turner, was going to convert it into a twenty-six-bedroom hotel. There were various staff cottages in the grounds that needed remodelling too. Our company (@baxtersettle if you want to check us out on Instagram) was gaining in reputation as dynamic

5

maximalist interior designers and Jack was looking for exactly that vibe rather than the classic Cotswold chintz. It was an exciting brief. The aim was to establish a signature style for the growing number of hotels in his portfolio. We were up against three other companies. We wanted it badly. It would put us into a different league.

Marcus and I worked day and night, putting together an original pitch, working with textures and shapes, mixing vintage chandeliers with mid-century modern furniture, velvets and leathers, buttons and fringing, fabric wall-papers, creating specific zones for eating, drinking, relaxing and working. We made the bold suggestion that the estate lent itself to a membership club. We went through to the second round. Then the third. Pop the champagne corks! We won!

As for winning Jack, well, I used to groan when people said they immediately knew so-and-so was The One. It's such a cliché. But when I walked into Jack's glass-fronted office on the day of the first pitch, nervous as hell, I took one look at him and knew I'd become my own worst cliché. I don't know what it was, his energy, his confidence, his glossy dark hair set against his bright blue eyes, but it was intuitive. Jack says he felt exactly the same – a connection across a moodboard! Although he assured me Baxter Settle won the job on merit.

On our second date, I made it no secret that I was keen to start a family.

'Maybe it's a little bold to say so early on but I'm thirty-four, I've always wanted children, and I'm not going to waste my time dating someone who doesn't.'

He'd picked up my glass and stared into it. 'Jesus! What's in this? If that's what you say after one Negroni, I hate to think what happens after two.'

'I'll tell you how many,' I said, laughing slightly awkwardly.

'Girls or boys?'

'That much I leave to the universe.'

'And is the universe kind to you?'

'I hope so!'

He'd smiled and leaned back, taking me in, letting me wonder. 'Well, you won't be wasting your time with me,' he said. 'But you might have to wait a couple of years. I definitely want kids but I'm committed to building my business. Then I'll sell it. I don't want to be one of those absent fathers who's tied to his career. When I start a family I want to be around to enjoy it.'

If I was a little bit in love with him before he said that, now I was hooked.

Of course, one hotel led to another and another and, in my own way, I was complicit in allowing the time to pass. Marcus and I had the monopoly on the design of every newly acquired site. We stamped our signature on them, Turner House's signature. Our business was growing in tandem with the group. We were carried along on the crest of the Turner House wave.

If ever I became concerned about the passing of years, which at times I did, Jack would sit me down and assure me it would be fine. That I had to trust him, that the universe would be kind to us and show us when the time was right. As a firm believer in Fate, I went along with him, easily absorbed back into the job I loved.

But time flies and the universe can be frustrating. If I'd wanted a baby in my twenties, worried slightly in my thirties, now, at the point of turning forty, I was all too aware of the biological injustice of my depleting hormones.

But what's the point of regret? Everything needed to

7

happen to get us here. Patience has paid off, the universe has finally given us the nod, and I was not going to beat myself up about having waited too long. Besides, being anxious about getting pregnant was the best way to fail.

'You're really not going to miss it?' I say, reaching the final line. 'The group has been so much a part of your life.' In a way it defines him. It defines us.

'I'm over it,' he says. 'Like I said in the article, hospitality burns you out.' He looks up from his phone screen. 'Besides, we have other plans.'

'We do!'

I had come off the pill a few weeks ago. We were still taking precautions – well, let's be candid, on the one occasion we actually had sex he wore a condom – waiting for my body to be free of any hang-over hormones. And we were holding back until after next weekend to go 'commando' because Jack was throwing a lavish party to celebrate my fortieth birthday at the Cotswold estate, the place that marked the beginning of everything. There would be champagne and cocktails on tap. We had much to celebrate. We were hardly going to impose self-restraint while watching our friends live it up.

'It's incredible, Jack. You come over really well.' I give him a round of applause and he bows his head.

'Thank you. If you say that, I know it's true.' His phone buzzes. 'Ha! It's your dad. *Just finished reading the interview. So proud of you.*'

I stare into the middle distance.

'I'm sure he's proud of you too,' he says.

'I know. I know. I was just . . . I was imagining our family.' It comes out on the hoof. Not so long ago I had to be careful not to overload him with my yearning. Now it was a relief to express myself freely.

He smiles, leaning back. 'And what does our family look like?'

'Two boys and a girl. But maybe I'm being a bit over-ambitious.'

He stands up and moves behind me, shaking my shoulders like he's shaking sense into me. 'What's wrong with ambition?'

'Nothing. Except I'm forty.'

'Everyone should look as good as you at forty,' he says, collecting our plates and putting them into the dishwasher.

'It's not the outside I'm worried about.'

'Stop worrying,' he says. He opens the fridge door. 'How about a glass of champagne?'

'Now? Before you go on a run?'

'Yeah! Why not? Stop being so sensible. We should celebrate. We need to get in as much alcohol and waywardness before we have to become no-thanks-we're-trying-to-get-pregnant bores.' He's already taking out a bottle. We keep champagne flutes in the fridge too. Our life is run like a hotel mini-bar.

'I can't wait until we become those bores,' I say, and the cork pops ceremoniously.

He hands me a glass, the frosty condensation making it look even more delicious. 'To a golden future,' he says, as we clink.

'To family!' I grin.

2

'Two violet martinis, please, bartender! And make them filthy.' My voice is hoarse from shouting over the constant roar of music. Up comes Ella Henderson with Sigma, 'Glitterball'. 'Toooon,' I shout at no one.

I watch as the bartender throws a bottle into the air. He catches it behind his back, then balances it on his dragon-tattooed forearm. He pours the vodka from a height into a cocktail shaker, adds the dry vermouth, then tips in a measure of crème de violette liqueur and a dribble of some secret ingredient I can't catch. I clap his theatrical action, his toned biceps on full display as he performs a maraca shake.

'There you go, birthday woman!' he says, placing two sexy cut-glass coupes in front of me.

The bartender is Flynn, my business partner Marcus's husband. Actually, he's not really a bartender – he's a world-renowned mixologist, highly sought after (@internationalmanofmixtery – look him up!). He's heading the bar tonight especially for me. I can't impress on you enough how generous that is.

Bee joins me. 'Even the loos are gorgeous,' she says, adjusting her blue silk maxi skirt, picking up her cocktail.

I hold my glass to the light, admiring it like a perfect purple jewel. 'See this? My blood is like this right now. Pure alcohol.'

'Mine too.' She giggles.

We look into each other's eyes and sip.

We shudder simultaneously.

'Whoooooaaa! That's evil,' I say.

I catch Flynn's smile. 'Evil,' I mouth, and turn into the room, my elbows keeping me propped against the marble bar, feeling the evil do its work, watching the general blur of party: friends chatting, mingling, drinking, dancing to the music. I give a nod to the DJ. Jack has booked Sigma. Actual Sigma! Cam nods back, with a thumbs-up.

'Fuck forty!' I yell.

'Yeah,' says Bee. 'Fuck forty!' She's thirty-nine and divorced a year. She was the one who walked away although it didn't seem to make it any easier. Suddenly she was a single mother to their three-year-old son. She's coming out the other side now. She's Bee again.

I turn my face up to the three massive pink Murano glass chandeliers that adorn the ceiling, the gentle spray of light highlighting the original mouldings. We had to have the ceiling reinforced to take their weight but it was worth it. Just look at them! When Jack and I move, I'd like to think I could hang one in our living room. Not that I have any idea where or when we're moving but it will be a big property. There's no point in pretending otherwise. That's what he wants. I really don't care about size. I care about design. I care about being surrounded by beautiful things, and you don't need huge to have beautiful. But most of all I want to be surrounded by children.

Now that the business is sold, Jack says he wants to trade in classic cars, something he can do from home, as soon as he's released from his contract. I'll carry on working. That's the joy of what I do. Of co-owning the company. It accommodates babies. I can create my own crèche!

I turn to Bee. 'How about we sneak away for a cheeky

little fag? A final salute to my sybaritic lifestyle before I become an abstemious bore.'

'Sure,' she says. 'You got a secret stash?'

'Are you kidding me? Wouldn't dare.'

I scour the room, looking for a smoker. My closest friend from uni, Caro, is dancing full on with Jack's mate Vincent. He definitely smokes, but I can't ask him because of Jack. Jack hates me smoking and Vincent is not known for his discretion.

Marcus is a drinker, not a smoker.

My eyes go full circle . . . There he is! 'Rob will have some.'

I shimmy across the parquet floor, my sequined frock sparkling under the pearly pink light, performing an ostentatious twirl, first because I like the sparkle but mainly because I'm high on life and cocktails.

'Have I told you you look gorgeous?' shouts Victoria.

'Yeah, but keep saying it!' I reply, sidling up to her.

'This place is ridiculous!' she says. 'You guys are such bloody great designers. I want to live here!'

I kiss her exuberantly, then sweep up my hair, fanning it to air my hot neck, pulling it over my shoulder so that it tumbles in a mangled twist onto my sequined chest. 'Got any ciggies? Going outside for some fresh air.'

She turns to Gina, making a fag finger sign. Gina shakes her head, holding up her cocktail. 'Lychee martini. Bloody amazing,' she shouts. 'Great party, Daise! Loving the dress and the blingy eye make-up.'

I flutter my long eyelashes, the feeling of falsies unfamiliar. 'Thanks, girlfriend! Gotta twirl!'

Arms aloft, I continue my shimmy towards Rob, a man so tall he reliably has to duck under doorways. He's clutching a beer, chatting to Ruth and Phil, who smile at me in a way that tells me I must look very drunk indeed.

'Mind if I interrupt?' I say.

'Hey, birthday girl!' he says. 'Interrupt away!' He's wearing a pale blue cotton shirt, sleeves turned up just below the elbows. He looks hot, in both senses of the word.

I crane my neck. 'Got a couple of ciggies?' I say quietly. 'Don't tell Jack.'

'Where is the rich bastard? I'll tell him it's time he gave his girlfriend an allowance so she can buy her own cigarettes.'

'I don't need an allowance. I'm perfectly capable of buying my own. It's just that yours taste nicer and Jack disapproves.' I cast up a big smile. 'My neck's aching. Please? I'll never ask again.'

'Yes, you will.'

'Okay, you've got me there.'

'Who's the other one for?'

'Bee.' I flip my chin in her direction.

Rob's eyes zone in on her as she dances unselfconsciously around her handbag.

'You're in luck. I'm liking Bee.' He puffs out his chest, pulls a squished pack out of his back pocket and quickly slips me two. 'Happy birthday, Daise. Being old suits you!'

I mock-slap him and he fakes pain.

Hiding my winnings in my palm, I slink away, dancing solo, joined by mates as I go, feeling like the hostess with the mostest sharing my mostess!

I share a quick glimpse of my bounty with Bee. 'And Rob has the hots for you.'

She sniggers.

'We need to get outside,' I say, and she grapples for her handbag as I grab her free hand.

'Where's Jack?'

'No idea. The grounds are huge. We'll be fine.'

When I say Jack hates me smoking, I mean JACK HATES

13

ME SMOKING. Even if I take a single drag of someone else's cigarette, it always leads to some silly row.

Bee and I skip outside, hunting for a surreptitious spot. We used to hide behind pillar boxes. Now we hide in the lavish grounds of expensive hotels.

'You got a match?' I say.

'I thought you had.'

'Shit. Martini head.'

She makes a boss-eyed face. 'I'll go back. Wait here.'

The air is cool. October cool. Leaves on the ground, the scent of damp grass. There's no lighting, I'm relying on the glow from the hotel, the moonlight and the stars. Oh, the stars! It's a clear night, and there are endless constellations. I stare into the magical depths of the vast open sky, celebrating the unknowable nature of the universe because we don't need to know everything, do we? My heart surges. I feel the rush of happiness. Or alcohol. Or both.

The torchlight on Bee's phone marks her return, the silhouette of her shape looming as she approaches. She produces a disposable lighter from her pocket. It's a fluorescent green. 'Rob's.' She smiles, a triumphant twinkle in her eyes. 'He wanted to join us. I told him he'd be too conspicuous.'

'Told ya!' I say. I put my finger to my lips. 'Listen . . .' There's a distinct sound of activity somewhere close by.

Bee snorts. 'Someone's having fun,' she whispers, mimicking the grunting.

I giggle. 'And we think an illicit fag is being brave.'

We light up. I take a long, deep drag, the smoke pluming from my mouth casting a silver pall in the damp autumnal air. My hair must be twice its normal volume. Bee's curls have curls.

'God,' I whisper, relishing the bitterness as it hits the back of my throat. 'I miss this so much.'

'Listen!' says Bee, shushing. 'They're really getting into it now. Fancy a peek?'

'Ew, no. Let's move away. Leave them to it.'

'Oh, come on. It'll be a good fortieth-birthday-party anecdote.'

I snort. 'Okay, then. Quiet, though. I don't want to be responsible for coitus embarrassus.' We attempt to stifle our amusement, treading carefully, pushing aside the bushes, holding our breath as though that will make our drunken advance quieter.

'They're there, I think,' says Bee, bending to a crouch. I follow her lead.

'Let me get a little glimpse.' I angle away my cigarette, squeezing my head through a convenient gap in the bracken, my eyes now acclimatized to the darkness.

'Fuck!'

'What?' Bee's cheek is now abutting mine. 'Fuck!'

I launch my entire body through the gap, shedding sequins, oblivious to the thin tracks of blood running down my naked arms. 'What do you two think you're doing?'

Jack jumps up, grabbing his trousers. 'Oh, my God! Oh, my God!'

Polly covers her tits, which spill over her splayed fingers. 'Sorry sorry sorry.'

Jack stares. 'What the fuck, Daise?' he says. 'Are you smoking?'

3

Where are you? Can you meet me in Reception?

I stare at my phone, biting my thumb, anxious for my brother Doug's reply, walking in a never-ending circle of despair around my carry-on, my weekend attire hastily thrown in – agonizing when you're a tidy packer.

'I'll go and look for him,' says Bee.

'Don't leave me!'

My phone pings. *On my way.*

Doug appraises me in a kind of horrified disbelief, my face an unapologetic mess of mascara and glitter, false eyelashes ditched somewhere along the path, arms looking as though I've had a fight with the resident cat and lost.

'What's happened?'

'Are you drunk?'

'No. Are you?'

'I was. Can you take me to Mum and Dad's? Please don't ask why.'

He starts to ask, then reboots. 'Let me find Eve and collect our stuff.'

I hold up my carry-on. 'No pressure.'

Bee and I wait on one of the velvet banquettes in the empty atrium, my chin lodged on her shoulder, her arm around mine. The thrum of music reminds us that the party is continuing, unaware of my drama. I'm shivering with cold or shock, glad the reception desk is unmanned, praying no one will walk through so that I have to proffer an excuse for leaving my own party.

As soon as I see Doug descending the grand staircase, his wife, Eve, in her long satin slip dress, tiptoeing in towering stilettos, I dash to open the heavy front door.

'Fuck. We're trapped,' I say. I can only rattle it. 'What's happening to me?'

Bee gives me a hand.

'Wow,' says Doug. 'Couldn't you even wait for me to get to the door?'

We walk down the drive towards Doug's car, which feels like a million miles away, to the cornflake crunch of our feet across the gravel. Bee walks with me, holding my hand, both of us shivering now. We hug goodbye.

'If anyone asks, tell them the truth,' I say.

'You're sure?'

I shrug my shoulders. 'If you do it, it means I don't have to.'

'You take care of you,' she says. 'I'll check in tomorrow.'

I let go of her, the last piece of my raft, feeling myself float adrift, untethered to neither past nor future. Lost. I climb into the back of Doug's car. The party is over.

The fathomless dark is caught in Doug's headlights, as my mind fills in the blanks, revisiting that moment again and again.

'I caught Jack fucking Polly,' I say, breaking the silence. 'Don't tell Mum and Dad. They love him.'

'Oh, Daise! I'm so sorry,' says Doug. 'Who's Polly? Do you know her?'

'An evil bitch,' I say. 'And I've just got to know her a whole lot better.'

'Noted.'

'I knew it would be something like that,' says Eve.

17

'Great. Thanks.'

My mind punishes me with the thought of people's reactions. I can't bear to be seen as a victim.

Jack and Polly? At her fortieth. Poor Daisy. Poor Daisy. Poor Daisy.

I am a victim.

I want to die!

For the first time, the tears start to fall.

'Don't cry, Daise,' says Doug. 'Nothing's over yet.'

'Everything's over.'

My phone vibrates.

I think it's Jack. It's Marcus: *Bee just told us. Flynn and I are leaving now. We're here for you, Daise. We love you. Work can wait. Whatever it takes!*

I send back several heart emojis then dissolve into uncontrollable sobbing. Doug puts his foot down on the accelerator. Kill me now.

4

I don't want to bother my parents with my misery but where else is safe to go? I can't go back to my home in Chiswick. It's Jack's. Everything is Jack's. Except my business, which was sort of Jack's.

Not any more.

It's nearly three in the morning before we arrive. My mother is waiting by the door in a floral dressing-gown, bed-head wisps of grey hair around her crown, the rest tied back in a loose top knot. Brewster, our black Scottie, lolls at her side. They've probably been standing there for the full two hours since Doug phoned to say we were on our way. Ma looks exhausted and anxious. Brewster looks bored. I bury my face in her neck. She smells of moisturizer and the fading breath of her perfume. Estée. The one she's worn for ever. I used to think such loyalty was boring. Now I'm grateful for boring. There's something soothing about familiarity.

I bend down and hug Brewster, who licks my chin. I try not to recoil from his unfading breath. I pat the top of his head.

'What happened, darling?' says my mother.

'Something too awful,' I say. 'Don't be nice or I'll cry.'

'I'll make us a pot of tea.'

I cry.

5

My phone buzzes. 'Leave me alone, Jack.'

I'm exhausted. I didn't think it was possible to cry so much, so hard. I wake up feeling a most profound grief, mourning the loss of something I still can't comprehend. Something I thought was inviolable.

I dive deeper under my duvet cover, encasing myself in the safety of its pink and purple *My Little Pony*.

'It's the only bedding of yours I've got,' said my mother, as I crawled into my childhood bed. 'I gave everything else to charity.'

'It was my favourite of all time, Mum.'

'That's why I kept it.' She sighed.

Another buzz. 'Will you leave me alone!' I say. It has to be Jack. I stick a hand out, fumble around my bedside table, grab the phone and look at the screen. Of course it's him.

Daise, phone me back! Please!

PLEASE!

There is a long list of his unanswered texts.

Forgive me.

The biggest mistake of my life.

Come on, baby!

Please forgive me.

He's nothing if not persistent. He phones. When I don't pick up, in comes another text.

I miss you!

I miss waking up to you.

I miss your deep brown eyes and your mischievous smile.

I miss the thwack of your hair on my face when you roll over (lolz).

No lolz, Jack! No bants. Not funny! Nothing is funny any more.

You have to speak to me!

Please pick up.

I can't Jack! Don't you understand?

I want to but I can't.

There's a bunch of flowers. Huge. Pricey. I wish the amount he spent was relative to the size of his remorse, not his credit limit. There's a card. *Sorry, truly. I love YOU! Please call me, Jack x*

I tear it into teeny tiny pieces, like flakes of salt, as unpalatable as his words, and divide the massive bouquet into small sections, about to crush them, one by one, into the bin in my bedroom.

My mother walks in at just the wrong moment and stops me. 'You may never get flowers like that again. He's trying so hard. Why won't you give him a chance?'

My parents think I'm making a big mistake. It would be better to tell them exactly what happened but I can't. It's too personal. I prefer to allow them to wonder, then listen to their opinion and ignore it. They tell me that to err is human. Everyone deserves a second chance. He's a good man. What more could I possibly want?

A man who doesn't fuck other women in bushes.

Jack texts again. And again. I'm tempted to block him but that might be unnecessarily cruel. When they go low, we go high. Thanks, Michelle Obama.

The days feel like years. I hibernate in my room. During

the day I sleep, sleep, sleep, like a dormouse, then toss and turn at night, fretting and cursing, getting up to stare into the void outside my window, wondering what's the point.

Brewster barks. The doorbell rings. It's Doug, Eve and their two sons, Monty and Eddie. My heart sinks, which is churlish of me, bearing in mind they're here for me. But I'm not here. Not the real me. The me who loves birthdays and anniversaries and Christmas. But not Mother's Day. I hate Mother's Day. Even more now. The me who loves dressing up for any occasion, including going to the supermarket. The me who loves presents, giving and receiving.

I'm not that me.

That me has packed up and gone AWOL. That me has left all her beautiful clothes on a beach and waded into the sea. That me has left behind another me, one who wants to wallow in misery, maybe for the rest of her life.

I hear my mother greet Doug in a low, funereal voice. His reply is equally sotto voce. Grief is everywhere. It pervades the house, rupturing everything, and I am its epicentre. Doug won't have told her what happened. He will have continued my he-did-something-awful-to-me line. I can trust Doug. He's my wingman.

I listen. There are no other voices and we all know without doubt when those two boys have arrived. I think Doug must be on his own, which is kind of a relief. I don't have to put on a show for perfect Eve. I don't have to be happy Auntie Daisy for my nephews. No jazz hands. Maybe I can stay in my jammies. No supreme effort necessary because I can't even manage half-hearted effort.

I want to die. I want to die. I want to die. I won't die. I'm too cowardly. I'm a waste of unmoisturized, crying-for-attention skin.

I certainly don't want to be at the family's celebration

22

of my birthday today. It was meant to be happening in a smart London restaurant. With Jack. Yes, him. When will that name stop showing up?

'We'll do that another time,' says my father. 'Shame. I was looking forward to it.'

Me too, I think. Shit happens.

'I'll make you a birthday cake,' says my mother. 'With icing and all the trimmings. I haven't done that in years.' She rubs my back, like I'm a magic lamp and the genie of the real me, the one she likes, the one I like, might appear. 'It will be just as lovely celebrating at home,' she says, with admirable conviction.

In between wanting to die and knowing I won't, I accept I have to be considerate. I mustn't allow my misery to ruin everybody else's day. It may be my fortieth but that means something to my parents too. I guess it's a milestone for them as much as it is for me. The fact that it's the worst birthday of my life is my own misfortune.

I'm going to have to get up but I don't want to leave this room. I don't want people to see me. I don't want to have to make small-talk. I wish my birthday would go away. Take a rain check.

I lie back on my pillow and stare at the ceiling. I am familiar with every hairline crack in the plasterwork. I'd like this year to be over. Which is like wishing away the last of the best years of my life, except they've already become my worst years. Fuck forty! What an initiation.

I googled Polly yesterday. I'd been avoiding it, knowing I shouldn't. I was right. I shouldn't have. She's forty-three. He's gone for the older woman, which lands like an insult.

It wasn't meant to be like this. I was meant to be starting a family. Who cares how many children now? One would do! One would be lovely, thank you. Was I being greedy?

Was I being complacent and the universe decided to knock me off my pedestal? Honestly, universe. I would have been happy with one.

I shrug off the duvet and sit on the edge of the mattress, staring out at my room. The wallpaper hasn't aged well. A south-facing room means the big pink roses now look pallid, and the background is sepia-tinged. There's a Wham! poster, which hasn't aged well either but, then, neither has Wham!. Poor George.

I lumber over to my hideously pink dressing-table, with its gilt moulding, and stare at my face in the triptych mirror.

My eyes are pink. In triplicate. They're bloodshot and raw. Do I have to get dressed?

I look at the lone jeans and jumper hanging in my wardrobe. The clothes I arrived with, meant for the remainder of the Cotswolds weekend. I gave the sequined dress to my mother for the local charity shop where she volunteers even though I loved it. It was so beautiful. I felt amazing in it. And then I felt like a dope, all dressed up, thinking I was sexy, when all the time my partner thought I wasn't sexy enough, getting his kicks elsewhere. From an older woman! I really shouldn't have googled.

I go to slip the jeans off the hanger. Nope. Can't be bothered.

I pad softly down the stairs. There's a conversation going on in the kitchen. The voices are horribly audible. I hover.

'We've spoilt her,' says my father. 'She's always sailed through life but this time it's not going to be so easy. Who's out there waiting for a forty-year-old? What's she thinking?'

I'm thinking, Whatever happened to unconditional love? Aren't your parents meant to have your back?

'I wish I knew what happened,' says my mother. 'Did he say something awful to her, Doug? She can be very sensitive.'

'I don't know,' says Doug. 'But Daisy wouldn't be like this over nothing.'

Thanks, Doug.

'She can't go on hiding for ever, though,' says my father. 'She doesn't even come down for meals.'

'I'm down now,' I say.

They turn round, looking at me like I've gatecrashed my own party.

'Happy birthday, darling,' says my mother, startled grin, flushed face, hair coiffed, like we're going out.

'There she is!' says my father, folding his arms across his chest. He casts a look at my mother, his face confirming his shock at my bedraggled appearance.

I wish I could tell you what happened so you could really understand but a part of me is terrified you never will.

'Happy birthday, Daisy!' says my brother. Today he's wearing a perfectly pressed checked overshirt with jeans. His weekend casual look, acquired since Eve took charge of his wardrobe. It's fine. I just hate it. My objection is more an Eve thing. She and I don't get each other. We both tried really hard at the beginning. Then we gave up.

I smile. 'Thanks, Doug.'

He moves to kiss me. 'I haven't showered in a week,' I say, holding up my hand to keep him at bay. 'Where is everyone?'

Doug looks at the floor and shifts on his feet. 'It's one of Monty's friends' birthdays. They're at his party.' I realize they're being kept away from me. Like the sight of children might upset me more. Like being more upset is even possible.

'Oh,' I say. 'I was looking forward to seeing them.'

'Let's have tea,' says my father.

He and Doug sit down at the scrubbed-oak table, its

mug rings and wine stains all evidence of a family life well lived, a life I apparently sailed through. I hang back, trying to garner some positive energy, running my hand along the oak worktop.

This kitchen used to be my fun place. The place where I'd retreat with friends after a night out, talking into the early hours, not wanting the night to end, shooting the shit, solving the world's problems – okay, the world's boyfriend problems – sobering up with cups of tea, until bed was the only option.

'Sit down, Daisy,' says my mother. 'I want to add the finishing touches to your cake. It should be a surprise.'

I'm over surprises, I think, but I sit down obediently at the head of the table, the traditional place for the birthday celebrant. When you're eight, it feels pretty exciting and grown-up. When you're forty, not so much.

'Happy birthday to you . . .' The singing starts and in comes my mother holding the surprise. A massive chocolate cake with two candles, a four and a zero, my name inscribed in pink icing on the top. 'Blow!' they shout, and I blow, trying to look enthusiastic. They clap like I'm the only person who's ever blown out two candles simultaneously.

My mother passes me the cake slice. 'Make a wish!' and I shut my eyes, knife in hand. I wish I could start all over again. I wish I could turn left where I'd turned right. I wish, I wish, I wish.

My mother retrieves the knife.

'I don't think Ma trusts you,' laughs Doug, and she tuts.

She cuts the other side of the slice and places it on my plate.

'Looks amazing, Ma, thank you.'

She cuts huge wedges for the men and a thin sliver for herself. She sits down and looks proudly at her crew. 'How is it?'

'Delicious,' I say.

We sit in a fork-chinking serenade of silence until my father perks up. 'So, birthday girl, what are your plans?' He demolishes a huge chunk of cake, the pink icing catching on the tips of his moustache.

I throw him my if-looks-could-kill stare, wondering what he's expecting me to say.

'Chill, Daise,' says Doug.

My mother fiddles awkwardly, chopping the cake on her plate into small pieces. 'I think it's a bit dry,' she says.

'Any thoughts generally?' perseveres my father, which is kind of admirable, the words slightly diminished by his pink-tipped beaver, which no one can be bothered to mention.

'Marcus is biking over my laptop on Monday. We've got some pitches to work on.'

'Excellent,' says my mother.

'Yes, but what about Jack?' says my father.

'What about Jack?'

'What's the thinking?'

'It's over, Dad.'

He sips his whisky. My father doesn't do Lapsang Souchong. 'Are you sure? I mean, I think you're being a bit premature.'

My mind flashes back to the grunting and the sighing. To their flesh shining in the darkness, to my partner fucking a woman days – just days! – before we were due to start trying for a baby.

'Trust me, Dad. What he did was devastating.'

'You don't want to talk about it?' asks my mother.

'I can't.'

My father glances across at my mother. 'Am I allowed another slice of cake, please, Sally?'

'Don't you think it's dry? I think it's dry,' she says, placing another slice on his plate.

'If you're worried about my future,' I say, 'Marcus and I will build up our business again. We'll survive.'

'Marcus is a lovely man,' says my mother. 'But I'm worried about you, Daisy. You can't just bury your head in work. Your father and I have talked about this. We really think you ought at least to see Jack. Hear what he has to say. He was your future and now you're throwing it all away at the moment of his huge success.'

My jaw drops. 'What's his success got to do with it?'

'Everything,' says my father. 'Security.'

It occurs to me that my parents treat love in the same way that they treat sell-by dates. Unless it's growing green bits or stinks, they won't throw it out. For me, Jack stinks.

I lean back in my chair, folding my arms firmly across my chest. 'Where's the security in witnessing my partner fucking another woman in the bushes at my birthday party?' I say.

'Oh, my goodness,' says my mother, her hand swinging to her mouth.

My brother looks at me in an I-thought-you-weren't-going-to-say-anything way.

My father raises an eyebrow. Literally. His reaction is to raise an eyebrow.

'So now you know,' I say.

My mother coughs and takes a sip of water. 'I don't know that it needed quite that language, Daisy. You could have said it with a bit more elegance.'

I laugh. 'It really wasn't very elegant, I can assure you.'

'Oh dear!' says my mother. 'I have to admit that was not what I was expecting.'

'That's certainly poor play,' says my father.

That's the best I can expect of him.

'Maybe now you understand,' I say.

'Except . . .'

'Except what, Dad?'

'Well, come on . . . I mean. I'm not saying he deserves immediate redemption but he wouldn't be the first to . . . you know. And he's such a good guy. Don't you think he at least deserves the opportunity to explain?'

'I don't think finding the good guy with his pants down, on top of a naked woman warrants an explanation.'

'That's enough, Daisy,' says my mother. 'We get it.'

'You think?'

'We need to let Daisy work through this in her own way,' says Doug.

'Thank you, Doug,' I say, nodding at him appreciatively.

'Fine,' says my father. 'So while you're working through it, where are you going to live? You can't stay here indefinitely.'

My mother throws him a withering look. 'I love having you here,' she says.

'I love it too,' says my father, wiping his mouth with a 'Happy Birthday' paper napkin, which finally removes the pink icing. 'But she needs a plan.'

'I have a plan, Dad. I'm working on it . . . I'll find a rental.'

6

'Such a waste of money,' says my father.

'What else do you expect me to do?' I say, then interrupt myself: 'Actually, don't tell me, I already know.'

'So you're definite, then?' says Doug. 'It's over between you and Jack?'

'One hundred per cent.'

'In which case you might want to think about picking up your stuff – you know, from the house.'

I shrug, unbothered. I haven't given my stuff a second thought. It's hardly forefront. 'Sure,' I say. 'In my own time. Once I've found somewhere to live.'

Doug scratches his lazy Sunday five o'clock shadow. 'Hmm, not necessarily,' he says. 'I heard from Jack today. He says he's called and called but you won't respond. He says that if you're done, it's only right you take your stuff. He should be allowed to move on.'

I push back from the table. There's an anguished screech from the floor. 'Are you serious? It's been a week!' My hands clench in tandem with my stomach. 'Why should he be allowed to move on? Shouldn't that be my prerogative? Like, shouldn't I be the one to decide when I'm ready to move out? Doesn't he deserve to sit in my shit for as long as—'

'Daisy, please,' says my mother.

I throw her my best eye-roll. 'Come on, Doug! Where's the justice in that? Didn't you say that to him?'

'I'll be honest, Daise, it didn't occur to me.'

My mother sucks her teeth. My father coughs. Brewster's collar rattles as he scratches at his neck like he knows this is awkward.

'I'm so sorry,' says Doug. 'Please don't shoot the messenger.'

'We're all sorry,' says my mother.

'There is one very simple solution, Daise,' says my father.

'How many times, Dad?' I say. How many fucking times?

7

My mother pokes her head around my bedroom door. 'Feel like eating?'

'Not really.'

She walks in, followed by Brewster. She's holding a mug of soup, looking elegant like she's going out for the evening. I'm in that weird place where I don't want company but I don't want her to go out either. My whole life has become a paradox. I don't want to talk to her but I like knowing she's there.

'You look nice,' I say. 'Are you going out?'

Brewster jumps onto the bed and I stroke him absently.

'Hardly,' she says. 'Your father's in a whisky mist.'

'Sorry,' I say. 'If that's my fault. Anyway, you do look nice.'

'I've taken off my apron.'

'You should do that more often.'

'I hate to see you miserable.'

'It won't last for ever.'

'I'm worried you're making a mistake.'

'I'm not.'

She sits down on the bed and the smell of soup, pea I think, makes me want to retch. 'But you're forty, Daisy. You were about to try to get pregnant. Jack has always been lovely to you. Looked after you, been ridiculously generous. He was trying so hard to put things right. Those flowers. Just beautiful. I'm worried you might be jeopardizing everything you've ever wanted, a family, a good life, an incredible life, in fact. I mean who gets that opportunity?'

It's interesting to hear the prism through which she sees my relationship.

Over the week, my mother has been nothing but kind, trying to allow me my privacy, poking her head around my door, (a) to check I'm still alive, and (b) to feed me. She brings mugs of homemade soup and bowls of pasta. 'You can't sleep your life away. You really must eat,' she'll say, looking at the latest bowl of untouched food. 'These always did the trick when you were a child.'

'I'm not a child,' I mumble, childishly.

'You'll always be my baby.' She sighs.

All I can think is I used to be Jack's baby.

Sometimes she'll lie on the bed with me to catch a few moments of the old episodes of *CSI* I'm watching on my iPad, distracting myself with other people's misery.

Sometimes I'll rest my head on her bony shoulder, and she'll pat my arm, saying things like, 'It'll all be fine. Life sorts itself out. It's how life works.' I've waited for her to say, 'Plenty more fish,' but she never has, hoping my fishing days are over.

She puts down the pea soup. 'Look at Hillary Clinton,' she says, tilting her head. 'She never gave up on Bill.'

'And you think she's a good role model?'

'They're still together, aren't they?'

'But are they happy, Ma?' I say, ruffling Brewster's neck. 'Bill looks very thin.'

She lets out a long, defeated sigh. 'Jack loves you. It's plain to see. Do you not think he deserves a second chance?'

'I've moved on.'

She frowns, then casts me a look of suspicion. 'You've

met someone else, haven't you?' She says it like she's caught me and it's started to make sense.

I groan. 'I've not been outside the door, Ma! I'm not Rapunzel. He doesn't climb up my hair.'

'There are apps apparently. Marianne's daughter uses them all the time.'

'Good for Marianne's daughter, but I have not been exchanging loving messages with random men on apps. It couldn't be further from my thoughts.'

'Well, if it's over with Jack, maybe it should be in your thoughts. If you want a family, you can't afford to wait.'

'Thanks for the memo.'

'I'm just trying to be helpful.'

I lean back against the pillow. Brewster nudges my hand with his nose and I carry on stroking him. 'You can be helpful by offering your unconditional support and yet I feel Jack's the one who's getting it.'

'We love you, Daisy. We only want the best for you.'

'Then you have to trust that I know what I'm doing.'

She lets out another long sigh and gazes at me in a way best described as pitying. 'I think you're in the wrong place to know what you're doing,' she says. 'Your father and I want to help. We can be more objective.'

'Wanting me to go back to Jack is not helping. And you're far from objective.'

She stands up, despairing of me, this daughter with whom she's always been so close inhabiting a new persona beyond her reach.

'Do you want the soup?'

'No, thanks. Give it to Dad.'

'Can I at least offer you one piece of advice?'

'You can try.'

'Perhaps you should think about having a bath and

34

washing your hair,' she says, moving towards the door. 'This room is starting to stink.'

Brewster jumps off the bed and she closes the door behind them.

I sniff my armpits.

I hear myself say sorry.

8

'This room takes me back,' says Bee. 'I haven't been here since we were teenagers. It still smells of school uniform.' She laughs.

'It's me. I haven't washed,' I say. 'Can't be arsed. Maybe tomorrow.'

'Oh, girlfriend,' she says.

I play with the front of my hair. 'I'm thinking of cutting a fringe. What do you think?'

'Don't!' she says, 'That's a classic break-up cut. You'll only regret it. It took months for mine to grow back.'

We juggle with the tray of tea and leftover birthday cake, sitting side by side on top of the duvet. I'm still in my pyjamas.

'I like being looked down on by Wham!,' she says, licking the icing. 'It's as though time has stood still.'

'If only that were true.'

'George was too young. He didn't deserve to go like that.'

'We don't always get what we deserve.'

'Quite.'

I look at George Michael and wonder whether there was a sliding-doors moment that transformed his fate for ever. If things might have turned out differently if, say, he hadn't been caught in that Beverly Hills lav. Or for me if I'd never sneaked out to smoke that cigarette with Bee. I wonder whether ignorance is kind. Whether bliss is everything it's cracked up to be.

She finishes the cake. 'I won't be able to eat for a week now.'

'Don't be daft, Bee. You're not fat. I wish you'd stop thinking you are.'

'I have to be careful,' she says.

'We stopped being careful when Leonie died of anorexia.'

'Too many people die young.'

'I wish I could die young. I'm already too old.'

'Now who's being daft?' she says, slapping my shoulder. She brushes her hand down her green polo-neck sweater. 'Sorry. I'm dropping crumbs. Your duvet will feel like Camber Sands.'

'Let's go to Camber,' I say. 'Run away.'

She throws me a sympathetic smile. 'Trust me, I'd love to be Thelma to your Louise but Patrick does his quota of childcare and no more. He's pissed off that I asked him to have Will again today.' She does a whiny voice: '*I had him last weekend so you could go to Daisy's par-tee.*' She gives it the big eye-roll. 'Sometimes I think he only loves his son every other weekend.'

She plays with a strand of my hair, weaving it through her fingers. 'You could fry chips in this!'

'Thanks.'

'Mr Big called me by the way.'

I frown.

'Your friend Rob. We had sex that night.'

I raise one eyebrow. 'Everyone was at it, then.'

'I think I was in shock and he was there and . . .'

'I get it.'

'He's asked me out. I'm going on a sweet old-fashioned date.'

'That's great!' I exclaim, trying to rally genuine excitement for her because I'm genuinely excited for her. 'He's a good guy.'

She narrows her eyes at me. 'You don't mind, then?'

'Why would I?'

'I thought you might hate men.'

'I hate Jack. That's all.' I lie down and punch the pillow in an effort to find a soft spot for my head. 'He called Doug, by the way,' I say, turning on my side. 'Said I need to collect my stuff.' My heart revisits the wound. 'It's official. I'm being booted out.'

Bee looks down at me. 'Brutal! What's it been? A week!'

'I know!'

'Oh, Daise,' she says. She polishes off her tea, places the tray on the floor and lies down next to me. We jostle for a comfortable position. She rests her hand on my hip. 'I'm so sorry. But better it's done. You need to move on . . . and you need to get out of this room. It can't be good for you.'

I shoot her a look of disappointment. 'I know I do. I want to. But sorrow and grief don't end just because you've all had enough.'

'No one's had enough. Everyone just wants you to be happy.'

'I want to be happy!'

Bee tucks herself into my body. 'I know you do. Hey, hey, hey,' she says, tapping her shoulder. 'Put it there.'

She holds me as I sob quietly. 'I'm so sorry, Bee. I don't understand what's happening. Everyone's losing patience with me and yet they've all the patience in the world for Jack.'

'No, they haven't.'

I wipe my nose with an upward sweep of my hand. 'Honestly . . . they do.'

'Here,' she says, feeling behind her and grabbing a tissue from the faded fabric-covered box that matches the faded wallpaper.

I blow. 'My parents seem to think that even though Jack's the problem he's also the solution.'

'Did you tell them?'

'Everything. Told them exactly what we saw.'

We stare up at the ceiling, trying not to see what we saw.

'My mother suggested I be more Hillary Clinton.'

Bee looks at me, horrified. 'No way.'

'You're so lucky to have Will,' I say. 'That's the worst part about all this. Not only have I lost the man I love, who I thought loved me, but I don't know if I'll ever have a baby now. I think I've blown my chances.' She stares at me for a long, anguished time. 'You think I've blown them too, don't you?'

She grabs my shoulders. 'Absolutely not. I was just working out how to say this without it sounding like a platitude because it's not. You've not blown anything. Women are able to have babies later now. Plenty of women are pregnant in their forties.'

'Yeah, but they're in relationships.'

'Not necessarily. They're also having babies on their own. Through choice. I've met two at Will's crèche. Two! Out of ten of us! What does that tell you?'

'That they're brave!' She looks at me like she's agreeing. I swallow hard. Bee has inadvertently articulated one of my more absurd thoughts. 'To be honest, it has crossed my mind.'

Her eyes pop. Her tongue lodges between her teeth. 'What? Really? You'd do that?' She looks impressed.

I shrug. 'Probably not. It's just an idea that's occurred to me.'

She rolls into me. 'Well, if there's one person I know who could go solo it's you. You're the most together person I know.'

39

I reel back. 'Look at me! I'm a wreck!'

Her eyes widen. 'You're sad. Of course you're a wreck. But you won't be like this for ever. You've always wanted babies. This is a setback. But it's not over. Sperm donation. Why not?'

'It's expensive.'

'Okay, so you may not be a gazillionaire now but you're not broke.'

'I'm homeless.'

'Do you want a baby?'

'More than anything.'

'Then stop putting up barriers. Think about it. You're one of the lucky ones. You've always said you'd work from home or take the baby into the office. Marcus would be brilliant about it.'

'Everyone else would think it was a mad idea.'

'What do you care about everyone else? Honestly, I've been thinking about sperm donation for when I'm ready for a second child. If I don't meet someone.'

'Really? But you've met someone.'

'I have a date!'

'I don't even want to date. Ever again. And I'd love to think that sperm donation is the answer to a life of celibacy but still . . . it's no guarantee.'

Her jaw drops. 'Nothing is guaranteed when it comes to our ovaries. Where was the guarantee that you could have babies with Jack? He might fire blanks.'

I laugh at the thought. I picture Jack as Clint Eastwood wondering why the hell the other guy isn't keeling over. 'It's possible. But unlikely. The man is one lucky bastard.'

'He's not. He's lost you. His luck has just run out.'

9

I take my laptop and charger out of the DHL box that Marcus had carefully packed and couriered over. I read his note. 'It's fully charged. No pressure. I miss you x'.

It's me who's not fully charged. I wish I could plug myself in somewhere. How useful would that be? Or resort to happy pills. Just for a boost. But I can't. Not if I want to get pregnant. I can't afford to get hooked on the chemical buzz of happiness.

I place my laptop on the desk that sits neatly inside one of my wardrobes. My parents had it installed when I needed to be encouraged to work for my GCSEs. It's pretty basic but I thought it was the bee's knees back then.

I connect to the house Wi-Fi. The laptop cranks out an endless list of emails. I look at them wearily. I'll deal with them tomorrow. I have other work to do today.

I click on Google and go to type in 'sperm donation' yet somehow find myself typing 'Why do men cheat?' Links gradually appear, loads of them. I click on one. A list pops up.

He fell out of love,

He was feeling unappreciated,

There was a lack of commitment,

An overwhelming sexual desire,

And on and on, making it sound like it was ALL MY FAULT.

It's not hard to deduce that these sites are compiled by

men. Not hard, that is, if you're in the frame of mind that makes you google why men cheat.

Jack hasn't contacted me since Doug arranged to move out my stuff. He has an end date. His future is sorted. He's moved on from the *biggest mistake of my life* into living his best life with everything he ever wanted: money! He is rich beyond his wildest dreams but that much he deserves. He worked damn hard and he was clever, spotting a gap in the market for boutique hotels and renovating run-down estates that otherwise would have been left to ruin. And, yes, I played my part. But my hopes and aspirations were very different. And *the biggest mistake of his life* has left me with nothing.

But I'm not going to let him defeat me . . .

I open Facebook. I search the names of previous boyfriends. And up they pop. I check their status.

Max is *in a relationship*.

It appears that the Felix I knew is not on Facebook.

Oliver is *married*.

Michael is *married*.

I give up hoping for the traditional route. What was I even thinking?

I google 'sperm donation'.

The slow house Wi-Fi wearily brings up every site available from the UK to the US to Denmark.

The US sites are overwhelming, like a beauty parade. A dating app without the swipes. It's all too much.

I go to a UK site. Click 'donor search'. It invites me to find my perfect match. I can choose everything. Everything! Eye colour, hair colour, height. It's like ordering a takeaway. I'll have blue eyes, blond hair, with six foot on the side. It feels weird. Like the list I put together in my teenage diary about the man I wanted to marry: handsome, generous, good job but not a stockbroker – boring – (*I have no idea where that diary is any more but I hope Dad never finds it*), long hair probably blond. Those were the things I thought were important back when I was sixteen. Now all I want is some decent sperm.

The process is daunting. Working around the site is daunting. It would be so easy to be put off and maybe that's the intention. I take a deep breath and delve into the mechanics, wading through a raft of well-laid-out information, realizing that before I even get over the hurdle of choosing my donor's eye colour, I need to appoint a fertility clinic. Delivery is synced with the clinic. Written in bold is the instruction to place your order two weeks before you start treatment.

At least I'm ahead of the game.

I lean back in my chair, visualizing myself, manifesting the process. I'm going to do this. I can feel it. First, I need to find a place to live. Then I need to sort an appointment with my doctor to know I'm going down the right route. Picking the right clinic. Making the right choices. I close down the site.

I sit back in my childhood chair and fold my arms with determination. I'm going to be a solo mother.

A single mother of choice.

I have a purpose.

Damn you, Jack! Damn my faith in *our* universe.

But it's no longer about us. It's about me. My time now, I say.

10

Doug has borrowed a van from a mate. It's obvious he's forgotten how to use a gear stick that doesn't say P, D or R. We bounce along the M4, no suspension, aware of every pothole, my stomach referencing air turbulence as I cling to the handle over the door, staring out of the window, trying to steady my focus, hoping to land as safely as possible.

Doug didn't want me to come because Jack didn't want me to come. So, precisely for that reason, I knew I had to. I don't trust Jack. Why would I? Despite his promise to my brother that he had packed everything of mine down to the last paperback, I wanted to be sure. Not that I could necessarily remember every *this is mine, this is yours* but I wanted to give it my best shot.

I'm sick on the pavement before we've even got as far as the front door. I could blame Doug's driving but fear and revulsion run equally high on the list of possibilities.

'Are you sure you're doing the right thing?' he says. 'Why don't you wait in the van? I mean, how important really are books and vases and sheets to you?'

'They mean everything,' I say. 'And I definitely want the coffee machine. Because he loved it. I don't want him to keep a single thing that's mine. He's robbed me of quite enough.'

He puts his arm around my shoulders. 'At least your clothes are safe. As far as we know.'

'Not funny.'

He holds out his palm and I willingly hand over my set of keys, looped to the key-ring Jack bought me when I moved in.

'Did Jack really say he didn't want me to come?'

'Look, Daise. Blokes are like that. When it's over, it's over.'

'Fine.'

'It was your decision, remember.'

'I'd like him to hurt, though.'

He looks at me. 'I think he does.' He holds up the keys. 'I have to post these through the letterbox when we're done. Do you want to keep the key-ring?'

'No, thanks. When it's over, it's over.'

I watch as he fiddles with the sticky lock, then pushes the door open.

It smells of home. Of us. Of me. Like the house has yet to realize I've gone.

'I can't go in.'

'You are kidding me?'

'I thought I could but I can't.'

I have an acute sense of smell – except for other women, it would seem. For me scent is powerful. Throughout the hotels, I always made sure there was a scent that was memorable. That would make people ask, 'What is that?' and buy the hotel candle.

The smell of this house is all too familiar. Part amber, part woody, part Jack, part me.

'I'll wait in the van,' I say. 'It's only stuff. What do I care about stuff?'

'A moment ago stuff meant everything to you.'

'I was going through my shallow phase.'

I climb back into the van, feeling useless and devastated.

Annoyed with myself for not being able to overcome a scent.

I watch through the wing mirror as Doug humps out a box, juggling a few clothes bags on top. I hear them thud, like a coffin, into the back of the van. This is it, I think, my heart crumpling. My entire life has been distilled into a bunch of boxes and bags.

He comes back out again with another huge box, weaving along the path letting out a loud groan of relief as he shuffles it into the back. Thud follows thud. Box follows bag. The Jenga pieces of my life.

A car passes. Something flashy. It holds my attention as it backs into a parking space further up the road. Intuition kicks in. It's Jack. I'm certain of it. I duck into the footwell. I don't want to see him. And, for Doug's sake, I definitely don't want him to see me. I wait. For a moment I think it might be safe to come out, then—

'Hey, Doug!'

The sound of his voice hits me bang in my solar plexus. I squeeze my eyes shut and swallow hard. I don't want to miss him. I'd rather be angry. Come on, Anger.

'Jack!' says Doug, taken by surprise. 'Sorry, I'm nearly done. Taking a bit longer than I thought.'

'No worries, mate.'

Tell him, Doug. Say 'I'm not your mate, Jack.'

'How is she?'

She? Who's she? The cat's mother?

'She's okay.'

She is NOT the cat's mother!

'Want a hand?'

'I'm fine,' Doug says. 'Last couple of boxes and I'll be away.' A box thuds.

'Want to see my new car?'

What the fuck?

'I'd best be getting on.'

Well said, Doug!

'It's a Tesla. Top of the range. Like a cockpit inside.'

You're the cockpit.

'Needs to be seen to be believed. You can sit in it if you want.'

What are they? Five years old?

'Oh!' says Doug, with a change of pitch. 'Yeah, why not? Never sat in one before.'

They are five years old!

Look at me! I'm crouched in this scuddy van and what does he do? He sides with the enemy. I hear their footsteps disappear into the distance, their chummy chat making me boil. My neck is hurting, back scrunched up against the metal underside of the dash, the smell of the filthy rubber mat in my face. My legs throb with the accumulation of blood that should be elsewhere. My chest hurts. Maybe I'll have a heart attack and I'll be discovered slumped in the footwell of this van. That'll teach them.

I start to count. When I get to a hundred, I'll go and find him. That's what we used to do when Doug was five.

At eighty-four I hear them returning. Doug jumps into the front seat.

'Daise?'

'Down here.'

He snorts. 'It's safe,' he says. 'He's gone inside.'

'I'll wait for you to drive away.'

He puts the key in the ignition. 'He was on good form. I don't think he'd have minded you being here, after all.'

My chin drops into the little space available. 'Well, maybe you'd like to call him back and we can all go and sit in his Tesla.'

'Yeah, right. Like you care about cars.'

He takes off his puffer jacket and drapes it over the back of the seat, turns the key. We lurch forward and my head knocks against the metal underside, jarring my teeth into my lower lip.

'Fuck, Doug! Are you trying to kill me?'

'Sorry,' he says. 'Forgot I left it in gear.'

A few minutes up the road, I venture out of my cubbyhole, rearranging my jacket, smoothing my hair, adjusting my facial expression, trying to feel calm. We stare at the road ahead.

'You all right?' he says.

'Why wouldn't I be?'

'Dunno. You just seem . . . uptight.'

'I'm fine,' I say, sounding uptight.

He turns on the radio, looking at me suspiciously.

'Tune it into something decent,' he says. 'Please.'

I fiddle until I find Radio 2. 'That do?' I say.

'What's up?' he says. 'I know something's up.'

I swallow. I have to say it, otherwise I'll be snippy the whole way home. 'I can't believe you went to look at his car.'

'*Whaaaat?* Seriously?' He laughs. 'It's a Tesla. He wanted to show it off. I let him. So what?'

The heat rises through my chest. 'If you don't know, I'm not going to be the one to tell you.' I look out of the window as we bounce along. 'No, wait,' I say. 'I am.'

'Oh, God! Here she goes!'

I turn towards him. 'Yes, Doug. Here she goes!'

I tell him, as if he didn't know already, that the man in question betrayed me in the worst way possible. By going along with him, he told him that betrayal meant nothing to him. 'You reinforced everything he already thinks,' I say. 'That he's a great guy. That he's done nothing wrong.'

'It was a car. What's the big deal? It doesn't mean I'm on his side.'

'Yes, it does.'

He looks at me for a second. 'I don't get it. But I'm sorry if I upset you.'

Whoever said 'sorry' is the hardest word to say got it wrong. It's the hardest word to mean.

'Okay. Let me explain it in words of not too many syllables.' I sigh. 'Jack has had everything – EV-REE-THING – his way. After six good years, I feel I-RRE-LE-VANT to him. You just made me feel A HUN-DRED times worse. And trust me, Doug, his ego does not need you to be its FLUF-FER.'

He scoffs, his hands gripping the steering wheel, the whites of his knuckles roaring. 'I went to look at his car. I did not rub his TUM-MY and tell him he was my FUCK-ING HE-RO.'

I stare ahead. 'It was the principle not the damned car.'

He shuffles his arse. 'Sorry!' he says. 'I'm sorry I fluffed his ego. I will never ever fluff anything of his again.'

I grunt, trying not to laugh but I can't help it. Doug laughs too, relieved.

'Fine,' I say, turning away. 'But I'm still angry.'

'Your prerogative.'

We continue to bounce along the route, my brother intent on shifting the gear stick from second to fourth and fourth to second like third gear's not worth the effort.

All I can think of is Jack, fulfilled and smug with Doug's admiration for his damned Tesla. I imagine him glad to see my stuff's no longer blocking the hallway, putting his feet up on what was once our sofa, his hands behind his head. Job done. I wonder if he'll phone Polly. Tell her she has the all-clear. But I mustn't have that thought.

'You should have told him he was a total shit,' I say.

Doug sighs because there are no words.

As we approach our parents' house he turns towards me and says, in a forced bright voice, 'I'll keep this stuff in my garage until you find somewhere to live. I'm assuming you'd like me to help you move in?'

'That would be great,' I say. 'Just sort out your clutch control.'

'And you sort out your anger.'

'Fuck off,' I say. I lean over to kiss him. 'And thanks . . . you know . . . for doing this.'

11

Eventually I settle for the flat in Shepherd's Bush. The rental process has been a nightmare. I've been outbid by every other renter across London. It's not perfect but I'm grateful someone's prepared to take my money. It's near enough to the office, in a location where I'm unlikely to bump into people I'd rather not see. No need for names. Jack and Polly.

And it's cheap. I'm having to be frugal for the first time in ages. But I have a creaking ceiling over my head and I'm grateful for that. This one-bed is on the first floor of a Victorian conversion in a little side-street off Uxbridge Road. It's inoffensive, painted throughout in a sort of cream, just the right side of magnolia, a bland backdrop on which to curate my own possessions. I'm trying to ignore the slight smell of damp. Everyone is being very polite about it.

'Nope, can't smell anything!' says Doug. Ma and Bee nod in agreement.

Once I get my candles burning and place my diffusers around, I'm sure it'll be fine.

As each box is opened, each bag emptied, I realize Jack has been incredibly fair. He's packed every single thing I've ever owned, like he had a forensic knowledge of what was mine. He's even put in a few extras. Towels he'd bought only recently in the Conran shop, which he knew I loved. My lip trembles as I unwrap the Moroccan dishes and the tagine we chose together in the souk on our last holiday in Marrakech. I take deep breaths. His fairness makes me feel worse. It's easier to hate someone when they behave badly.

'You okay?' says Bee.

'I will be,' I say.

'Where do you want this?' says Doug, holding up my favourite French vintage table lamp.

'That's lovely,' says my mother, in her Cath Kidston apron, looking across from her position on the stepladder, duster in one hand, paperback in the other, leaning against the built-in shelves that flank the faux fireplace.

'You have some lovely things, Daisy. And some interesting books.' She holds up a copy of *Fifty Shades*.

'Yeah, well, I never got past the first chapter.'

'Liar, you read all the filthy bits,' says Bee.

'Sorry to interrupt the intellectual banter,' says Doug. 'Lamp, anyone?'

'By the bed, please,' I say, unwrapping a mug. Jack has wrapped everything meticulously. I never knew he was so capable. I wonder if he had help. Of course he had help. I'd put money on it. I'd put money on it that that's why he wanted me out so quickly. It makes me feel sick. I try to push her name out of my head and remind myself this is purely conjecture. I remind myself that the house still smelt of me. Then I remind myself that Polly is wily. She doesn't leave a scent.

Bee is helping me unpack all the kitchen gear. She lifts something heavy out of one of the boxes. 'Aha!' she declares. 'He's given you the famous coffee machine. Welcome! You're home safe and sound, baby.'

'This is just temporary, isn't it, Daisy?' says my mother.

'Temporary for a while,' I say. 'I've got a six-month break clause.'

The last of my possessions is unwrapped and put away. My clothes are hung up in the freestanding wardrobe, the pine laminate doors left open to allow it to air. Doug makes loud noises of exasperation as he breaks down the boxes, like he wants to ensure we all know he's being incredibly helpful. Eventually I'll play around, arranging things exactly how I want them. For now, we're all trying to get comfortable on the two-seater navy-blue sofas that sit either side of the fireplace.

'I never knew cushions could feel like concrete,' says my mother, shifting around as if one spot might feel magically less solid than another.

'They're called made for rental,' I say. 'It's a sign I shouldn't get too comfortable.' I look across at her, sitting in a rigid posture, her weariness from the past few weeks lodged on her face. She unties her apron and neatly folds it up.

'That's better,' I say. 'Knocks years off you. You've just made seventy the new sixty.'

She rolls her eyes. 'Oh, Daisy. I'm going to miss you.'

'You left off *and your miserable face*,' I say.

'I'm not going to miss that,' she says.

'I'll miss you too,' I say. 'And Brewster. I genuinely think he knew I was leaving. He looked so sad.'

'He's a dog,' says Doug.

'Never say that about Brewster again!'

'Who wants a glass of wine?' says Bee.

'That sounds very appealing,' says my mother. She glances at her watch. 'Oh, gosh. It's only three. It feels more like midnight.'

'It's wine o'clock,' I say. 'Although I'm not sure there is any unless Jack slipped in a bottle as a farewell gesture.'

'I think he slipped into Polly as a farewell gesture,' says Doug, giving himself a high-five.

'Doug!' says my mother.

'Ho-ho!' I say.

Bee is going boss-eyed, trying hard not to laugh. 'I think I spotted an offy up the road,' she says. 'I'll go. You guys grab some family time.'

I feel we've all had quite enough of that.

Soon Bee returns with two huge bags of crisps and a bottle of red. 'You've got a nice corner shop,' she says. 'Very handy.'

Doug unscrews the wine. 'Feels wrong to drink it out of mugs,' I say, putting the mugs on the counter.

He checks the label. 'Trust me, you could drink this from a bucket.'

I roll my eyes. 'Ignore him, Bee,' I say. 'He's a wine smartarse with a cellar. We're grateful, aren't we, Ma?'

'We're all grateful,' says Doug. 'Sorry for being a smartarse, Bee.'

She laughs, tearing open both bags of crisps and placing them on the coffee-table. 'Lunch and supper,' she says.

We sit around the table, taking handfuls of crisps, apart from my mother, who happily downs the wine.

'To new beginnings, Daisy,' she says, stemming a yawn.

'New beginnings,' we chorus.

* * *

Doug takes the boxes outside to the recycling bins and my mother kisses me goodbye as we stand in a huddle in the hall.

'You're not going to cry, are you?' I say.

'I'm the one who's going to cry,' says Doug, walking back in. 'I need a hug.' He wraps me in his slender muscular arms.

'I couldn't have got through this without you. Thank you,' I say.

'I'm glad I could be there for you. You've always been there for me. At least, I think it was you.' We squeeze each other tightly.

I hug Bee. 'See you soon, please?'

She gives me her you-sure-you're-okay look.

I nod, yes. Not sure at all.

* * *

I creep around the flat as though I'm not meant to be here, as though I'm an interloper. I keep finding excuses to move things around, until I'm so tired I have no choice but to go to bed. The bathroom feels too cold, the bedroom feels too warm, yet when I climb under the covers, the mattress is freezing. I read for a while, the same page again and again, taking in nothing, trying to relax, but I can't switch off. I can hear the tread of my upstairs neighbour. I wonder who they are. I hope they're decent. I hope they don't stay up all night.

Finally I give in, turn off my bedside light, grateful for the familiarity of its twisted vintage wire, the flick of the old-fashioned switch. This is your lamp, I tell myself. This is your home now. Not perfect but not for ever.

I lie there, eyes forced shut, trying not to look into the darkness, aware of the shadows that shift every time a car passes. There are new noises. The clunk of a radiator. The creak of a floorboard. I pull my duvet over my eyes.

How did I end up here? Where is my old life?

I turn onto my side and reach across the bed feeling the emptiness of the freezing mattress. This is what solo feels like, I tell myself. Get used to it.

12

'I've decorated hotels for as long as I can remember,' I say. 'I don't know if I can do a standard residential project again.' I'm holding my portfolio, heavy with swatches and mood-boards, resisting leaving the office for my first commission since returning to work.

Marcus looks at me. 'We've won the job on the back of your design, Daisy. It's an interesting house. You loved it when you saw it. You loved Camilla. Said you couldn't wait to work with her.'

'I did?'

'I'm not thrilled about the Hoxton apartments either but, at the moment, beggars can't be choosers.' Marcus has won a commission at a boxy new development of flats, great for financial reasons rather than aesthetic. 'Besides, nowadays everyone wants their home to look like a hotel. You can do this!'

'You mean I have to do this!'

'That too.'

I head out to face the grey December chill and somehow, in a girl-starting-a-new-school daze, manage to navigate the route to Peckham. I wander into the nice Danish café I'd discovered the first time, grateful for some warmth, knowing I need to bolster myself with a coffee. 'Latte with oat milk to go, please,' I say to the barista, trying to establish a sense of belonging.

'Would you like a loyalty card?'

And just like that, with the stamp of a card, I belong, my loyalty rewarded with a free coffee after six purchases.

Grey unwelcoming skies shadow my walk along the Georgian streets. I'm sipping my coffee through the lid, humping my portfolio, looking at the neglected buildings that nestle against shiny neighbours, wondering who minds most: the ones living in the crumbling wrecks or the ones who've invested their life savings in their reinvigorated home.

I miss Jack. The thought pops into my head from nowhere. Old habits die hard. I'm starting something new and daunting and I want to share with him. I wonder where he is and what he's doing. I think about how my days used to be. And then I see the cloak of scaffolding. Deep breath. You can do this.

Before my clients, Camilla and her husband Tim, bought this house, it had been owned by the same family for more than eighty years, which gives you a clue as to its condition. The good thing is, it wasn't adulterated during the seventies and eighties when elegant panelling, marble fireplaces, beautiful balustrades and elaborate cornicing were casually ripped out, making way for the plain, often ugly. The bad thing is, the heating and electrics have not been updated since God knows when. We're taking everything back to basics, then reviving the delicate Georgian grandeur while bringing the utilities into the twenty-first century. Most of this initial work will be hidden in the walls and floors, which is the part the client finds most difficult. They hate paying for work they can't see.

There's plenty to keep me busy over the coming months. The original features might still be in place but the cornicing has been painted too many times, layer upon layer, blurring the fine egg-and-dart detail. Every one of the five floors is overrun by ill-thought-out stud partitions as though it needed to accommodate a family of ten. And maybe it did.

This over-painted, over-partitioned rabbit warren of three and a half thousand square feet is a glorious challenge. Not exclusively mine, of course, since this level of structural refurbishment also requires the skills of an architect. Camilla and Tim have hired Benedict Shaw, whom I've never worked with. He was entirely their choice – sometimes the client consults you but on this occasion they chose Benedict long before they chose me. The job was put out to tender about three months ago, planning permission granted, and the appointed contractors are actively on site. Benedict is very efficient – he certainly has a good reputation, if the testimonials on his impressive website are anything to go by. No presence on Instagram that I could find, which is unusual in today's need-to-be-seen, need-to-be-liked world.

I'm greeted by the large boards bearing Benedict's name alongside Baxter Settle's. I always get a buzz when I see our sleek logo: it makes me feel like we're part of a huge concern rather than just a two-man band.

I gather some fake confidence, walk up the front steps and stand in front of the original panelled door, with its beautiful arched fanlight, my portfolio in one hand, the empty coffee cup in the other, butterflies breaking free in my stomach.

The door is opened by a blinking Camilla, in a hard hat, wiping her eyes.

'Welcome to the dustbowl,' she says apologetically, like she's responsible. 'Builders obviously took down more walls yesterday. It's thick with it. It smells weird, too, but they tell me it's something to do with disturbing the lead paint.' She has the taut body language of someone highly strung.

Her face is lined, etched with dust, no make-up. Her wavy mid-brown hair peeps out from under the hat. She's wearing red jeans that sag at the knees and a cable-knit navy polo-neck under a sheepskin donkey jacket. 'Benedict's on his way. He got held up at a previous meeting – the man never stops. I mean, who has meetings at seven in the morning?'

'Benedict,' I say.

She laughs, ushering me in.

'He's bringing coffees and cinnamon buns from the Danish bakery as penance, bless him.'

'Ah!' I say, chucking my cup into one of the many rubble sacks lining the hall. 'I feel bad now. I should have asked if you wanted anything.'

She shrugs. 'Don't be silly.'

'How's it going?' I say, taking a hard hat off a hook on the wall.

'Good.' She smiles. 'They started on the foundations for the extension last week, which was exciting, and most of the partition walls are down so it all looks huge. Of course it'll shrink again once the new ones go up.'

I'm impressed by the progress. The builders are moving ahead nicely but the early stages of demolition are always the most rapid. 'Now's the time to change your mind if you like the open-plan look . . . particularly that wall between the dining room and the kitchen. I've been thinking about it. I mean, it'll make a real feature of that glorious marble fireplace in the dining room, sharing it with the entire space instead of locking it away in a room you might seldom otherwise use.' Her eyes widen as she registers the idea. 'I know you don't like the smell of cooking travelling, but if we can install a decent extractor, the general feel will be so much more inviting and convivial. Imagine! A glorious log fire on a winter's day as you're cooking breakfast.'

'You're keen to keep down that wall, aren't you?'

'Your call, though,' I say, and she manages a half-hearted shrug.

'It's all so overwhelming.' She sighs. 'So many decisions. And Tim's no use at all. He just cares about how much everything costs.'

I smile. 'Someone has to. Anyway, that's what we're here for. To help you make those decisions as well as keeping an eye on your budget. Let's see what Ben has to say.'

'Oooh, Benedict!' she says. 'Have you worked with him before?'

'I haven't, no.'

'He's very dashing. The mean, moody type.'

'Is that what you look for in an architect?'

She laughs. 'I suppose I should be more serious. But I like the fact that he's nice to look at. It helps me get through the boring bits. I'm looking forward to when you get started.'

'Not long now,' I say.

She ushers me into the sitting room. 'We've set up an old wardrobe door on some trestles so we've got a makeshift desk to work on.'

I look around, reminding myself of the potential.

'It's going to be great, isn't it?' she says, as though seeking reassurance that the mess and dust and horror of it all will end.

'I'm very excited about it.'

There's a creaky ring at the door, like the bell has a sore throat.

'Here he is,' she says, her eyes lighting up. 'Come and meet the gorgeous Benedict Shaw.'

'Stop that now,' I say. 'And we need to get the doorbell fixed.'

My nerves are immediately on edge. It's always weird

at the beginning of a project, getting used to working with new people, knowing you're about to put your ideas out there to be judged. I'm more nervous about the architect judging me than Camilla. Another professional's opinion is far scarier than that of the person who's paying you.

She opens the door to reveal his tall, imposing shape. He's older than I'd expected. Late fifties, maybe, but in good nick. He has thick grey hair, which sweeps elegantly away from his forehead. In fact, everything about him is elegant. If someone had asked me to guess his profession I'd have said barrister, city job, then architect. He's wearing an expensive navy coat, which takes guts on a building site, yellow cashmere scarf looped at the neck. Black-leather-gloved hands hold a cardboard tray of coffees in a way that says he'd rather not.

'Welcome back to the dustbowl,' says Camilla, with a coquettish giggle, flicking the ends of her straggly hair, which remain motionless.

He strolls in, all straight-backed hauteur, and grabs a hard hat.

'Sorry I'm late,' he says, sucking in his cheeks, staring at the rubble sacks. 'They need to get rid of these before they take over the hall.' He looks at me. 'I'm guessing you're Daisy Settle.'

I smile awkwardly at his formal greeting. 'And you're Ben Shaw.' My voice comes out weirdly high-pitched, set against the deep resonance of his.

'Benedict,' he says, his face registering surly impatience as he holds out the tray to Camilla, who takes the cup with a black C on the disposable cap.

'Oh, right! Sorry.'

'I braved the decision you were a cappuccino type,' he says crisply.

'Great, thanks.' I take the one marked D. I'm not going to bother contradicting this guy. He throws the tray into a rubble bag.

'Sugar?'

'Not for me, thanks.'

'Sweet enough,' says Camilla. She's incorrigible. And brave. With very, very poor taste in men.

He produces a paper bag speckled with greasy blotches and shakes it open. 'I bought us each a bun. We need the carbs in this cold.' The house is colder inside than it is out.

Camilla and I take one each, and we all move into the sitting room, arranging ourselves around the makeshift desk.

'So cold,' says Camilla, as we sip our coffees.

'Next time, we should all wear cashmere scarves,' I say.

Benedict throws me a withering look.

'Well done for being prepared,' I bluster.

His demeanour is dismissive of me as he starts talking, taking us through the work that has happened to date, the confidence and gravity of his voice holding our attention. He explains how everything is going to be reconfigured as he flips through the 3D drawings on his iPad.

Waiting for our comments, he twiddles his wedding ring, a thick gold band, pressing it between middle finger and thumb. I find it unnerving. I have a feeling that's his intention.

Camilla asks if he thinks we should leave down the kitchen wall.

'I think that would be a good decision,' he says.

I'm relieved, although architects hate walls so I should have known. He draws his finger over his iPad screen and shows us how it would look with this configuration. 'There are some pretty decent extractors on the market,' he says, 'if you're worried about the transfer of kitchen odours.'

'That's what Daisy said.'

'She's right.' He nods at me.

I smile, flattered.

He nods again.

'Oh, right!' He's giving me my cue. I riffle through my handbag searching for something with which to wipe my hands.

'Have you lost something?' he says archly, twiddling his ring.

I hunt even more feverishly. 'Looking for a tissue. Cinnamon fingers!' I waggle them in the air.

Camilla is licking hers. 'Very sticky,' she says, 'but delicious, thank you.'

'I have some wet wipes,' says Benedict, pulling a packet out of his satchel. 'Here!'

Of course you do, I think. 'Perfect,' I say, taking one and wiping my hands.

I pull out my boards, laying out the swatches in an orderly display, slowly feeling a welcome calm come over me, like an actor whose stage fright disappears as soon as they enter stage left.

I talk them through each board, handing them the relevant fabric swatch, the sample flooring, giving Camilla an opportunity to get a feel for texture, tone and pattern. It's my turn to pull up the images of each room on my iPad, fully dressed versions of the empty configurations that appeared in Benedict's presentation. I watch Camilla grow more and more excited, seeing my interpretation of our discussions for the first time. In direct contrast Benedict seems to be incrementally withdrawing, an unequivocal disdain for my maximalism. I remind myself he's an architect. They hate anything that gets in the way of their own clean lines. Ignore him! The client loves it.

We start to walk around the house, through what will eventually be the actual rooms so that I can hold up the images in situ and Camilla can visualize, to some extent, what the final look will be.

After a full hour, going through everything, she actually applauds, bouncing on her feet with enthusiasm. 'I'm overwhelmed,' she says, patting my back. 'I was terrified, wondering what you'd come up with, thinking I might have been mad to tell you to go for it, but this is beyond anything I could ever have imagined. I'm glad you pushed us out of our comfort zone. Your designs have such . . . I don't know . . . pizzazz!'

Benedict gives a tight smile. 'Very nice,' he says.

* * *

'Heading back to the Overground?' he asks, as we make to leave.

'Yes.'

'So am I,' he says, neither of us thrilled at the prospect. As we walk down the road together, he's frenetically punching the keys on his phone. 'I asked the contractor to get rid of that rubble immediately. It shouldn't be sitting there blocking the hallway. We've got so many deliveries coming. They should have ordered another skip.'

I nod. 'I'm sure Camilla wasn't worried about it.'

'It's not Camilla I'm concerned with.'

'Right.'

We carry on walking, no interaction, his face in his phone most of the way.

'Mind the dog shit!' I say.

'I saw it,' he replies.

Next time I hope he walks straight through it.

As we reach the station, he says, 'I'm going to Bermondsey. Where are you heading?'

'Back into town.' Thankfully it's in the opposite direction. 'I'll see you at the next one.'

He grunts, slipping his phone into his coat pocket, and heads towards the bridge.

'Look forward to it!' I say to no one.

13

I've bought myself a set of Moleskine notebooks. I use them for work. I love the feel of them, particularly when you open a fresh new one, peel back the first page and seal it at the crease. But now I'm going to start journaling. I want to train myself to write every day. It doesn't have to be important. Nothing of any significance. Merely stream-of-consciousness thinking. Whatever comes into my head. It's meant to be healthy and I'm determined to improve my mental wellbeing.

I sit on my bed and my pen runs away without my brain even having to shift into gear, like it already knows what to do:

Shitty first day at the Peckham house. Got to deal with a ghastly architect. Why? Why, when it would be nice to have a smooth transition back into real life, do I have to deal with an arrogant, stuffy ego? Who likes minimalism. He fiddles with his wedding ring, like he wants you to know. Or to keep Camilla at bay, which he's definitely not. Camilla actually flirts with him. Why do some women find rude men appealing? I don't get it. I certainly don't get him. Perhaps I do hate men. I don't. I know I don't. I just hate that kind of man. I pity his poor wife. And it's not just because he doesn't like my designs. I know he doesn't, even though he

didn't say as much, but what can he say when the
client is loving everything? It's like his distaste springs
from his pores. But it's Camilla who matters. I do
not have to seek his approval. I do not have to seek
anyone's approval. It's a very bad habit.

I close the notebook and smile. Laugh to myself. In laying out my thoughts in a few scribbled paragraphs, I've taken away his power. What could be more important?

14

The Coburg bar at the Connaught Hotel is as expensive as its Mayfair address would suggest. And just as beautiful. I hadn't wanted to come out but Marcus insisted. I'm glad he did. Being here makes a much-needed change from another night in with a takeaway, or a bowl of soup, or some cereal in front of the not-brilliant TV that seems to pixilate every time something crucial happens so I miss it. I need to make a list of problems for the landlord but I keep telling myself I'll be out of there as soon as I can trigger the six-month break clause. I still have a lot of months to wade through before that happens.

I look at him.

He smiles. 'Do you miss them? The old haunts?'

We're seated in low armchairs in front of a glass-topped art-deco table. I run my hands across the deep pile of amethyst silk velvet, aware of the shift in colour, intense to pale, pale to intense, with every sweep of my palm. 'In a way. The familiarity. People knowing who you are. Feeling part of a team.'

'Me too,' he says. 'All those things.'

Behind us is the handsome, heavily panelled bar which gleams invitingly, bathing you in the promise of superlatives. The wood-encased glass shelves, their backdrop of illuminated mirrors, are home to a chorus of spirits and rare vintages waiting for their moment to perform. Champagne bottles tantalize in ice buckets, glasses sparkle and the bartenders busy themselves, mixing and shaking and pouring.

'Where's Flynn this week?'

'Berlin,' says Marcus. 'Lucky bugger. What you having?'

'Back on Negronis. If I never touch another martini it'll be too soon.'

The head bartender spots Marcus and comes over to say hi. He shakes his hand, a polite glance at me, smiling with a hint of recognition, before taking our order. Everyone knows Flynn. Marcus gets excellent service practically wherever he goes. He loves it. Loves the attention. Dresses up for it. This evening he's wearing a navy-blue Paul Smith suit, lined in his trademark patterned silk, a blue pinstriped shirt, M.B. embroidered on the pocket, the cuffs neatly turned back with elegant gold-knot cufflinks. His outstretched legs, crossed ankles, reveal bright-crimson socks above Church's black leather brogues. His look for site meetings is a tatty faded Rolling Stones sweatshirt, the tour dates printed on the back, which he loves, and a pair of baggy trackie bottoms worn with some Nike trainers or Dr Martens depending on the weather.

I've not been on site. I'm wearing high-waisted Prince of Wales check trousers, a green jungle print satin blouse and black suede ankle boots. I'm grateful to have retrieved my decent wardrobe. Particularly for unexpected evenings out like this.

Our drinks are put down in front of us, on leather coasters. There's a bowl of crisps, and green olives, which look like they've been polished, alongside the perkiest, saltiest mixed nuts. It's all so lush. Turner House was never so classy, I tell myself. Not in the same league. The fact that I'd have argued convincingly in its favour until recently is not the point.

Marcus throws a nut into his mouth and holds up a cut-glass tumbler of whisky. 'Cheers.'

'Cheers, partner!'

'How you feeling about working with old Not-So-Shaw now?'

I laugh. 'Are you kidding? He's properly sure of himself.'

'He's an architect.'

'Yeah. Old school. I get the feeling he's more of a man's man. Although Camilla loves him. Really loves him. She told me she likes them mean and moody. He certainly fits the brief.'

'You can deal with mean and moody. Jack was no pushover.'

'No. But he was Jack. I knew how to navigate around him.'

'Just remember never to call the man Ben and you'll be fine.'

Marcus had loved it when I'd told him that Benedict had been insulted by my shortening his name. He'd chuckled about it on and off for the rest of the day. 'Arse!'

'To be fair, it would be like him calling me Daise. I'm not sure I'd like it either.'

'True, but worth a laugh. And what about Jack?' He spears an olive, chews it. I look at him questioningly. 'You seem fine but I get the feeling you might just be putting on a good show.'

Large glug. The bitterness of the Campari lingers, which is the point of Campari. 'I'm better for working. A lot better.' I look across at him. 'What about you? No regrets? You could have tried to woo the new owners.'

'Don't be daft. We're a team.' He scratches his chin. 'And we have some decent projects. They're not Turner House budgets but it means we have to be cleverer in our thinking. I like that. We had it fairly easy for a very long time.'

I nod. 'I like the challenge too. I'm so over hotels.

Peckham is the first time in ages I've been able to think outside the box.'

Marcus clears his throat, hesitant. 'Jack phoned me last week.'

My stomach flips. 'What about?'

'I think it was just an excuse to chat. He claimed he wanted some advice on flooring in the Regency Club that needs attention. Frankly, I think he misses you.'

'Good.'

'I take it you don't miss him?'

'No.'

He waits a beat. 'Yeah, you do.'

I snicker. 'Okay, sometimes. But I don't miss the hairs in the sink . . . or when he leaves the loo seat up, or picking up his underpants, or the apple cores he leaves lying around. Wondering what to cook for dinner or what time he might be coming home.'

'You're describing my life. Apart from the loo seat.'

I laugh. 'A lot of people's lives.'

'So, what do you miss?'

'I don't know. I try not to think about it.' I smile. He knows I'm obfuscating, that I know he wants to know. Another healthy slug of Negroni. 'I miss sharing with him. Work in particular. He would have been good at understanding Mr Oh-So-Shaw. I miss the nights curled up together in front of the TV . . . you know, glass of wine, foot massage. I miss my garden. I miss my gorgeous bathroom, lighting candles, sharing a bath with him. I miss sex.'

Marcus feigns amazement. 'Six years and you were still having regular sex?'

I scoff. 'Jack was the only one having regular sex. I was the one used for occasional pregnancy rehearsal.'

He presses his lips together. 'Sorry.'

'I miss the idea of a family.'

'Of course you do.'

We sigh simultaneously. I swirl the pink drink. 'Let me try this one on you,' I say. Deep breath. Voice dropped to a whisper, indicating for him to lean forward.

'I'm thinking about . . .' nervous pause '. . . sperm donation.'

His mouth falls open. 'Really?' Beat. 'Who with?'

'Don't know yet. Got to sign up to a clinic first. An anonymous donor.'

Marcus shifts in his seat, taken aback. 'Wow!' he says. He looks into his whisky, biting his lip. 'Honestly, Daise, I'd offer, only . . . I'm not sure Flynn . . .'

'Of course. I'd have asked if . . .'

'Yeah. I hope you would have.' He turns his head, side-eyeing me. 'You think you'll do it?'

'What do you think?'

'I don't know, Daisy. It's not up to me.'

'You'll be involved, though. Not your genes obviously but you might have to look after it, if it works, of course, when I bring it into the office.'

'That was always the deal. Even with you-know-who.'

An involuntary pang of regret. 'Then I might do it.'

He puffs out his cheeks. 'Wow!' He looks around the room, nodding slowly, trying to work out how he feels. 'You've really thought it through?'

'I've looked into it.'

'What do you think Jack will say?'

'Do I care?'

'No, of course not. It's just . . . I think he genuinely misses you.'

'Don't, Marcus. You're not helping. I'm really trying to move on.'

He taps his foot. 'You don't want to wait to meet someone?'

I shake my head. 'I don't have time. Or the inclination. I don't want to risk being hurt again.'

His face melts into a concerned frown. 'You'll have to risk it sometime, Daise,' he says, grabbing a handful of nuts. 'You can't die a spinster. Think of all that sex you'll have missed. What a waste.'

I crunch a crisp, the tiny glistening flakes falling into my cupped hand. 'I'm putting sex on the back burner for now. I'm going to try to be a virgin mother.'

'You're a fucking saint, darling.'

I watch him steeple his fingers under his chin, looking at me in amazement.

'I have to accept it might not happen, though,' I say. 'Even to saints. But I can't not try.'

He offers small, thoughtful nods. 'What do your parents think?'

'I haven't told them yet. I'll tell them when they've had a few drinks. Probably over Christmas, which will be here in a blink.'

He blinks and holds up his glass. 'For my part, whatever you choose to do, whatever happens, I want you to know I'm with you all the way.'

I hold up my near-empty glass to his. 'I love you, Marcus. Will you marry me?'

'Sorry, darling. Already taken.'

'The best ones always are.'

15

My Moleskine is starting to fill, my thick scrawl crinkling the pages.

Big day. HUGE. Going to the doctor, really nervous. This could be a defining moment. It's certainly a huge step. Wish me luck! I underline the final three words.

* * *

Dr Baldwin looks at me with her serious expression. I know she's about to say something awful. Back in the day, if something horrible was about to happen, an injection, an examination, Dr Keene, our family doctor, would distract me by giving me a fruit pastille or a few Smarties from a supply in his desk drawer. But Dr Keene is dead and I'm too old for fruit pastilles. Too old for Smarties. From the look on Dr Baldwin's face, I think I may be too old for everything.

'I think you ought to get yourself checked out by a specialist first. Just to make sure your eggs are in good shape. I'm sure you'll be fine but . . .' she pauses '. . . at your age it's worth looking into before you embark on such a huge emotional and financial investment as sperm donation . . .' she scratches her neck '. . . which will prove fruitless if your eggs aren't up to the job.'

'I've been off the pill for a few months. My periods are still regular.'

'That's good. But there are still a few more hurdles for a woman of your age to overcome.'

A woman of my age. What age is that? Should I be pensioned off? 'Is there anything positive about this?'

'Hopefully a baby,' she says, 'but statistics aren't on your side.'

'That sounds very positive.'

She tucks her short highlighted hair behind her ears. She wears small pearl studs. She likes the classic look. Her jumper is Jaeger, no doubt, or something similar. 'You need to hear this, Daisy. You're embarking on a major journey with no guarantees. What I can tell you is there are some excellent fertility clinics out there. And I have had patients who've been successful. But more often than not it's taken several goes, which is both emotionally challenging and expensive.' I nod. 'And they've all been in relationships.'

I almost fall off my seat. She certainly knows where to land the blows.

She carries on regardless. 'I'm wondering if you're really fully prepared for this. Do you have any back-up at all?'

'How do you mean?'

'Friends. Money?'

'My friend Bee. My business partner Marcus. They're the only ones who know right now. And I have some rainy-day savings.'

'Good. And your friends are happy to support you?'

'Yes.'

'Do they know what that support entails?'

'Bee is the mother of a three-year-old.'

'She'll be busy, then. Don't rely too much on her.' She picks up a pen on her desk and starts twirling it between her fingers. She looks at me with concern. 'I'm really sorry you find yourself in this position, Daisy. I just want to be sure you're aware of what you're embarking on. I mean, it's unfortunate, but things do change quite dramatically for women who want to get pregnant once they've hit their forties.'

'You've made me fully aware, thank you.' I knew I was erring on the side of old, but she's made me feel decrepit.

She closes her eyes for a second. 'Good. Then I'll email you a list of clinics. Try to set up an appointment soon. And don't just rely on Google. Come and discuss things with me if you need any advice. I'm here for you too. Going it alone will be tough. I may be the one saying the things you don't want to hear right now but I promise I can be a gentle, supportive hand.'

'Frankly, I'd rather that hand.'

She laughs. 'Most people would.'

I wander home preoccupied with the what-ifs. What if my eggs aren't up to the job? What if I need IVF? What if it fails? I'd be putting my life savings, every ISA, every Premium Bond, into something that's not guaranteed. It's scary. I have rent to pay now, utility bills, food, Tube fares, things I never used to think twice about. And, yes, thank goodness I'm working, and Camilla and Tim are good clients, plus we have more job pitches coming through but, unless you're on the level of the Mahdavis or the Collinses or the Brudnizkis, being an interior designer is not as well paid as everyone imagines. Face facts: I'm no longer on the generous terms I had with Jack. I may have savings (thankfully) but now I realize how much I've frittered away over the years because I never thought I would end up being so financially exposed. And now, thanks to Dr Baldwin's unpitying directness, I know I've probably frittered away my best eggs.

I've always felt maternal. But what does that mean? I'm

not a little girl playing with dolls, imagining motherhood. What does it mean in the cold light of maturity? I know it's not the holy grail – I see how demanding it is for Bee. I've lost friends along the way because they've had families and started to lead different lives. It's what happens. Your priorities change. But no one I know has ever done it on their own.

My mind races. I dive deep into my soul. Knowing I want a family is not a rational decision, it's emotional, visceral. I might always have known I wanted to be a mother but I never imagined I would be forty and single.

Does that change things?

Should it?

Do I have to adjust my thinking, realign my expectations?

By the time I get home, Dr Baldwin has sent through the promised list of fertility clinics. I stare at them. I write:

I'm not sure I'm ready to find out how good my eggs are. I read Dr Baldwin's email and poured myself a glass of wine (of course I did), then looked at the different websites. I've already decided I don't want to start this journey before Christmas. I don't want to have any test results hanging over me in case they're not the results I want. I want a merry Christmas. I want a new year full of optimism and promise. I desperately need to leave this old painful year behind. And I need my eggs more than I ever realized.

16

It's my first Christmas without Jack, I write. *I don't want to think about him but firsts are always difficult. I can't help but wonder if he is with Polly? Polly's family? If he's having a different sort of first.*

I scribble out the last bit. I don't want to give either of them the power of destabilizing me. I need to focus on the positive: I've booked an appointment at a fertility clinic in Harley Street for the first week in January. I write that down instead.

* * *

I spot Doug's car in the distance and wave furiously, a kind of in-joke, as if I'm not the only person standing at the appointed spot, on the side of the empty street. He draws up beside me, his window sliding down. 'Are you the elf we ordered?'

'No. She was double-booked.'

'Do you do good Christmas?'

'I can peel sprouts.'

'Climb in,' he says.

'What about these?' I hold up two bags full of wrapped presents, mainly for the boys. 'Should I put them in the boot?'

Magically his boot opens without him leaving the car. I watch it descend over my gifts.

Doug is wearing a red and white Santa Claus outfit.

'Doesn't that spoil the illusion for the kids?' I say, buckling up. 'Don't they realize Santa is Daddy?'

'Ho-ho-ho!' he says, slipping on a white beard. 'I can be very convincing.'

'Yeah, well, so can they. They're probably humouring you.'

'Are you going to be a mean little elf, in which case I'll have to send you back to the factory?'

'It's my first Christmas without Jack,' I say.

'Of course it is,' he says, tapping my thigh. 'I'm sorry. But try not to take it out on us.'

* * *

The smell of the log fire greets us, layered with the scent of Jo Malone candles, enormous three-wick ones that sit on the two big sideboards, one in front of the stained-glass window on the landing, enveloping us in a bouquet of cloves, cinnamon and orange.

My mother is in the kitchen, which smells of turkey and roasting potatoes, wearing her statutory apron over a smart puffed-sleeve navy wool dress, the round neckline embellished with her favourite Tiffany chain given to her by my father for their silver wedding anniversary. Only it's white gold. He insisted she knew that. She greets me, looking hot and flustered.

'Need help? Hi, Eve!' I say.

Eve is assigned to sprout-peeling – she's usurped my elf role. That woman gets everywhere. She looks up from her knife work, 'Hi, Daisy!'

'Not in the kitchen,' says my mother, wiping her forehead with the back of her hand. 'Check who else needs help.' She reverts to her list, which she diligently ticks off as she goes along even though she's done this for at least the last hundred years, hand in hand with Delia.

The boys charge in, screaming at each other, high on E numbers, and we haven't even begun.

'Merry Christmas, boys,' I say. 'Have you been good this year? Did Santa fill your sacks with goodies?'

'Yes!' they scream, rolling on top of one another, tugging at hair and clothes and noses.

'Get off me!' shouts Eddie.

'You get off me,' laughs Monty, sitting on top of him.

Brewster, fascinated, tries to join in the fun, making the error of licking Eddie's cheek. 'You stink,' he cries.

'How about we play a game?' I say.

'We are playing a game,' says Eddie.

'Play with your own friends,' says Monty.

'Come on, Brewster,' I say. 'It's you and me, mate.' Brewster casts me a bored look and happily trots back to his bed.

With no obvious friends, I head for the tranquillity of the vast wood-panelled Arts and Crafts sitting room to place my gifts under the tree that overwhelms the space, both visually and aromatically, as soon as you walk in.

'Santa's been busy,' I say to no one, upending my bags and placing the presents among the ridiculous melee of riotous wrapping and embellishments.

'Merry Christmas, Daisy!'

I look behind me into the back of the room with its wide bay window, the pinch-pleated Colefax & Fowler curtains drawn back with gold-coloured, heavily tasselled rope sashes. My father is standing hunched over the mantelpiece, navy-blue shirt, mustard corduroy trousers, brown leather belt, poking the fire, shifting the logs, which spit and wheeze, the flames emitting swirls of smoke that are swiftly sucked up the chimney. He has it swept every year. He's on first-name terms with Keith, the chimney sweep. He's very proud of its 'strong draw'.

'Merry Christmas,' I say. 'You okay? You look pained.'

'Bloody back,' he says, standing up and curling over his hips. 'Picked up Eddie. He's getting too big for that now.'

He leans awkwardly to grapple another log from the huge pile neatly stacked, like Trivial Pursuit wedges, by the side of the fireplace and throws it into the grate. 'Ooof.'

'Careful,' I say, watching as it catches. 'Let me. You'll do yourself more damage.'

'I'm fine, I'm fine,' he says. 'Just a twinge. Nothing to worry about.' He puts his arm around my shoulders and kisses the top of my head for which I'm grateful: when he kisses my cheek his moustache brings me out in a passing rash.

Doug comes in. 'Anyone for eggnog?'

'That's the plan,' I say.

'I'm sticking to whisky,' says my father. 'My back.' He points.

'Coming up,' says Doug.

I see my poor father wince. I feel his pain.

* * *

'I can't believe you put this out,' I say to my mother, when I discover Jack's card, a glittery number in aid of Shelter, sitting proudly among the impressive collection that occupies every window ledge.

'It's a Christmas card. I think he's being very thoughtful. We were his family.'

'"Were" being the operative word.'

'Honestly, Daisy. This is a time for goodwill to all men.'

'And women,' I say. 'Try not to forget the women.'

She leans against the sideboard. 'I don't know how I'm meant to behave with this. I liked him. He was practically my son-in-law. I feel like I've lost someone too.'

'Oh, Ma!' I say, heavy with sarcasm. 'Sorry for your loss.'

She looks downcast. 'You were such a great couple. It's such a shame. I can't tear it up. It's sacrosanct.'

'Not when it's from the Devil, Ma.'

I hand her his card and she slips it into the drawer of the desk, with its letter slots, shelves and recesses. It's still full of pens and stationery, the things I would love to sift through, the thrill of finding the odd stale Sobranie cigarette, admiring its jewel-coloured beauty, sneaking it away to share with Bee. Choking on it. 'I'll put it in the recycling with the rest of them on January the sixth.'

Jack will be recycled. Pulped. It gives me a sense of satisfaction. How weaselly of him to send my parents a card.

* * *

The Arts and Crafts dining-table has been extended to its full length. The red linen runner stretches from end to end, dotted with decorative trivets. There's a floral centrepiece, adorned with holly berries clustered around a flickering white church candle; there are the old place mats with their impressionist prints, the cutlery, the red napkins, some smart gold-embossed crackers all waiting for the fun to begin.

'Can we pull the crackers yet?' says Monty.

'Wait for Grandma to sit down,' says Eve.

'Hurry up, Grandma!' shouts Eddie, cupping his mouth to form a foghorn.

'I'll go and see what's she's doing,' I say.

My mother is in the kitchen fussing over the turkey. 'I need to let it rest. I'm running behind.' She checks her list. 'What am I talking about? We've got the pâté to eat. I'm so befuddled today.'

'Ma,' I say reassuringly. 'Stop worrying. It will all be delicious. It always is.'

'Okay, okay,' she says, tucking the foil around the huge turkey.

'I need to talk to you later,' I say. 'Privately. I've made a decision about something.' As soon as I say it, as soon as I see her even more befuddled face, I know I've made a mistake. I'm so keen to put it out there that I've misjudged the timing, but since I made the decision, having booked the appointment, I can think of little else. And I'm desperate to share. Most of all with my mother.

She looks up at me, her face hot and pink, then goes to the sink and washes her hands. 'What decision?' she says. 'You have to tell me now. I can't sit through Christmas lunch wondering what decision my daughter has made.'

'It's best I tell you later. I just want to find some time with you.' My mother is the mediator for my father: when there's something he might not approve of, you have to get her backing first. You can then leave him to her. She wins him round. That's how it works.

'Why?'

I laugh uncomfortably. 'All right. I'll tell you now. I'm going to try to get pregnant. In the new year.'

'What are you saying? Have you met someone?'

'I'm using sperm donation. Going solo.'

I watch her face darken as she absorbs the news, and try to take her hand as a gesture of reassurance. She avoids me, choosing to pump out some moisturizer from beside the sink, rubbing it vigorously into her palms then stroking it through her fingers. 'I have no idea what you're talking about.'

'The father will be sort of anonymous.'

She looks back at me. 'What does that mean? Sort of?'

'All right. I'll be using an anonymous donor.'

She screws up her face and inhales deeply. I wait for her to exhale.

'Fine,' she says. 'Just don't tell your father.'

'Why not?'

'He won't understand.'

'Well, maybe he should. It's my last crack at having a baby. How can he object?'

'Because he believes Jack is your last crack at having a baby.'

'And so do you, don't you?'

'It's certainly a better option than this.'

I wait a beat. 'Tell Dad when you think he's ready to understand.'

She purses her lips. Her nostrils flare. I hold my position.

'You take the smoked mackerel pâté and I'll take the Melba toast.'

* * *

We pull the crackers, the adults as eagerly as the children, all rushing to put on our paper crowns, simultaneously screaming as we grab the novelties that drop out. My mother holds up a tiny measuring tape, gazing at it with disdain. 'I bought expensive ones this year and the gifts are just as awful,' she says.

'They did look pretty, though,' says Eve. 'Expensive.'

'An expensive pile of rubbish now,' says Doug.

'Remind me not to do it again,' says my mother.

'Oh, you'll do it again,' says my father.

* * *

There's a moment when I catch my mother looking at me. As our eyes meet she glances away. I feel deflated by her reaction to my plan, hoping that the passing of weeks had allowed her and Dad to let go of Jack. I wasn't expecting to find them still clinging to the wreckage.

After lunch Eve and I help clear the table while Doug entertains the children and my father slips into his study for a bit of peace and quiet, meaning a glass of whisky and a snooze on the couch.

'Daisy and I can do this,' says my mother. 'You go and help Doug.'

'He's fine,' says Eve. 'He loves fooling around with his boys.'

'No, no, honestly. I'll wash, Daisy will dry, and the dish-washer will do the rest. Off you go!'

Eve seems strangely miffed. She has no idea why my mother is being so unusually forthright. Her head drops as she leaves. For once I actually feel sorry for her.

'So, come on, then,' says my mother, handing me a tea-towel. 'Explain. You're going to have a baby using a man-you-don't-know-from-Adam's sperm. Is that right?'

'That's the objective, yes.'

'Hmm. Philippa's daughter, Emma, did something simi-lar because her husband was shooting blanks but I've never heard of this.'

I gulp, horrified on behalf of Emma and her husband. 'I get the feeling you discuss everything with your book club except books,' I say. 'I'd rather you kept this between us.'

'Trust me,' she says. 'This is not going anywhere. Have you even considered who's going to look after this baby when you're at work?' She pours boiling water into the roasting tin, adds a squish of Fairy Liquid and leaves it to soak, turning her attention to a saucepan, which she scrubs with indecent aggression.

'Assuming I'm successful.'

'Of course you'll be successful. You've never failed at anything.'

She is my mother. That's how she thinks. She slots the saucepan into the draining rack. I pick it up and start drying. 'When it's small, I'll be able to take it into work. Eventually I'll find a crèche. Babysitters. You and Dad,' I brave, and she gives me a testy look.

'And what about in the middle of the night when the baby has a temperature, or it's cutting teeth and keeping you awake and you're exhausted? Who are you going to share that with? How are you going to manage the crying and the vomiting and the worrying on your own?' She brings a yellow Marigold-gloved hand to her forehead and pushes away a loose wisp of hair.

'I'm guessing you're not in favour.'

'I'm merely asking. I'm wondering if you've considered anything beyond the romance of having a baby.'

'I'm under no illusions, Mother.'

'I'm not so sure.'

'I've always wanted children. You know that.'

'Yes, that's true. You always wanted to hold every baby you ever saw. But babies grow into Montys and Eddies. How are you going to manage when they're not sweet and compliant any more, when they have minds of their own?'

'I've thought about all the pros and cons, as far as I can anticipate them, and I'll manage. Because I'll have to. I'm on my own now and I'm managing far better than I ever thought I would.'

She looks like she's running everything through a processor and the algorithms are coming back unfavourably. 'Well, that's good for now,' she says. 'But you're managing one person. You! A baby is something entirely different. Ask Bee. She's not exactly had it easy this last year. And meeting someone once you have a baby is going to be difficult.'

'Bee's met someone.'

She glances back at me, surprised. 'Oh,' she says. 'I'm pleased for her. Why can't you wait to meet someone?'

The kitchen door swings open.

'Why is Eve so upset?' says Doug, bursting in. 'What did you say to her?'

My mother tuts, turning back to the roasting tin, her shoulders bent inwards. 'Nothing. I just wanted some private time with Daisy. I think that's allowed?'

He stands at her side. 'Couldn't you have said so? Without making her feel as though she was persona non grata.'

'Oh, God!' I say. 'I knew she'd take it to heart. It wasn't intended. Tell her to come back in.'

'Why would she want to come back into this welcome? Look at you in your huddle! Would you prefer me to leave too?'

'It's not what you think,' I say, hating that he feels excluded. 'I'm trying to get pregnant.' My mother flashes me a dark look. 'We're keeping it under wraps for now. Not telling Dad.'

My brother actually laughs.

'If you're going to be rude, then forget I said anything.'

He puts a conciliatory hand on my shoulder. 'That was just my shock reflex. What's occurring, sister?'

'I'm doing it alone. Sperm donation.'

His head tips back. 'You're playing with me?' he says, turning to my mother.

'Don't look at me!' she says.

Doug stares. 'Daise!' he says, with wide-eyed incredulity. 'You're serious?'

'Do you object?'

He shakes his head adamantly. 'Of course not. What you do with your body is up to you. I'm just . . . you know . . . This is huge.'

'This is madness,' says my mother.

'Thank you.'

'Having a baby is wonderful but it's a tough call. Eve was an emotional wreck.'

'I'm not Eve.'

'No. You're not. But a lot of the time I was an emotional wreck too. It was one of the toughest things we've ever been through. And we were in it *together*.'

'That's what I've been telling her,' says my mother. 'It's no easy ride.'

'Which is why you had Eddie, right, Doug?'

He sneers, like What's that got to do with anything? 'Yes, we had Eddie but that was tough too.'

I can see my mother willing him to come up with more that might deter me.

'But you went through it again because you wanted a family?' I say.

'Of course.'

'So you accept that occasionally you have to wade through the tough times to get what you want?' His face registers. 'It's what I want, Doug. It's what I've always wanted.'

He puffs his cheeks. 'Fair point,' he says. 'But why won't you wait to meet someone?'

My mother looks at me. 'That's what I said.'

'The clue is in my age. I don't have time.'

I hear her quiet scoff. 'There are women in the *Daily Mail* in their sixties who've had babies.'

'I don't want to be in the *Daily Mail*.'

'Then we have to get behind you,' says Doug.

'Do we?' says my mother. 'I don't necessarily feel inclined to encourage something I think is a very bad decision.'

'Well, I'm here for you,' he says.

I put down the soggy tea-towel and walk over to kiss his cheek. 'Thanks, bro. I couldn't love you more. Do you mind keeping this from Eve? I know you two have no secrets but I'd be grateful. I've got to have my eggs checked out before I do anything else anyway. It's not a given.'

'Oh, Daisy,' says my mother. 'What on earth are you letting yourself in for?'

Christmas not a resounding success. My plan did not get a great reception from Ma who is determined to shield Dad from the so-called terrible idea. I told Doug too. After some cajoling, no instantaneous round of applause, he came good. I REMAIN RESOLUTE.

17

Caro's Clapham flat – with fairy lights, Happy New Year banners, music thumping, the smell of the evening's buffet – is bursting at the seams. Despite the freezing cold, well-oiled guests head out onto her tiny balcony as the beer, Prosecco, tequila and rum punch spill from disposable glasses. The floor is sticky beneath our feet.

I'm standing at the side of the room, wondering who to talk to next, which unfamiliar face looks the least intimidating.

It occurs to me I no longer know who Caro hangs out with. I only ever go out with her on my own: to bars, for dinner, the cinema, the theatre. We're a happy twosome, rarely cross-pollinating, apart from birthday celebrations or the occasional wedding. It never occurred to me I might feel alienated, barely knowing any of her friends, that finding myself in a sea of unrecognizable faces, including the ones from university I should probably know, is rather disconcerting. It's hard work on an evening I wanted to be easy, hoping it would soothe my wounds.

Caro's obviously better at staying in touch with people than I am. A number of uni folk here fell off my radar another lifetime ago. I wonder if it's a singles thing that when you're on your own you make more of an effort to keep in touch with people. When you're with someone, you neglect the friends peripheral to your immediate circle, losing whatever you once had in common. Guilty! And now my guilt has caught up with me.

'Hey, Daisy!' says a vaguely familiar face. 'Étienne. We were in the same year.'

'Of course,' I say, trying to hide my amazement. He used to be really handsome with long sexy hair that went perfectly with his sexy name. I quite fancied him, although he was in no doubt that every available female fancied him. Not any more. In middle age he has lost his hair and acquired a small paunch.

'Lawyer! But I guess I was always heading that way.'

'Right.'

'Married to that beautiful woman over there.' I follow his finger. I don't want to be mean but his wife is better preserved. He's obviously punched above that extra weight. 'Three kids,' he says.

Punch in the gut.

'Wow!' I say. 'Life's been good to you.' He nods, with a smirk that says it would be hard to disagree.

'What about you?' he says. 'Husband? Kids?'

'Not that I know of.'

He laughs. 'Still the wit.'

I smile casually, hiding the hurt, managing a dismissive shrug to make out it's not even on my to-do list while feeling a complete failure. Why do people have no compunction about asking such intimate questions? I mean, we all want to know where old friends have ended up but does it have to be the first question asked?

A woman joins us, saving me. 'Hi, Daisy,' she says. She's another I should know but I'm struggling to place her. 'Julia Pottinger,' she says. 'We were in the same halls.'

'Of course,' I say. 'Sorry. Yeah! Remember you now. You look great!'

'You don't have to flatter me,' she says, with a sigh. 'I'm a doctor. I'm positively exhausted. Let alone married with two kids. I'm fully aware it shows.'

'It doesn't,' I say, my stomach literally starting to churn.

'Juggle, juggle, juggle,' she says, throwing her hands around like she has several balls in the air. 'What about you? Married? Kids?' She looks over my shoulder as if some imaginary husband might appear. 'Divorced? We're at that age now, aren't we? Can you believe it? I can't. I don't think I know a single mate from our year who isn't divorced. Except Étienne. And Caro, of course, but she's defiantly single. And looks amazing on it. Maybe she's the only one who's got it right.'

I nod. 'Yeah, maybe.'

'Daisy hasn't married or had kids,' Étienne throws in, like he's now in charge of my CV. 'Which surprises me since you were once the hottest girl on the planet.' He says this without any misgivings.

'Really,' I say. 'Well, we can't all be hot for ever, can we?'

Julia smiles awkwardly, her eyelashes fluttering, trying to ignore the underlying truculence in our exchange. 'So what's your story, then, Daisy?'

I clear my throat. 'I've got an interior design company. Baxter Settle. Sounds fancy but it's just me and Marcus Baxter. We met at design school.'

Étienne nods. 'My wife dabbles in interiors.'

I groan inside at the all-too-familiar comment.

'More of a career girl, then?' says Julia.

For some reason I feel compelled to justify myself. 'I was in a long-term relationship but it came to a natural conclusion a few months ago.'

Her jaw juts forward. 'Oh, Daisy! Sorry to hear that.'

'I'm fine about it,' I say.

'We ought to mingle,' says Étienne.

I mingle aimlessly, finding I'm happier observing the activity from a discreet corner of the room. Caro is wandering around with a bottle of Prosecco, making sure we're all completely off our heads before midnight.

I see her spot me. 'You playing at being a wallflower?' she says, filling my glass.

'Do people constantly ask you why you're single?'

Her lips curl. 'Is that what's happening?'

'Seems to be the only thing people are interested in. That and how many kids I have.'

'Sorry about that,' she says. She takes a swig from the bottle as I look on in horror.

'Don't worry,' she says. 'It's only the dregs. I won't be serving up my spit!' She lets out a snort. 'Unless someone wants it!'

'I think I'll pass, thanks.'

'To be honest, I think it's because you look so good, no one can believe you're on your own.'

'So what's your excuse, then?'

She leans against the wall with me. 'Everyone knows I have no interest in getting married or having kids. They've given up asking. You shouldn't take it personally.'

'Caro,' I say, 'it is personal.'

She grabs my face with her perfectly manicured left hand, her long nails pressing into my cheeks, making my lips go Donald Duck. 'How many of these people are you going to see again?' she says.

'Probably one,' I quack. 'You!'

'Fuck 'em, then. Tell them you're married and your husband is at home babysitting your four children.'

I laugh. 'If only,' I say.

She kisses me on the lips. 'It'll be better next year, babe,' she says. 'Promise . . . sorry for sharing my spit!'

* * *

Later, having mainly managed to avoid further assaults on my status, I find myself huddled between a bunch of people's backs, clutching another disposable flute, sipping the final dregs of a warm Prosecco, wondering whether I can slip away before midnight.

'Daisy, isn't it?'

I smile at the attractive face that breaks into my internal plotting, hoping he isn't just another guy from university I've forgotten about who will go on to press all my vulnerability buttons. 'Sorry,' I say. 'I'm really bad with names.'

'Oh, don't worry, you don't know me. But Caro talks about you a lot so I feel as if I know you.' He has no idea how much relief this comment brings. 'Glad to finally meet you.'

'Nice to meet you too!' I say.

'Oliver,' he announces coyly. 'I'm guessing she's never mentioned me?'

I clench my jaw. ''Fraid not.' More's the pity, I think.

As my eyes study his face he becomes more and more handsome. The most beautiful glowing skin, deep brown eyes, head perfectly shaven. I never imagined I might find a bald man attractive but he really is. I wonder why Caro's kept him a secret.

'Fair enough. No reason why she should.' He smiles and tips his head at my empty glass. 'You look like you need another drink. Can I get you one? I was just going to get myself a top-up.'

'Great, thanks,' I say, smiling. Suddenly, a little glimmer

of New Year's Eve hope is lighting up my darkest year's end.

I watch him weave through the crowded room, before marking his return, drinks held aloft, avoiding being bumped and elbowed, as he heads back to my spot. 'Cheers,' he says, handing me the Prosecco. 'Happy New Year. Nearly.' He checks his watch. 'Very nearly.'

'Happy Very Nearly New Year.' I grin, trying to contain my excitement.

'I suppose you're glad this year's over?'

'Oh!' I say, checking myself. 'Do I take it Caro told you?'

'She did.' He looks at me uncomfortably. 'I'm not being indiscreet, am I?'

I laugh in a gesture of reassurance. 'No, no! Not at all. It was never a secret. I reckon the whole of my birthday party and beyond knew about it. It was a pretty hot story. Although I'd rather I hadn't had the leading role.'

He grits his teeth. 'I'm so sorry,' he says. 'But you look happy.'

'Getting there.'

'So . . . are you dating yet? You must have them queuing round the block.'

I sip my drink, trying to hide my irrepressible glee at his obvious delving. 'Hardly,' I say.

'A bit soon, I guess.'

'Not really. I just haven't met anyone is the truth.'

'A new year always helps. You can put all the crap behind you!'

'That's the plan.'

'And who knows?' he says, flashing his eyes. 'Maybe you'll meet someone tonight.'

'I'd like that,' I say, trying desperately hard not to seem too keen and yet be open.

'I don't know how you didn't murder him.'

'Who?'

'Your ex!' He laughs. 'I think my wife would definitely have murdered me.'

I swallow hard trying not to gag. 'Oh. Yes, well, I would have liked to murder him, trust me.' I flash an upbeat smile as my heart sinks into my feet. 'So is your wife here?'

He looks around. 'Over there.' He points. 'The one with the long blonde ponytail. She's one of Caro's yoga buddies but we go out together quite a lot after their sessions. Which is why I suppose I know your story.'

'Oh, right,' I say.

He rolls forward on his toes. 'I guess I should get back to her or she might start to plot my murder.'

Wild laugh. 'Of course. You should.'

'But glad to have met you.'

'Likewise,' I say. 'Have a good new year!'

What was I thinking? What made me think that Caro wouldn't have told me about a single guy in her entourage? Of course he'd be married. And of course she'd have a long blonde ponytail and a ridiculous yoga-honed figure. I guzzle the rest of my drink. Fuck it! I need to get a grip. I'd come with no expectations other than to have a good time, and because I didn't want to be the loser who stays in. I chose not to go out with my loved-up friends. Rob and Bee, Victoria and Gina, Marcus and Flynn. I thought I'd feel more comfortable here, with Caro, my lone single mate, my ally in singledom. But I didn't think it through. I didn't think how I'd feel when people inevitably asked me about my relationship status. That I'd be feeling left behind by people I really didn't care about who have partners and children, and suddenly I care deeply. I'm angry that I believed I wasn't looking to meet anyone, then one kind smile from a bloke and I'm excited. And now I feel deflated because I misinterpreted someone's kindness for interest. Worse still, I wanted it. Am I telling myself one big lie? Is my determination to be a solo mother as precarious as a new year's resolution?

* * *

We're fifteen minutes away from 1 January. I can go home soon. If I can get a cab.

I watch Caro getting ready for the Big Ben countdown, rushing around in her role as best hostess, making sure everyone's armed with a drink.

She turns up the music, which pumps through the speakers, and everyone starts bouncing and bopping on the sticky wooden floor, the sound of feet, like thunder, pounding through my head.

I'm back in my corner, standing with the non-dancers, a guy next to me, loudly spouting economics at a woman who looks bored out of her skull. Where are the decent men? The witty entertaining ones? The ones without wives? Who look like Jack but don't act like Jack. Do they even exist?

The music is turned down and the bongs blast out of Caro's TV.

Ten! Nine! Eight! I yell in tandem with the crowd elevating my mood. It's a new year. Allegedly things can only get better.

. . . Three!

Two!

One!

HAPPY NEW YEAR!

I watch as everyone mixes, hugging and high-fiving and fist-bumping, noisily toasting a new year with all its drunken optimism, finding myself, back against the wall, looking at Étienne and his wife kissing and laughing because what do a paunch and a bald head matter when you love someone? At Oliver and his wife doing a highly sexy jive. At the guy next to me, who was spouting economics, snogging the face off the woman who only a moment ago couldn't have been less interested, and I wonder how relationships work. Whether I'm better off being a loser on my own than a winner with a cheat. Whether I'll be happier in charge of my own destiny. Or with Jack.

His face filters into my muddled thoughts. Where is he now? Is he kissing Polly? Or is he thinking about me the way I'm thinking about him?

Should auld acquaintance be forgot.

18

'This place is quite gorgeous,' says Bee. 'You'd think we were entering a spa. It must be costing you an arm, a leg and a kidney.'

'Just the kidney.' I take her hand as if to prove I still have limbs.

We approach the reception desk.

I'm nervous. I'm excited. My mouth feels dry. This is really happening, I tell myself.

The fertility clinic is discreetly housed on London's Harley Street behind a highly polished front door. The reception area is neutral and elegant. It smells beautiful. A huge scented candle is flickering in an ornate glass pot sitting at the end of the long marble desk.

The high ceilings with their intricate cornicing are painted something akin to Elephant's Breath. The herringbone parquet floor is undoubtedly original. There are several crescent-moon sofas, generously spaced, covered with a greige leather. The smartly dressed receptionists, slick make-up, headsets with mics that don't interfere with their perfect blow-dry, give an air of super-efficiency.

If the designer's brief was *We want to convey a sophisticated operation where clients can feel professionally managed while cocooned in a beautiful environment*, they've nailed it. Bee is right: this could definitely pass for a fancy spa.

I check in at the desk and we're pointed towards one of the sofas. 'The nurse will be with you shortly.'

'You okay?' asks Bee, as we sit on the edge of the smart sofa.

'Terrific,' I say. 'Actually, delete that. Insert terrified.'

She grasps my hand firmly. 'You can make a run for it,' she says. 'There's time.'

I breathe deeply. 'Not gonna happen.'

She pats the back of my hand like it's going to be okay.

'I know,' I say.

'Daisy Settle?'

'That's me!' I jump up. Bee jumps up. We're no different from the well-behaved school kids we used to be. 'Okay if my friend comes?' The nurse, brown hair tied back, no make-up, pristine uniform, white plimsolls, tells us to follow her.

We are taken into a small room with two chairs and equipment laid out for a blood test. I sit down opposite her and Bee stands in the corner.

'I'm going to take some blood to check your AMH levels.'

'Right,' I say. Dr Baldwin has filled me in on this.

'Your AMH levels determine how many eggs you have in reserve so that we know how well you might respond to IVF if needed.'

'Okay.'

After a search for a decent vein, she tells us to go back to Reception and wait for the sonographer.

We don't have to wait long. The sonographer, about six foot tall, making me feel very small, white coat, white plimsolls, short blonde hair, takes us down a long corridor, then another, through to a large, windowless room. There's an examination bed draped with the usual rollout disposable paper. The equipment and screens look very twenty-first century.

'Slip into the side room and remove your lower clothing, please, including your underwear. I say that because everyone always asks. There's a gown hanging on the back of the door for you. Leave your shoes in the room and come out when you're ready. '

I sit on the chair, unzip my boots, wondering what the hell I'm doing. I take off my tights and knickers and breathe.

And breathe.

And breathe.

I laugh to myself because I'm here. Because I'm starting this process. And I can't quite believe it.

'How do I look?' I say to Bee, coming back into the room, twirling in the gown, giving her a glimpse of my buttocks. 'This is my mooning outfit.'

She smiles. 'I particularly like that colour on you.'

I lie down on the bed, watching as the technician puts a mega sheath over what can only be described as a huge dildo. I look on in horror, lying prone, legs like jelly.

'This might hurt as I enter,' she says, po-faced, 'But don't worry. If you relax, focus, take deep breaths, it will soon feel fine.'

'That's what they all say,' I mutter.

Bee, who is standing at my head, stiffens. I know she's trying not to laugh. I love Bee. Right now I couldn't love her more.

'Just breathe, please, Mrs Settle. Try to relax.'

I take a deep breath then blow out slowly. 'I'm a Ms,' I say.

'Sorry,' she says, pushing a hot poker up my vagina. 'Easy. You see. Not that bad after all.'

For whom? I think, legs akimbo, wishing I'd had a leg wax, or at least shaved them. Thinking I'm neglecting myself because there's no one to notice me any more. Because there's no one. I'm here because I have no one.

'You okay?' asks Bee, as if reminding me I have someone.

'Terrific,' I say. She knows what to delete and insert.

I lie back and think of England.

* * *

'How do you feel?' says Bee, as we walk out into the cold, dank air.

'Messed with.'

* * *

That evening I pace the room, obsessing about my results. I pour some wine to try to calm myself. Sit with a magazine, trying to read but not really caring, then start pacing again. The moment I see Dr Baldwin's name light up on my phone I put down my glass as though she can see me. Or in case I take an unthinking sip and she hears. I told her my wine consumption was minimal. About three units a week. What I meant was a day. Slip of the tongue. I'm not proud of drinking alone but what choice have I? I'll stop as soon as I need to. I will.

My hand trembles as I swipe to accept.

'I'm afraid it's what I suspected, Daisy,' she says. 'But please don't castigate yourself. It's the same for most women over forty. You need to have your eggs stimulated. You're at least fortunate. Your AMH reading was good. Adequately high. That means your reserve is good, which is positive. If it was low, IVF is not necessarily recommended.'

I stare at the phone as if the call is not intended for me. I reach out for the wine, then resist. 'What exactly does stimulated mean?' I ask.

Dr Baldwin tells me precisely what it means.

102

Hormones, basically. Self-injecting. Maturing my eggs on speed.

'Fine,' I say, trying to stop her making me feel the very opposite of positive.

'I'm so sorry,' she says. 'But let's be honest, it's not totally unexpected.'

'No, of course not,' I lie. For whom?

IVF.

My most dreaded acronym.

Well, apart from STD. And UTI. And now AMH, although that's a good one, for me at least.

I guess I should be grateful the option even exists. But I'm not. I'm scared and angry with myself. Angry that I left it too long. Angry that I allowed Jack to lead the way.

Why did I not prioritize what I wanted?

Why did I trust him?

On everything.

Because I loved him, that's why. But love is a losing game. You were so right, Amy Winehouse. Look where love has got me. Wait! Look where it got you. Which somehow makes me a winner. A pyrrhic victory.

Once upon a time, IVF was for other people. Now I'm other people. I'm in the category of women over forty for whom it is inevitable. Why did I not know this? Was I so dazzled by the excitement of my life that I failed to inform myself of the facts of life other than the ones I already knew? Failed to be curious about something so important and vital to my very existence? How could I have been so naïve? Or am I merely human?

I loathe myself. I feel like my body isn't fit for purpose. Everything is going wrong. Everything.

Bee tells me to take my time before making a decision. She thinks I haven't given myself enough distance from the trauma of my fortieth. That I need time to heal. But maybe I'll never heal. Maybe none of us do. We just bury the pain, hoping to forget it, hoping it will go away. But it never does. Pain memory is smarter than we are. It sits patiently, waiting to pounce. And it knows all the best moments.

'IVF is a big decision,' Marcus says. 'You're putting chemicals into your body. IVF messes with your pathology. You have to be really confident it's what you want to do. At the end of the day, the only one putting pressure on you is you. It's your choice. No one will judge you if you change your mind.'

Why did I think I'd sail through sperm donation? That it would be just a few clicks away. I hate to admit it but maybe my father was right. From exams, to boyfriends, to business ventures: they all fell into place, lulling me into a false sense of security, into believing that a good life was what happened if you were a good person who played by the rules. If you were kind, loyal, hardworking. If you were nice to animals and children. Turns out the universe is not a meritocracy after all, and the tectonic plates of my future have shifted.

I never signed up to this. I'm not programmed for it. Fuck it! Fuck it!

I pull out my Moleskine, full of my random scribbles.

But this isn't going to be random. I have to think this through seriously. I need to write a list – a Fuck It list – of all the pros and cons, challenging my feelings:

1 *Is it a baby I want or Jack's baby I wanted?*
2 *Am I strong enough to cope on my own with what lies ahead?*
3 *How will I cope if I fail?*
4 *Will a baby change my life for the better? Is that what this is about?*

5   *Will I be capable of looking after a baby on my own, being a solo mother?*
6   *Is it enough to know Bee and Marcus are there?*
7   *Is this a time when I need the support of my family? Not just Doug, for whom I'm forever grateful, but Ma. Do I need to have a proper adult conversation with her? Should Dad be involved? What to do, Universe? Give me a sign!*

I sleep with the notebook under my pillow. Maybe what I've written will enter my subconscious and give me the answers. I wake up, feel under my pillow and grab my pen. The answer is unequivocal.

Yes! I want a baby. I will be capable. I will be a good solo mother. The longing has always been there and, in the end, I know myself better than anyone.

It's not about Jack. It's not about my family and what they might think. It's about me.

And if IVF is what it takes, fuck it! I'm going to face down my fears, ignore the naysayers, and listen to my heart.

19

My sterile flat feels far cosier with another person here. Bee brings warmth and familiarity into my weird new single life, making it feel less alien.

She looks at the Thai menu on my laptop. 'If you're having chicken green curry, I guess I'll have prawn pad Thai and we can share.'

'Perfect! Add it to the order. What about a starter? Spring rolls.'

'Yum! You're sure?'

'Yes! You've paid for a babysitter. This is my treat.'

'Added!' she says.

I bring over the plates and put them on the coffee-table. 'It's eat on laps, I'm afraid. That's the system here. How long before they deliver?'

She checks. 'Forty minutes. Let's do this thing,' she says. 'You call up the sperm website.'

'Bee!'

'Sorry. But that's what it is, isn't it?'

She slides the laptop across to me. It feels warm on my thighs.

I call up the site and log in. I've already filled in my details, confirmed my physical choices, stated my priorities (health), checked them a thousand times, but haven't uploaded the form yet. I wanted Bee to be here so that she can help me make the final decision once they send through the three donors, which they do very quickly.

This particular site doesn't send through a beauty parade to overwhelm you. Its algorithm picks out what it considers to be the best three donors specifically for you. God help you if their algorithms go rogue.

It's a British site, one preferred by my clinic. They were incredibly helpful, giving experienced counsel but entirely happy for the decision to be mine. They can handle sperm from anywhere! In the end, their advice made sense.

UK donors don't get a fee, just expenses. It's not that I object to paying – honestly, I'm ready to give up my life's savings and practically already have. It's just that I like the idea that the donor is doing this altruistically.

He must also accept that the child can contact him, should they wish, once they've reached eighteen. I think that's important. Some children may not care but others may find themselves unfulfilled by the wondering. It's fair to let them have the choice.

Another stand-out was that UK sites impose a limit on the donor of ten donations. Your child won't be one of a family of, say, thirty-five, as it may should you happen to choose some prolific American benefactor. Or if you go with a private donor. Bee found someone on Facebook the other day. 'He'll do it for sixty quid,' she says.

'Sounds dodgy, no?'

'For some people it may be their only hope.' She giggles. 'Of course, the child will have the biggest family tree they'll never know!'

'Right,' I say decisively, my completed application checked one final time. 'Let's order my sperm takeaway. I'm pressing send.' I reach out my hand and grab hers. 'One – two – three!'

'Done,' she says. 'Now what happens?'

'I guess they send me the three guys they think are a match.'

'Spermmatch.com.' She snorts.

'You love that word, don't you?' I say.

'Sperm, sperm, sperm!' she says. 'Come on! Let's get with the program.'

We sit there staring at my screen. We jump at the ping of a new email, even though that's exactly what we're waiting for.

'You look,' I say. 'I can't.' The laptop slides back to her.

'It's from them,' she says. She hits the first link.

I stare. 'Is that it?' I say, as various childhood photos pop up.

Bee moves the cursor around. 'You just see them as babies and children, apparently. I guess that gives you an idea of what half your child might look like. Before you add half of you.'

'And stir!' I flip through the photos. 'He's sweet. I like him.'

'Oh, wow!' she says. 'Look! He's written letters to you and your future child. This is so emotional, Daise.'

'I know!' I say, welling up.

'Wait! Here are his documents detailing his medical background. It's very thorough.'

'It has to be,' I say. 'It's not Facebook.'

We wade through the three profiles, every photo, every detail, the information about their background, every medical fact, their letters.

Finally, I look at Bee. 'It's him, isn't it?' I say. 'I know it's him. What do you think?'

'No question,' she says. 'It's him.' I stand up and come back with two glasses of water. 'Read his letter to me out loud. I want to hear it as though he's speaking to me. In your voice, obviously.'

'Okay, because I'm not going to put on some random man's voice.'

She clears her throat and starts reading:

I come from a family of four siblings. We are two brothers, two sisters. My mother conceived easily. She says she could have gone on having children for ever. We were very loved. Only economics held her and my father back. So when I became old enough to appreciate that not everyone enjoys my parents' fertility prowess, I decided I wanted to help. I knew that if a couple or maybe a woman on her own ['That's you,' interjects Bee] were so sure they wanted a child that they would choose to embark on this difficult route, then that child would be loved. That the partner was generous enough to overcome ego and know their progeny would not have their genetics, that the mother was prepared to enter into a pact with a stranger that might bring about the gift of a longed-for child. To know that I've helped would feel like I had done a wonderful thing. Not that I will know the results in the short term but, hopefully, statistics will be favourable and maybe some time in the future I'll know of my success. And I'll get to meet them as young adults. So this is why I'm on this site. I want my sperm to help you create the child you long for, the child you will love. I hope it works for you. Adam

She puts down the laptop and holds her arms open for me. 'Congratulations! It's Adam,' she says.

'So long as he hasn't been maxed out.'

'That sounds gross!'

'They warn you that you might pick someone who's reached his ten limit in the time you take to get back.'

'Let's do this quickly, then!'

We watch and wait. I get up and walk around.

'Oh my God! Affirmative!' Bee cries.

'Hello, ADAM!'

'Adam sperm!' screams Bee, and we dance around the room, hugging each other, jumping up and down, buoyant with the sense of success. The sense of possibility. The sense of hope.

The intercom rings.

'Here's the other takeaway,' she yells. 'Thai sperm rolls.'

'Stop it now, Bee,' I scoff. 'You'll put me off my meal.'

20

I wake up every morning and try to ignore the sense of anxiety in my stomach. It's so reliably there that it's become a part of me. As familiar as my morning routine. Anxiety, journal, tea, teeth, shower, get dressed, put on make-up, check phone, go to work, different anxiety, come home, reverse rinse, repeat.

But now there's an even greater anxiety to add to the list. My daily routine is getting an addition that will sit somewhere between reverse rinse and repeat. I'm at the beginning of my cycle. I have to start self-injecting. It needs to be done in a regular window and I've elected to do it between seven and nine in the evening. I don't know how I'm going to feel but I don't want to feel sick on my way to or during work. Better the hormones do their magic overnight. I imagine them like micro ants, pummelling away, stimulating my eggs, knocking them into shape. 'Come on, guys! Wake up! Get your act together.' Then I think of my eggs, lazy and deluded. 'Fuck off, ants! We were fine before you got here.'

I've turned my tiny bathroom into my own private clinic, boxes of syringes neatly stacked as if they're no more incongruous than my cotton-wool dispenser, sitting happily next to my make-up remover, my very expensive nearly empty moisturizer, my pink Himalayan bath salts and an Amber candle. Next to my bathroom pedal bin is the mini sharps box I'm about to christen with my first emptied syringe.

This is momentous. What has, until this singular point in time, been nothing more than an idea thrown around in my head, a discussion with a doctor, a clinic, a demonstration on YouTube, a book I'm reading, is about to become reality. As soon as I take the first of those syringes in my hand, as soon as the needle pierces my skin, as soon as the magic potion is released, then in the most chemical, most prosaic, most unromantic of ways, I will be realizing a passionate, ardent dream.

I sit down and stare at the syringe in my shaking hand.

I'm such a coward. At the doctor's I look away. How am I ever going to inject myself? I'm hoping that by creating a peaceful ambiance I will keep calm and con my brain into telling my body this is all a delicious treat.

To set the scene, I've put on some gentle background music.

I've lit a scented candle and turned off the light. This, I tell myself, is an act of self-love. It's going to be a short, sharp shock and then done. I'm going to ace it. Yet every part of me wants to black out.

'You can do this,' I say quietly, my insides slightly cramping.

'Yes, you can!'

'Thank you, Mr Obama!' Where the hell are *you* now?

My heart pounds. My breathing is shallow and fast. My hand is still quivering unrelentingly. I'm going to fail. I can't do it.

'Yes, you can!'

'Okay, Barak! I hear you, man!'

Deep breath. Focus on one spot. Exhale. Inhale. Long and slow. Long and slow . . . I'm feeling slightly high. Pinch my stomach, hold thick fleshy bit between thumb and finger, take aim . . . FIRE!

Fuck!

Plunge, pull out, fumble for sharps box, quickly sit down on side of bath, stick head between legs and breathe.

There's a burning tingle.

It subsides.

I remind myself to keep breathing.

I look around.

I haven't fainted! I'm still conscious. I am alive.

I've done it! Barak! Mate! I've only gone and bloody done it!

Note to self: Next time ensure you have a glass of water next to you.

Note to self: Well done!

I tick 1 and 2 on my Fuck It list

21

This month has felt like nothing but rain, not helped by exceptional winds that batter the poor trees and everything else in their path, lingering malignly in waiting, whipping up when you least expect, keeping even the meteorologists on the back foot. Happily the scaffolding at the Peckham property has held up. As did Benedict Shaw's and Baxter Settle's company signs. They were well tethered.

My umbrella keeps blowing inside out, the broken spines flapping annoyingly in my face. 'For fuck's sake!' I scowl. 'Do your job. The one I paid for you to do!' Admittedly not that much. You get what you pay for.

In the end, I give in and face the elements. The wind pummels my body, driving the rain into every nook and cranny. I'm drenched within seconds. My hair sticks to the sides of my face.

I can see Benedict in the distance, large black umbrella, arriving ahead of me, wearing his usual coat and what looks like a khaki beanie hat. I put on a pace, trying to catch him before he goes inside.

'Hey!' I shout, and he turns with the look of a haunted man.

'Oh, it's you,' he says, as I approach, still running. He clocks my rain-sodden appearance. 'Have you ever thought about putting up that umbrella?'

I let the offender drop on the outside step. 'It's a cheap one. It looked pretty. Turns out it's only skin deep.'

'I see,' he says, and somehow, with just two tiny words, I feel chastened for being cheap.

Brushing his coat of the excess beads of water that have bravely managed to find their way past his obviously expensive model, he rolls up his umbrella with concentrated precision, pressing the popper to hold it in immaculate place. I find myself engrossed, as if he's showing me how it's done. Dutifully, I observe the master. He grabs a hard hat and hands one to me, putting it on over his beanie. 'I always forget how freezing this place is,' he says, then pulls out a fancy camera from his perfectly beaten-up satchel, and slings it round his neck. 'Ready?'

'For my close-up, Mr DeMille?'

'Let's start at the top of the house.' Deadpan.

'Why not?'

The task ahead is as dull as he is humourless. We're deciding on the positioning of the new fuseboard, the switches and sockets, the lights, where to conceal the speakers for the sound system, which will be run discreetly throughout the house. We have to commit to the best placing of nearly thirty radiators. (The notion that this job is purely about glamour is nonsense.) Little details, small but crucially important, need to be established. Where we put the smart thermostats, one on each floor, which will make them efficient but not intrusive. Things that most people think have landed by magic, the architect or the designer, or both in this case, have sweated over, although there's not much chance of us working up a sweat today. I'm wearing thermals, which feel wet and sticky, a thick coat, ditto, a scarf (cashmere, please note, Benedict! He doesn't), thick socks and warm gloves. There's nothing I hate more than the cold apart from wet clothes.

'You can see there's been quite a bit of progress since you

were last here,' he says, taking photographs. 'The bones are nearly done. Almost ready for the flesh.' He nods at me, like I need reminding that's my department.

Maybe it's the way he says 'flesh' but my purple and blue stomach reacts with a pulsating throb. I quickly rub the area that has become a pincushion for the needles I now administer with practised ease.

'Problem?' he says.

'Just a stitch.'

'Not a runner, then?'

I want to punch him. 'No,' I say.

We work through the tasks quickly and easily. There's not much dispute about where things need to go. The way Benedict has designed the bones and I've fleshed them out, there's a natural logicality.

He may be dull and lacking in humour but he's actually good to work with. Decisive. Specific. Says what he thinks but is open to suggestion. Haughty, yes, but in the end it makes it easier. Everything is very professional. Let's get on with the job.

'Let's go to the Danish bakery,' he says, as we wind up. 'We can complete the plans somewhere warm.'

The thought of sitting opposite him in a café I rather like is oddly unappealing. As though he might sour my enjoyment by association.

'Sounds good,' I say.

We walk together, me trying to keep my umbrella from folding in on itself until Benedict grabs it from me and chucks it into a bin we're passing.

'I might need that later,' I say.

'For what exactly?'

We continue under the protection of his, our coats billowing, the wind practically blowing us into one another.

He offers his arm, a pragmatic gesture, and I take it in a pragmatic response because I need to stay as dry as possible and not get blown away.

* * *

We find a seat at one of the raw wooden tables, slapping at our arms trying to get back some feeling.

'I'll get this,' he insists. He slings his satchel onto the bench. 'Cappuccino, right?'

'Great, thanks!' Let's keep the conversation simple. Not disabuse him of his sense of control.

I take off my gloves and blow on my hands. My fingers are rigid with cold, throbbing with pain. I pull out my copy of the plans, a scale ruler, pencil and rubber from my tote. Digital is fast and probably technically more accurate but on some things I remain old-school.

The place is half empty. People are working on laptops at a couple of other tables, but London is still waking up to the fact that Christmas is over. Trees may have been dismantled and discarded, the cards may be in recycling bins (bye-bye, Jack!), but all that's left to look forward to is the looming threat of February, real winter, and no one's rushing into that, least of all January, the longest month of the year.

I look at Benedict, who's standing alone at the counter chatting easily to the barista. She's smiling at him, a twinkle in her eye. I can't believe she's flirting with him. Surely not. I can understand Camilla but a pretty young woman? Perhaps it's me. Perhaps it's hormones. No! I'm right. Someone might be nice to look at but not necessarily nice to hang out with, and as far as Benedict is concerned, I know the truth. Sorry, barista. The truth is disappointing.

I stamp my feet under the table, and clap my hands

trying to revive my extremities. Benedict looks towards my noise and I immediately stop. Jesus! Lighten up, man! I sit down and blow quietly into my cupped hands, the blood slowly starting to return to my fingers. He wanders back with coffees.

'Here,' he says. 'Wrap your hands around that.' He hands me a mug – I wish I could curl my entire body around it. He sits down opposite me, takes off his beanie, revealing his full head of salt-and-pepper hair and puts on a pair of glasses with thick square black frames. I find myself doing a double-take. He looks good.

'Is there a problem?' he says.

'Sorry, no. I was just . . . I like your glasses.'

'Thank you.'

'They suit you,' I say, not knowing why I'm even bothering.

'Right,' he says, like a full stop, and dives into his satchel, placing his plans in front of him. 'Let's do this. I'll draw up the CADs in the office.'

'That's the nicest thing you've said all day,' I say.

He looks at me suspiciously and we carry on with professional efficiency because, in the end, there's a natural symmetry to dislike.

22

'How are you feeling?' Bee asks. 'Used to the injections yet?'

'It appears you can get used to anything.'

There's definitely a greater intimacy about speaking to someone when you're tucked up in bed, just before you fall asleep.

I slide under my freshly washed duvet cover. I'm also getting used to the local launderette. It doesn't look very appealing from the outside, sandwiched between two charity shops with chaotically cluttered windows but I quite like the monotony of the process, the noise, the heat, the folding, the robotic nature of it that allows you a kind of meditative state. I just hate the fight with the duvet as I try to put it back into the cover.

'I'm actually looking forward to the egg extraction rather than worrying myself silly over it. I mean, each stage happens in such swift succession you don't have time to worry.'

'Good,' she says. 'Because . . . and there's no easy way to say this so I'm just saying it.' She allows a moment to pass, leaving a tense vacuum, contradicting herself.

'Go on,' I urge.

I hear her suck her teeth. 'Polly moved in with Jack. Just before Christmas.' She says this at ninety miles an hour.

'Whoa!' My brain is an instant pile-up, every thought slamming into the one in front. I crawl further under the duvet wishing it was sand and I could stick my head in it.

'Shite,' I say, my demons tearing at the patched-up pieces of my heart. 'I mean, it's not like it's a surprise but having it confirmed is . . .'

'You're sounding very muffled,' she says. 'Where have you gone?'

'To Hell,' I say, from under the duvet.

'Sorry,' she says. 'I just thought it better you heard it from me.'

I curl into the foetal position. Visions of Polly hanging her clothes in my wardrobe, placing her things on my bedside table, filling the bathroom with her stuff, Jack bringing her a cup of tea in bed in the morning. 'It's not even as though I want him back. It's just . . .'

'You know what men are like,' says Bee, putting on her reassuring voice. 'He's used to being with someone. He's probably lost without you. He got Polly to fill the gap.'

'His Pollyfilla!'

We giggle gamely and, for a moment, it's funny.

'You've got to laugh, right?' says Bee.

'Not really,' I say.

I reach my hand out from under the duvet, feeling for my book, *Relaxation and Meditation During the IVF Process*, opening it where I left off. 'I'm learning how to meditate,' I say. 'I'm very zen about everything.'

'Right.'

'Which, of course, is a lie. If I'm honest, I have moments, like now, when I immediately feel the need to do something with my life.'

Bee gasps. 'You are doing something with your life! You're trying to have a baby.'

'I know, I know. What I mean is maybe I should try to meet someone. I mean you're with Rob. Vic is with Gina. Marcus has been with Flynn for ever. And now Jack is with

Polly.' Exhale slowly. 'So everyone I know is hooked up, barring Caro, who's bloody great at being single. And sometimes I think I'm getting there. Then news like this comes along and I realize maybe I'm not getting anywhere.'

'Nonsense,' she says. 'You're so much happier. This is difficult news to take in.'

'I know,' I say. 'This too shall pass.'

I disconnect the phone, close the book and reach for my Moleskine.

Polly has moved in with Jack. I hate how that feels. Bee thinks he's just replacing me with her, that she's a temporary fix, but that's hurtful too. Like it doesn't matter who's there so long as there's someone. Like I just happened to be that someone for six years. What does that say about me? It confirms he didn't love me. I thought he loved me for what we shared. Our interests, our humour, there was mutual respect. But it all turned out to be bullshit because the only person he loves is him. He just said what I wanted to hear because it meant he got what he wanted. And now he's probably telling Polly exactly what she wants to hear. He knows the strategy works. And for a while it will. But then he'll move on, which at least is some consolation.

But it hurts. Plain and simple. It shouldn't, not now, but it does. It will always hurt.

23

I talk to him – Adam, I mean. In my head I've turned him into a real live person who needs to know everything that's happening. I'm telling myself a story by way of making this experience less lonely. In my head, I'm one of those couples walking hand in hand down Harley Street, going through it together. 'It's egg-extraction day, Adam,' I say. 'Your moment has arrived.'

'I'm excited,' he replies. 'Good luck. Let me know what happens.'

I've printed both of his letters and stuck them on my fridge with Andy Warhol *Heinz Tomato Soup* magnets. I've decided Adam eats Heinz tomato soup. My story is very detailed. I know Adam intimately because, in a way, I'm about to.

They sedate you to aspirate the eggs. You have to fast the night before so I'm pretty hungry. During the procedure I feel kind of high, woozy but nice woozy, and then I feel a bit crampy. And hungry. So hungry.

On leaving the clinic, Bee not Adam by my side, facing the freezing night, she asks her customary question of how I feel, holding my arm like I may fall over in the street, which I may.

'Glad to be emptied of the golf balls,' I say, feeling the twinge of a cramp. 'And I need to eat.'

'Italian?'

'Why not?'

The West End streets are buzzing with people getting on with their lives, couples holding hands, women who look pregnant, whether they are or not. My brain is over-manifesting. I've had my eggs extracted. I'm excited. I'm high in a world where everyone is pregnant. I can't finish my spaghetti.

* * *

Today I'll know how successful the procedure was. It's that fast.

I keep looking at my phone, willing the clinic to call before I leave for work, like it's even faster than fast. I need to relax. I need to forget about it, but it's hard.

When I arrive at the Peckham house, I reluctantly put my phone on silent and slip it into my pocket.

'They'll call. Be patient,' Adam's voice tells me.

'Very wise,' I say.

Two seconds later Benedict joins me on the doorstep. I hope I wasn't talking out loud.

'Looking forward to this?' I say.

'Not much,' he grunts. 'This is really your call but I don't think Camilla understands the parameters of our different jobs.'

'Maybe, because she sees you as site manager, she thinks you have to be involved in everything.'

He rolls his eyes.

'You should be flattered.'

'I don't need flattery,' he says.

Good, I think, because you'll get none from me. I smile up at him politely.

Camilla opens the door. 'Come in, come in,' she says,

in a rushed voice. 'Thank you both so much for coming. I need to address this. It's been bothering me. I haven't slept for days.'

It shows. Her face is that of a woman totally stressed. That's what this sort of project does to you. If it was easy, everyone would do it. It's stressful enough even for a professional. Those brave enough to embark on a huge refurbishment often have no idea what they're wading into. It starts with a burst of excitement, then halfway through all the worries pile in, the escalating budget, the choices they were so certain of which now they doubt, the sleepless nights, the rows with their partner. Everything culminates in blame-calling, and guess who bears the brunt?

But that's what I'm for. I don't think Benedict does brunt. He's made of Teflon. He has about as much feeling in his body as a frying pan. Although a frying pan feels the heat. I need to remember that. Write it in my journal. Get rid of the frustration.

Camilla's hair sits raggedly around her shoulders, no longer hidden by a hard hat: the demolition complete, they are no longer required. We're still bundled up in winter coats and scarves. The house is still colder inside than out. And that's saying something.

We follow her through to what will become the kitchen-diner, now a large open-plan space, the new pipes and wires chased into the wall ready for plastering. Benedict walks around inspecting everything, making use of this waste of his time, while I hover around Camilla, waiting for her grand reveal.

'I wish I could make a decision but it's proving impossible,' she says, sighing. 'I loved the kitchen you designed, Daisy. Loved it! But now that I've seen Jan's I'm in a real quandary. I'm so sorry to be a pain.' She sweeps her hand through the top of her hair, her fingers getting enmeshed in the neglected knots. 'Oh, for goodness' sake,' she says, wincing.

'You're really not being a pain,' I say, with sincerity, relieved that it's merely neighbour envy. 'It's just part of the process. As each decision is signed off, it gets scarier.'

She looks at Benedict, who approaches the table. 'You have to recognize that Jan's renovation is a couple of months ahead of ours and it's always easier to see things in real life rather than visualize them from moodboards and printouts.'

'I know, I know . . . Look, I have photos.'

We stare at the supposed beautiful kitchen that has thrown our client into doubt. I look at Benedict. He looks at me. For once we are united in our repugnance.

'Jan's house is quite different,' he says. 'Yours is Georgian. Hers is later, probably Edwardian. It invites that kind of kitchen which is not necessarily compatible here.'

That's the most helpful contribution I've ever heard from him.

'That said, if that is the style you feel more comfortable with, and you're the one who has to live with it, I'm sure Daisy can adapt her design.'

I feel my face freeze. What a cop-out!

'Would you do that, Daisy?' she says.

'If that's what you want.'

'I'm not sure.'

I breathe in. Her hesitancy has handed me a lifeline. 'Let's talk this through, Camilla,' I say. 'I think you need to be one hundred per cent certain.' I'm avoiding looking at Benedict. I'm too angry. As much as he doesn't want to be here, I'd rather be sitting somewhere quiet, staring at my phone, waiting for the clinic to call. But I'm not. I'm dealing with Camilla, like she's the most important person in my life right now. I'm taking her angst seriously while protecting the integrity of my design. Because that's what interior designers do. I'm not choosing the easy option of agreeing to adapt my design so that we can all pack up and get on with our day. This is important to me. I want it to be right and I want Camilla to know that I want it to be right for her. Even though I'd far rather be talking eggs and pregnancy. You bet I would.

I pull up the original kitchen moodboards. The ones Camilla and Tim had approved. My cabinet maker has already started the initial work. Halting it will cost time and money. But I'm not going to mention that yet. She'll feel like she's being backed into a corner. She needs to feel she has made the decision based on personal choice, not because I'm frightening her with the extra cost.

'This is a beautiful kitchen, Camilla. It will be. I think you may have lost confidence in your choices because you made them what seems like a long time ago. But I can assure you, this kitchen fits this house. That said, if you like Jan's kitchen, I can adapt it for you. But don't you want to feel unique? Do you really want to copy your neighbour? This has been designed uniquely for you. No one else. I think you should try to recall your excitement when you first committed to it. You and Tim were both totally enamoured.'

I can feel Benedict's eyes flit from me to Camilla.

'Maybe we were,' she says.

I bring out the chart of classic Georgian paint colours. 'If it's the paint colour that bothers you, we can change that. I want you to feel comfortable.'

'I just don't know any more. What do you think, Benedict?'

Benedict casually picks up the chart. Glances over it, then

puts it down. 'It's your decision. But I'm not sure colour should be your issue. You either want to go with the country look or the Georgian look. Maybe try to visualize yourself living in each. Which one feels like home? Daisy and I can guide but, in the end, it has to be your decision.'

I nod in agreement. Still pissed off.

'So you think this is nicer than the oak?' she says, looking at me.

'The oak is okay,' I say, 'but in your house, this design is more appropriate and I honestly believe it would look stunning.'

'The oak is pretty stunning.' She sighs.

Benedict fiddles with his wedding ring.

'Oh, gosh,' says Camilla. 'I'm so confused. I think I need a drink.'

'Shall I leave you to sleep on it?'

'I won't sleep!' she says. She gazes at me, imploring.

'Do you want me to make the decision for you?'

'Daisy,' says Benedict. 'Can we just pause a moment?' Patronizing shit. 'That'll make her too hasty.'

Camilla smiles at him, grateful to her hero.

I hate him. I hate his surly arrogance, his imperiousness. If Camilla can't read him, I can. 'I'm not making her be hasty. I'm trying to help her. But if you want to leave it for a few days, Camilla, that's fine.'

She pulls her chin into a tight grimace. 'I'll go with your kitchen,' she says.

I want to kiss her.

I want to give Benedict the finger. I want to rip off that damn wedding ring he so enjoys flaunting at the slightest opportunity. I don't care if it's a nervous tic. Wait! It can't be. He has no nerve endings.

'You're sure?' I say calmly. 'I don't want to push you

into anything you might regret down the line and then it becomes an expensive mistake.'

'No, no. I'm sure. I should go with unique. I shouldn't copy Jan. I don't think she'll thank me for it anyway.'

* * *

Benedict and I leave together. I'm still angry with him. I'm not sure if he knows but I don't care. We walk back to the station in silence.

As we approach the entrance, he says, 'You handled that well, Daisy.'

'Thanks,' I say, poker-faced.

'You do know I had to play it that way, don't you?'

I seize the moment. 'No, Benedict. I'm not sure you did. I don't think you were helpful at all.' I can feel my cheeks reddening. 'She could have ended up choosing that ghastly kitchen and then it's my work that looks terrible. Not yours. And you don't even have an Instagram page! I'm glad she listened to me not you.'

He looks awkward. The first time I've ever seen him out of sorts.

'Then I apologize,' he says. 'I just felt she should be the one to make the decision. Otherwise it could backfire on both of us.'

'But we needed to help her make the right decision. To help her choose what she should want, not what she thinks she wants. I had confidence in my kitchen. That was the right decision.'

'Yes,' he says. 'Yes, of course. You're absolutely right.'

'Thank you.'

I walk away, completely fired up. Amazed at myself. Proud of my reaction. I can't allow him to knock my confidence. I don't have to defer to him just because he's so self-assured. Enough!

I take a deep breath and pull out my phone. I have three missed calls. One from the clinic. I knew it. I listen to the message on voicemail and press dial.

'Daisy Settle,' I say. 'I'm returning Ellen Baker's call.' The noise of the train approaching on Benedict's side mangles their words. I stick my finger in my ear.

'Date of birth, please?'

They put me on hold. I really don't need to hear their piped music.

'Ellen Baker.'

'Hi, Ellen. Daisy Settle returning your call.'

'Ah, good! Thank you, Ms Settle.'

I hear her computer keys click. There's a pause. It seems to last for ever.

'I have good news,' she says. I hold my breath. 'We extracted thirteen eggs.'

'Thirteen?' I repeat the number, wanting to make sure I've heard it correctly.

'Yes. It's good,' she says. 'But, of course, you do know they won't all be viable.'

'Right,' I say. I didn't know and if I did, I don't remember. But I'll remember this moment for ever.

'We'll call you every day with an update. Let you know how many survive. Don't be upset as the number goes down. It's normal.'

As I disconnect, I let out a silent whoop and punch the air. THIRTEEN! Today I have thirteen chances. Today I fought for myself at work and won. Today has been a good day.

I text Bee, pressing the egg emoji thirteen times.

24

My mother is making cucumber sandwiches.

'Cucumber sandwiches? Are they still a thing?'

'Your father likes to have a proper tea when he comes back from golf. He has his lunch at the club.'

'And he needs tea?'

'Please don't question it,' she says. 'It's what we do. Would you like one?'

'No, thanks.'

'Stop watching me! Go and sit down.'

I sit on the sofa in the sitting room, waiting for my mother to bring in our tea. We both know I'm here for a reason but only I know the reason. My father is out playing golf. The atmosphere is different when he's not around. It has a different energy, as if the house is relaxing.

'How lovely! I've got you all to myself,' she says, bringing in the tray. Brewster settles down in his tartan bed. 'What a treat.'

'I'm glad I'm still a treat.'

'Of course, dear. Always.'

She sits down and smoothes her skirt.

'Shall I pour?' I say.

'Yes,' she says. 'You be mother.' She taps her thigh. 'That's why you're here, isn't it? You're going ahead with the baby project. You want my blessing.'

I look at her, then back at the teapot. I continue trying

to pour steadily over the strainer into two cups and ignore the insinuation of 'project', although it's an improvement on 'terrible idea'.

'Am I that predictable?'

'You're my daughter,' she says. 'I hope I know you.'

I pass her a cup and sit back with mine. It tastes good. Real tea.

'So?' she says.

'I am going ahead, yes. I've been regularly self-injecting.'

'Oh, Daisy! That's awful. I couldn't do that.'

I shake my head. 'You would if you had to. If you wanted something that badly.'

She studies me for a moment. 'You really do want this more than anything, don't you?'

'I thought you knew me.' I smile. 'I'm at the point where I've had my eggs extracted.'

'Good God!' she says. 'And what exactly does that mean?'

'It means they aspirated eggs from my ovaries.' She cringes as if this is physically painful for her. 'They extracted thirteen but every day some of them die off. There are now seven. They're waiting to see how many survive, if any, which means they're ready for fertilizing. I have to wait and see. I get a daily update.'

She takes a deep breath. 'That can't be easy,' she says.

'It isn't.'

'Then what? If none of them survive?'

'I don't know,' I say, but this is a distinct possibility. 'I probably will give up. And that's why I'm here.' I breathe out. 'I know I've tried to be independent and self-sufficient. And I can be. I've proved that to myself over these last few months.' She looks at me intensely, one eyebrow slightly raised. 'And I know you're not that keen on the route I've taken but ultimately I'd like you to be there. I'd like your support. Whichever way it goes.' Dramatic pause. 'Because you're my mother.'

She gets up from her armchair and comes to join me on the sofa. 'Shift up a bit,' she says. She puts her arm around my shoulders. 'I'm so sorry you have to go through this,' she says. 'I didn't imagine this would be how your life would turn out. But I guess we have to move along the path we're given. I'm glad you've asked me because I'd like to move along that path with you. I really would.'

'Really?' I tip my head briefly onto her shoulder. 'I'd like that,' I say. 'I'd like that very much.'

'Good, good,' she says, and leans forward to pour us more tea.

I sip, relieved with the happy outcome. 'And, by the way, you can put away any hopes of Jack. He's moved in with "that woman".' I make a sneery face.

She looks unbothered. 'She was his publicist, right?'

'Yes.'

She nods slowly. 'You see,' she says, 'you simply can't trust that kind of woman.'

'What kind of woman?'

'An ambitious working woman. You can't trust them. They've always got their eye on the main chance.'

I laugh. 'So what am I, if not an ambitious working woman?'

She looks at me askance, as if this is news to her. 'It's just I never think of you like that. I know you're successful. And I'm proud of you. But to me you're just my daughter.'

25

Doug and Eve's wide four-storey Edwardian house sits happily among the other properties on the street. All well cared-for, with polished door furniture, all security conscious, with state-of-the-art video doorbells and security cameras. I could probably name every door's paint colour. Mole's Breath, Lichen, London Stone. Sometimes I wish my interior designer brain would give it a rest.

I ring and smile at the camera, readying myself. I love spending time with my brother, but Eve and I are polar opposites. I couldn't live her life for a second. As much as I want children, I know I want to carry on working. I want to be able to hold a conversation about more than just schools, buggies and where to get a good blow-dry. I think Eve looks at me with the same wonder in reverse: that I'm obsessed with work, that she couldn't bear my life. I think she'd be amazed to know what I'm currently putting myself through. That I want a child so much I'm prepared to go it alone.

Eve opens the front door and the sound of warring boys is immediately unleashed.

'Would you please calm down!' she shouts. 'Come in,' she says. 'It's a mad house today. Your parents aren't coming – your dad's got a cold.'

'Oh, shame!' I say. 'Well, at least we've been spared his sneezing. The foundations shake when that man's nose explodes.' She locks a white-tooth smile on me.

I hand her the bottle of wine, which she takes with the same smile. 'Don't forget to take off your trainers – oh, Veja, nice – then come through to the kitchen.' Even though they've been married for eight years, lived here for five, she tells me to take off my footwear every time I come round. I don't think it's personal. I think she says the same to everyone. It's part of her welcome/unwelcome script.

'Sorry,' she says, walking away. 'I have two boys to separate before they kill each other.'

I make amused eyes. 'Where's Doug?'

She shrugs. 'I think he's still in the shower.'

Hurry up.

The hall smells of roasting meat, root vegetables, and a family with kids. I hang my coat on a spare peg between the small duffels, Monty's red school blazer with blue trim, and the puffer jackets. Then I take off my trainers and line them up next to the collection of welly boots and wander into the vast kitchen-diner.

The boys are sitting at the long marble breakfast bar, which stretches the full length of the island, on leather bar stools that swivel, with big drawing pads in front of them. They seem to be squabbling over who should have the yellow felt-tip pen.

'Say hello to Auntie Daisy,' scolds Eve.

'Hi-yaaaaa,' says Eddie, the three-year-old.

Monty, the nearly six-year-old opportunist, seizes on Eddie's distraction and grabs the yellow pen.

'No, Monty!' yells Eddie. 'It's mine! Mummy! Tell him! I need it for my sun.'

'Monty, give it to him.'

Eve is stationed over the massive stainless-steel Wolf range, several saucepans on the go. Her hair swishes perfectly every time she swings her head, the product of an expensive blow-dry. She has a regular Friday appointment at a West End hairdresser followed by lunch with friends. It's her special day. In this household it's not Friday, it's Eveday.

Behind her is a wine fridge, a Sub Zero fridge, a paper-thin sixty-inch television screen on the wall (there's a screen in practically every room), which operates through the concealed Sonos sound system, with integrated speakers in the ceiling, all of the twenty-first-century essentials for the status-conscious middle classes.

She's wearing a posh tracksuit with a green and white side stripe and what appear to be matching glitter socks inside red furry slippers. She looks like she's permanently Instagram-ready. Because she is. All of her friends follow her and some bots, which she doesn't mind so long as she gets the likes. Her friends dutifully like everything.

'Hello, boys,' I say, kissing the top of their heads.

'Have you brought us something?' asks Monty.

'You don't ask that,' scolds Eve.

'I have!' I say. 'I've brought you both something for later.'

Eve looks at me. I mouth, 'Chocolate.' She nods, giving me the okay. I once brought Haribo. You never make the same mistake twice.

'She said chocolate,' says Monty.

'But only if you're good,' I say.

'You see?' says Eve. 'Everyone wants you to be good.'

'I'll be good as gold,' says Eddie. I want to eat him.

'Anything I can do?' I ask.

'All under control, thanks,' she says. She bends down and opens the oven door, throwing a beam of light onto a gleaming leg of lamb.

'Looks good enough to eat,' I say.

'Did Doug tell you I'm veggie now? Feel much better for it. I'm contemplating going vegan.'

135

'Right.'

'Obviously I still make meat for him and the kids. Rarely, though. We certainly don't do a roast every Sunday any more. This is a special treat.'

'I would have eaten veggies.'

'It's fine.' She smiles. 'Like I said, it's for Doug and the kids too.'

'Yes, of course.'

I wander back to the boys and perch on the bar stool next to Monty, who's scratching away at his piece of paper with the yellow felt-tip. It looks like he's drawing his family. From the numbers, I'm thrilled he's including me although it's hard to tell since we all have yellow hair in the picture even though only Eve does in real life. Perhaps he's drawing everyone in Eve's image.

I smile, aware of Eddie staring at me. It's slightly disconcerting.

'How old are you?' he says.

'I'm forty, Eddie.'

'You're older than our daddy!'

'Yes.'

He looks back at his drawing, then up again. 'Why don't you have children?'

Eve looks horrified. 'Eddie!' she says. 'We don't ask questions like that.'

He adds a few green lines to the circumference of his sun. 'Are you going to die soon?' he asks casually.

'Oh, Eddie.'

'I hope not,' I say.

'Our nana died,' says Monty, embellishing his Eves.

Eve's mother died a couple of years ago. She wasn't terribly old. Younger than our mother.

'I know she did,' I say. 'That was very sad.'

'Mummy was sad,' he says. 'Daddy wasn't.'

I suck in my cheeks in an attempt not to laugh. Eve looks at me with resignation.

'Hey!' says Doug. His hair is dripping onto his shirt. 'How's it going?' He kisses me on both cheeks. He smells of man shampoo.

'Yeah, good,' I say, wiping my wet cheeks.

'Sorry I'm late to the party. I went to the dump. Got rid of a load of shi—' He looks across at the boys. 'Shizzle-dizzle. I'd have been back sooner but there was some accident – pretty major – which delayed me. Why does everyone slow down to look at an accident?'

'You obviously did,' says Eve.

'Shame about Mum and Dad.'

'Except we don't have to suffer his sneezing.'

I laugh. 'That's what I said.'

'Can I get you a drink?'

'Shit,' says Eve. 'I never even offered you a glass of water. Oops! Shizzle-dizzle.'

'Did you say a naughty word?' asks Eddie.

'She said "shit",' says Monty.

'Monty!' says Doug.

'She said it first.'

'Glass of water will be fine.'

'No way!' says Doug. 'It's Sunday. You're having wine.'

'Daisy brought that bottle of red over there,' points Eve.

'I'll get a nice one from the cellar. No offence! We haven't had a roast in ages. I feel it's a celebration. Why don't you come and help me choose, Daise?'

Eve inhales, her shoulders tensing. The one chink in her armour is when Doug throws his light on me. Or any woman who isn't her. What does she think is going to happen? He loves her. That's plain to see. But, then, I thought Jack loved me . . . Aha! I get it.

'Do you need me?' I say, wanting Eve to relax. 'You know I have zero wine nous.'

'Just come and look at how cool it is down there,' he says.

'I've seen it. It's beautiful.'

'That was ages ago. We've put in new casing.'

We trot down a spiral staircase to their underground cellar, which immediately lights up via a sensor. It is beautifully built with elaborate brick patterns and walnut racks.

'Looks great!' I say. 'Can I go now?'

'So tell me,' says Doug, conspiratorially, 'is there something to celebrate?'

'Not that I'm aware.'

'Oh! Right. Sorry, it's just you mentioned the other day you weren't drinking . . .' He's running his fingers along the bottles, deciding which vintage to choose. '. . . and I wondered.'

'I've not been drinking since I started IVF.' I flash back to Eddie. 'Have you discussed this in front of the kids by the way?'

'Of course not. Not even Eve knows.'

'Thank you. Only Eddie asked why I don't have kids.'

'Eddie is obsessed with babies right now. Pure coincidence.'

'Classic stuff,' I say, raising my eyes heavenwards. 'That's how conspiracy theories start.'

'It's just . . .' Doug pulls out a bottle and examines the label. He stares at me hesitantly.

'That one's perfect,' I say. 'Pour me an inch in order not to arouse Eve's suspicions. I'm going back up. She hates us being on our own together.'

He looks at me like I've lost it. 'No she doesn't!'

I groan. 'You really have no idea, do you?'

'Because she doesn't.'

'Fine,' I say. 'Have it your own way. I'm still going back.' I turn and run up the stairs.

I think I hear him say, 'Shizzle-dizzle.' It makes me laugh.

The lamb is out of the oven, resting. Eve is putting the roast potatoes into a white oval dish.

'Did you gasp in wonder?' she says, her cheeks perfectly pink from the heat.

'Of course.'

'Sometimes I think he loves that wine cave more than he loves me.'

'It's the wine caveman in him,' I say.

Doug walks back in. He kisses Eve on the forehead as if to prove he loves her more. 'That looks incredible, darling. Right. Let's get this beauty aired.' He opens a drawer and pulls out an elaborate corkscrew.

'Want to watch Daddy open the wine?'

'No,' comes the chorus.

Undeterred, my brother makes a big song-and-dance about withdrawing the cork.

'Only a drop for me,' I say, and he pours an inch into a glass, then pours another for himself.

'What about Eve?' I say.

'Oh, I'm not drinking.'

'Mummy's having a baby,' says Eddie.

Doug winces.

My insides contract. I'm frozen into silence before realizing I'm expected to react. 'Congratulations,' I say, holding up the wine that I'm not going to touch. 'Great news.'

'Thank you! Early days.' She looks at Eddie. 'Eddie,' she remonstrates. 'I told you. It's our family secret for a while.'

He screws up his little face and both children stare at me in bewilderment.

139

'Auntie Daisy is family,' says Monty.

'I am,' I say. 'But it's a little different.' It occurs to me that the extra figure in his drawing wasn't me after all. It was another baby.

I feel scribbled out. I feel like a non-person. How can it be so easy for some women to fall pregnant and so tough for others? Okay, so she's younger than me but so what? Damn her! Damn her perfect body and her perfect uterus and her perfect ovaries. And damn her for making me envious. I don't want to be envious. Least of all of someone's right to have children. Ever!

If this procedure doesn't work, I might just have to scribble myself out for a very long time. Run away. Escape somewhere where no one and nothing can harm me. No words innocently spoken out of place. No quizzical looks that, intended or otherwise, question my womanhood.

Doug puts his hands on my shoulders and gives me a consolatory squeeze. He whispers in my ear, 'I tried to warn you.'

Did he? He didn't try very hard. I force a smile. 'Are you trying for a girl or a football team?' My words sound brittle.

'Girls play football.'

'You're right, Eddie,' I say.

'Just healthy,' says Eve.

'Of course,' I say. 'That's all anyone can hope for.'

* * *

We sit around the oval marble table. I'm eating on remote, thinking about my eggs, how I dread the daily call from the clinic, how thirteen has whittled down to five. My fear is I'll end up with none, that this lunch, this news, is setting me up for disappointment.

'Knock, knock, Daisy,' says Doug. 'Are you with us?'

'Sorry,' I say. 'Momentarily distracted.'

'I only asked if you were busy at work,' says Eve.

'Oh, yes! Very,' I say. 'Fortunately.'

'Any new trends I should know about?'

'For nurseries?'

'Not necessarily.'

I think for a moment. 'There's a new cot you might like,' I say. 'I'll send you the link.'

'Daisy!' she says, in a jokey patronizing tone. 'I don't need a cot. I have had babies before, you know!'

'Of course you have,' I say.

* * *

I'm doing up the laces of my trainers, getting ready to leave. There's a tug at my arm. 'Where's the chocolate?' says Monty.

'Sorry, Monty. I nearly forgot.' I delve into my tote and pull out two bulging bags. Eddie appears at my side and I hand one to each boy. Monty opens his, his eyes incredulous as he inspects it.

'Wow!' he says. 'Will you come to my birthday party, Auntie Daisy?'

Eve groans, retrieving the bags from the boys, who groan louder. 'I'll put these in the treat drawer,' she says, shaking her head like I've overdone it.

'You should come, Daise!' says Doug. 'It'll be fun.'

'No adult wants to come to a child's birthday party,' tuts Eve, 'least of all if they don't have children.'

'I'd love to come!' I say, to spite her.

She's clearly surprised. 'In which case we'd love you to be there.'

'It's a circus theme,' says Doug. 'Fancy dress.'

'Lovely,' I say, already feeling like a clown.

26

It's today. And my mother is going to be there. I feel the signs augur well. I'm thinking positive. I tuck my journal under my pillow with a nervous shudder.

My mother places her brolly in the umbrella stand, rubs her neck, hovers momentarily, like she's wondering what she's doing in London, let alone in a fertility clinic. She glances around, squinting, searching for me. I'm sitting with my hand up, a slight wave, but she misses me, instead approaching the reception desk, slipping the handles of a leather-bound carpet bag over the crook of her arm, looking like Mary Poppins. As she's pointed towards me, her face lights up, and she rolls her eyes, like 'Of course, silly me overlooking my own daughter', an air of startled relief.

I stand up as she strides towards my corner, leans to kiss me, and puts her bag beside the sofa.

'Oh, goodness, I thought I'd be late. Couldn't get a cab from the station. I guess everyone wants one when it's raining.'

'You're here,' I say. 'And you're on time.'

She smiles. 'I am . . . It's filthy out there.' She brushes down her skirt, then tries to revive her flattened hair with her fingers.

'You look fine, Mum,' I reassure, because she does.

She sits down next to me. 'You okay? You look a bit

pale.' She lifts my face, giving it a maternal inspection. 'You sure you're not anaemic?'

'I'm good. Don't make me more nervous than I already am.'

'Daisy,' she says, under her breath, 'I am twice as nervous, I can assure you,' adding, after a considered pause, 'You do know you don't have to do this?'

I snort. 'You know what I'm going to say to that, don't you?'

'Good, good,' she says. She shrugs and looks around, taking in the room. 'It's very smart here,' she says, with tempered enthusiasm. 'I wasn't expecting it to be this fancy.'

'Were you expecting some kind of backstreet abortion clinic?'

'I don't know what I was expecting.'

'Has Dad asked why you're staying with me tonight?'

She sits back and crosses her legs. 'He just thinks the show ends late. He was more concerned I'd left full instructions on how to heat up his supper.' She gives a knowing laugh.

'What show are we going to see?'

'*Les Mis*. Your father and I saw it together a few years ago so if he asks me any questions, which he won't, I'll be able to give an informed answer.'

'What about if he asks me?'

'Just tell him you loved it.'

'You've got it all worked out.'

She sucks her teeth and shudders. 'I lied to him. Can you believe it? In all these years I've never lied to him and now I must have lied to him at least three times on your behalf.'

'We could tell him, you know.'

Her mouth crinkles. 'No. Not yet.'

'Anyhow, you have lied to him.'

She stares at me.

143

'Sure!' I say. 'All the outfits and shoes and handbags you've sneaked in over the years, and when he asked if something was new, you'd say, "What – this old thing?"'

'Ohhh!' She chuckles. 'That's allowed. Everyone does it.' She taps her palm on my thigh. 'Do you realize he and I have practically never spent a night apart?'

'That's very adorable,' I say.

'We have to be clever about how we tell him this news. Break it to him in the right way.'

'What – this old thing?' I point at my stomach.

She looks into the middle distance. 'No. But something will occur to me. I'm sure he'll be fine. Let's just get you pregnant, shall we?'

'Statistical results are not great, you know,' I say, preparing myself for the worst. 'I might not get pregnant. You might never have to tell him.'

It's clear she still doesn't know Eve is pregnant. She'd have mentioned it by now. I'm impressed they're managing to keep it under wraps, maybe bribing the boys to maintain the secrecy. I'm not sure why. She must be past twelve weeks.

'Thanks for coming today,' I say. I slip my hand through her arm and she squeezes it into her ribs. 'Do you want a cup of tea? They do nice teas here. That's what Bee says anyway. I can never face anything.'

'I had a cup before I left home.' She looks at her watch. 'They're running late.'

'Two minutes!' I say. 'Stop making me nervous.'

'So, just the one, then?' she says.

'One what?'

'Embryo,' she says, under her breath. 'That's what you told me, right?'

'Yes.' I say. 'They call it a blastocyst.'

'I'll never remember that.'

'You don't have to.'

'What happens to the other two?'

'They freeze them.'

'Good God!'

In the end, there were five viable eggs of which three were successfully fertilized by Adam. Who was delighted. I danced around the room, 'Shape Of You' blasting out of my iPhone at full volume, celebrating with him. He's a good dancer! The clinic had asked·me if I'd wanted two blastocysts implanted. It was one of the toughest decisions I've ever had to make. What if they're right and having two implanted gives me a better chance? On the other hand, what if I choose to have two implanted and lose one? How will that singular loss feel? Or I lose both? That would be untenable. Then again, what if I have two and both reach term? I simply wouldn't be able to cope on my own.

'Daisy Settle?' The voice comes from nowhere and my stomach lurches.

I stand up. 'That's me.'

My mother gets up with me. 'Good luck. I'll be waiting right here.'

'Thank you,' I say, and we hug. 'If you get bored, you can pop next door for some Botox.'

'Can you imagine?' she says, her fingers pressing into her face. 'Your father will definitely think I'm having an affair.' She pulls out a paperback from her handbag. 'Don't worry. I came prepared.'

'When have you ever not been prepared?'

'Well, I wasn't prepared for this,' she says.

* * *

When we get home I make us hot chocolate. My mother looks through my cupboards and says I need to start eating more sensibly. She asks about the letters on the fridge and I let her read them.

'Charming,' she says, confessing she'll never completely understand my choice but at least she understands a bit better now.

My mother says I should ask the landlord for a more supportive mattress but manages to fall asleep straight away. I blame my lack of sleep on her snoring, which, in truth, is a kind of gentle purr. Really I'm too excited.

27

There was no need for Ma to stay that night.
Everything was fine (still is – phew phew phew!) but
we shared a cup of tea in the morning, which was
nice, and she grabbed a cab to the Tube. Ever since
she left, I've wanted to buy a pregnancy test. Not to
use – way too premature – but to know that I have
one to hand for when the time comes. I've withstood
on the grounds of delayed gratification or delayed
disappointment whichever is to be my fate. But
we're two weeks on, so no point avoiding potential
devastation. Failure is going to hit hard. I know it is.
Unless I wait to see if I have a period, I may as well
confront the outcome. The time is now.

I can't go to the local pharmacy: it would make me feel they
know too much. The one I find is conveniently quiet. I sidle
up to the counter, glad to be unobserved.

'Excuse me,' I say. 'Do you know which of these is best?'
I slide three pregnancy-test kits across to face the man,
olive skin, silver-framed glasses, wearing a white lab coat,
whose white badge with four stars tells me his name is
Murray. Today, I'd rather not know. I find the whole thing
embarrassing.

He looks at me like I'm disturbing him, like there's a long
queue behind me, which obviously there isn't.

'They all do the same thing,' he says dismissively.

'But which is the most reliable?' Try making this easy for me, Murray. Please!

He picks up a packet, raises his glasses to look at it with a naked eye, bringing it right up close to his face, reading the small print. He briefly scans the other two. 'They all say ninety-nine per cent accurate.'

'Then I'll take all three,' I say.

His head cocks as if he's wondering why I bothered to ask him in the first place. He yawns as he scans them into the till.

'Loyalty card?'

'Nope.'

'Want one?'

'No, thanks.'

'It's quiet. It only takes a minute. You'll get a ten per cent discount and earn points.'

'I'm in a rush.'

'Carrier-bag? They're ten p.'

'No, thanks,' I say, and tap my credit card, still amazed at the efficiency of contactless payments.

He hands me the tests and I slip them into my tote, clutching them closely to my side like they're precious cargo. Right now they feel more precious than my purse. If I got mugged I'd say, 'Here, take everything but leave me the tests.'

* * *

I sit down on the cold toilet seat, which shifts slightly to the left, the way it does every time, even though I descend gently in order not to take it by surprise. Amazing the habits you adopt to accommodate badly behaved sanitaryware.

I've tried tightening the screws at the back but they refuse to behave too. It's a bathroom conspiracy.

I get comfortable. This is a serious business. I turn over one of the packets in my hand, examining it nervously. Weighing it up like I'm checking it for quality. Like I don't trust the 99 per cent accuracy endorsement even after the chemist's assurance. Even though I'm counting on it.

I feel my breasts. They don't seem any different. If I was going to predict the outcome it would be negative. Let's face it: it never happens the first time anyway and I have no expectations. Which is a lie because I'm hoping I'll be one of those rare people for whom it does happen the first time. Because wouldn't it be nice if something went right?

I fight with myself, fumbling to open the packet, wrestling the white stick from the tight blister mould, my hands shaking, like I'm having a sugar rush without the sugar. I delve inside the box and pull out the instructions. I read them. Three times.

'So I have to pee,' I say. 'Mid-stream. I have to guess where mid is in my stream.'

I start to pee.

I place the stick under it, in what feels like mid-stream.

I pull it out and breathe.

I wait. I stare at it. Then I put it down because if I stare at it it will never happen. I wash my hands and set the timer on my phone for two minutes forty-five seconds on the basis that I might have taken fifteen seconds to wash my hands. Accuracy is everything!

I shuffle two paces forward, two back in the tiny space.

I check my phone.

I shuffle and check again.

I sit down on the loo seat, which lurches to the left. I stand up.

I tuck in my blouse for something to do.

I jump at the sound of my phone alarm and press stop.

I go to look.

I can't look.

I look.

I look away. Heart pounding.

Then look again.

Just to be sure.

There's a second line. A SECOND LINE. It's there. It is! It's definitely there.

I'm pregnant.

Seriously?

Am I?

No, wait. I need to be certain. I grab the instructions, look at the illustration. There it is. The only bit I need to know. A second line, no matter how faint, means you're pregnant. I throw the box down.

Shut! Up!

'Shit! Shit! Shit!' I say out loud.

I start to spin even though there's barely room to spin a cat, then realize I might be spinning it out of my body. I don't know what to do first. I'm beyond excited. I pick up the stick again. The lines are still there. Should I do another? Just in case? No! Fuck it. They are 99 per cent accurate.

I AM PREGNANT, ADAM! WE DID IT!

And then it comes over me. Anger surging through my veins. A feeling of injustice and yet justice being served. 'Fuck you, Jack!' I scream at the ceiling. 'FUCK YOU!'

PART TWO

28

There's a woman at the door to take my coat. She gives me a numbered ticket. It seems incredibly well organized for a six-year-old's party. So very Eve.

She looks at the carrier-bag in my hand, a big blue bow poking out of the top. 'We're putting all the presents in the snug, which is at the back of the house to the left-hand side, before you go out into the garden.'

'Thanks,' I say, catching myself in the hall mirror, aware that I look ridiculous. I've gone for the full immersive experience: a bright-red curly wig bought from the local wholesale wig shop, my own application of exaggerated blue and green eye make-up and huge red lips that overhang my own by at least two centimetres. No longer disguised by my coat, I feel exposed in the pair of baggy trousers I found from days when I'd happily paint walls, a blue and white loud-check shirt from the charity shop and yellow braces bought on Amazon. I hope Monty appreciates the effort. I have absolutely no doubt that I might be disappointed.

I bend to remove my trainers, only to realize this is obviously a shoes-on party. How will Eve cope? I'm surprised she hasn't supplied everyone with those funny white hotel slippers. I know people who do that.

I put the present on top of the already substantial pile, fold up the carrier-bag and throw it into the bin which I know sits behind the sofa-bed.

The bi-fold doors from the snug are fully opened onto the garden and I trudge across the lawn into the marquee.

There's a small sea of miniature clowns, fairies, princesses, wizards, a dragon . . . Adults are dotted about, some in fancy dress, clutching coloured cocktails, some with little people clinging to their legs.

For a moment, I stand there, in all my clownlike glory, taking in the scene that's playing out in front of me, daring to imagine a future. From the pea in my stomach, I manifest a tiny being clinging to my calves, sensing them slowly letting go, running off into the distance, playing with their cousins, having a ball. My skin tingles. It's possible. It's very nearly possible. I'm pregnant, I think, and I've done it entirely on my own. Well, with some help from Adam and a clinic, but still. I place my hands on my stomach, then quickly remove them. That's such a classic pregnant-woman pose.

Waitresses are walking around with canapés on trays. I grab a baby quiche and a baby pizza. Suddenly everything is baby-baby-baby.

Doug is managing the bar, which is draped in red-and-white striped fabric, like a Punch and Judy tent. He is surrounded by jugs and bottles. Behind him on a ledge there is a Slush Puppy machine. They've thought of everything.

'Are you Mr Punch?' I say. 'You look very profesh.'

'You look like—'

'A drag queen. I know. Don't judge me or I'll get Judy to thwack you.'

'You still pretending to drink?' he says, holding up a jug draped with slices of orange, and maraschino cherries. 'Fancy faking a glass of Doug's famous Sangria?'

'Nope. I might sip in error.'

His eyes gleam at me. 'Oh. My. God?'

I suck in my cheeks. 'Don't jump ahead,' I say, looking

around. 'It feels like ages since I had a drink. Actually, it feels like years.'

In his quiet voice, he says, 'Oh, well. I was hoping we may have ended up being vaguely in sync.'

I tilt my head and shrug.

Do I want to be in sync with Eve? I reprimand myself. I would love to be in sync with anyone! Including Eve. Mainly Eve. Bring it on.

'Don't tell Ma and Pa about us. Not yet,' he says.

'Why?'

'Eve wants to wait as long as poss. Until she shows.' He drops his voice. 'It's a girl. She's so thrilled she's terrified she'll jinx it.'

'Totally get it! Oh, Doug. That's exciting.'

'Don't let on that you know,' he says, with a conspiratorial wink.

I try to ignore the creeping feeling of envy. It's automatic. It has to stop. What is there to envy other than that she must be over the twenty-week mark, the scan when they can tell the sex? I feel like a pregnancy encyclopaedia. I've read too many books.

'Here! Have a Slush Puppy. Cup and straw recyclable. Bins over there.' He waves towards a run of wheelies.

I sniff it. It smells sickly sweet. Nothing could tempt me to drink it. 'Where's the birthday boy?'

Doug gestures towards a child dressed in what looks like silver foil, jumping up and down with two other kids on a huge trampoline, surrounded by netting. 'He's the astronaut. He didn't want to be a clown.'

'A boy with ambition,' I say.

I walk over to the trampoline, holding onto the Slush Puppy I won't drink: it spares me the effort of saying I'm not drinking every time someone asks.

155

I stick my face into the netting. 'Happy birthday, Monty.' He carries on jumping, ignoring me. Eddie is lying on his back, spread-eagled on the red rubber floor, being bounced around by Monty's jumps. He's wearing what looks like a blue tutu. 'How are you, Eddie?' I say.

No reply.

'Are you alive?' I ask.

He turns to look at me 'You look ugly,' he says.

He's alive. 'No fooling you!'

I look around the vast marquee. Eve is standing with a group of other mothers, one of them decidedly pregnant, none of them in fancy dress. Not in the official sense anyway. Eve is unusually low key, a baggy jumper, designer, of course, and cropped jeans. They're taking selfies, pouting and swooshing their hair. Laughing. Approving. The best will no doubt appear later on Eve's Instagram. We catch eyes. I force myself to go over and say hello.

'Hi!' she says, and air-kisses me – there's a lot of make-up to avoid. 'This is my sister-in-law, Daisy.'

'Hi,' they all go, giggling awkwardly. I feel them scrutinizing me.

'Sorry,' I say, adjusting my red wig. 'Came straight from work!'

'She's joking,' says Eve. 'She's an interior designer. Hotels.'

I feel the hit in my solar plexus. 'Not exclusively,' I say.

'Of course not. Sorry. Habit. Nicky's just done up all her kids' bedrooms and they're gorgeous,' she says.

'Thank you, Eve, darling,' says Nicky, who evidently has several children. 'I take that as a real compliment coming from you. Your whole house is gorgeous.' She looks at me. 'With your help, I assume?'

'No, actually,' I say. 'Eve's work entirely.' I know this not to be true. She hired an interior designer but didn't want me to know in case I got offended. I was relieved.

Eve gives a dismissive flick of her wrist, playing at being humble.

'Oh, look!' I say, spotting the perfectly timed arrival of my parents. 'I'm off to frighten the folks! Catch you all later.'

* * *

'What do you look like?' my father says, as I air-kiss him.

'At least I made an effort.'

'You look . . . terrific,' says my mother.

My father looks around. 'Where's the birthday boy?'

'He's the astronaut,' I say. 'The streak of silver that's just left the trampoline.' I watch Monty's little foil frame hurtle towards the ball pit, throwing himself in head first.

'He's a lunatic,' says my father, laughing. He fishes into his back pocket and holds up a ten-pound note. 'Better go and give him a birthday hug.'

'Is that a bribe?' I say to my mother, watching my father trying to attract Monty's attention.

'Of course not,' she says. 'We've got his bribe in the car. Dad likes to give him something personal, to make him feel special.'

'I don't think there's any issue in the special department, Ma.'

'How are you?' says my mother. 'Any . . . you know . . . signs?'

'Are you sitting down?'

'Obviously not,' she says, confused. Her eyes light up. 'Should I be?'

'You might want to.'

'You are kidding me?'

'I am not.'

We flash excitement at one another. No big scene.

'Oh, Daisy,' she says. 'Oh, wow!'

A dramatic cry emits from near the trampoline. 'Is that Eddie?' she says. She sets her hand to her forehead, shading her eyes. 'Is he wearing a dress?'

'I think you'll find he's Elsa.'

'Who's the clown?'

'That's your son, Ma,' I say. 'I'd be careful how you phrase that.'

Doug has rushed over to Eddie, who is wailing. As we get closer we can hear the familiar problem. 'But I wanted a go first,' he yells. 'I never go first.'

'Do not bite me,' says Doug, pulling back his hand.

'What's wrong, Eddie?' says my mother. 'Give Grandma a kiss.'

'No,' says Eddie, sticking out his tongue.

My mother pretends to cry.

'Do you want to bite Grandma?' I say.

Eddie looks at me in wonder. 'Can I bite you, Grandma?'

'Honestly, Daisy,' says my mother. 'I'm not sure that's the best child psychology.'

'It stopped you ugly-crying,' I say.

'Aunt Daisy is being funny, Eddie,' says Doug. 'She thinks she's a clown.'

'I need a drink,' says my mother. 'Point me towards the bar.'

Doug stands up, nursing his hand, as if he's been mortally wounded. 'My domain! Now stop being a girl, Eddie, and go and play nicely.'

'I am a girl,' he says, running off. 'I'm Elsa!'

'Oh, goodness,' says my mother. 'It's all got so complicated.'

29

Sunshine is streaming through the office window, making the world feel like a better place. Marcus jumps up from his seat.

'Happy Valentine's Day,' he says, handing me a bunch of roses from behind his back.

'Oh Marcus,' I say, embarrassed. 'I'm trying to forget about it. It's officially cancelled as far as I'm concerned. I haven't got you anything.'

'I wasn't expecting anything,' he says. 'I was hoping to cheer you up . . . you know, in case you hadn't forgotten. But you don't look like someone who needs cheering up so let's just consider these flowers for the office.' He takes them back, hastily fills a jug of water and drops them in, still in their brown paper wrapping.

I kiss his cheek. 'You are the sweetest man alive.'

I lean my tote against the leg of my desk and wander back to the kitchen area. 'Coffee?'

'No thanks,' he says. 'But I've made a fresh pot for you.'

'Thanks, Valentine,' I say, pouring myself a mug then cutting the stems off the roses and arranging them properly. 'Very lovely,' I say and place them between our desks.

'You're welcome.'

I sit down and turn on my screen.

'You're pregnant, aren't you?' he says.

'What on earth makes you say that?'

'Don't go coy on me. I can tell!'

'What can you tell?'

'Two clues. One, you're in a very good mood considering, you know . . . what day it is. Two. The delicate way you're walking. Like someone who's trying to protect their body, which, under normal circumstances, might mean you've hurt your back or something. But knowing what I do, well, it's obvious.' He does a 360-degree turn in his chair, like a spin of triumph. 'I'm right, aren't I?'

'I don't know what you're talking about,' I say, hiding my face behind my mug.

'Fine,' he says. 'Let me know when you're twelve weeks.'

I put down the coffee and throw my hands in the air. 'Damn you, Marcus!' I say, immediately relenting. 'Yes! You've got me. I'm pregnant!' I shake my head, disappointed at my pathetic inability to keep up the pretence. 'I so wanted to wait until it was safe to announce. I don't want to jinx it. But you've guessed. You always guess.'

'You're so easy to read.'

'Why can't you be dyslexic?'

'I could read you backwards.'

'Fine. But I'm serious about not wanting to jinx it. Can we pretend you don't know?'

He grins at me. 'Am I allowed to congratulate you before we go into denial? I mean, that's pretty amazing, first time around.'

'I'm pretty amazed. But it's like a minute. Anything can happen. Let's wait until I'm twelve weeks before we celebrate.'

He jumps up, comes over and gives me a gentle hug. 'No celebrations, just a hug,' he says.

'Thank you.' I hug him back.

My mother and I had to downplay our excitement so

160

it's uplifting to feel Marcus's enthusiasm, even though it's premature.

He allows a few minutes to pass, then looks over the top of his screen. 'So am I allowed to ask how you're feeling? Any sickness? Mood swings? Sorry, I can't help it. Let's face it, it's out there!'

I look at him, knowing that now he's opening up the subject, it's all I want to talk about. 'I'm guessing you'll tell me about the mood swings. But no. No sickness. I don't really feel pregnant, if I'm honest. Not yet.'

'You might be one of the lucky ones who doesn't get sick.' He studies me. 'I admire you. I don't think I could ever have done those injections.' He makes to vomit.

'Yeah, you would,' I say. 'If you had to. And I still have to. For at least another twelve weeks. Anyway, it's become as automatic as cleaning my teeth.'

'You're pregnant, Daisy Settle!' He grins. 'And from now, until you're official, my lips will remain sealed.'

I, too, keep my lips sealed but it's frustrating. You're holding in a piece of news so exciting you want to share it with the world, yet caution dictates you can't. Work helps. The project is quickly moving into second fix. All the essentials are installed if not yet commissioned: the boiler, the Megaflo system, which will ensure reliable hot water is swiftly pumped throughout the house, the rather hi-tech digital programmer and the Bluetooth smart meters. Everyone is so preoccupied with their own issues, no one notices anything different about me. Besides, externally there's nothing different about me.

The other day, standing in one of the smaller bathrooms with Camilla, admiring the installation of the floor tiles, a beautiful pea-green ceramic, I suddenly came over slightly dizzy. For a nanosecond, I thought I might throw up and, since I haven't had a moment's sickness, it took me by surprise. I reached out for the wall as though casually leaning, feeling Camilla's gaze, praying she wouldn't say anything.

'I love this tile,' she said.

I think if I'd turned the colour of the tile, she'd have said the same. We carried on.

This afternoon, while gently trying to explain the somewhat complex heating programme to her, Benedict entered the hallway. 'I'm never going to be able to work this system,' she said turning to him. 'I'm definitely leaving it to Tim. Can you run through it with him?'

'Happily,' said Benedict, which made me laugh because he never does anything happily. But I'm happy. I don't think I could be happier.

* * *

Going home, I look at the young girl sitting opposite me on the tube, eating from a packet of almonds, wiping her salty lips with the back of her hand. I envy her youth: her glowing skin, plump pink cheeks, her perfectly rounded bump. I wonder if she can tell that I, too, am pregnant. If there's some kind of internal osmosis among the pregnancy tribe that responds, perhaps to a scent, a coy smile, when nothing about my physique gives away the slightest hint. To be honest, I know this is merely an amusing distraction. Deep down, the sensible part of me is fully aware that even though I was uncovered so easily by Marcus, a man who knows me too well, there is absolutely no reason for anyone else to sense a change in my physiognomy. The secret is all mine to enjoy.

* * *

162

Today I can relax. Marcus and I have managed to sort some time together in the office. Baxter Settle has three projects we're pitching for. We sit side by side at the glass trestle table, which runs perpendicular to our desks, mugs of coffee, decaf now, a plate of Digestive biscuits. We face the shelves and cupboards, which are full of swatches, fabric books, reference books and paint charts from every supplier imaginable, both UK-based and abroad.

The table is covered with velvets and chenilles, wools and silks, plain sheers, embroidered sheers, in every possible colour and weight you can imagine, specifically focusing on a pitch for an apartment in Mayfair. There are flooring samples: patterned tiles, plain tiles, different woods of all shades, engineered, reclaimed, bamboo, and we play around, mixing, matching and mismatching, deciding how best to create something new and original that excites us.

I move on to a pile of books that range from mid-century modern to art deco, as well as some French and Italian architectural influences, to see if they help inspire the vibe we should go with. Once we nail a style, it's much easier to grow the vision, whether that is around a colour palette or an inspirational piece of furniture from which we can build the total concept. Marcus is tapping away on his iPad, googling ideas for lighting and furniture from places like 1stDibs, Vinterior and Pamono.

For a second, I look up and stare into the middle distance, imagining a possible scheme.

'I'm not sure your heart is quite in this,' says Marcus, without lifting his head from his iPad.

'Excuse me?'

'Well, I wouldn't blame you. I mean, I'm sure your hormones must be—'

'Don't you dare start second-guessing me. Or blaming

my hormones. I'm totally on board. I was just having a brief moment of visualization and you're on me like I'm slacking.'

'Sorry,' he says. 'Just checking. It wasn't a criticism. I thought maybe you might want a bit of a break.'

'It was a criticism!' I say. 'You're testing me. You think that now I'm pregnant my priorities have changed, but they haven't. I'm not ill. I'm still capable of work. I may have moments when I'm tired, not on top form, but you have those moments too. And I may have moments when I'm actually enjoying myself. Like now! Before you ruin them. So, give me a break, buddy.'

He laughs awkwardly. 'Whoa. Okay! That put me in my place.' He grimaces. 'Sorry, Daise! That was the bloke in me speaking out of turn.'

'Well, put that bloke away.'

'I never liked him anyway,' he says.

* * *

That night I scribble:

Secrecy is such a strange state to be in. I'm grateful to the people around me who notice nothing and ungrateful to Marcus who notices everything. Really it should be the other way round.

30

I spot Bee walking from the station towards our agreed meeting point in front of the flower shop that sits in the middle entrance to Liberty. She's easy to pick out, her curls bouncing in time with the spring in her stride, her mid-length baby-blue bouclé coat over navy culottes, and baby-blue suede ankle boots. When she clocks me, her happy face turns to apologetic. 'Sorry,' she mouths, picking up her pace. She's ten minutes late but it's been no problem sharing the pavement with beautiful buckets of perfectly behaved flowers, heads all upright, showing off their colourful blooms as if heralding the fact that spring is on its way.

She's breathless. 'Sorry! Tube was on a go-slow. Let me look at you!' She grabs each side of my trench coat, opening it like a pair of curtains.

I snort at being manhandled, knowing she's about to be disappointed. 'Bee, I'm ten weeks and three hours.' I laugh. 'That's according to Google which is very precise obviously.' I let out a sigh. 'I'm not even growing proper tits yet. When does that happen?'

She rolls her bottom lip. 'It may only have been a few years but, honestly, I don't remember those things any more. I just remember the end, when I was huge and uncomfortable and couldn't wait for him to come out.'

'I look forward to that feeling.' We walk into the main hall. 'You might have to steer me clear of the sofas. I'm actually quite tired today. Happy tired. Glad of an actual symptom. It's practically the first time I feel like I might be genuinely pregnant.'

She smiles broadly and clutches my hand. 'I'm just thrilled to hear you say those words. I know how much this means to you.'

'Yeah, you do,' I say.

We start to wander among the tables, all beautifully arranged with designer handbags sporting designer price tags, which not so long ago might not have seemed so outrageous to me.

I check how I'd look with a thousand pounds dangling from my arm. 'What do you think?'

'You buying today?' asks Bee, picking up a silk scarf.

'Yeah! A lipstick,' I say. 'I'm not in this league. I just fancied some playtime with my buddy.'

'Me too. Do you miss that league?'

'Nope.'

I slip my hand through her arm and pull her towards the next arch. 'Let's treat ourselves to an uplifting lipstick.'

We move into the make-up hall, where an array of concessions invites us to play with their wares.

'Going somewhere nice tonight?' I say, in my best hairdresser voice, using a disposable brush to apply a bright red tester to Bee's Cupid's bow.

'No,' she says, puckering. 'Patrick's bringing Will back early. Not sure why but I don't mind. Rob's coming round. We're having a Netflix-and-Will night. You?'

'I'm seeing Caro.'

'Oh, wow! You telling her?'

'Not yet, although she might wonder why I'm not drinking.'

'She may not notice. You know what she's like.' She checks her face in the mirror. 'Very nice,' she says.

'Can I tempt you, madam?'

'Not today, thank you.'

'Right! In which case, let's pretend to buy some sexy cushions for my unsexy flat.'

We stand waiting for the lift, watching the floor number change slowly.

'Why have you never pursued Jack for money?' she says. 'Don't you think he owes you? He's full of guilt. He'll want to buy himself absolution.'

I fiddle with the collar on my coat. 'Well, he's not getting it from me.' I look at her. 'Anyway, why would I want his money if I don't want him?'

'I can think of several dollar-sign reasons.'

The notion of taking anything from him is completely obnoxious. 'Accepting his money will allow him to think that everything I do, everything I achieve after our split, is down to him. And it won't be. It'll be down to me. I don't want to give him any power over my life. Money is power. So, no, I'd rather struggle.'

'And you do it so well!' She laughs.

We exit the oak-panelled lift into the furniture department and I head towards my favourite corner display of extravagant cushions, velvets and silks, exotic patterns, geometrics, some edged with fringing, some with tiny feathers. I love feathers. I pick one up.

'I could happily wear this,' I say.

I pick my way through a pile, stroking and admiring, longing for the day when I own a flat and can calmly scold my child for the line of felt-tip shakily drawn across luxurious silk. 'Mummy worked hard for that!'

'I love this one,' I say, picking up a silk floral with navy fringing. 'It's perfect.' I check the price tag.

'Put it down,' says Bee.

'Don't make me!' I say, clutching it to my breast. 'I just want to hold it and feel as though ownership is possible.'

Bee scoffs. 'Don't make me feel sorry for you.'

'I'll put it down in a bit.'

We wander across the floor, me clutching the cushion to my stomach, like a safety shield.

'Actually, I'm going to buy it!' I say.

'Daisy, no! Think baby,' Bee whispers.

'That's all I think,' I say.

We approach the till, coming up behind a woman with a neat choppy bob in a red A-line coat, hunting through her Gucci handbag.

Bee grabs my arm, stopping me in my tracks. 'Shit!' she says, nodding wildly. 'Let's do a quick reverse.'

'Why?' I say, bemused.

'That's you-know-who!' She coughs.

I scrutinize the woman's back. Listen to her voice as she apologizes for the hold-up, then pulls out a neat cardholder. 'What a relief,' she says. 'Thought I'd lost it.'

'Oh!' I say, instant revulsion. 'I didn't recognize her with her clothes on.'

Bee snorts. We go to make a U-turn.

'No, Bee!' I say, as if a switch has been flicked in my brain. 'We're not the ones who should have to slink away. We're going to do this.' I grab her hand. 'It's serendipity. The universe has spoken to me.'

She digs her nails into my palm. 'Come away!' she says. 'I distinctly heard the universe say something different.'

'Hello!' I say, before Bee can stop me.

The woman swings round.

'Oh!' Her eyeballs practically burst from their sockets. 'Daisy,' she says, her red lips tightening. 'Hi. How are you?' She gives Bee a cursory glance.

'This is Bee,' I say. 'Remember her?'

'Stop it, Daise,' whispers Bee.

'I'm not sure I do.'

'It was a dark night,' I say. 'Just not dark enough.'

She fidgets, her eyes flitting to the cushion I'm gripping tightly under my arm. 'How funny,' she says. 'I just bought two of those! Not that colour, though. Beautiful, aren't they?'

I sideswipe Bee with the cushion, not intending to be quite so fierce. 'Sorry, Bee,' I say under my breath. 'Would you mind putting this back on the shelf?'

Bee looks at me, imploring eyes loaded with fear.

'Oh, Daisy,' says Polly. 'Don't let me put you off it.'

'Stay calm,' says Bee, under her breath as she slips away.

The assistant ahems. 'Whenever you're ready, madam.' She's holding out the card terminal.

'Of course,' Polly says, and pops in her card. I boil watching her, wondering if her Amex is in fact Jack's, trying to discern the pattern of her fingers over the keys but she's too fast.

The assistant finishes the transaction – oh, how I wish it had been declined – and Polly quickly throws everything into her handbag. She picks up the two purple carrier-bags.

'Listen,' she says. 'Better dash. Nice to see you.'

'I hear you're living with Jack.'

She stalls, trying to look coy but somehow managing to look simperingly smug. 'Yes.'

She's just confirmed where those cushions are heading, confirmed that I absolutely do not want one. We stare at each other. She looks away first.

'Don't you think you owe me an apology?' I say, a fiery heat rushing up my oesophagus.

She pouts with awkward uncertainty. 'I think that's down to Jack, isn't it? I know he's tried.'

'He has,' I say, mimicking her patronizing tone. 'But I'd like to hear it from you. You know. For the sisterhood.'

She scoffs. 'I'm sorry then. For the sisterhood.'

'Not accepted,' I say, with the same glib sarcasm. 'Listen, there's one thing I need to know and I want you to be honest with me. Which is probably a high expectation.'

Head tilt. Jaw shift. Pout. Slitty eyes.

I swallow bile, knowing I'm about to cross a line. Then again, all boundaries were broken the second I saw her naked tits. 'When did it start?' I say.

She rolls her narrowed eyes, sighing with weary disdain. 'Do you really want to have that discussion here?'

'Where else would you like to have it?'

She pushes her hair behind surprisingly pointy ears. 'It started that night.' She looks at me in a way that says, Happy now?

I gawp with theatrical surprise. 'Really? Because that's not what Jack said.'

Polly's eyelids flutter. Her jaw swivels. 'I didn't think the two of you were still in touch.'

I return a broad, satisfied smile. 'Well, we are.' It's one of those little white lies that feel acceptable under the circumstances.

She rests her arse cheeks against the desk and drops the two bags. 'So if you know, why ask?'

'Because I wanted to hear it from you. I knew you were a cheat but I wanted to know if you were a liar. Are you?'

She sighs, stares, mumbles to herself. 'Six months,' she says. It's a punch in the gut. 'And by the way . . .' she dips to pick up the bags '. . . I was lying to protect your feelings.'

I laugh in shock at her temerity.

'And, in case you were wondering, he was the one who made all the moves.'

170

'That's funny,' I say. 'Because Jack said you made all the moves.'

She screws up her face. 'He's the liar then.'

I laugh again, even though I want to cry. 'You might like to remember that when he cheats on you.'

She lets out a dramatic groan. If she was ever hoping to forget my existence, the former lover, the ex, then those two cushions sitting on that sofa are going to be a constant reminder. Of everything. Of her cheating, her lying, of her total lack of remorse – but that, of course, assumes she has feelings.

'Have a good life, Daisy,' she says, her voice clenched, throwing her Gucci bag back over her shoulder, turning to leave, nose in the air.

'You too!' I say, watching her dash towards the stairs. 'And send my love to karma!'

I feel Bee standing at my side.

'I caught the end of that. You okay?' she says.

My heart is pounding. I'm shaking. 'Do you think getting something off your chest is good for a baby? I feel like I might faint.'

Bee grabs a wooden chair from next to the till. 'Sit down. Head between knees.'

I breathe deeply, trying to regain my equilibrium. 'Six months, Bee. It had been going on for six months. Do you realize that if your train had been any later, we might never have bumped into her? I was meant to find that out!'

She kneels down and hugs me to her chest. 'I think I just heard the universe call closure,' she says.

31

Caro is staring at her phone when I arrive, her standard G-and-T, slice of lemon, loads of ice, sitting at her elbow. She's wearing a leopard-print silk headscarf around her Afro, her leopard bustier top revealing toned glossy shoulders. I slip onto the velvet barstool next to her.

'Welcome,' she says. 'Give me a minute.'

The bartender wanders over to help me fill the minute. He smiles in a bartender *What can I get you*? kind of way.

'Lime soda, please,' I say quietly, hoping Caro is too immersed in her phone to be listening. 'Easy on the ice.'

'What do you think of him?' she says, holding her phone screen underneath my nose.

'Swipe left.'

'No like?'

'Oh, no, sorry. Swipe right. What do I know?'

She looks at me in horror. 'Are you not on the apps yet, babe? What are you waiting for? The Grim Reaper?'

'Not my type.'

'For real.' She stares at me, waiting for an appropriate explanation.

I quickly think of one. 'I'm starting to get used to this single life,' I say. 'It's okay.' My drink is put down on a coaster in front of me and I drop in a swivel stick from a stainless-steel holder to my side, stirring like I need to mix the alcohol.

'Single is fine, babe, I'm all for it. But don't be a nun.'

'Cheers,' I say.

'To your single life! You'll soon get bored.'

'Thanks. And how are you?'

'Fine,' she says, slipping her phone back into her handbag, which is hanging from a hook under the Nero Marquina marble bar top. 'Although my mother's not been great. Been staying with her. Juggling work hasn't been easy. Beauty shops need managing, I'm lucky it's not our busiest time.'

Caro has turned her psychology degree into something completely unexpected. She's become quite the entrepreneur, with a chain of beauty salons. I helped with the design of the first, long before we'd set up Baxter Settle. She felt that all high-street salons looked the same and wanted hers to be standout, to offer a luxury experience at an affordable high-street price on the basis that investment in the design is a one-time outlay, worth the stretch, particularly when you have a girlfriend fresh out of design college and keen. I created a luxurious space: a reception desk that looked expensive but was actually a lot of MDF clad in pretty ribbed tiles, and funky lino flooring. We sourced beautiful mirrors, chairs in robust wipeable fabrics that were still comfortable and inviting, all cocooned in a relaxing palette of paint colours. It was to become her signature. In exchange I got a lot of free treatments. It was a fun time.

'You look good, though.'

'I'm a bit tired but nothing that a night out with you can't fix.' She winks.

I raise my eyebrows. 'Oh, yeah, I'm a regular bundle of laughs. Sorry about your mum. Will you send her my love?'

She nods, places her fingers one by one around her drink, her long perfect manicured nails clink-clink-clinking against the glass. 'She says she's better but I think she just wants to

get rid of me. She likes her own space. I admire her for it.'
She smacks her lips loudly. 'But, we're not seventy yet. Get
on those apps, babe!'

I proffer a reluctant smile. 'I will. When I'm ready.'

'You'll never be ready. You just have to do it. Honestly.
Have fun with it. Don't take it too seriously. You need to
get out there again. I'll write you a profile, if you want.'

I scoff. 'Really? What would you say?'

She glances upwards, thinking. 'I don't know . . . something like 'Unexpectedly back on the scene, I'm a complete
dating-app novice . . . Hoping for a kind, witty, loyal guy
who's interested in design, good-looking . . .'

I laugh. 'Doesn't that make me sound a bit shallow?'

'No. Play it straight, babe. The ugly ones reply anyway!'

Snort. 'Okay. Carry on.'

She nudges me. 'You see? You're enjoying this. I'll get
you hooked yet.'

'Maybe.'

She gives a long hmmmmm. 'So, help me out a bit here.
You got any preferences? You know – he has to like dogs
or Chaucer or Nietzsche?'

I make to fall off the stool. 'I think I'm happier being
shallow,' I say. 'Is that what you've got in yours?'

'Nah! Obviously not. I'm playing with ya, cos you're
playing with me.'

I sip my drink. 'Sorry. I might brave it some time. Just
not in the mood quite yet.'

We sit for a moment, both staring towards the rows of
brightly coloured bottles. I find myself absently reading the
labels inside my head.

'Don't you ever want to settle down?' I ask, curious.

She pffs, shaking her head, looking like someone who
knows she's got it right. 'Nope. Having too much fun. I see

what happens to people like you, good people, you know, who commit to someone and get fucked over. I don't want to put myself in that position. I'm gonna love 'em and leave 'em wanting more.'

'Good for you,' I say, wishing I could love and leave anything without a sense of deep regret. 'But aren't you ever lonely?'

She shrugs, the sinews of her shoulders flexing. 'Sometimes. So what? We all get lonely. For me it's not enough to make me fall for the trick of heating soup for someone when he's sick, doing his washing, wiping his beardy bits out of my sink, constantly putting down the loo seat, then having him ditch me when he fancies a newer model. I respect myself too much.'

I hold up my drink. 'Respect to you, girlfriend. You are definitely one of a kind.'

'I am of womankind, baby!' She grins. 'You'll all get there in the end.'

I laugh from the pit of my stomach. 'Oh, Caro!' I splutter. 'I love your womankind.'

She smirks. 'You see, people?' she says, looking around as if she's hoping for applause. She laughs! 'What the fuck, babe?' She giggles. 'Fuck loneliness! Stare it down.'

I nod. 'Or phone a friend,' I say.

'And here we are,' she says.

We stare at each other, like we're drinking each other in. Recognizing what we represent: the years of friendship, bolstering each other up from exams to careers to men. The comings and goings, the highs and lows that only a long-term friend can know to remind you of.

'But what about when you're in your fifties and single, or your sixties?' I say. 'Doesn't that bother you?'

She rolls her eyes and groans. 'Are you kidding me? I'll

be a hell of a lot happier than those poor women stuck in marriages, wondering what the hell happened to the cute guy they pledged themselves to, sleeping at opposite sides of the bed, watching different TV shows in different rooms, barely talking over a dinner she no longer cooks with love.'

I grin. 'That just assumes everyone gets it wrong.'

'Most of them do, babe. Trust me. Most of them do.'

I rest my chin in my hands. 'Well, I can hardly talk, can I?'

She playfully pokes at my ribs and I flinch as it tickles. 'What about you?' she says. 'Isn't it time you started having some fun?'

'I bumped into Polly today.'

'That sounds like a lot of fun!'

'She moved in with Jack. Before Christmas. I hate her.'

'You're human, babe. It's understandable. But she'll get what she deserves.'

'I don't know that she will. She's buying cushions. She's there to stay.'

'Only you could classify a situation by some cushions.' She puts her hand on my arm. 'Listen to your friend. It's out of your control. Move on. You can't hold on to the pain. You have to release it. Have some great sex, for God's sake! Even some not so great sex!' She stretches her neck. 'Holding on to pain is not healthy. I see it every day.'

I swivel my stool closer to the bar and lean my elbows on it. 'You're right. I was doing quite well until I saw her. She looked so damn smug. She admitted they'd been having an affair for six months. I thought knowing would help but it doesn't.'

She shakes her head, mouth downturned. 'You still want them?' she says. 'Kids?'

I look at her, bemused by the tangent, panicked she's

about to challenge me. Like she's noticed I'm not drinking. 'Yes. Of course.'

'Good,' she says. 'I'm glad you haven't given up on your dream. I'd hate to think the shit stole that from you too.'

'Oh, he stole everything,' I say. 'But hopefully I can redeem what matters most.'

She smiles. 'Don't you think it's funny? We're so different yet we still manage to be great friends.'

'We have shared history.'

She gives an upward nod. 'Maybe that's it.'

'Anyway, how can you be so sure you won't meet some guy who blows you away and suddenly you want to have his children?'

She puffs. 'It's a vile world. Why would I want to bring kids into it?'

'To make it a better world.'

Her face suggests otherwise. 'Always the optimist,' she says. 'Don't ever change!' She holds up her emptied glass at the bartender, who gives a thumbs-up. 'Listen,' she says, studying my face. 'I love you, babe. I've always loved you.' She fiddles inside her handbag and pulls out her phone. 'But no one is ever going to convince me to change my mind about my solo status. It's too precious.'

She swipes up her phone and hits some keys with the speed of someone well practised, her long nails more accurate than my stubby jabs could ever be.

'What do you think of him?' she says, and I laugh at the unapologetic contradiction, how she defies logic, defies convention, happily flouts all the rules, playing the game exactly as she wants to.

'Go for it. Swipe right.'

'You learn fast,' she says, with a wink. 'Take my word for it, Daisy babe. Get on the apps.'

32

Marcus is on a site visit at Hoxton. The job is moving forward, taking up more and more of his time. I miss him. I never used to feel this way before when he was out of the office. I quite liked having the place to myself. Now I hate the silence. It's become too familiar, like an unwanted friend.

I try to focus on chasing contractors and suppliers. I have a long, long list sitting in front of me with only a few ticks and an awful lot of spiralling doodles. I think I'm better at working when Marcus is around. His presence, his sense of focus, grounds me, stopping my mind wandering into the depths of my doodles.

My phone is on silent but it catches my attention in my peripheral vision. I casually look across, seeing the screen illuminate with a message.

It's from Jack.

My whole stomach flips. I hate that his name still has that effect on me. That he has an ongoing hold on my emotions without any right.

I debate whether to delete it without reading it, but that's like promising yourself you won't eat chocolate – it's inevitable.

I click.

I hear you bumped into Polly. She told me what happened. That was a cunning ruse, Daise. But I guess you would have found out sooner or later.

I put down the phone feeling guilty. Then pick it up again, because the guilt does not belong to me.

Do you think now is the time for us to meet and have a proper conversation? I'd like to apologize in person.

'Oh, for goodness' sake,' I say aloud, standing up and pacing. 'Why do you need my forgiveness, Jack? So you can feel better about yourself? Well, you're not going to get redemption from me. There are three of you in that relationship. You, Polly and betrayal. Not forgetting two very silky, very plump cushions. I hope it's overcrowded.'

I sit down. Maybe I'll text that.

I look at my phone. I won't.

Another message pings through.

I beg you to give me the chance to explain. I think you'll understand. I really do. I miss you, Daisy. I can't tell you how much, but I'd like to. Because I still love you. I need to see you. Jack x

I gasp out loud at his clever manipulation. I'm not going to fall for it. I'm not! I am *not!*

Flopping like a puppet, I push my feet against the foot bar of the desk so that the wheels of my chair roll backwards. My hands dangle at my sides, and I'm still clutching the phone. How dare he play with my feelings like that? He got caught in flagrante with the woman who's now officially replaced me yet he has the temerity to say he still loves me. Isn't that called having your cake and eating it?

I won't reply. Not even with something clever. I won't delete the messages either because I want to remind myself of his tactics. How am I supposed to work when he bombshells me with that? How am I expected to draw a decent doodle? I let go of my phone and it drops softly onto the coir matting.

I sit in a foggy, limp-limbed stupor for an indeterminate

amount of time, my mind a mush of thoughts, roaring through the entire spectrum of emotions from anger to self-blame to anger and self-blame. I write my own narrative, imagining what has prompted him to say this. He's playing with me. He's lonely. He's bored. He's remorseful. Strike that last one.

The click of the door breaks my thoughts and I sit up, relieved to be able to share my self-flagellation with Marcus, who walks in, talking on his phone, taking off his coat one-handed, hanging it on the back of the door. I stare at him, willing him to end his call. He carries on, oblivious, his problem with a contractor taking precedence.

Finally he ends the call and heads to pour himself a coffee. He looks round and catches my expression. 'What?'

'Can you believe what Jack has just texted?'

'I don't know. Can I?'

I reach down for my phone and read out both messages.

He looks at me, like it's a good thing. 'I told you. He misses you. What are you going to do about it?' He sits down in his seat and flips open his laptop.

'Let's talk when you're not distracted.'

He flips down his laptop and rolls his eyes. 'You've got me. I'm all ears.' He looks at his watch. 'I actually need a distraction. Fucking window delivery's delayed again. I might achieve more if I calm down before I yell at them.'

'Sorry. It's just I—'

'Daisy. Let's talk this through. Jack misses you, right?'

'Maybe, but not in the way you think.' I scrape up my hair and swing it over my left shoulder.

Marcus sits back in his chair. 'Go on.'

'I've been running over everything in my head. He's no longer the big boss. We're not around him for all those meetings we used to have. He's surrounded by new people, living with Polly, whom he barely knows, apart from carnally. He's got no continuity. He must feel lacking in purpose. I guess he thinks that being with me will ground him again. But it's too late.'

'Really, Freud. Interesting.' He sips his coffee. 'Why too late?'

I point at my stomach. 'Hello, Jack! I'm pregnant with Adam's baby. Still love me?'

'I see what you're saying. So we're allowed to talk about it now?'

'In this context, yes.'

He wheels his seat from under his desk and travels over to mine. He leans into me. 'You're not regretting anything, are you?'

I gulp in distaste. 'God, no! I mean, and I feel weird for even saying this, but I actually feel a bit sorry for him.'

Marcus plays his fingers across his chin. 'What? The man with a gazillion pounds in his bank account?'

'Yeah!' I say insistently. 'Because of that. What does he do now? He's forty-five years old. He's not going to be starting a family any time soon. He's probably wondering who loves him for him or for his money. I feel like he's flailing around, which is why he's reaching out to me.'

He puts his hand on my forearm. 'Daisy. Don't do yourself down. I think he's reaching out to you because he loves you. And, by the way, no one with a gazillion pounds flails around for long. Trust me.'

'What are you saying? That a million women will be gagging for him?'

'At least.'

'I hope Polly knows that.'

Marcus puts down his mug on one of the brightly coloured china coasters decorating my desk. He crosses his arms to his chest. 'Listen, we've never had this conversation but now that you're pregnant, and you're never going to get back with that poor little rich boy Jack, I think we should. Because something tells me that, at some point in your life, you're going to meet someone and you're going to be expecting monogamy and I don't want you to be disappointed.'

My stomach gurgles. I've not eaten for too long. I open my drawer and pull out the packet of Digestives, which is depleting rather too quickly. 'Want one?'

'Don't mind if I do.'

I hand him a biscuit, then return the packet to my desk drawer. 'Explain, please. What's the problem with wanting monogamy?' I bite and chew slowly.

Marcus demolishes his. He picks up his mug, polishes off the dregs of his coffee and runs his tongue across his teeth. 'I don't think men do monogamy. I can understand why you ended the relationship with Jack. No one wants to witness the love of their life fucking another woman.' He clears his throat again. 'That must have been awful.'

My eyes close. I bite down hard on the biscuit. 'And?'

'I think expecting any man to stay monogamous in a long-term relationship is tough.'

I laugh. 'Tough, then. I'm really sorry but I don't see why a man can't keep it in his trousers if he loves someone.'

Marcus stretches out his limbs and crosses his feet at the ankle. He steeples his fingers under his chin. 'Because I think the sort of man you're going to fall for, probably dynamic, entertaining, bright, can't. He just can't. Even though he might want to.'

I look out of the window at the office buildings across the street. It's starting to get dark. 'I'm doomed, then,' I say. I put my head into my hands. 'Or . . . maybe I'm not. Maybe I don't want to meet a man.'

'Everyone wants to meet a man, darling,' he says, smiling.

'And even though I like the sound of dynamic, entertaining and bright, if playing away is the inevitable outcome, then maybe I'm better off on my own. Happy with one . . . possibly two children,' I lift my eyes to Heaven as though praying to someone who might be listening, 'In whom to invest my love.'

Marcus raises one eyebrow. 'What? And no sex?'

I shift in my seat. 'I'll pay for it. That way I'll know exactly where I stand and there will be no disappointments.'

'Oh, yeah, sure. I can just imagine that.' He swivels in his chair. 'I'll buy you a Rabbit. And I don't mean the sort with dodgy front teeth.'

'Just buy me some batteries. Anyway, I have to disagree with you. I think it is possible to meet a man who can stay monogamous. But I'm guessing you and Flynn aren't.'

He eyeballs me, flapping his hands on either side of his head, like 'Has that only just occurred to you?' 'Of course not. It's what keeps us together. But we're open about it. We agreed from the get-go we could have sex with other men but we weren't allowed to fall in love.'

I look at him with muted surprise, even though part of me always wondered what their arrangement was. 'Honestly, I don't think I could do that. I'd always be suspicious, always wondering. What would that do for my mental health?'

'It does wonders for mine. Keeps me on my toes.'

I stretch out in my chair. I look at the text on my phone and put it back on the desk.

'What if Jack says he's happy to play father to your baby?' he says.

I laugh in surprise.

He tips his chin. 'You never know.'

'Listen,' I say. 'Maybe I'm being unrealistic, or stubborn,

or overly romantic in my expectations but for me Jack is yesterday. Tomorrow is about me and my baby. He's too late.'

He pushes his chair right up next to mine, his face so close he's practically abutting my chin. 'Gazillions might be nice,' he says, with an amused wink.

'You sleep with him, then.'

33

Bee and I are reporting in from under our duvets. I read her Jack's message. I need to dissect it from a woman's perspective.

'I told you, he misses you. You sure you don't want to see him? Just get it over and done with. Put him out of his misery. Tell him you're done! Won't that feel great?'

I stare at his words. 'Then I'll have to tell him I'm pregnant.'

'Why?'

'Because it's the honest thing to do.'

'Where does honesty come into it?'

'It's my playbook, even if it isn't his.'

'Fine. Then don't see him. But don't reply. If you reply you're keeping the window open. You need to close the conversation down.'

I press delete. 'That conversation is officially closed.'

'Well done.' I hear the plumping of a pillow. 'Okay. I have a question.'

'Uh-oh.'

'I've been wondering . . . I mean, I know what I'll tell Will about what happened between me and his dad when he's old enough to ask, but what will you tell your child?'

Your child. My heart springs into a flutter as my mind replays the words. *Your child. My child.* No bigger than an apricot, becoming more and more formed. Not just connected to my body but connected to my life, our futures soldered together.

'You go first,' I say. 'What are you going to tell Will?'

She laughs. 'You're playing for time.'

'I'm not. I've genuinely thought about it but you go first.'

Bee tells me what she'll say to Will about the breakdown of her relationship with his father. How they loved each other when they got married. How Will was born out of love. How people sometimes grow in different directions. Some towards the light and some towards the dark. And she preferred the light.

'Don't you think that's a bit damning? Patrick liking the dark side?'

'He does, though,' she says. 'Come on. What about you?'

I roll onto my back and stare at the ceiling, listening to my neighbour padding about, hoping he can't hear my conversations, like I can sometimes hear through next door's walls when they row.

'I guess I'll just be honest with them. I'll tell them their conception was magical, that they have never been more wanted because I had to be determined and courageous to go down this route. I'll show them the photos of baby Adam, give them the letter he wrote to them and say, "This is your dad, and when you're ready, after you've reached eighteen, he says he's happy for you to be in touch."'

She takes a beat. 'Wow! That's really charming, Daisy. You make it sound positively romantic.'

I laugh. 'Good. Because the whole procedure was quite the opposite.'

She blows her nose.

'Are you weeping?'

'Absolutely not.' She snuffles. *She is!*

'Anyway,' I continue, 'by the time our children are old

enough to be interested in their parentage, schools will be full of kids of divorced parents, solo mums, solo dads, kids with same-sex parents, and they'll take it as the norm. The unusual ones will be the ones whose straight parents are married! The world will be a very different place for our children. A better place, perhaps.'

'Let's hope,' she says.

When we finish chatting, I think about what we've discussed.

Our children.

Her children.

My children.

It sounds so fantastically positive.

I record our conversation in my journal. For posterity.

It's the final page. I close it wondering where to keep it safe, shutting it away in the bedside drawer.

34

I open a fresh Moleskine. I love it when you start a new one, when it's all virginal, the pages uncrimped by writing.

I've always hated Mother's Day. Partly because my mother loves it so I have to make sure I remember to buy her a card and write ridiculous things in it to remind her that I love her when frankly everything I do for her should remind her of that. But mainly I hate it because we always have to go out en famille and, if I'm honest, in recent years, with my younger brother overtaking me on the en famille front, I've always felt a bit of a failure. Because I am not a mother. And I've wanted to be one since my first Cabbage Patch Doll. So I hate Mother's Day. Until now!

I look at the two letters on my fridge and wonder if Adam's going out with his mother today. Or the mother of his known child? If there is one. Or more. The entire anonymous nature of this procedure remains unfathomable to me, even though I'm steeped in it. It conjures up too many questions that will never be answered. And maybe they don't have to be. I should try to be content with where I am.

Whatever Adam is up to, in my head or otherwise, my family is going out for lunch to celebrate. Which is *what we do*. Lunch is booked at Dinner. I know! What do marketing guys think when they dream up these names? Dinner is Heston Blumenthal's restaurant at the Mandarin Oriental Hotel in Hyde Park. It was where we were supposed to be celebrating my fortieth and, being the sort of man who doesn't like to let eventualities defeat him, my father has chosen it as the place to celebrate Mother's Day instead.

'Do you think it's time to break my news to him?' I ask my mother. 'I mean, he'll be relaxed. He'll be head of the table, in charge, which is his favourite disposition.'

'With whisky, lots of whisky,' she says. 'Because we're getting a cab into town.'

'There you go. Perfect. A whisky-filled happy father. And it's Mother's Day. What could be more appropriate?' I let out an uneasy sigh. 'I guess I should be allowed to bend the twelve-week rule for family. I'm so nearly there.'

'If you're okay with it, I think it's the perfect opportunity, darling. I'll make sure I act surprised. I don't want him to know that I know anything about it, let alone that I was there for the conception.'

I laugh.

'Or whatever it was. Don't say anything to Doug, that way he'll be genuinely surprised. And, by the way, I'm sure Dad will be delighted.'

'Yeah, right.'

'True. I'm not sure of anything any more. Of course he's thrilled about Eve.'

We all know she's pregnant now but only I remain privy to the fact it's a girl.

* * *

I'm first to arrive. Hanging about in the lobby. My anxiety building for the conversation yet to happen.

My parents appear next, very refined and Mayfair-ready, my father in a dapper tweed suit, my mother in a wraparound Diane von Furstenberg dress, one of my favourites from her wardrobe. 'Card,' I say, slipping it into her handbag.

'Looking good, daughter!' says my father, kissing the top of my head. 'I'm liking your pink suit. Better than I've seen you look for a very long time.'

My mother shoots me a knowing nod. I think she might have to hold back on them or he'll suspect something.

'Thanks, Dad,' I say. 'Not so bad yourself.'

There's a small commotion. 'And here they are,' says my mother.

My brother is holding Monty's hand. Eve is holding Eddie's.

'But I'm hungry!' says Monty.

'I told you to eat your breakfast,' says Doug.

'We'll be eating soon,' says Eve.

'I ate my breakfast and I'm still hungry,' groans Eddie, practically swinging off Eve's hand.

She's wearing a body-hugging block print dress that shows off her great legs with their perfect sprayed-on tan, no tights, just cowboy boots. Her teeny baby bump looks like it could have been sprayed on too. She's the sort of woman who would happily show her bare midriff, were it not that in this weather it would be covered with goosebumps. In a few months' time, now that it's official, guaranteed it will be out for all to see.

The boys are neatly turned out, with brushed hair, little navy jackets with the Ralph Lauren logo on the breast pocket, pale blue shirts, striped ties, stone-coloured chinos for Monty, a pink net tutu for Eddie. I like his style. My father is not so sure. 'Shush,' says my mother.

Doug is looking his usual cool, relaxed self, even though he's smartened up by wearing a jacket and tie and a normal shirt he's actually tucked in. I don't suppose you can expect your children to wear a jacket and tie if you don't. We exchange grand hugs of excitement as if we haven't seen each other for months. 'Happy Mother's Day!'

We follow the maître d' into the dining room and my father hangs back, waiting for me. 'You approve of the design?' he asks, in a rare acknowledgement of my professional skills.

I take in the stunning lighting, the backlit glass jelly moulds grouped in threes that cast an ethereal glow against the walls, the elaborate sculptural construct of the chandeliers, like Spirograph circles within a circle, the beautiful leather-upholstered benches and chairs, which flatter the rich dark wood of the tables.

'Not too shabby,' I say, and my father nods, like he's done a good job.

'Where do you want us?' Doug asks, as they hover round the table.

'I want to sit next to Grandma,' says Monty, and my mother flutters with the excitement of grandchild approval.

'*I* want to sit next to Grandma,' says Eddie.

'Well, that's Grandma sorted,' says Doug. 'I want to sit next to Mummy. Who else wants to sit next to Mummy?'

'I do!' they say.

'Who wants to sit next to Auntie Daisy?' I say, swooping in to avert a meltdown, recognizing that only one of them can sit next to Mummy *and* Grandma.

'I do,' says Eddie.

I tap the seat next to mine. 'Your throne awaits you, Princess Eddie.' He happily skips round to it. Helping him up, I notice his slightly chipped pink-painted nails.

'Aperitif, anyone?' asks my father. Somehow I have

managed to place myself next to him, even though it's not necessarily the safest position today.

My mother nods heartily. 'What's that cocktail we had in New York, Ted, that I liked?'

'Mimosa,' says my father.

'One of those, please.' She does a little shimmy of excitement in her seat.

'Not for me,' says Eve, tapping her stomach.

'Doug? Daisy? You'll join your mother and me?'

'Damn right I will,' he says. 'Dirty Martini.'

'Daddy!' says Monty.

'It's a real name, Monty. I'll let you have a sip.'

'No, you won't,' says Eve.

'He'll find it disgusting. It'll put him off for life.'

'But I want a Dirty Martini,' says Monty.

'Me too,' says Eddie, and Eve throws my brother a withering look, like he's her most difficult child.

'You can have a sip of my Mimosa,' says my mother.

'Now that would definitely be a mistake,' says Doug. 'They might actually like that.'

Eve groans. 'They can try my non-alcoholic cocktail. I'll have a St Clements, please, Ted.'

'Make that two,' I say. 'You can try some of mine, Eddie. It's very pretty.' He grins up at me, his little teeth all white and perfect and pointy.

'Oh, for goodness' sake, Daisy. Have a real drink,' my father insists. 'This is a celebration. Eddie can have some of Eve's. She has no choice.'

'I'm fine, Dad,' I say, and he rolls his eyes.

We're handed the Mother's Day menu. Doug requests some bread 'to keep the boys quiet'.

'Very sophisticated menu for children,' my mother says, casting her eye over the short list of offerings.

'Very sophisticated children,' says Doug. 'Anyway, I'm sure they'll do some kids' options. And if not, they'll happily eat the triple-cooked chips.'

'Triple-cooked chips for me,' says Eddie. 'Wicked!'

'I want the beef,' says Monty.

'I told you,' says Doug. 'Sophisticated.'

'Are you still veggie?' I ask Eve.

My father looks revolted. 'Veggie? Don't be ridiculous.'

'Ted!' scolds my mother. 'Are you, Eve?' she queries gently.

'Yes,' she says. 'But there's plenty here for me.'

'She can have the triple-cooked chips,' says Monty.

'She doesn't like chips,' says Eddie.

'But she eats them.'

'Sometimes she eats meat,' says Eddie.

'I do not!' exclaims Eve.

'Yes, you do! You ate my sausage yesterday before you put the plate in the dishwasher.'

'That's called tidying-up,' says Eve, as the bread arrives. She quickly pushes a slice into each of the boys' hands probably wishing she could push it straight into their mouths.

My father blows a raspberry. 'Well, I'm glad you're not being strict about it,' he says. 'It's complete nonsense.' And before anyone can counter him, he goes into lecture mode, pontificating about some article he's read in the *FT Weekend*, which had statistical proof of the vitamin deficiency risked by vegetarians. 'And don't get me started on vegans,' he says.

Eve meets him with a beatific smile, then hands the kids their iPads, helping them set up their screens, Monty first then Eddie, turning the volume to low rather than mute 'because he likes to hear the sounds a little bit'.

'You're pregnant, Eve,' says my father, like she needs a

reminder, as she sits down, expressionless. 'You need to be sensible.'

'She takes supplements, Dad,' says Doug. 'She's absolutely fine.'

'Well, don't say I didn't warn you.'

'You're hardly one to boast about healthy habits, Ted,' says my mother.

'Here she goes,' says my father, rolling his eyes.

I play with my food, the nerves messing with my stomach, while Eve finds useful diversion from my father's lectures by fussing over the boys. She tries not to betray her annoyance when my mother corrects them on how they're holding their knives and forks.

'It's a knife not a pen, Monty.'

'It's a fork not a shovel, Eddie.'

I remember all too well the days when it was 'It's a knife not a pen, Daisy,' and 'It's a fork not a shovel, Doug.' But for Eve it feels like a personal failure.

'You okay?' says my father, looking at me quizzically. 'You're not eating or drinking. Are you not well?'

'I'm fine,' I say. 'I'm taking it slowly. I've read it's good for the digestive system if you chew everything thirty times.' It's always helpful to mirror my father's tactics back at him. He actually enjoys it. He likes to joust. But he likes to win.

'Hmm,' he says, now quite well oiled, at least two whiskies, a few glasses of red under his broadening belt. 'I've read that too.' Not a man to be outsmarted. 'Who wants dessert?'

The kids want ice cream, Doug will choose the most chocolaty thing on the menu and my mother will order whatever my father wants, take one mouthful and pass it over to him. Unsurprisingly, neither Eve nor I can face it.

I nip to the loo and prepare my little *Guess what? Happy*

days! I'm pregnant speech in the mirror, checking my facial expression as I wash my hands, making sure I look positive and upbeat, not shitting myself, which I am, despite being constipated. I put it down to stress or pregnancy. Or both.

Desserts have arrived. My father has ordered a bottle of Sauterne, which he pours for everyone barring Eve.

I sit down, putting my hand over my glass.

'Just a drop, for goodness' sake. For the toast.'

'Fine.'

He holds up his glass and we all hold up ours.

'Happy Mother's Day to my beautiful wife and beautiful daughter-in-law. You are the best mothers anyone could ever wish for. I'm very proud of you.'

My mother and Eve look appropriately coy.

'Thank you, Ted.'

I HATE MOTHER'S DAY. I can feel my face flushing. In that moment, I feel so excluded. Do the marketing men ever think about that? The women who want to be mothers but can't. The women who are hoping to be mothers, living on a wing and a prayer and injections. The people who have lost their mother. The people who have never known their mother. Is this day really necessary?

I muscle in, pinging my spoon against my glass. 'Announcement,' I say.

My mother sits to attention, her face a picture of interested innocence.

'Don't tell me,' my father says. 'You're pregnant.' He laughs. 'That's a joke obviously.' My mother's eyebrows virtually fly off her forehead.

'Why is that a joke?' I say defensively.

Eve shoots me a weird look.

My father looks at my mother. 'Well . . . obviously you're not pregnant.'

'Why obviously?' There's an awkward silence, barring whispered Candy Crush noises and the peripheral buzz of the surrounding tables, happily oblivious to the little domestic drama that's about to erupt at our table.

'Actually, I am pregnant,' I say. 'I was going to say it a bit more elegantly but you've ruined that opportunity.'

'Don't be ridiculous,' scoffs my father. 'I meant it as a joke.'

'Oh, my God!' says Eve. 'Seriously?'

'Seriously.' I nod.

'Congratulations,' she says. She mouths, 'Jack?' and I shake my head.

We all look differently confused.

'Bravo!' says Doug, his eyes slinking towards our father.

'Yes bravo!' says our mother. 'This is wonderful news. Congratulations, darling. Isn't that lovely news, Ted?'

I think she's overdoing it.

My father is busy checking the general reaction, not sure if everyone's pulling a fast one on him.

'Are you messing with me, Daisy?' he says, placing both hands firmly on the table, in full confrontation mode.

'This is not something I would mess with you about, Dad. It's too important to me.'

He frowns, still hesitant, then breaks into a smile. 'Well, if you're back with Jack, why didn't you say? That's marvellous news. He should be here with us now.'

'It's not Jack's,' I say.

His face switches, his hands clench. 'Whose is it, then?' He looks at my mother again, as if he's starting to guess by her relaxed appearance that she's in on this. 'Is there something you've failed to tell me, Sal?'

'I'm using an anonymous donor,' I say.

'What are you talking about? Anonymous? What the hell does that mean? Sally, did you know about this?'

'Well, I do now,' she says, remaining unfazed. 'Explain to us what anonymous means, please, Daisy.'

'It means I'm pregnant using sperm donation. I know everything about the father, I just don't know him.'

My father's entire face screws into an ugly red moustachioed ball. 'Have you gone mad?'

I throw a pleading look at my mother, who's still in role, looking innocent. 'No. I'm pregnant, Dad. I thought you'd be happy for me.'

'And why would you think that?'

'Because if I'm happy you're happy. Isn't that how parenting works?'

'Not for this parent,' he says.

'I'm happy for you,' says my mother.

'Me too,' says Doug.

'Me three,' says Eve. 'This is great news. Boys, Auntie Daisy is going to give you a cousin,' which gets no reaction from their Candy Crush-focused faces. Of all people I have Eve as an ally. I throw her a grateful look.

'How many weeks, Daisy?' says my mother.

My father sighs in disbelief that she's even dignifying me with a question.

'Very nearly twelve. Probably should have waited until I was over that mark but Mother's Day felt like a good time to tell my family.'

I stare at his angry face. I knew this would be his reaction. I was prepared for it and yet somehow, foolishly, I'd hoped things might turn out differently. I'm angry with myself that, at forty years old, I still want his approval for something not even my mother really approves of. But at least she's open to it. At least she's trying.

Eve smiles and gives me an excited handclap.

'Twelve weeks,' says Doug.

'Nearly,' I say emphatically.

'Fantastic news,' he replies.

'Is it?' says my father. 'Have you really thought about what you're doing?'

'I have.' I stare him directly in the eyes, stern, holding my core together. Not about to let him bully me! He blinks at me awkwardly, unused to mutiny.

'Listen,' I say. 'It's Mother's Day. It felt like the appropriate day to tell you all but if you're unhappy about it, Dad, we can discuss it another time. For now can you just pretend to celebrate with me? I don't want to be responsible for ruining everyone's meal.'

'I need a poo, Mummy,' says Eddie.

Eve jumps out of her chair. 'Okay, little one,' she says. 'Let's go to the loo. Want to come, Monty?'

None of us has noticed that Monty has fallen asleep, head to one side, lolling against my mother, iPad propped up in front of him.

'Leave him,' says my mother. 'He's fine.'

Eve whips round the table, adjusting her dress so she's not showing her knickers, takes Eddie's hand and runs towards the loo.

My father is chewing the inside of his finger, as though longing for the days when restaurants allowed him to chew on a cigar. 'Am I the only one who's finding Daisy's announcement a shock?' he says.

'Seems so,' says Doug.

'Right, then. I'm going for a walk.' He stands up so violently, his chair tumbles back. 'Bugger!' he says, and picks it up. We're all waiting for him to slam it into the table but he resists.

Monty springs to life. 'Where's Eddie?'

'Gone to the loo,' says Doug.

'Where's Grandpa going? Can I go with him?'

My mother puts her arm around him. 'You wait here, darling,' she says.

'Maybe you should go with him, Ma,' I say.

She shakes her head. 'He'll work it out better by himself. If I go, he'll think I'm putting him under pressure. And he'll suspect something. Which he probably already does.' She fiddles with her napkin, looking strained beneath the surface calm.

'Why is Grandpa angry?' asks Monty.

Because Grandpa's a dick, I think.

'He's not angry,' says my mother. 'He's just trying to adjust to a new idea. You know, like when you want to watch *Britain's Got Talent* and everyone else wants to watch *Strictly* and you feel angry and frustrated. You need time to adjust.'

We resort to silence as Monty resorts to his iPad. I feel bad that I've ruined a lovely lunch. Eve comes back with Eddie.

'Everything okay? Where's Ted?'

'Grandpa's angry,' says Monty, not bothering to look up. 'Because everyone wants to watch *Strictly*. We should send him to the naughty corner. He needs to learn to control his temper.'

'Well said, Monty!' I say.

Eddie climbs back into the chair next to me. 'You okay?' says Eve, moisturized hands placed on my shoulders.

'I'm good,' I say, and she gives me a small squeeze before returning to her side of the table.

We can feel the air shift as my father returns.

'I'll get the bill,' he says. He scrapes out his chair and sits down with a thud.

'It's just a TV programme, Grandpa,' says Monty.

'What?' says my father.

'Never mind,' says my mother. 'Let's get the bill.'

'Are you paying, then?' he says.

'For goodness' sake, Ted,' she says. 'Grow up.'

Eddie sniggers. 'Grandpa's nearly a hundred, Grandma,' he says. 'He's very grown-up.'

'You'd think,' says my mother. 'But sometimes even grown-ups act like babies.'

35

I look out of the murky windows of my flat, streaked with what looks like years of residual rain and dust, trying to decide what kind of day it's going to be. The grey clouds hang low in the sullen sky, barely shifting. I'm guessing at least we've been spared the wind. It feels like everything is a bit grey and purple, including my stomach, but next weekend the clocks go forward. Spring! Reasons to be cheerful.

I throw on a jumper, thick tights, a pair of wool trousers which once felt generous at the waist but now fit, suede ankle boots, grab my coat and my tote bag, lock up and skip down the stairs. As I make the final turn, I'm greeted by my upstairs neighbour, coat over his pyjamas, his balding grey pate shining under the timed hall light, lingering over the post table, clutching a litre of milk.

'Mr Henderson!'

'Miss Settle,' he says. 'Okay, dear?'

'Yes, Mr Henderson. Good, thank you. You?'

He nods, wipes his nose with a scrunched-up tissue. 'Cold out there. For the time of year.'

'Good to know!' We squeeze past each other, one of those awkward moments when you'd rather not know what he had to eat last night.

The welcome appearance of daffodils in full bloom signal that I'm over the worst: the freezing, miserable weather, the penetrating bone-numbing cold of the flat, the scary, vulnerable weeks that hang over the viability of my baby. So very nearly there. My twelve-week scan is tomorrow. It feels like for ever away, even though I'm so very nearly there. Be still, my beating heart. Beating two hearts. I'm genuinely, outrageously happy.

In the office, the Peckham house preoccupies most of my morning. Chasing deliveries. Chasing an elusive electrician. Keeping Camilla calm. I've been trying to stop her going to the house for the past week, until I've checked it's ready for inspection.

Installation of the kitchen is almost complete, the island, clad in polished statuary marble, is standout. The tiles should be delivered this afternoon. A pale grey mother-of-pearl fish-scale mosaic, which will cover practically every space available on every kitchen wall. I told Camilla it would be worth it. The open-plan kitchen-diner is going to be a massive oh-wow! I know Benedict doesn't agree. His taut face tells me he thinks my designs interfere with his clean architectural lines and, in a way, he's right. I soften those lines because this is someone's home. It's not a submission for some architectural award.

Once the tiles have been mounted, we can finish decorating the dining area and up will go the beautiful vintage wallpaper, with its delicate silver florals and birds, which we're customizing by running antiqued silver metallic braid down the seams. So very not Peckham. So very not Benedict. So very exciting!

I've bought a stunning antique French refectory table from 1stDibs, and I've got my eyes on eight dining chairs on eBay that will work perfectly with it once they're re-upholstered. I've already chosen the fabric, which Camilla 'love-love-loves!' I can't wait to see everything in situ. But no rush. Plenty to do yet.

The bathrooms are first to be finished. They're being cleaned up ready for the big reveal tomorrow evening. Any issues need to be sorted out ahead or Camilla will see one minor problem and start assuming there are problems everywhere, scrutinizing every brushstroke, every millimetre of grout, every tile, building up an excessive snagging list that might have been avoided.

All I can think of as I approach the house is that as soon as the inspection is done I can get straight home and have a relaxing evening, a bath, candlelight, anchovy pizza, in anticipation of tomorrow morning's scan.

Benedict opens the door.

'Hello!' I say, trying not to let his mere presence quash my positive spirit.

He looks at me in his usual way. 'I was about to leave but since you're here, maybe once you're done with your team, we can have a quick run-through of everything. The extension is so close to second fix, we can start to consolidate your plans.'

'That's good news!' I say. 'But I may be quite some time.'

'I can find plenty to do, I can assure you.' He follows me through to the kitchen on his way back down to the extension. 'By the way, your kitchen tiles have arrived. They're beautiful.'

I practically fall over in shock. A compliment! From Benedict Shaw. That's like getting a handshake from Paul Hollywood on *Bake Off*.

'Oh, good,' I say. 'I'll check them out.'

'Hey, Daisy! I thought I heard your voice.' The arrival of my decorator, Graham, his big ruddy face always smiling, wearing his navy overalls, dappled with paint and grout, allows Benedict his exit. Graham and Bonnie are one of the freelance teams we used at Turner House. We worked so well together that I contacted them to see if they would be available, if they hadn't had any warnings not to work with Baxter Settle. They were available. And they hadn't.

'Just looking at these stunners,' I say, pulling out a sheet of tiles.

'They're going to be a beautiful challenge,' he says. 'Popping out to the not-so-beautiful Portaloo. We've cleaned up all the bathrooms ready for you. Bonnie's just tidying the en-suite. I'll be up in two.'

I wander up to find Bonnie hoovering with the big old reliable incredibly noisy industrial Henry.

'Hello, Daisy,' she shouts, turning off the motor. She stands back, taking in her work, waiting for me to do the same.

'Wow, Bonnie!' I say.

'I know,' she says. 'Just wow!'

This vast en-suite to the main bedroom is, along with the kitchen, one of the highlights of my design. I take in the effect of the marble floor tiles, laid in a chevron pattern, set against the olive-green-painted panelling; the glorious ornate Georgian mirror, which hangs above the Georgian sideboard, which we've had refurbished and repurposed with two marble basins and antique brass taps; the high-cistern loo, with its antique brass chain and black teardrop-handle flush; and the stunning copper bath, which takes centre stage. It's all pulled together perfectly. It looks incredible, super-chic yet warm and inviting. I check everything right up close, running my hands along surfaces, seeing if there are any overlooked streaks or bubbles or gaps, or if an extra polish is needed, but since they are both perfectionists I'm pretty confident about the standard of finish. Graham strolls back in.

'Beautiful work, guys,' I say. 'As always.'

'It's been a dream,' says Bonnie. 'I love it when the client has actually embraced the creative flair of the designer instead of playing it safe. So much boring beige abounds nowadays. We knew this was going to be exceptional because of the hotels. Always loved your and Marcus's work.'

'Mutual,' I say. 'Thank you.'

She leans against the bathroom window, which will eventually be framed with an olive velvet pelmet. 'This is one of those houses I'd actually like to live in. In fact, I wouldn't mind living in this bathroom alone,' she says. 'It's bigger than my sitting room.'

'There are two armchairs on order. It will be like a sitting room when it's done.'

Graham nods, laughing. 'Put a beer fridge in that corner over there and I'm made!'

I think of my current home and yearn for the space to enjoy a little of my own creative flair. 'I'd happily curl up with a duvet in the copper bath,' I say.

'You always find such great pieces,' says Bonnie. 'I wish I had your eye.'

We wander into the main 'family' bathroom, which is more youthful and fun with its modern matt white Agape taps, an ocean-blue lily-pad tile, running in a scattered wide stripe down the wall, surrounded by white hexagonal tiles so that it has the calming effect of a waterfall. It looks so exciting, making you want to plunge into the bath for a long soak and visualize yourself somewhere exotic. I feel vindicated. I was right to ignore Benedict's silent dismissal of my designs. Right to hold on to the sense of my own skills. If Bonnie is reading my mind, she looks at me in a way that says she agrees.

We go up to the top floor. The shower room looks

incredible. A pea-green Moroccan porcelain tile with the occasional randomly placed white star tile is beautifully enhanced by the installation of the brass sanitaryware.

'Very happy,' I say. 'Now go home! I'm going to run through stuff with Benedict. I think we can allow Camilla back in to inspect the bathrooms tomorrow night but don't let her near the kitchen.'

'Oh, she hangs out here all the time,' says Graham. 'But mainly around the architect.'

'Which is probably why he looks so miserable.' Bonnie smirks.

'Oh, well,' I say. 'I tried.'

I follow them down the stairs, which echo noisily, waiting for the stair runner to be fitted with its antique brass rods. But it will have to wait: carpet is one of the last things to go down.

Bonnie slips into her oversized satin bomber jacket, Graham into his beaten-up leather jacket and they pick up their backpacks.

'Fancy a drink, Bon?' says Graham.

'Thought you'd never ask,' she says.

'See you, boss!' they say, and I watch them leave, admiring their effortless camaraderie.

I wander down the short flight of stairs from the kitchen to where the extension has been boarded up to stop the dust encroaching on my beautiful kitchen units. That's when I feel it. A warm trickle. No cramps so I'm not overly bothered. Could be nothing. Could have imagined it. I've done that enough times before. I ready myself for whatever Benedict has to say, looking forward to seeing the effect of the extension he has guarded so closely.

I'm about to go through the makeshift plywood door, when a sudden hot cramp overwhelms me. I hunch, clutching my searing stomach, leaning my head against a kitchen cabinet, holding on to the plastic dust sheet that's protecting the worktop. My forehead breaks out into an instant sweat. There's more than just a warm trickle now. It's not my imagination playing games with me. I know I need to get to a toilet. There are six here, including the Portaloo, which officially I should use, but Benedict's through there and I don't want to alert him to my distress. It may just be a passing anomaly. It may be nothing.

It's nothing, I tell myself.

It's nothing.

It's nothing.

It's nothing.

But if it's something, the last place I want to be is in a Portaloo.

I cautiously climb the stairs, my face burning, holding onto my stomach, clenching the tops of my thighs, then slip into the en-suite, closing the door.

I rush across the marble floor, flip up the loo seat, tug at my clothes, wanting to rip off my trousers, struggling with my tights and knickers not daring to look, sit down and hear the unmistakable sound that every pregnant woman must dread. A loud splosh.

Blood.

Lots of it.

Please, Universe, say it isn't so. Say this is a nightmare and I'm going to wake up in my bed.

I'm properly cramping now, wanting to cry, wanting to howl, to scream, but not to be overheard. I allow myself the release of a low groan, which comes up from the very depth of my stomach, through my jaw, emoting the visceral pain. I breathe deeply, long, slow breaths, trying not to faint.

I put my head into my hands, waiting for the pain to

subside. Waiting. Not daring to look down into the toilet bowl.

The pain recedes but somehow I know it's going to return. I look. If I needed any evidence, there it is, spattered around the white china, the sort of blood pattern that on an episode of *CSI* tells the precise details of a murder, only this is my crime. My murder.

Have I been doing too much? Have I eaten the wrong things? Am I being punished for becoming smug? Was I even smug? Happy, yes! Excited, yes! But smug? What did I do wrong? Am I not mother material?

It doesn't matter because, beyond doubt, somewhere in that mess is my tiny, apricot-sized baby. Adam's and my baby.

It's over, Adam, I whisper. *Over.*

I crawl onto the cold marble floor.

I curl up knowing that's it.

The curtain has just been drawn on my chance of a family.

My solo crack at creating a life for myself beyond forty, beyond needing a partner, has died in that toilet bowl.

I lie still, foetus position, no coincidence. I want to bring the baby back by sheer force of longing. I want not to have seen what I saw. Not to have pulled that long brass-chained flush. Not to be here, in this beautiful bathroom, which has suddenly turned so heartless and ugly and cold.

I want not to be me.

36

'Daisy?'

I've almost forgotten where I am until I hear Benedict's voice.

I will him to leave, to give up the search and go home, to think that I left without realizing he was still here. But that would be out of character for me. And just as out of character for him.

I sit up, shuffling my back against the toilet bowl, trying to make sense of what's just happened.

The reality is almost inconceivable.

I flushed away my baby.

How is that possible? That one, two flushes and all evidence of the life I once carried, one with which I had bonded with such intensity, has disappeared around a U-bend. How ignominious can it get? A life so easily flushed away.

In my despair, I somehow managed to call the clinic, finding their contact through a blur of tears.

'I've lost my baby,' I whispered to the receptionist.

'You need to come in straight away.'

I can't talk. I merely sob into the phone.

'I'm so sorry,' she says.

'Daisy. Are you up here?' I hear his footsteps climb the bare echoing wooden stairs. I'm shivering. Shaking. Spaced out. In shock. I don't want him to find me.

'Daisy?'

But he's going to find me. He's going to keep calling my name until he finds me. Oh, God, Benedict. The worst possible person in the world to find me. The most unsympathetic man I've ever met. How cruel and mocking of the universe.

I stand up and collect myself, put a wad of tissues between my legs (I've always kept a full supply since my first encounter with Benedict) held in place by my knickers and tights, and pull up my trousers. The waist is still tight. How heartless and confusing the body can be.

'I'm in here, Benedict.' I can't even think to say where here is. My mind is barely functioning. 'I'll be with you in a second.' My voice is so weak, I can't imagine he can hear me. Maybe he'll go.

He knocks on the door of the en-suite. 'Daisy?'

'I'll be out in a second, Benedict.'

'I've found you!' he says, from the other side of the door. 'Are you okay?'

'I'm fine,' I say. 'Had a bit of a turn.'

'Do you need something? Can I do anything?'

I splash water on my face, straighten my clothes and open the door.

His face drops. 'Good God!' he says. 'You look like you've just seen a ghost.' He beckons me towards him. 'Come and sit on the stairs.'

Not with you, Benedict. It shouldn't be with you.

I'm still shaking as we walk through the empty bedroom out to the staircase. I'm light-headed, drifting with a sensation of weightlessness, yet my heart is leaden. I breathe deeply, trying to pull myself together. We sit down on the top stair side by side.

'I'm sorry to do this to you, Benedict,' I say, feeling the call of desperation, 'but I need to get to a clinic in the West End. Would you mind coming with me? You don't have to come in, just accompany me in the cab. I'll feel better if I'm with someone.'

He looks awkward. I hear him swallow. He's not going to come.

'Of course,' he says. 'I'll order a cab now. What's the address?'

My mind can't focus. The address eludes me. 'Somewhere. Harley Street. I can't think of the number.'

'Don't worry.' He punches his phone in the way he does. Bang-bang-bang. 'Five minutes,' he says.

We stare ahead.

'Do you want to talk about it?'

'Not really.'

'Understood.'

I take a deep breath. 'Let's just say you're taking me to a fertility clinic.'

He throws me a look that matches my devastation. 'I'm so sorry,' he says, and he spontaneously places his arm around my shoulders and pulls me into his side. It feels strangely acceptable for me to sink my head into his neck. I breathe him in. This unknowable man who suddenly feels like my safety harness. I try to forget that this is Benedict. I imagine this is someone entirely different. Someone warm and kind and caring. This is Adam.

'Do I smell of blood?' I say. 'That's all I can smell. Blood.'

'You don't,' he says. 'I promise.'

I sob into the neck of this man, this colleague, a man who has been nothing but difficult, for whom I'm so unexpectedly grateful.

'I'm so sorry, Daisy,' he says again, with such sincerity that I sob even harder.

He delves into his satchel and hands me a Kleenex.

'Thank you!'

He pulls out a pack of Tic Tacs. 'Want one?'

'Does my breath smell?'

'Daisy,' he says, 'you don't smell. I just thought it might help.'

'It will,' I say. 'I have a metallic taste in my mouth.'

He flips two onto his palm. I take one. He pops the other into his mouth.

'Is there someone you should phone?'

'Not really,' I say, sucking like my life depends on it.

He looks at me as if maybe I'm not thinking straight.

'If you mean the father,' I say, 'he's not around.' I realize this offers up several connotations not all of them flattering. But I don't want to talk. I'm in pain. I'm in shock. Please don't make me talk. 'It's complicated.'

'No problem,' he says. 'You don't owe me an explanation.' His phone pings. 'Can you manage to get downstairs? The cab will be here in one minute.'

'Yeah. I think so.' I stand up and wobble. I feel blood. I smell blood.

'I'll hold onto you.' He holds my arm, picks up my tote and slings it over his shoulder, then picks up his satchel.

We walk to the cab, which is double-parked outside the front door. What started as a grey day has carried out its threat, ending in rain and misery. Pathetic fallacy. Benedict puts me into the near side, then walks round and jumps in. The metronome beat of the windscreen wipers pounds along with my head. Swish swoosh. Swish swoosh. I stare out the window, aware that my hand is in Benedict's. Or Adam's. I don't care now. Whoever he is, I'm glad he's here. His warmth reassures me. I don't want to think of how embarrassing this is going to be when we're back to being professional. For now, I'm grateful for his presence.

Swish swoosh, swish swoosh, swish swoosh.

I want this to be over.

I want to curl up in my bed and forget.

The taxi draws up outside the clinic. 'Thanks,' I say awkwardly, relinquishing his hand. 'I've taken up too much of your time. I'm really sorry. Your wife must wonder where you are.'

He clears his throat. 'Don't worry about it.'

'When I next see you, can we forget this ever happened and go back to fixtures and fittings and beautiful tiles?'

He smiles. I register how rare that is. 'Of course. Are you okay for me to go? I can wait for you, if you want?'

'Honestly, not necessary,' I say. 'You've done quite enough. You should get home.'

In that moment, I can't help myself. I lean across and kiss his cheek. I avoid his gaze. I already know he hated that moment.

37

'I'm really sorry,' says the sonographer.

I cry quietly on the crescent-moon-shaped sofa, armed with a supply of sanitary towels and paracetamol, which is all they can give you, apart from 'I'm really sorry' looks. I'm glad that the place is empty, barring a pregnant couple who are sitting well away from me.

This has always been a place of such optimism and now it feels like the room of doom.

I can't bring myself to call Bee. She'll want to rush to my side. I don't want to call my mother. I know she'll be devastated for me but I don't want to catch any hint of relief in her voice. I pick up my phone to order an Uber.

There's a text from Benedict: *I'm still outside. It felt wrong to leave you but I will if you'd rather. I'll wait to hear. Happy either way.*

He sent it half an hour ago. He must have gone by now.

What a turnaround. This man. This miserable, aloof, unsentimental man. This man is actually capable of such kindness.

Thanks for being so thoughtful, Benedict. I hope you've given up on me and gone home. I'm fine. Really. Thank you.

I feel my nose tingle and burn as I try to stop the tears. Kindness is such a trigger.

He texts back: *I'm fine is the most ridiculous brush-off in the English language. And I don't give up that easily.*

38

'I'll make you a cup of tea and some toast and go,' he says.

'I'm fine, honestly . . .'

'Daisy!' he scolds lightly. 'I'm here. Let me do something for you. Besides, I make a good cup of tea.'

We climb the stairs to my flat. 'It's just a rental. Temporary. Please don't judge me.'

Benedict scoffs. 'I'm sure it's charming.'

'You might be disappointed.'

I throw on the hall light. Suddenly I hate this place. I hate everything about it. I hate what it represents: my life held in limbo.

We dump our bags and take off our wet coats. He follows my lead and hangs his on a spare hook. He looks through to the sitting room. 'It's perfectly charming,' he says.

'You're being nice.'

'I'll confess I had you somewhere different.'

'Me too,' I say.

I hover, wondering what to do first. 'Do you mind if I disappear and get out of these clothes?' I'm desperate for a shower. I can't bear to smell myself any more.'

'Go ahead. I'll navigate my way around your kitchen. Tea and toast enough or can I make you something more substantial? You must be starving.'

'Just tea is perfect. I don't think I can face eating.'

I sit down on my bed and a horrible sense of loss crushes

my shoulders. An iron band of pain sits around my stomach. I'm still reeling with disbelief. Part of me wants to blame Jack but I can't. I can blame him for my weary heart. I can blame him for this shitty flat. I can blame him for the fact I had to go solo. But I can't blame him for the loss of my baby.

I slip into the bathroom and stare at the stack of syringes. The sharps box. What was the point? What was it all about? All that effort. All that discipline. Yet in the end my body failed me. I failed me.

In the shower, I scrub as hard as I can to rid myself of the pain, the disappointment, the blood.

When I walk back into the kitchen, hair wrapped in a towel, having thrown on a comfortable old tracksuit, Benedict is standing at the kitchen worktop, stirring two mugs of tea.

He looks at me. 'Tea one sugar. You need the energy.'

'Thank you.'

I spot Adam's letters on the fridge door and whip them off, hastily folding them and slipping them into my back pocket. It feels like the fumbled solemnizing of an ending.

'I'm sorry,' says Benedict. 'I couldn't help but notice. I'm guessing they're from your donor.'

I blush. I'm not sure whether I have a right to be angry with him or merely embarrassed. 'I should probably just tear them up.'

'Wait until you have a clearer head.'

We move towards opposite sofas and I sit down tentatively, still feeling crampy and vulnerable. I wish for feather cushions instead of concrete. I wish. I wish. I wish.

'Do you need pain relief?' he says.

I shake my head. 'Just taken some, thanks.'

I notice his reaction to the non-responsive seat cushion. 'I know,' I say.

'It's only temporary,' he replies.

For a moment, it's slightly awkward. We're not meant to be here. Him still looking smart. Me like a wreck. It feels wrong.

'Do you want to talk about it?' he asks. 'You don't have to.' He shifts a cushion from behind his back, trying to create a deeper space so he can stretch out his long legs. 'We can always discuss the weather. Or Peckham.'

I smile. 'To be honest, this is the only thing I can think about right now.'

'Then talk to me,' he says gently.

'I have no idea what to say.'

He allows my silence. I'm grateful. I gather my messy thoughts, trying to work out how to articulate something so painful it's close to unutterable.

'This was my first attempt . . .' Pause for reflection. Pause to gulp, to swallow, to hold back the tears. 'I was due to have the twelve-week scan tomorrow.' His face says what my heart feels. 'Thought I was on the home run. I felt great. I knew there were more obstacles ahead but I thought I'd conquered the magic twelve-week mark.'

He nods, listening.

'There were absolutely no warning signs. You'd think your body might give you some kind of alert.' Involuntary tears, warm and thick, stumble down my cheeks. 'Sorry,' I say.

He gets up and comes to sit next to me. 'Daisy, you're allowed to cry. You've just been through a major trauma.'

I nod in acknowledgement. I reach out for his hand and he takes mine. I squeeze thank you and release him. I realize how much I've missed tenderness, the simple act of reaching out to someone, of someone reaching out to me. A hug. Someone to curl up with. How I've missed those moments with Jack because there really were those moments. Lots of them.

I am racked with sobs. Benedict looks on silently, with kindness. I try to pull myself together.

We sit, no talking.

He turns to face me. 'I may be speaking out of turn but don't give up,' he says. 'If it's any consolation, I know of a few couples, friends' kids, who have been through this and it's never been easy. Never. I don't think there was anyone who managed to stay pregnant first time around.'

'They do warn you the chances are slim,' I say.

'So, if this is what you want . . .'

'It is. At least it was. I can't go through it again. Maybe I'm being defeatist but the fear of miscarriage will just be hanging over me all the time. The stress will be enormous. You talk about the couples you know, and that's the point. I think it has to be easier if you're doing it with someone. I can't shoulder this again by myself. It's too huge. And even though my parents did their best, well, let's be honest my father didn't bother, I don't think they understood, and that's tough. If you're doing it alone, you need people around you. Family.'

'No friends?'

I smile at how pathetic that sounds. 'Yeah. I've told a couple of friends. And they've been great. But it really is quite an isolating experience.'

For a moment, he closes his eyes. 'I still think it's early days,' he says. 'You need to allow things to settle. You need a bit of distance. This is tough. But you'll come to the right conclusion.'

I feel the room move, as though it's about to slip away.

'You okay?' he says. 'You look a bit pale.'

'A bit giddy,' I say. 'It will pass.'

He stands up and I think he's going to leave and suddenly I'm panicked. 'That's it. You need food. If I make perfect tea, you need to experience my world-renowned buttered toast. Only architects can concoct toast with the necessary precision. You'll see.'

He made me laugh. This is surreal.

* * *

'Delicious,' I say, wiping the corners of my mouth. 'Architect toast. Who knew?' I speak with a weary tone.

'Not even me,' he says.

I laugh. Again!

'I do feel bad about christening Camilla's en-suite.'

'Oh, don't,' he says. 'Because you didn't. I've christened Camilla's en-suite a couple of times.'

I splutter. 'Shut up! The main thrust of your work now is in the extension. Right next to the Portaloo!'

He grins. 'Sorry not sorry.'

We finish the toast. I'm suddenly aware of how hungry I must have been. I put the plate down and catch his look. I think he wants to leave but I'm not ready. I don't want to face up to what's happened yet. I don't want to be alone.

'So tell me about you, then,' I say, trying to sound casual.

He flinches. 'What about me?' For a second I see the familiar Benedict reappear.

'I don't know.' I sigh. 'I'm just bored with me.'

He twiddles his wedding ring.

'So tell me about your wife, then. Do you have children?'

'That's pretty personal, to be honest.'

I'm strangely offended. 'Well, we're in pretty personal territory, but if you don't want to go there, then obviously we won't.'

'My wife is dead, Daisy.'

* * *

The atmosphere in the room holds its breath in tandem with mine. All the vile thoughts I've ever had about him, my disappointment, my looking for praise, like a child hoping for his approval, my concern for my own feelings, never questioning the source of his. How could I be so self-absorbed not to notice someone's pain? To only see their anger.

'I'm so sorry, Benedict. I just assumed . . .' I look at the finger of his left hand. 'The ring . . .'

He shrugs his shoulders. 'I'm not ready, you know, to let go. Not yet. Maybe never. It's a talisman. We remain connected.'

I nod. I understand.

'Lisa died nearly two years ago.' The contour of his Adam's apple bounces, down then up. He sits there in dignified control. I want to cry for him but I mustn't.

'That wound is still very fresh, then?'

'It was a long illness. Her death was expected. But even when you're ready, you're never ready. We'd known each other since we were eighteen. I'm sixty-one. That's a lot of years.'

I can see he loved her very much. I have so many questions sitting on the tip of my tongue but his body language tells me now is not the time. Nor is it my place.

'I'm so sorry, Benedict.'

'Thank you,' he says. He looks shrunken, his hands cupped around the mug of what must now be tepid tea. He looks like he's weighing up what he wants to say. Or maybe what he doesn't.

Finally, he speaks. 'I don't tell many people. I don't really want to answer questions. And I don't want anyone's pity. I just want to get on with my work. That's my best escape.'

He looks back at me. 'But, for some reason, it seems we've been put in a place where we can share heartache. And I'm not going to lie. It's been quite cathartic. Even in this brief unburdening.'

My stomach twinges. This is now a room overflowing with loss. And yet, for all the darkness, I see Benedict in a new light.

'Do you need a hug?' I say.

'I think we both need a hug.'

We stand up, shifting awkwardly.

We hold each other closely, his arms wrapped around me. I feel so small.

'I've had architect toast, and now I'm in an architect sandwich,' I say, and we both attempt a laugh, releasing each other.

'I should let you get some sleep,' he says.

I watch as he puts on his still-wet coat and picks up his satchel. I feel sad to see him leave.

'I'm sorry for your loss,' I say.

'I'm sorry for yours, Daisy.'

I close the door behind him, listening as the sound of his footsteps fades, followed by the slam of the front door. I sink to the floor, aware that now I have no choice but to face up to what happened, left alone in this cold, unfeeling space. Alone to face my grief. I think of how stoic and silent Benedict has been. Two years of avoiding his loss, burying himself in his work. Wanting to remain connected to his wife of maybe forty years. How wonderful to have been so loved. I think of the brief time I was connected to my baby, and yet it too was loved. Deeply.

I remember Adam's letters and pull them out from my back pocket. My tears drip onto the pages as I read them one last time.

'I'm sorry, Adam,' I say, speaking into the silence. 'It's the only way.' I rip into the pages and listen to the sound of torn dreams, watch his beautiful words break apart, floating, like paper snow, into my lap.

39

The early morning brings with it the rawest feeling of grief. My eyes heavy and swollen, I know I've been crying in my sleep. The thick pad uncomfortably wedged between my legs serves as a further reminder. It's gone.

I curl up around my stomach and tug the duvet over my head. I sob into the darkness of my unforgiving mattress. Can today, tomorrow and tomorrow and tomorrow go away, please? So much for my Fuck It list.

Eventually I manage to drag myself up, my heavy limbs slowly making their way towards the bathroom. I don't want to look at myself. I know. I don't need the mirror to tell me. Between sobs, I sort myself out as best I can and resolve to get on with it. I have a job to do. I can't ask my mother to phone the school and make an excuse so that I can have a duvet day. I'm a grown-up when sometimes I really don't want to be.

Walking to the Tube I check my phone for the first time.

A text from Benedict making sure I'm okay.

I hold down the rising grief that never fails to follow kindness.

I wonder if he regrets telling me about his wife, whether the catharsis was short-lived and now he hates having allowed someone – me – into his private grief.

I'm fine, I write. *I hope you are too*. I attach the ironic emoji, trying to rally some humour at least by way of my phone. It pings again and I smile sadly, expecting some sort of witty admonishment, knowing today is already different. We won't ever have that connection again.

Do I take it from your silence you are not prepared to give me a second chance?

Do you hate me that much? I wouldn't blame you. I hate me too.

I miss you so much, Daise. I miss us.

What a jerk! Jack x

Delete! Delete! Delete!

40

Marcus throws open the office door, greeting my arrival with a huge smile and a bottle of champagne, which he opens grandly in my face. I hold up my palms to protect myself. Pop! He laughs as the cork hits the ceiling, then pours the fizz into two glasses with exaggerated flair.

'We won Mayfair!' he squeals. 'We're back at the top of the Monopoly board baby! They love you! They loved our plans.' He hands me a glass, which I take absently. 'You must be allowed just a teeny tiny sip and then I've bought some lovely fresh orange juice just for you. The star of the moment!' He stops his exuberance mid-flow.

'Oh, God,' he says. 'What?'

I try to smile but I can feel the giveaway crumple of my cheeks. 'I lost the baby,' I say. 'Win some, lose some. At least I can drink the fizz now.'

His face drops. 'Oh, darling,' he says, shrinking back, taking away my glass and putting everything safely down on the worktop. 'You poor, poor love.' He wraps me in his arms and I allow myself to collapse into him. 'What happened? When?'

I gather my fortitude and peel away, my head pounding. 'Yesterday evening. Peckham. At least it was in a very smart bathroom.'

'Ouch,' he says. 'Oh, Daisy. Is there anything I can do to make you feel better?'

I shake my head. 'Nothing. Sorry I pissed on our fireworks.'

'Shit!' he says. 'I really thought it was going to happen.'

'Me too,' I say.

He puts the bottle back into the fridge. He turns to look at me. 'You'll try again, right? You've got two more what-are-they-called? Blastocysts?'

I'd be impressed if I wasn't so desolate. 'Yeah but . . . I don't know. I don't think so. I don't think I can face going through all that again. All the angst, the hormones, the excitement, then more angst. Maybe I have to wait to meet someone after all and if it happens it happens. I'm not doing it on my own again.'

'Let's not think about it. I'm sorry I asked. You're griev-ing. I'm sorry.'

'Well, I have to face up to it sometime.'

'Not now, though.'

I think of the women who go solo and marvel at them. The ones who try again and again. I know I don't have what it takes. It takes everything.

41

My father never answers the phone but, today of all days, he does.

'Hello,' he says brusquely. 'How's it going?' He's still angry. It hurts even more.

I take a long glug of the cheap wine in my glass hoping it will make me sound more resilient.

'Daisy?' says my father, to my silence. 'Did you mean to call us?'

'Yes, sorry, Dad. Mum there?'

He shouts for my mother. 'It's Daisy,' he says. I hear him whisper, 'She doesn't sound very happy.'

My mother swoops onto the receiver. 'You okay, Daisy?' she says.

'Not really. I lost the baby.'

'Oh, darling! Oh, that's awful. I'm so sorry. When?'

'What?' says my father.

'She lost the baby.'

'Yesterday evening,' I say.

'Yesterday evening,' she repeats. 'Oh, darling! Why didn't you call me?'

'I was just dealing with it, Ma. I couldn't.'

'No,' she says. 'Of course not. How are you feeling?'

'How is she?' says my father.

'Stop interrupting,' says my mother, shushing him. Weirdly their sideshow serves as a helpful stopcock on my

227

emotions, a mess of voices crowding out the devastation in my head.

'Not my best.'

'No, darling. Awful. I totally understand.'

Why did she say that? I know she's trying to be empathetic but for some reason it really annoys me. This is my pain and mine alone.

'You don't understand. How can you possibly?' I say.

There's a long silence but I don't care if I've offended her. 'Because I miscarried too, Daisy,' she replies quietly. 'Twice.'

Her tone is mournful, as though she's instantly reliving the terrible moments, making me reel at the insensitivity of my rebuke. 'Oh, God, Mum! I'm so sorry.' I press my phone into my shoulder, wanting to reach out and hug her. Wondering at the secrets we keep. At the loss we choose to hide in our souls. 'You've never said.'

'Not something one discusses as a rule,' she says.

'I'm really sorry.'

'But you mustn't give up hope,' she says swiftly. 'Look at me. I went on to have you and Doug.'

'What's she saying?' says my father.

'Nothing,' says my mother.

'I'm saying I can't go through with it again.'

I imagine my father's relief as my mother relays my words. I hate his relief. I want him to hurt with me. To hurt with the residual pain my mother still carries. I want him to take her in his arms and hold her because this hurt has never left her. Yet it probably bounced off him.

'Do you want to come over?' my mother says. 'Should I come round? Your father can drive me.'

'Sally! It's late.' Beat. 'Sorry, of course, of course.'

'I'll be fine, Ma. But thank you.'

I take another long slug of the numbing liquid in my glass. My red morphine.

I phone Bee.

'Oh, my darling girl,' she says. 'I'm so sorry. So, so sorry!'

'Please don't get upset, Bee. I don't want to cry again.'

'Why didn't you call me?'

'My mind was barely functioning enough to call the clinic.'

'I can't begin to imagine. That's just the worst. I'm so sorry.'

'Thank you.'

I want to finish this conversation. I'm emotionally drained. Exhausted. I want to curl up in my bed, which was where I've wanted to be all day but I had to carry on. And tomorrow I have to carry on again. Despite this cruel blow to my body.

'You'll try again, right? When you're ready.'

I don't answer. I can't.

I hear her suck in her breath. 'You've been amazing, Daisy. The whole way through. Don't forget that for one moment, please. You'll get your mojo back.'

What the fuck is a mojo anyway?

42

Somewhere along the way, without my even noticing, my so-called mojo sneaks through a crack in my armour and re-establishes itself. Without any grandstanding or discussion, it's helped along by Benedict, as we carry on working around each other, managing to slip back into previous boundaries, knowing they are not as tightly drawn as before. There is no more mention of what happened, just the occasional look, a nod in passing that says, 'Are you okay?', a smile that says, 'I know.' The intimacies we shared are put back in the box marked 'Personal'. Life must go on. But I'm glad of these small shifts. I will always be grateful to him.

The mother-of-pearl tiles are up in the kitchen, looking even better than I could have hoped. It's not long before the entire house will be ready for the finishing touches: the curtains and blinds, the carpets in the bedrooms, the rugs, the stair runner and rods, all the pieces of furniture, from the newly commissioned headboards to the antique chairs and sofas from auctions and websites around the globe. Everything is ready to be delivered as soon as I give the go-ahead. Out with the single bulbs on dangling wires, in with the vintage chandeliers and sconces, every room ready to be styled and dressed.

The extension is nearly finished, the temporary partition down, the freshly plastered walls dry and ready for painting. The retractable glass ceiling retracts with a steady hum, the Crittall doors, which open onto the back garden, have been installed; the massive concrete-style floor slabs have been laid, flowing from inside to the patio outside. It is absolutely on point, according to the spec. It's now down to me to turn Benedict's clean, sharp lines into something softer with bookshelves, lighting, sofas and rugs.

Before, I think he would have had to hold his nose, knowing my designs are out of his comfort zone, but now he's being a little more generous. To the point I actually risk sharing.

'What do you think of this sofa?'

I see his face react to the geometric patterned fabric.

'Actually, I can see how that will work. I'm starting to understand your style, Daisy. I won't go as far as saying I like it, but I can appreciate it.'

Which is pretty good where I'm concerned.

My brother arranged the delivery of a good bottle of wine, a vintage.

'I have a little something for you,' I say, handing him the brown-paper bottle-bag, the minimalist styling especially for him. 'A thank-you. I hope you like it.'

He looks aghast, his hands fluttering hesitantly, reaching out, then resisting. 'I told you, you don't have to thank me. I was glad to be there for you.'

'Take it,' I say.

He gives an embarrassed smile, runs his fingers through his thick hair. His expression, as he checks the label, says he's impressed and flattered as well as embarrassed. 'As long as you agree to drink it with me. We can celebrate the end of this project.'

'Deal,' I say.

'Thank you, Daisy. You've lifted my spirits. The weekend after next is not a good one for me.'

'Oh,' I say, and we both know what he means. He must count the days.

My own loss still sits heavily in my soul. I have resisted entering the en-suite but the passing of time, the ongoing work, the sense of achievement in the design means I finally decide to brave crossing the threshold into its glamorous portals. I stand there, held for a moment, knowing I'm still sad, knowing I will never forget the loss of my baby, knowing I will always live with this strange, hard-to-articulate grief, unfathomable to those who have never experienced it, which, for me, comes hand in hand with the reluctant acceptance that I will never be a mother.

And possibly for the last time I close the door, taking comfort in the knowledge that the baby I nearly had will be with me always. But that place, with its beautiful copper bath, its Georgian splendour, is no one's grave. It's merely a bathroom.

43

Tempting as it is to go back to my tiny, uninspiring flat and withdraw with a takeaway into my misery, I am lucky to have friends who care deeply for me, who indulge my sorrow but won't allow me to drown in it. I have evenings out with Caro, with Victoria and Gina, with Bee and Rob, with Marcus, occasionally accompanied by Flynn. For a while I'm glad to lose myself in their company, in their laughter and gossip. Their interest – 'How are you? No, *really* how are you?' – has started to taper off, which, in some way, is a relief: I can pretend to myself that I'm getting better because they believe I am.

'I'm hung-over,' I tell Benedict, when he catches me rubbing my temples.

'Good for you!' he says.

'Maybe you should try it,' I say. 'Honestly. It's everything it's cracked up to be.'

He laughs. 'Are you suggesting I'm leading a dull life?'

'I don't know. Are you?'

'Maybe I like dull.'

'Then maybe we should do something about it.'

He holds my gaze, laughs dismissively, and we carry on.

I understand how hard it must be for him to disengage from the comfort of his misery. The need to stay connected in whatever way possible to the person you will never see again. Even now there are times, at the end of an evening with friends, returning to my echoing flat, that, no matter how hard I try to ignore it, or how good I am at talking the talk, my misery returns like an old friend. Welcome, loneliness. Welcome, loss. Welcome, grief. Make yourselves at home.

And then, because I shouldn't, sitting on my unforgiving navy sofa, glass of wine in hand, I read Jack's old texts, the ones I've never deleted, reminding myself that once upon a time, I felt loved. Often I pull up his number on my phone in a wistful move to call him, knowing I don't have the guts. I'm too proud. Too afraid of rejection. What if he's with Polly?

I finish the bottle of wine. This, too, shall pass.

Tonight, in the corner grocery/offy, I stand quietly next to the familiar rows of sweets and chocolates, the endless bags of crisps, the opposite shelves of cleaning products, queuing to pay for the bundle I'm clutching. If I was asked to give an accurate description of this place as part of a memory test, to describe the layout, the order of stacking, I'd probably get an A*. It's not much to be proud of but it sums up the excitement of my life.

I know the man behind the till really well. I know his name although I never use it. I've heard his wife calling him – at least, I assume she's his wife. I know that on most days he wears a brown hoodie over a T-shirt, the hood up. Sometimes, when he comes out from behind the till – rare – he's wearing a pair of faded denims with black socks inside open-toed sandals. I also know that, despite my awareness of him and his sartorial habits, he makes no attempt to know me. Not even a smile of recognition. Nothing. Ever. I'm just one of a hundred different faces he sees in a day. I'm a blank image.

'And a packet of ten of those, please,' I say, pointing to

the cigarettes, handing over my can of tomato soup and a bottle of their best £5.50 house red.

I hand him the cash.

'Bag ten p,' he says, staring at me blankly.

'Sorry, yes, of course.' I fiddle around in my purse, hunting for a 10p coin among the millefeuille of receipts. A bloke, maybe three behind me, groans. This makes me even more fumbling. 'Sorry, sorry,' I say.

Inside my flat, trying to ignore the heavy aroma of Mr Henderson's Indian takeaway, intrusive yet appealing, I throw off my coat, rip off the lid of the can, empty the soup into a bowl and place it in the microwave.

As soon as I hear the soup start to spit, I press End.

'Ouch, ouch, ouch! Shit.' The bowl is burning hot. I stir the soup, use an oven glove to put it onto a tray and sit down to eat. It's decidedly tepid while the bowl is still a burn hazard. I don't know why I have yet to learn that the same method ends with the same result. I eat it despite myself, deciding it's purely transactional, unlike Mr Henderson's undoubtedly delicious takeaway, and put the bowl into the sink, pour the wine into a glass, neck it, then fill it again.

Opening the window, I set up a chair, balance my wine on the ledge and light one of my cigarettes. It's a non-smoking building but I'll take the risk. If I'm challenged, I'll plead ignorance and if that doesn't work, I'll plead desperation.

I blow the smoke out into the evening air.

I'm sure Mr Henderson smokes. He has the pallid skin of a smoker and that musty smell about his clothes. Poor lonely Mr Henderson. Or maybe he isn't. I wonder if he thinks, Poor lonely Miss Settle. Tonight he'd be right.

I stare out of the window into the anonymous rooms across the street, flapping my hand regularly, dissipating the illegal spirals of grey smoke. A light turns on and I watch the shadowy shape of two people, a couple maybe, moving behind yellowing nets before the front curtains are drawn and the hope of a show disappears. I continue it in my head, wondering what they're doing, if they're sitting down and chatting happily, curling up on a sofa in front of the television, the way I used to curl up with Jack. I have an aching, ill-advised longing for the house that used to smell of me, of us, for the all-encompassing soft featheriness of our sofa, for the warmth of Jack's arm as he holds me until his arm goes dead and we have to shift around.

Or maybe this couple are sitting oceans apart. In the middle of a fight. One that may not end well.

I light a second cigarette and then a third, drinking more wine. Slowly now.

It's still there, the morose feeling, but not quite so close to the surface. Cheap alcohol works. I look at the filter tips of the cigarettes, feeling a bit the worse for wear, head pounding with a nicotine throb, then close the packet, knowing I mustn't overdo it or tomorrow morning will bring too many hours of regret.

Ping! Phone lights up. Ignore!

I throw the cigarette packet onto the table, sitting down to finish the last few sips of wine in my glass.

Ping!

I glance reluctantly at my phone screen.

Then glance again in disbelief.

Jack. He knows I'm smoking. How is that even possible?

Call me, Daise. I'm really missing you tonight. Three *please* emojis *xxx*

I'm weak, I'm weak. I miss you too.

I mustn't . . . Stuff phone down side of sofa.

Why are the wrong people always there when you're feeling at your most vulnerable? I pick up the packet of cigarettes and light just one more, moving back to the window, my mind racing. Fuck him. Fuck him for having the balls to admit his feelings, the courage to put it out there, courage I don't have because my pride (and Polly) gets in the way. My racing mind stills, lingering on Polly. Why is he missing me when he has her?

It occurs to me that perhaps the universe is telling me that the wrong people are often the right people. That Benedict was the last person I expected to be the right person but he was. It occurs to me that you can justify anything when you want to. It occurs to me that I want to.

I fiddle down the side of the gap in the cushions, ignoring the crumbs, fishing out my phone. I hold it to my chest, knowing this is a dangerous moment. I finish the cigarette, throw the butt out of the window, gasping at my mistake. I neck the wine straight from the bottle. Who cares about dignity. Who cares about mistakes?

Tomorrow, I think. Remember what you might regret tomorrow.

If you want to talk, I'm ready. Daise x

I delete the kiss.

44

I allow my phone to ring for six peals, watching his name flash on my screen, knowing that on the seventh it will revert to voicemail.

'Hi,' I say.

'Thank God you're there! I was waiting so long, I thought I was going to voicemail.'

'Please leave your name, number and any message. BEEP!'

He laughs. 'Jesus, baby, you sound very drunk.'

I rest my ear against the phone. I like the sound of his voice. I like the way his tone makes my skin tingle. He's right. I'm drunk. My head is properly muzzy. I'm capable of liking anything.

'Can I remind you? I am not your baby.'

He laughs again. 'Old habit.'

'Bad habit.'

I'm not going to tell him I'm pleased to hear his voice. I'm not going to tell him I'm miserable. I am definitely not going to tell him about the miscarriage.

'How are you?' I say.

'Pleased to hear your voice.'

'You lonely, Jack?'

'No,' he says. And why would he be? 'I genuinely miss you. I miss us.'

I'm in a kind of daze, listening to his breathing,

deconstructing his words, which, inside my muzzy drunken head, is difficult.

'I want to see you,' he says, misinterpreting my silence for strength. 'I need to explain. You never gave me the chance.'

I snort at my phone. 'To be fair, I didn't need an explanation. I saw what I saw. Polly kindly explained the rest.' I'm starting to fire up. 'Out of interest, how does Polly fit into your "missing us" scenario?'

'Where are you? I'm coming over.'

'Answer the question, caller.'

'I will, face to face.'

'I don't want to see you. Besides, it's late.'

'It's a good time for me. My days are busy.'

'Oh, busy-busy-busy. Good for you. But you can't come over. I've just smoked a hundred cigarettes.'

'Daisy! Please! Give me your address.'

* * *

It's like I've been transported into a metaverse that somehow allows a scenario that doesn't really exist to play out in front of me. Opening the door, seeing his face, his hair appealingly dishevelled, seeing him in jeans and a bright blue jumper I certainly would never have picked for him but which suits this avatar, I look at him looking at me standing in the hallway of a house where I shouldn't really be. And neither should he.

Only he's not an avatar. He's real. His lips brushing my cheek, his arms holding me for as long as I allow are all real. His smell, still the same familiar scent, is real. It's disarming. I tell myself this is why I didn't want to see him ever again. He's dangerous.

'Can I come in?'

'Briefly.'

'I've brought wine.' He hands me a bag. I look inside. There are two bottles wrapped in tissue.

'That's not brief.'

'We'll drink quickly.'

'Do you want to get me completely wasted?'

He raises his eyebrows. 'You're already completely wasted. I'd like to catch up. But you can join in. That's the general idea anyway.'

He walks into the sitting room, taking it all in. The lack of charm, the size, the cheap furniture, the cream-coloured paint, the smell of the refusenik cigarette smoke, which overrides the Grapefruit candle hurriedly lit, burning in the corner. I'm seeing them all through his judgemental eyes. Sensing the smell through his censorious nose.

'I wasn't expecting this,' he says.

'You're not alone.'

'What are you doing here?'

'I like it here.'

'No you don't.'

'Have it your own way.'

He wanders behind the kitchen counter, looking at everything.

'Please don't, Jack. I feel like you're judging me. It's not fair. This is just temporary.'

I see him clock my tomato soup bowl in the sink and cringe inside, wishing I'd remembered to wash it up and put away the evidence of my solo slovenliness.

'Where do you keep your glasses?'

'I drink straight from the bottle nowadays. It cuts down on the washing-up.'

'Be serious.'

'That cupboard there.'

He takes out a wine glass. I hand him the corkscrew from the drawer. It feels so strange seeing him standing here. I feel my heart speed up, ignoring the *Danger! Toxic hazard* signs.

We sit down on opposite sofas. 'Is this a sofa or a tombstone?' he says.

'Are you going to be snarky?'

'Sorry.' He takes a long sip of wine and puts down the glass. He leans forward, elbows on knees, hands clasped. 'You look good,' he says.

I frown dismissively. 'You don't have to go the other way either.'

'You do. Your hair has grown. I always liked it longer.'

I swing it over my shoulder, like I'm worth it. 'Yours has grown too. I like it. And that's the nicest thing I'm going to say to you.'

He laughs. 'God, I've missed you,' he says.

* * *

He pours his second glass of wine. 'It was a difficult time,' he says. 'Intense. We were looking for the right buyer. You had no idea of the pressure I was under.'

'Actually, I did,' I say, drinking water, starting to sober up. I'm holding back on the alcohol for the sake of self-preservation. 'I was feeling the pressure with you. I thought I was supporting you through it.'

'I needed to let off steam.'

I stand up and move to the window, trying to breathe in some fresh air. 'Most people do that in the gym, Jack. You own three. Did you forget? Or was it just me you forgot?'

His head sinks into his hands.

'It was at my party, Jack. In plain sight.'

He looks up. 'I was off my head. We all were.'

'We didn't all throw our keys into the proverbial bowl, though, did we?'

'I was going to end it that night. I really was.'

I squint at him. 'So it was like a fuck-off fuck?'

He snorts. 'In a way. Before you and I started making a family. Honestly, I was going to end it. And then, well . . .'

I can see it all playing out in front of me, in painful slow motion. 'And you fought really hard for me by running away.'

'I told you, I was wasted. I didn't know what I was doing.'

'You knew who you were fucking. You managed to see I was smoking.'

'That was different.'

'Why?'

'Because I hate it when you smoke.'

'I hate it when you fuck other women.'

'It was only ever Polly.'

'It was only ever one cigarette.'

'I'd have forgiven you.'

'I am never forgiving you!'

* * *

The second wine bottle is half empty. Or half full. Depending on the angle at which you're looking at it.

Jack's lying down, his calves dangling over the end of the sofa arm, loafers now off, navy socks with small bright blue spots, as though he's given due consideration to his jumper. His face is turned towards me. I am sitting firmly upright on the opposite sofa.

'Polly moved in because she was pushing for it.'

'Nothing to do with you?' I swirl the wine in my glass, my resistance to holding back having withered over the hour.

'Of course to do with me. But she was pushing for it and

I felt like it might be a way forward because I was getting nowhere with you.'

'That's pathetic.'

'Probably.'

'And you weren't prepared to live on your own?'

'I didn't like it much, no.'

'So she was your Pollyfilla? See what I did there?'

'Very funny.'

'I enjoyed it.'

'Anyway, she's gone now. It was wrong. It wasn't easy to end. It was upsetting, more for her than for me—'

'Which is how you like it.'

'No, Daisy. That's not true. Stop trying to make me out to be some misogynistic bastard.'

'I'm not the one doing that.' So he's no longer with Polly. 'Hang on! Is that why you're here?' I say. 'Because you don't like living on your own and you thought you'd give it one final crack at getting me back to fill the void?'

He rolls off the sofa, crawls round the coffee-table on all fours and sits cross-legged in front of me. 'I've been totally transparent with you, baby. Sorry, you're not my baby.' He grunts. 'No, I don't enjoy living alone but that doesn't mean I'm not capable. And it's not as if there aren't plenty of available women out there. Trust me, there are.'

'That's precisely why I can't trust you.'

His eyelids flutter. 'But they don't interest me. You interest me. You excite me. We were a good team and I blew it. I want you to give me another chance.'

'Have you not heard a word I've said?'

'Yes. But I love you. And I miss you.' He rolls forward onto his knees, takes my face in his hands and looks at me with probing eyes, forcing mine to meet his. 'I'm sorry,' he says. 'So deeply, deeply sorry.'

I wrestle free. 'No, Jack! I'm not falling for it. I'm not sure what you're sorry for. So far all I've heard is you blaming it on the intense pressure you were under. Or on Polly putting on the pressure. What about when you're under pressure again? Because there will always be an excuse, Jack, if you want to find someone else to shag. The truth is I'm not enough for you. I've learnt to accept that.'

He puts his hand on my arm. 'Are you kidding me? You were always enough for me. You were my everything.'

'Until I wasn't.'

'It was a mistake.'

'So own it. You were entirely responsible for what you got up to over those six months. You were entirely responsible for moving Polly in. I'd feel sorry for her if I didn't not feel sorry for her.'

He swallows a laugh.

'I'm serious. You have created this situation. I'm over you now, Jack. Please leave.' I hate him. I hate him because I know I love him.

'No!' he says. 'Because I don't believe you.'

'That's funny, because I'm not sure I believe you.'

He stands up and starts pacing the room, running his fingers through his hair.

'I don't believe you're over me. You and I have too much going for us. Yes! I accept I was an idiot. I take full responsibility for that. But fuck it, Daisy, I'm human. I made a mistake for which I could not be more sorry. But it's a mistake I want to rectify. Am I not at least entitled to try?'

His eyes and words rip through me. Marcus's monogamy lecture re-enters my head. I push it away.

'Not when I've spent the last six months getting over you, Jack. It's too late. Don't you understand how much you hurt me? The betrayal? The humiliation? The opportunities lost. My vital years all fucking lost.'

'I tried—'

'We were getting ready to start a family, Jack. What could be more of a commitment to one another than that? And I'd been waiting and waiting for that commitment and then you blew it. I'd invested my heart and soul in us. In your business. In your life. Trying to make your dreams come true. But what about mine? What happened to your investment in me? If you don't approve of where I am, this lousy apartment, then ask yourself why I'm here because I ask myself that question a lot. And sometimes it's fucking lonely. It really is. Like tonight. Tonight, of all the nights you choose to call, I felt really fucking lonely. Miserable. Pointless. And why?'

He grimaces.

'Because of you. You and Polly. Someone who didn't even seem to matter that much to you made you risk everything we'd built together. And now it's too late. Read my lips. It's too late, Jack.'

I get up from the sofa and weave towards the box of tissues on the kitchen worktop.

He walks over and takes a tissue for himself. 'Fuck, Daisy. What do I have to do to win you back? I'll do anything. Just tell me.'

'I don't want to be something you win, Jack. You win everything. I want you to earn me.'

* * *

We're sitting on the same sofa, two feet apart.

'I just think, if you'd let me explain, it might not have gone as far adrift as it did.'

I look across at him. 'You see what you do? You're saying it's my fault.'

He shakes his head. 'Not that I cheated, no. I accept that. I told you. *Mea culpa.*' He holds up his palms. 'I just think that if you'd given me the chance to explain, to have the discussion we're having now, it would have saved a lot of agony.'

'You have no idea of my agony. None whatsoever.'

'A little bit, though?'

'Not even a little bit.'

* * *

'Shall I go and get some more wine?'

'I've had enough. I'm tired. I really think you should go.'

'Okay.'

I let out a long sigh. I don't want him to go. What the fuck?

He stands up, stretching out his arms, clicking his knees, easing his neck. 'I have one more thing I just need to say and then I promise I'll go.'

I look up at him.

'I still don't understand why you won't give me another chance. What have you got to lose?'

I rub my eyes. I can barely see straight, let alone think straight. 'I don't know, Jack . . . It's late. Can we do this another time?'

His face lights up. 'Is there going to be another time? Seriously? You're not just trying to get rid of me?'

'I am trying to get rid of you but, yes, I think there's going to be another time. Don't ask me why. Don't push your luck. Good night, Jack.'

* * *

246

Before I climb into bed, I check my phone. It's an annoying reflex I have before I turn it to silent. Like I'm always expecting something amazing to land in my inbox. I'm not sure why. But there it is. Jack has texted a date. *For your diary x*

I plug my phone into the charger, a smile in my heart. I'll let him wait for my reply. Exhausted though I am, I have to record this moment. I might have forgotten the context in the sober light of day. I write with a flush of triumph.

I was sad. I got drunk. Jack phoned. I saw it as a sign. Of course I did! Anyway, he was very persuasive so, against my better judgement, I let him come round. We drank. Both of us vulnerable. We fought it out. I got to say what he needed to hear. I think he heard. Who knows? Polly has left. Or been asked to leave. He misses me blah-blah-blah. I want to believe him. What's funny is how keen he is to meet up again. Suddenly the balance of power has swung in my favour. I should enjoy it while it lasts because inevitably it will swing back.

I close the journal, turn out the light and pull up the duvet. I lie there, my mind still buzzing with alcohol and excitement. It's no good. I have to get this down . . .

I reach out, turn on the light and open to the last written page.

Is that our problem? That the ball always seems to be mainly in his court? Mainly in the man's court? Are truly successful relationships built on equilibrium? Or is equilibrium where boredom and complacency lie?

45

I walk along his street. In a way I'm not surprised to discover a row of fifties detached modernist houses, big square windows, plain frontages. I ring his doorbell. I know this is a risk but I also know this is a bad day for him. I want to help but I'm prepared for him to tell me to go away and I'm not to take it personally, even though I know I will. I must respect his space.

I hear footsteps approaching and the latch being unlocked. Benedict opens the door, merely poking his face out. Unsurprisingly he is shocked to see me. I try not to react to the fact that he looks terrible. His face is as grey as his hair. His eyes are sad but I don't think he's been crying – he's not that sort of man, more the type to keep everything tucked deep inside. Which is kind of why I'm here. Wearing my Superwoman cloak, metaphorically speaking.

He eyes me with suspicion. 'Am I expecting you?' His polite way of saying, 'Fuck off.'

'I wondered if you fancied going for a walk.' My insides are wincing, watching his expression. This is properly awkward.

'No, Daisy. It's not a good day for me.'

'I know,' I say. 'You told me.'

'I did?'

'In passing. That was why I wondered if you wanted to go for a walk.'

He presses his lips together. Swallows. 'No, but thank you.'

'Understood.' I turn to leave.

'Wait!' he says. I look back at him. 'Since you've come all this way . . .' He harrumphs. Shuffles open the door and motions me forward. '. . . I'll get my act together. Forgive the mess.' The only mess is him, in so far as he's not dressed in his usual smart attire but his jeans are neat, his black sweatshirt tired and faded. They smell freshly washed.

The house is spotless and tidy. I follow him beyond the porch, walking into a huge open-plan living room. The blockwood floor looks regularly polished. There's an un-usual mid-century olive-leather sofa, a long mid-century sideboard bearing very little: a simple stone carving, a tall straight glass vase, no flowers, one chrome-framed photo I'm not quite close enough to examine or feel I should. In the corner, with a few books neatly piled on the floor next to it, there is a brown leather Eames chair and footstool. It screams original. Everything here looks methodically chosen for its vintage. Like walking back in time. There's an oval dining-table, with seats that probably haven't been occu-pied for at least the last two years, and a massive kitchen at the opposite end, with a large central island, the worktop half wood, half stainless steel. The sink, stainless steel, is centred on one side, opposite, to the right, a chrome five-burner gas range.

There are a few cups on the draining-board, a frying pan leaning in the rack, which is what I imagine to be Benedict's idea of a mess. Other than that it is perfectly kempt.

He swiftly rushes to put the cups in the dishwasher, its wood-veneer décor panel in keeping with the other units, all with half-moon routed handles.

He looks round at me. 'Sorry, Daisy. I didn't mean to be rude.'

'You do know I understand, don't you?'

He stands up, scratches the top of his head. 'I suppose that's what bothers me.'

I smile. 'If you want to be miserable, I can leave you to it.'

He peers back at me, his dark brown eyes weighing me up. 'I do. But somehow I'm not sure you're going to.'

I laugh. 'I think we're getting to know each other quite well, aren't we?'

'Yes.' He inclines his head, frowning. 'How on earth did you find me?'

'I have my methods. Your Companies House listing.'

He makes a long humming sound. 'How very Agatha Christie of you.'

The walk takes us along the towpath of the Grand Union Canal. The day is one with blue skies and clouds, a gentle breeze, classic spring. There is blossom on the trees, thick bunches of pink and white, so glorious. I comment on the display of canal boats, all brightly painted, golds, reds, pinks, blues, names splashed alongside roses, horses and castles, lined up, nose to tail – 'Bow to aft,' corrects Benedict, as they bob happily in their moorings. 'I would probably have come out for a walk here later,' he says.

'Sorry I dragged you out early, then.'

'You know what I mean. I'm just saying I wasn't going to be a sad old grump all day. I would have ventured out eventually but I'm glad you're venturing out with me.'

'I'm glad, too,' I say. I tell him anniversaries are tough. That I'm probably going to hate the anniversary of my miscarriage for the rest of my life.

'But you mustn't,' he says.

'Then neither must you.'

He crooks his arm so that I can slip mine through it. It feels friendly. No longer merely the pragmatic option.

We continue the walk and he tells me about some of the boat owners he knows. 'Not well enough to have a coffee with, but we exchange brief chats, updates on the weather, missing cats, you know . . .' He trails off.

'Sounds fascinating.'

He looks at me, eyes scolding my sarcasm. 'Politics too. Bigger stuff.'

'Sorry,' I say. 'I wasn't taking the piss. I'm very keen on discussing the weather. And missing cats.'

'You were taking the piss,' he says.

'Yeah,' I say. 'I guess I was.'

We laugh, at ourselves and each other.

Walking in silence for a bit, I become aware of the freshness of the air against my face, the sound of our footsteps in tandem, that my arm through his feels oddly natural. Fatherly. I think he would have made a lovely father.

'Did you never want children?' I ask.

He slows our pace, pausing before replying, absently playing with his ring. 'In my youth probably,' he says. 'You know, a natural presumption. But when I met Lisa, she told me quite early on that she couldn't have children. She gave me the option of leaving her, finding someone with a better life expectancy, with prospects of a family, but there was no way. So, I guess I put any thoughts of children out of my head.'

'I admire that you were prepared to do that for her.'

'It wasn't hard,' he says. 'I loved her.'

I wonder if they realized how blessed they were, even though they carried such a cruel curse.

We stop for lunch at a café that overlooks the water.

'I find water very calming,' he says, as we sit down. 'It's nice to watch its ebb and flow. To see its colour and movement change with the seasons.'

We share a large bowl of spaghetti with fresh tomato sauce. He's pleased that I'm capable of twirling it with just a fork. 'Normally people ask for a spoon.'

I don't want to tell him I very nearly did.

'That was good,' I say, wiping my mouth, checking the front of my blouse for unsightly specks of tomato.

'Simple, honest food,' he says. 'And the chef is from Naples.'

'It tasted authentic.'

I look out over the water, pleased that I risked coming out to find him today. That I risked rejection. That he took me on this walk and brought me here, to this simple restaurant with its delicious simple food. Who needs bells and whistles when the food is this good, when the chef is from Naples, when you can look out over water and feel the calm?

I glance across and catch his wistful expression, the gentle sadness in his brown eyes, the defined squareness of his jaw, the pronounced dimple in his chin. In that moment, I want to reach out and tell him it will all be okay. That he really is very lovely.

'I'll settle up,' he says. 'Fancy an ice cream? They do really good Italian *gelato* just up the road.'

'Do you have Italian roots?'

He laughs. 'No. Just a love of their country. And their food.'

'*Gelato*'s on me,' I say.

We stand in line behind a couple with two children and gaze beyond the glass counter at the displays of metal trays, an array of different flavours and colours.

'Not Mr Whippy, is it?' I say. 'What are you having? So many to choose from.'

'I'm afraid I'm a creature of habit.'

'You surprise me!' I nudge his arm and he nudges me back.

'Stracciatella and mint, please,' he says.

We move to the front of the queue and I order 'One stracciatella and mint. In a cone?' I look at Benedict to check and he nods. 'And can I try that one and, erm, the hazelnutty one, please?'

The man passes me a spoon, first with the sorbet, then another with the creamy hazelnut. I like the hazelnut. 'And can I try the dark chocolate with orange?'

Benedict fiddles with his wedding ring. 'Are you going to work your way through the entire selection?'

'I want to get it right!'

'And so you should,' he says, rolling his eyes. 'It's important.'

'You rushing somewhere?'

'No,' he says. 'Carry on.'

I realize that's not going to be possible without him twisting his ring off his finger, so I settle for hazelnut and the dark chocolate with orange, which is mind-blowing, and watch as the soft scoops are pressed into the cones. Benedict grabs plenty of white napkins from the dispenser. He hands me half.

'Want to try some of mine?' I say. 'I made a very good choice, even under pressure.' We stop further along, cross arms and try each other's.

'Nice,' he says. 'But I don't think you've converted me yet.'

We carry on wandering along the towpath, which is becoming busier, occasionally having to avoid a cyclist or an over-friendly dog, which Benedict responds to, stroking the top of its head.

'You've not got pets?' I say.

'We had a cat but she died,' he says.

'Oh, God, sorry!'

He laughs. 'It was a long time ago and she was twenty, which in human years is about a hundred and ninety-six. You don't have to be sorry. You?'

'We have a dog. Well, my parents do but he's kind of the family dog. Brewster. A black Scottish terrier. I adore him. But obviously I don't get to see him that often.'

'You're not close to your parents?'

'Oh, I am. Just not in location. We're a close family. I have a brother, Doug. And a sister-in-law, Eve, and they have two boys who are adorable rascals.' He smiles. 'She's pregnant again.'

He glances down at me. 'Is that tough?'

'It is, yeah.' It's such a relief to be able to come clean and know whatever I say, however it might sound, will not be judged. That it stays between us. 'But . . . well, you know, it's not her fault I can't have kids, is it?'

'You don't know that you can't have them. You've only given it one shot.'

'Don't make me feel bad for being a quitter.'

'Sorry. You're not. That was unintentional.'

We carry on walking, finishing our ice creams. Benedict doesn't bother with the end of his cone, throwing it into a bin.

'That's the best bit,' I say. 'The soggy bottom!' He shows no recognition. Not a *Bake Off* fan.

'I should have given it to you. Next time,' he says. 'If you fancy doing this again?'

I smile. 'I'd like that,' I say.

We pass a beautiful narrow-boat, decorated in grass green, a red roof, and yellow shutters with grass-green four-leaf clovers in the panels.

'I bet you like that one,' he says.

'I do. Tell me, would you like to talk about Lisa?' It

springs spontaneously from nowhere. I check his face, panicked that I'm pushing too heavily against his boundaries.

His face says he's wondering. 'I don't really feel the need to talk about her.'

'Fine. I just thought I'd ask. You know. It might help. Maybe when you're ready.'

'Want to go over the footbridge and head back along the other side?' he says.

We walk across the slatted wooden bridge and stop for a moment, leaning against the parapet wall, daubed with graffiti, looking out over the shifting dappled water.

'Everything's inside my head,' he says. 'Everything's in that house, I feel her presence with me all the time.' He pushes his hands into his trouser pockets. 'It's so strange. I feel uncomfortable talking about her. But thank you for asking.'

We start our return, looking at the boats, stopping briefly when someone, a short woman with grey hair wearing dungarees, comes out to say hello.

'This is my friend Daisy,' he says, introducing me.

'Nice to meet you, Daisy,' she says. 'Glad he has some friends.'

'Thanks very much! See you later!' says Benedict, laughing.

'You see?' I say, further on. 'That's what people think.'

'Daisy,' he says. 'I don't care what people think.'

Yes you do, I want to say. Everyone cares what people think.

'I know what you're thinking from your silence,' he says. 'And I don't.'

There's a gap in the buildings across the water and he points out the view towards the city.

'You ever worked on any of those?' I ask.

'During my apprenticeship. But not for myself. Nothing

that grand. I admire Richard Rogers hugely. He's inspirational. But I never wanted the kind of commission that would require a large company. I always wanted to keep it small. So that I could be around if needed.'

I want to tell him that, with each layer he peels away, I find him more and more impressive.

As we approach the slip road that leads up towards his house, he says, 'I think you'd have liked her.' I try not to overreact, wanting him to continue. 'She was funny. Smart, sharp, never let me get away with anything. If I was immersed in a job she'd let me get on with it, but not to the point where she felt I was neglecting her. Or myself. She'd reel me back in.'

'So you need reeling in?'

He looks at me and smiles. 'Sometimes, yes.' His eyes focus on the middle distance. 'I can be overly absorbed in my work. I don't think I need to tell you that.'

'So what do I have to do to reel you back in?' I say. 'To life. Outside work.'

He laughs. 'What are you trying to tell me?'

'I think you should start dating,' I say boldly. 'I don't know, and forgive me for being presumptuous, but I get the feeling that's what Lisa would have wanted.'

He flinches. 'Oh, we had that conversation many times,' he says, standing back to allow a girl of about eight on a bike, wearing a pink helmet, to pass on the pavement, followed by a young guy I assume is her father. 'She said she wanted me to meet someone. She was insistent.' I ask him why he hasn't acted on it. 'Because that's not how my life has evolved.'

He goes to sit down on a wooden bench and I follow.

He crosses his legs and rests his elbow on the arm. 'It's similar to what you said to me that night.'

I shrug my shoulders, wondering what I'd said.

He looks at me. 'That you couldn't imagine going through another attempt at pregnancy because it was too hard. Because the pain was untenable. That's how I feel about relationships. The risk of loss is too great.'

'I hear you,' I say.

We sit and gaze ahead.

Eventually he says, 'Listen, you don't have to worry about me. I'm content in my work. I don't need to go out dating. The very thought of it, at my age, is abhorrent.'

I twist towards him. 'You do know you're a very attractive man? Don't you?'

'Maybe I was once,' he says.

'You still are. Look at Camilla!'

'What about Camilla?'

'She's constantly flirting with you.'

He frowns. 'Don't be ridiculous.'

'Fine,' I say. 'But I promise you, there will be women out there who would kill for a man like you. And they'd be right.' He scoffs. He has no idea he's allowing himself to go to waste. 'It might be time, Benedict.'

'Don't you think I should decide when it's time?'

'Not really, no. I sometimes think it's easier from the outside looking in. And I think, from where I'm sitting, it's time.'

He looks at me, uncertain how he's meant to react, his lower jaw shifting from side to side, his eyes brimming with discomfort. 'Would you like to come back for a cup of tea?' he says. He's being polite. We've reached his fuck-off moment.

'I think maybe I should be getting home.'

46

The Everyman are putting on a retro evening, and Bee, Rob, Victoria, Gina and I are gathered outside, queuing to pick up our tickets for the 11 p.m. screening of *Some Like It Hot*. Being out so late, our evening only just beginning, feels vaguely decadent.

'When was the last time you saw it?' says Rob.

I try to recall but it feels like for ever. 'I haven't seen it in years. Can't remember.'

'Well, it's lucky I can,' he says. 'Because it was with me fifteen or so years ago. You were dating that ghastly blond prick, whatshisname?'

Bee laughs. 'I remember him. Oliver Ghastliness.'

'Thanks for the reminder.'

'How come if you were around then I never met you?' Bee says, tugging Rob's sleeve.

He slips his card into the automated machine and it splutters out two tickets. 'Because the universe that is Daisy compartmentalizes her friends.'

'No, I don't.'

'Where is Caro, then? We only ever see her on birthdays.'

I think about it for a second. 'True. I don't know why that is. We just like to see each other one on one. No other reason.'

I put in my credit card. The machine ejects my single ticket.

'That's so sad,' says Victoria, with a theatrically down-turned mouth.

I look at her. 'What? That I didn't invite Caro? I'll invite her next time.'

She puts her hand to her face, shrinking back.

'What?' I say.

'Sorry,' she says. 'I just felt sad seeing your single ticket.'

* * *

We exit onto the alleyway, hit by the smell of urine and weed, and walk out towards the burger bar.

'That was so good!' I say. 'I barely remembered it.'

'You don't remember it because you were too busy snogging Oliver Dumb-Blond,' says Rob.

'Well you must have been snogging Shelley Big-Tits with one eye on the screen.' I huddle up to Bee. 'Sorry, Bee, but he had a life before you. I know. It's hard to imagine.'

* * *

We sit around the Formica table waiting for our order.

'I never realized Tony Curtis was so handsome,' says Bee.

'He was hardly our era,' says Victoria.

'He was gorgeous,' says Gina. 'Not as gorgeous as you, though,' she adds turning to Victoria and pecking her on the lips.

'Damn,' says Rob. 'I thought you were going to say me.'

'You *are* gorgeous!' says Bee.

'But Tony Curtis was beautiful,' I add.

Victoria nods. 'Listen, I have an apology to make,' she says, looking at me. 'I'm sorry I mentioned the singleton thing. I don't think it's sad. I think it's admirable. It's just old-school conditioning. You know how it is. We were all fed the fairy tale. That happy-ever-after means a husband and two point four children. I mean, I'm the last one entitled to make that kind of judgement. And yet somehow it's planted in our consciousness.'

'Don't worry,' I say. 'I get it.'

'I blame fucking Cinderella,' says Gina.

The waitress interrupts the moment, placing our burgers in front of us. 'One with cheese?'

'That's mine,' says Rob.

'I think I asked for medium rare,' says Gina, peeling back her bun and pressing the patty with her knife.

'That is medium rare,' says the waitress.

'Appropriately reprimanded,' says Gina, making an eek face.

'So come on. What was Oliver's surname?' asks Bee, biting into her bun.

I groan. 'Wheeler.'

Bee laughs, wiping her hands and picking up her phone. 'Let's google him!'

I put my hand on her arm. 'I already have,' I say, 'and he's fat and bald, married or in a relationship. Can't remember. Didn't cross-check his wife/partner. I looked him up on Facebook in one of my more desperate moments. Please don't feel sorry for me. I don't need anyone's pity.' I glance at Victoria.

Bee pulls a disappointed face and puts down her phone. 'Aren't you lucky you still have hair?' she says, looking at Rob.

'Do you mean if I was fat and bald you wouldn't love me?'

'Have you told him you love him?' I say, acting swoony.

Bee looks at Rob, smiling. 'Maybe.'

'Oh my God,' I say, in a controlled yell. 'Pay attention, everyone. They love each other!'

'Stop it,' says Bee. 'Why are you in such a good mood?'

'Does there have to be a reason?'

'No, I'm delighted.'

'But now you come to mention it, maybe it's because . . . erm . . . because . . .'

Rob frowns. 'Because what, Daisy?'

'Because I'm seeing Jack again.' I blurt it out as quickly as I can. 'And before you say anything, it's just a date.'

The atmosphere around the table changes in a millisecond. If ever there was a response that was coordinated yet entirely unplanned it's the 'SHUT UP!' that follows.

'When did that happen?' says Bee, choosing not to disguise her dismay.

'It kind of evolved. I was needy. The universe sent him over.'

'Oh, God!' says Bee. 'You're so dangerous when you're needy.'

'And you're not?'

'You see?' says Victoria. 'There we were, thinking you've got this single life sorted, you're happy as fuck, but really it's because there's a bloke back in your life.'

'Not true!' I object. 'He's not back in my life. He's on trial.'

'Even so, what this proves,' she continues, 'is that at the end of the day, we all want to be with someone. Because none of us wants to die alone.'

I feel in my pocket and pull out the stub. 'Or maybe because none of us wants to be the one holding the single ticket.'

47

Jack's text says, *Outside!*

I slip into a leather jacket, grab the 'warm scarf' he's instructed me to bring, throw on the 'good walking shoes' and head down the stairs, glancing at the post sitting in my pile, organized neatly by Mr Henderson, that I've been ignoring, trying to forget that bills have to be paid.

'Good morning!' He smiles as I climb into his car.

'I thought you'd be in a Tesla.'

'Nah! Didn't want to risk having to charge it. Brought the Maserati. Could have brought the Ferrari—'

'Fine,' I say, buckling up. 'I get the picture.'

'You'd hate the Ferrari. Not your kind of car.'

'I'm not sure I have a kind of car,' I say, and he says, 'Exactly,' and puts his foot down as we roar away.

He asks how I am and I say fine and I ask how he is.

'Going to be a beautiful day,' he says.

I look out at the heavy grey skies. 'When exactly?'

'From around eleven thirty – at least, where we're heading. Apparently it's a bit of a microclimate.'

'Am I allowed to know where we're going?'

'That will spoil the surprise,' he says. 'What do you want to listen to? We can do radio, Spotify, nothing? We can talk?'

'How long is the drive?'

'Couple of hours.'

'Let's start with Spotify.'

He calls up his Spotify library.

'Do you still have our old playlist?'

'That's what I was going to play.'

'Are you going to be extra-super-charming all day?'

'Yes,' he says.

Our favourite tunes accompany us along the boring monotony of the motorway and we sing along as we always did. To Ed Sheeran, Adele, Lewis Capaldi, Lady Gaga, Elbow.

'We're so middle-of-the-road,' I say.

'Speak for yourself.'

'What about Polly? Did she like our taste in tunes?' I ask, like it's the most natural question in the world.

'Can we not discuss Polly?'

I tell him we have to discuss her. There are things I need to know. He asks what things. And I say was she good in bed? He tells me there are some things I don't need to know and I say, 'That means, yes.'

'You're good in bed,' he says.

'But I wasn't enough.'

'It was stress-driven,' he says, and I wonder if he thinks he's now going to have a stress-free life.

We listen to our middle-of-the-road tunes and look at the road ahead. I try to decipher where we might be heading, checking the road signs, which give nothing away. Maybe Faversham. Definitely Kent. 'We've been there before? You've been there before?'

'I've been a couple of times. It's a location we're looking at for another hotel.'

'Are you still that involved?'

'I'm still a consultant, Daisy. For at least another eighteen months.'

'I just didn't know precisely what "consultant" would mean.'

'Whatever I want it to mean,' he says, and he shuffles his eyebrows provocatively.

'And what do you want it to mean?' I ask.

He looks at me, then back at the road. 'I just want to have fun, Daisy. I think I'm entitled to enjoy myself for a while. Otherwise what's it all for?'

'Whitstable?' I say, spotting the sign. 'You're taking me to Whitstable.'

* * *

I can see the sea on the horizon as we descend the hill towards the town. The promised blue sky is painted above it. It's uplifting.

Jack pulls into a car park adjacent to the shingle beach. 'Want to go for a walk first?' he says. 'The restaurant is just there. Table won't be ready for about an hour.'

I look across at the large Georgian brick building with its white-painted sash windows, facing out to sea, proudly bearing its name 'Royal Native Oyster Stores' above a crest that hangs over the dark-green-painted door. The fame of this restaurant dominates the town.

'I've always wanted to go there,' I say.

'I know,' he says. 'That's why I brought you.'

'You really are going to be charming, aren't you?'

He casts down his eyes. 'I'm just being me, Daisy!' He waits a beat, like he's expecting me to agree. 'Come on, let's discover the British seaside.'

We get out of the car, which beeps quietly as he locks it, the wing mirrors slowly rotating inwards. The fresh air is welcome, warmed by the sun; the smell of the sea, seaweed and fish tells me that we have definitely left behind cloudy grey London. We start to stroll. There are small boats tethered outside the Neptune pub, people sitting drinking beer, eating chips, enjoying the microclimate.

Further along, Jack suggests we dip our toes into the sea and we sit down on a groyne and kick off our shoes. I take off my socks, stuff them into my sensible walking shoes, and roll up my jeans. We stand up and the uneven layers of the shingle press into my soles so that within three strides I'm in pain.

'Race you,' he says, rolling up his trousers over his hairy pale-skinned calves, running, then turning around, egging me on to 'stop being such a wuss'.

'My feet hurt!' I say. 'Why don't yours?' He runs back to me, lifting me up, throwing me over his shoulder as he rushes towards the waves. 'There,' he says, putting me down in the freezing cold estuary. 'Door-to-door service.'

'It's fucking freezing!' I yell, immediately trying to leap back into his arms.

'It's good for you!' he cries, laughing, holding me above the rippling water. 'People swim here every morning, whatever the weather. They live to be a hundred.'

'Not my people!' I say. 'And I don't want to live to be a hundred.'

He lowers me in slowly. 'There. Not a shock this time.'

My toes are hurting, and my ankles are bright blue. 'It's fine. Let go of my wrist!'

'Your body gets used to it. It warms up,' he says.

'When I'm a hundred?'

He throws his head back, like I'm being hilarious. 'You're hating it?'

'Not hating it, no. I'm just letting off some repressed emotion.'

'Oh, I see,' he says. 'This is payback.' He holds his hand to his heart, like he's been shot.

I splash around, shifting from one foot to the other, trying to warm up.

We start to venture deeper. 'If there are any jellyfish I'm out of here!' I say.

'If there are any jellyfish, I'll be out of here with you.'

He kicks some seawater at me.

I jump back, horrified, then laugh, kicking some back at him to lesser effect. 'If my first experience at the Royal Native Oyster Stores is with soaking wet, sticky jeans, I'm telling you, I will not be good company.' I make a second attempt to kick water at him. It's barely an improvement.

'Come here,' he says, and pulls me into him. He grabs my face. His hands are freezing. 'I love it when you're angry.' He looks at me, his eyes even brighter blue, squinting against the sunlight.

'No, you don't,' I say.

'This kind of angry,' he says. 'Messing-around angry.'

'How do you know I'm messing around?'

'Can I kiss you?' he says.

'Messing-around kissing?'

'I don't mess around kissing,' and his lips press softly over mine and we stand, freezing cold, up to our mid-calves in the flapping swell of seawater, stones pressing into the softer parts of our feet. In that moment, everything drifts away; the discomfort, the fear of jellyfish, the spectre of Polly.

His face pulls back and I open my eyes.

'I love you, Daisy,' he says. 'I want to spend the rest of my life with you.'

I push him away, suddenly freezing, shivering, teeth chattering. 'No! No! No! No! No, Jack! That's unfair.' I feel my numb cheeks. 'You can't bring me here, kiss me and make me fall in love with you again. It's too soon! You can't expect the sea to wash everything away. Please, Jack. I'm still raw.'

I turn away and hurriedly splish-splosh out of the freezing sea, over the beach, my feet roaring with the shooting pain of the cold and the shingle and the upturned, sharp-edged shells, and sit down on the groyne, staring at my shoes and socks. He looks at me, like a boy wondering what the hell he's done wrong.

'How can I ever love you again?' I shout, my teeth chattering. 'My feet are frozen and you didn't even bring a damned towel!'

He smiles, breaks into a run and swoops down in front of me.

'Which one is the coldest?'

'Too numb to tell.'

He picks up my right foot and massages it, warming up my toes, rubbing his palms over my whole foot.

'I'm sorry,' he says.

'For what exactly?'

'For forgetting a towel.'

'You're forgiven.'

'And for trying to make you fall in love with me again.'

'Yeah,' I say. 'Don't get ahead of yourself.'

* * *

We are shown to a corner table and they immediately bring over a carafe of water and a basket of warm French bread, which they put down on the white-paper square that hangs over the red-and-white chequered tablecloth.

I butter a piece of bread and bite into it, ravenously.

'Better now?' Jack says.

'You have no idea.'

'Admit it, though, it was fun.'

'It was freezing, Jack.' I look at him, mid-bite. 'Okay,' I say. 'It was fun.'

'Oysters, then?' he says, and I nod, feeling the warmth starting to return to the marrow of my bones, some sensation finally returning to my feet, the reward of carbohydrates entering my stomach.

A glass of white wine accompanied by the silkiness of oysters sliding majestically down helps assuage my mood.

'So how's work going?' he says, adding some vinegar dressing. 'I'm sure it's not been easy.'

'Actually, we're doing rather well, thanks,' I say. 'I'm just finishing a really successful job in Peckham.'

'Peckham?'

'Don't look so shocked. Like most of London, it's changing. Some parts are beautiful. I've just updated a magnificent Georgian house. It's turned out really well.'

'Of course it has. You're good.'

He's always thought I was good. He's always told me, encouraged me, reassured me. I watch as he swallows another oyster, watch his eyes widen with appreciation, watch as he takes a sip of the wine. It's like I'm seeing him, the man I used to see, before he became the man I never wanted to see again. I remember you now, I think. And my heart clenches with the pain because I realize what I've lost. Him. Time. Babies. But maybe there's hope. Maybe.

I rinse my hands in the small bowl of warm water and squeeze some lemon over them. 'What about you? How does it feel to have relinquished control of the hotels? Is it odd?'

'Not while I'm still involved.' He wipes his mouth, rinses his hands and moves his chair nearer to the table, pushes his plate aside, then puts out his hand, palm up, waiting for mine. 'I'm not trying to make you fall in love with me. I just want to explain something to you and I want to hold your hand.'

'It's sticky.'

'I want to hold your sticky hand.'

I place my hand in his.

'My life has changed beyond measure. It's good, Daisy,' he says. 'Life is very good and I feel funny saying that to you after everything I've put you through, but at the end of the day you know exactly why I can say it. You know I'm not boasting when I tell you I probably won't have to work for the rest of my life because it's the truth. For several lives. I don't know how to explain to you how that feels. It's taken me to a level beyond the already pretty privileged existence we had together. It's almost scary.'

'Why scary?' I say pithily. 'It's what you always wanted.'

'Yes. Yes. But until you have it, you don't appreciate how it's going to feel. You can merely imagine. Anyhow, my point is, I wanted it for us. And somehow, having it, without you, I don't know . . . I don't know. And I'm not begging you, I want you to take your time, but I really want you to give this another chance.'

'I'm here, aren't I?'

He puts his other palm on top of mine, closing around it like an oyster shell. 'But you don't trust me, do you?'

'Not yet, no.'

He jiggles his leg under the table. 'I understand. You're entitled to that.'

'Thanks!' I go to remove my hand but he holds on tighter.

'I have a proposal,' he says. 'What say we go back to regular old-fashioned dating? Get used to one another. Slowly. Take our time.'

'Maybe,' I say.

His face brightens. 'Let me take you to Paris. Or Rome. Wherever you want to go.'

I laugh at his interpretation of slow. 'No, Jack. That's not taking our time! I don't need dates in Paris or Rome. Let's keep it simple.'

His jaw drops. He runs his fingers across my open palm and it tingles. 'Paris *is* simple. Rome *is* simple. That's the point. We can go wherever we want. Whenever we want to. Don't you see what's opened up to us?'

I pull away. 'What if I don't want it to be like that? What if it makes life too easy?'

He doesn't even try to hide his disgust. 'Don't be ridiculous. Everyone wants it to be like that. What do you want, Daisy? To struggle for the rest of your life? To live in some ghastly rental? You want to do up houses in Peckham for ever? Are you crazy? This could be our life. Your life.'

'I know it's hard for you to believe but I'm okay with the life I've got.' I can see it's a rather pointless argument to have with someone whose life has changed in the complete reverse direction from mine. 'Not that I don't like nice things. I love Paris, I love Rome, but let's keep the dating simple.'

He shrugs. 'That's my point. I was trying to keep it simple.' My dismissal of his grand gesture is incomprehensible to him.

In that moment I intuitively know not to bring up the subject of babies. It would mean telling him about the sperm donation. The pregnancy. The miscarriage. He would have to appreciate its significance and his part in it. He's not ready for that information. He's flying too high in his new orbit. Neither am I ready to trust him with it. I don't want to be told how crazy I am. Because it wasn't crazy. It was brave.

* * *

I lie down in the car with my jeans button open. 'I can't believe I ate so much.'

'I'm bloated too,' he says.

'But it was worth it.'

He smiles across at me. 'It was,' he says. 'Listen, there's a charity ball on Thursday. In London,' he adds, in case I doubted it. 'It's important to me. I'd like you to be there. Say you'll come?'

'Can't we just go out for a burger?'

He laughs. 'Anyone can go out for a burger.'

'Okay, Prince Charming.' I smile, knowing I have already fallen. 'Just a regular old-fashioned date, right?'

'Something like that,' he says. 'It's black tie.'

'I don't think I have one of those.'

He laughs. 'Leave it to me.'

48

It's a time of endings, which is always sad yet fortunately heralds new beginnings. Time to close the door on the Peckham house and open the door to the Mayfair apartment.

'So this is it,' I say, as Benedict and I do our final rounds, photographing every room for our respective websites, me for the Baxter Settle Instagram account. 'We can now officially hand over this home to Camilla and Tim. Our work is done.'

'It certainly is, Daisy.'

One of the main joys of being an interior designer is seeing the transformation of a worn, tired, neglected old building into a beautiful, warm and welcoming home. I love interpreting what the client wants, what they envisage, how they live, what's important to them, then ramping everything up, giving them more than they bargained for and toning it down until it fits their life and the way they see themselves. When I leave a project, I want to leave behind a home where the family can put their feet up and say, 'This is ours and it's beautiful.' Camilla and Tim can happily do that.

'Selfie, Mr Shaw?' I say.

He lets his camera swing down to his chest and takes my phone from me. 'I have longer arms,' he says. 'Say cheese!'

'Gruyèahhhhhh.'

'Gruyèahhhhh,' he mimics, then takes a couple of shots.

We look at them together.

'We make a charming cheesy couple,' I say.

'Send them to me.'

He packs his camera into its leather case and puts it into his satchel.

'I feel strangely sad leaving this place. A lot has happened here.' I stand back, taking in the glorious kitchen-diner, watching Benedict organizing himself, checking his pockets for the keys, checking the contents of his satchel.

'It may surprise you to learn that I try not to be emotional about jobs but, in this case, it has been an exceptional experience.' He pulls out a bottle of wine. 'You haven't forgotten this, I hope? I think now is an appropriate moment to enjoy it.'

'Ah!' I smile, recognizing the label on the vintage wine I'd bought for him. 'That bag of yours is quite a Tardis. Corkscrew? Glasses? Bar?'

He proudly produces two glasses, removing the bubble wrap, which makes me smile, and a wing corkscrew. 'That's as much as this Tardis could manage. Let's sit outside on the garden step. That can be our makeshift bar.'

It's a beautiful spring evening. We make our way through the stunning extension with its retractable glass roof gleaming in the sunlight, the virgin linen sofa, the tall open bookshelves yearning to be filled, the uninitiated glass coffee-table, the beautiful handcrafted wall lights, the smell of paint still fresh. Benedict unlocks the massive Crittall doors, sweeping them open.

'Good work,' I say.

We wander out onto the patio. The garden is starting to take shape in the hands of the next expert, the smell of the freshly laid grass, the lavender bushes bordering the path, the rosemary, the clematis, the jasmine lined up in pots waiting to be planted. A work in progress. It will be beautiful in time.

We sit on the step and I watch him unscrew the cork and hear the quiet release of pressure from the bottle. He passes the cork under his nostrils. 'Smells good,' he says.

'Everything smells good now, doesn't it?'

'I'll let the bottle air for a bit.'

'Fine,' I say, leaning back against the brick wall. 'Happy just to wait at the bar.'

He chuckles, placing the bottle carefully on the concrete slab. 'So what's next on the agenda for you?'

'A rather grand but dilapidated flat in Mayfair.'

'That's a distinct change from Peckham,' he says.

I raise my eyebrows, agreeing. 'I'm looking forward to the change. It stimulates the design process. Working at the hotels became quite stagnant creatively. I say that in hindsight, of course. While we were living it, we enjoyed it. It seemed like we'd landed the best job you could ever hope for. But in the end that was merely from the perspective of financial security.'

'Nothing wrong with financial security.'

'No. But I've quite enjoyed rising to the creative challenge again. Okay, so my income is down but my creative juices are right back up there.'

'I understand that.'

I smile, believing he does. 'What about you?'

'New-build house,' he says. 'Steel-and-glass-framed. Super-slick pavilion construction. It's complicated but very pure.'

I clap. 'You must be in your element.'

'I am,' he says. He picks up the wine bottle and pours. 'To a happy ending,' he says.

I clink his glass. 'Happy endings!'

The wine trickles nicely down the back of my throat reminding me of what decent wine tastes like.

'I've never said this before,' I say, braving what I've wanted to say for a while, 'but you made the start of this job bloody miserable for me.'

He looks at me startled. 'Did I? In what way?'

I study him, trying to work out if he's being disingenuous or whether he genuinely has no awareness of how intimidating he can be. 'Oh, come on. You knew you were being difficult. You refused to engage with me. You hated my designs.'

He swirls the wine in his glass, absorbing the motion, then looks at me with an air of contained bemusement. 'I didn't engage with anyone. I'm not proud of it. It was how I coped.'

'Of course. I know that now.'

'And I wasn't being difficult, Daisy. I just wasn't sure your designs were entirely right for this house. They were very bold.' He sips slowly. 'But you're bold. And you proved me wrong. That's how it works, isn't it? You stuck to your guns and I had to adjust my opinion.'

'Am I bold?' I'm surprised to hear him say this.

'Sure you are. It must have taken a lot to knock on my door when you did.'

It did, but I'm not sure that was anything to do with feeling bold. 'Not really. It was simply something I wanted to do.'

He smiles. 'And that's why you're bold, darling.'

We quickly turn our faces towards the sunlight, both registering how alien that word rang against our ears. His shoulders give a tiny almost imperceptible shudder. 'Thanks for coming over by the way,' he says. 'That really helped.'

'It's what friends are for.'

He smiles.

He holds the bowl of the glass in his palm, sipping, and we both lean back against the wall, revived by the warmth of the sun soothing our wearied skin, easing the stress, the pressure that has weighed on us over the past several months.

I marvel at life's surprises. That this man, who once could disrupt my confidence by saying nothing, is now the source of trust and assurance, the man with whom I can share everything. Total, open-hearted conversation.

'I had an unexpectedly good weekend,' I say. 'A rarity.'

'Really?'

I glance across. 'I guess it's time I told you what's been happening in my life.'

He looks awkward, drawing his knees to his chest. His shirt, unbuttoned to just above his sternum, widens to reveal olive-toned, hairless skin. He turns to face me. 'I've wanted to ask you about that part of your life for a while but haven't felt entitled to pry.'

'Why not?' I say. 'I've done nothing but pry into yours.'

'Yes, but I don't have your charm.'

I laugh. 'I'm not sure that's true.'

I fill him in on the back story and he listens intently as I relive the horror of my fortieth birthday party. He gives nothing away. Voices no opinion until I open up about my route to solo parenthood.

'That makes total sense now,' he says.

'It does? You don't think it was crazy?'

He frowns at me, picks off a spider that's landed on his trouser knee, allowing it to spool its way to the ground. 'I think it was admirable,' he says.

'Not so admirable to give up so quickly, though?'

'Daisy. I told you at the time. You know yourself. You

have to do what feels right for you. And now I understand the pain you were carrying I can see how hard it would have been to try again.'

We sit quietly, drinking.

'So what about this unexpectedly good weekend?'

'Oh, right,' I say. 'I completely forgot why I was telling you. I met Jack again.'

'Ah. Okay.'

'He wants to be given a second chance. For us to give it another go.' I'm expecting Benedict's face to switch to disappointment in me, but he holds the same open expression, waiting to hear what I have to say. 'He took me to Whitstable. It was fun.'

'I'm pleased for you,' he says.

I shift my bottom, numbed by the concrete slab that is my bar stool.

'And you're willing to take it further?' he says. 'You can trust him?'

'I don't know. I'm going out with him again this week. To a charity ball. I think I need to see what it feels like being with him, among other people. To see his new world. To try it on, if you like, and see if it fits.'

'That sounds sensible.'

'To see if it's what I want,' I add. I hunch my shoulders looking down into my lap. Wondering if I even know what I want.

He stands up and stretches his legs, looking across at me, as I sit, still hunched. 'Do you know what you want?' he says gently, and I laugh.

'Is that funny?'

'No. I was just asking myself the very same question.'

I feel glad of his gentle interrogation. That his words are respectful rather than impatient. I'm grateful for the opportunity to articulate the thoughts that have been whirring around my head, dutifully recorded in my journal.

'I know some things,' I say, with certainty. 'I want a family. More than anything else. Even more than the glamorous life Jack promises. I want a child. Maybe even children. And if I'm not going to use the two blastocysts and I can't, I just can't, then Jack is my last hope.'

He raises his eyebrows. Cocks his head, considering me, skewering me with his gaze. I feel strangely exposed. Like he can see me too well. He sits back down, picks up the bottle warming on the step and holds it up so that I put forward my glass.

'Well, I'm keeping everything crossed for you,' he says. 'I really am. He's a very lucky man.' He pours generously. 'We should finish this, don't you think?'

'Rude not to.'

49

I stare impatiently at my phone, listening to the ringing tone, waiting for my mother, or maybe my father, to pick up.

'Hello?' she says.

'It's me.'

'Everything okay?'

I smile. 'Yes,' I say, 'Probably better than okay.'

'What's happened? You sound excited.'

'I am,' I say, thrilled to be able to share something positive at last, which I know she'll be delighted to hear. Something that will put an end to my parents' angst about me. That will unite them around me, the way they always were. And that's a lovely feeling because, at the end of the day, life is easier when your family are as one. 'You're going to be very happy,' I say, 'but I don't want you to get overexcited because it's still in the early stages.'

'You're pregnant?' she says, with a sharp intake of breath.

I laugh. 'No, ha!' I should have anticipated that. I dangle the carrot for one more millisecond. 'I'm seeing Jack again.'

There's a long pause. 'You're joking?'

'I'm not. I've already had one date with him and he's taking me to a charity ball tomorrow.'

I hear my father walk in. 'Ah, there you are, Sally. I was calling you to say the phone was ringing.'

'Not the one at the Grosvenor House?' she says, ignoring him.

'Yes!' Slight sinking feeling. 'Are you and Dad going?'

She laughs. 'I wish! That's the charity ball of the year, darling. I read about it just this morning in the *Daily Mail*. All the great and the good will be there.'

'You mean the stinking rich.'

'And my daughter is going to be right there with them. With her boyfriend Jack.'

'Is she back with Jack?' says my father. 'What's happened?'

'Yes, Ted!' she says. 'Stop hovering! Sit down! Oh, Daisy, you're back together. That's the best news in the world, darling. I'm so pleased for you. I just want you to be happy.'

'That's funny,' I say, 'I just want you to be happy.'

'Ted!' she says. 'It's the news we've been praying for. They're together again.'

Oh, wow! I think. They've even been turning to prayer. 'We're dating, Ma. Early days.' I have to stem their enthusiasm. Maybe my need to share is somewhat premature. But there is no twelve-week rule here.

'Oh, wonderful!' says my father. 'Let me have a word.'

Suddenly it's my father at the end of the phone.

'Daisy, darling, I couldn't be more thrilled. At last. This is how it's meant to be. How it was always meant to be.'

'Well, it's not quite how it's meant to be yet. But, hopefully, it's a new beginning.'

'A good new beginning,' he says. 'I'm handing you back to your mother.'

'I'm elated,' says my mother. 'I want to hear all about it. Come over at the weekend. With Jack. Oh, my goodness, we'll be one big happy family again.'

'No promises,' I say. 'We're not—'

'What are you going to wear, for goodness' sake?' my mother says, sounding panicked. 'It's going to be so glamorous.'

'Jack organized a personal shopper to call in some dresses for me. I'm looking at them now. They're beyond glamorous.'

'You see, Daisy? You could have missed out on all this. What a lucky girl you are.'

I'm not sure this is the most important thing I might have missed out on. 'Yeah, lucky,' I say.

The strange thing is, their excitement is exactly the reaction I wanted, even though I might have been being premature in telling them. I so want them to be happy. (When does one stop trying to make one's parents happy?) I long to be that big happy family again. Life will be so much easier. I long for normality. To be where I fit.

What this has done is prove I know Jack cares deeply about me, which is all I could possibly ask for. That you can sometimes forgive something you thought was unforgivable. And maybe we know each other better now. Maybe that was what this was all about. That we had to break up to come back together even stronger. Like Japanese *kintsugi*. We are a golden repair. I can relax into his arms and feel held, knowing I'm home.

50

Jack is late. Held up in traffic.

I check my phone for his regular updates, rubbing my arms against the draught that seems to accompany every turn of the revolving door, each flash of the cameras that line the red carpet, every appearance of a couture dress, a Versace, a Gucci, an Alexander McQueen. The great and the good, if that's how you define them, are most definitely here. Welcome to the Grosvenor House Hotel.

I look at my fake tan, wondering how it shapes up against their genuine Monte Carlo bronze.

* * *

'I need to know what you're wearing?' Caro says, as soon as I open my front door.

'I'm fine, thanks. And how are you?'

'Busy. Come on,' she says. 'I'm fitting you in.'

I usher her into my bedroom and show her the three dresses Jack's had couriered over, hanging precariously from the frame of the freestanding wardrobe.

'Which one do you think?'

'This one,' she says admiringly, putting her hand through the bottom end of the asymmetric single sleeve and fluttering it. 'Rich people love sequins and feathers.'

'I like sequins and feathers and I'm not rich.'

'Yet,' she says. She purses her lips. 'Are you letting him dress you now?'

I fiddle with my hair, pinning it up so it doesn't get in the way. 'No. I gave my birthday frock to charity. He just wanted to make it easy for me. It's not like I'm drowning in ballgowns and there was no time to shop. He briefed some personal stylist.'

'These are very nice clothes, babes. Lucky you! Right. Take off that dressing-gown. I'm gonna give you the best fake tan you've ever had.'

'What if I've never had one?'

'Semantics,' she says, pushing me into the sitting room.

'Let's do it in the bathroom.'

'Too small, babes. I'm not going to ruin anything. Not here anyway!' She laughs. 'I've got a very good aim. Now hold out your arms and keep still.'

I love the sensation as she rubs up and down my arms in swift perfect circles, hand in a bright-pink glove.

'It'll get deeper over the next couple of hours. Do you want me to do your hair and make-up?'

'I thought you were in a rush.'

'I am. But I want you to look amazing! I want you to blow that cheat away!'

'You might have to stop thinking of him as *that cheat*.'

She laughs. 'Babe! That's your job not mine!'

* * *

Traffic awful, not moving.

Hurry up, I think. I feel so conspicuous even though I'm barely noticed.

The women continue to glide through, wearing the highest of heels with immaculate ease, wafting their pricey perfume, hair perfectly blown, foreheads glowing with an expensive sheen, flaunting a confidence borne of money and powerful husbands, surreptitiously appraising each other's outfits, two air kisses, sometimes three because that's what foreign royalty do and they adore royalty. Their powerful husbands, who look twice their age, tans as leathery as their wallets layered thick for tipping, exchange extravagant man hugs, patting each other's backs enthusiastically, kissing cheeks baked with cologne from Clive Christian or Creed or maybe Tom Ford.

Jack throws himself through the revolving door and charges towards me. 'Darling! I'm so sorry! Oh, my God. I thought I'd never get here.' He's sweating, agitated. He looks around, quickly checking out the company, smoothing back his hair. 'You should have let me pick you up, like I suggested. You wouldn't have had to wait here on your own and I'd have been less stressed out. The traffic is shocking. Gah! I feel terrible.'

'Never mind. You're here now.'

'Let me look at you.' He takes a moment, trying to draw breath. 'Wow! You're beautiful,' he says.

'Thanks.' Note to Caro: You blew him away.

'Let me whizz to the Gents. I'll drop off our coats.' He looks for mine.

'I've already checked mine in,' I say.

He comes out looking calmer, less sweaty, handsome in his black tuxedo.

'You look good, too, Jack,' I say. 'Here, let me straighten your bow-tie.'

'Jesus,' he says, puffing his cheeks. 'Is it tilting down again? I thought I'd sorted it.'

I tighten the bow so that it's fixed, stable. 'There.'

We look at one another and smile.

'Are we good?' he says.

'Yes,' I say. 'We're good.' Butterflies in stomach. A kaleidoscope of them.

'Let's go in. I need a drink.' He takes me by the hand. The gesture feels reassuringly natural.

'Negroni?'

I nod.

He wends his way through the hordes and I watch him engage with the bartender, feeling the sense of pride I used to have when I watched him and he was unaware of it. He's laughing, obvious banter, then his tall, slim frame, so elegant in the tux, is returning with two Negronis.

We sip, his eyes darting around, taking in the room.

'Hey, Nick, mate!' he says, to a passing older man, grey hair, elegant.

'Aha! Jack, my boy! Good to see you.'

'This is my girlfriend, Daisy.'

I try not to react, secretly thrilled even though it's presumptuous.

Nick checks me out, his eyes shamelessly sweeping over my body, like an airport scanner. 'Heard a lot about you, Daisy,' he says, taking my hand, brushing away the feathers and kissing it.

I smile politely, wondering what he's heard.

'Where's your lovely wife?' says Jack.

He looks around, searching across the heads of the crowd, then points. 'Flirting with the resident celebrity, Justin Doyle. Look at him! Every woman lapping him up. What is it about these celebrities? I'm tempted to flirt with him myself.'

'Justin Doyle is doing the auction,' Jack says, and I nod excitedly because I know he wants me to be impressed. 'Can you believe it? Boy Doyly.'

'Amazing!' Not my favourite celebrity, that's for sure, but he's one of the highest-paid presenters, so I guess that's why he's here.

'Got my eyes on the Piaggio,' says Nick.

'Come off it, man!' Jack sniggers, and Nick gives him a faux slap on the cheek. 'He's a cheeky bugger, your boyfriend,' he says, turning back to Jack. 'It's not for me. It would be for my son. What about you?' he says.

'I quite like the sound of two weeks on the private island.'

'That's a busman's holiday!'

'Not until I own it.'

'You should get residency in Monte Carlo now.' He taps his nose. 'Think about it.'

Jack laughs. I laugh louder.

A plate of canapés passes by and I reach out enthusiastically to grab one.

'God, you must be the only woman here who eats,' Nick says. 'Congratulations, Jack. I'm impressed.'

I feel myself stiffen, not sure whether to put the tiny duck-in-pancake into my mouth or shove it into his. I choose mine. It melts into nothing. I wish I'd grabbed two. I'm so hungry.

'See you later,' says Nick, and sets off in the direction of Justin Doyle, in an attempt to out-flirt his wife.

'And who is Nick?' I say, dabbing at my lips trying not to ruin my lipstick, which I've already reapplied three times (nerves, waiting, and needing something to do).

'One of the board members of the PE house.'

'PE?'

'Private equity. They bought the company.'

'Should I have curtsied?' I chuckle.

'He'd have liked that. He'd have got a better view.'

'Of what?' I say, my jaw clenching.

'Nothing. Never mind.'

I take a deep breath.

He introduces me to a few more men, some standing with their wives, who smile at me with aloof politeness. I feel I should engage in conversation with them, break the ice, break into this set, but I can't think of a single thing to say to them. Evidently it's mutual.

I drink my Negroni too quickly, sensing it spread to my cheeks, relieved when the master of ceremonies, with ruddy face and slicked-back white hair, in full crimson frock-coat regalia booms, 'Ladies and gentlemen, kindly make your way to the ballroom. Dinner is about to be served.'

Jack takes me to one of the huge table plans inscribed in gold-and-black calligraphy and scans it for our names. 'We've been placed in pole position,' he says, thrilled. 'Table six.'

'Wow!' I say. 'Big night!'

'It is, Daise. We've made it. We've fast-forwarded straight to the top. We're officially members of that elusive club.' He looks at me, as though waiting for my applause. 'Look around you! Look at the world we've moved into. It's going to be such fun.'

I smile broadly. 'You don't have to try to convince me, Jack.' It's me who has to try to convince me.

'Good,' he says. He pulls me towards him. 'Can I just say this now before I get too drunk?'

'Is that your plan?'

He inhales deeply and his nostrils pinch. 'You look beautiful. I'm glad you came. And I know this is just a date but . . .' He holds my shoulders a touch too tightly so that I can feel his hands quiver. 'This is us, isn't it? It's as if we've never been apart. Right?'

'This is definitely us,' I say. 'And this us is very hungry.'

He laughs, dropping his hands to my sequined waist. 'Looks like all of the women here are hungry, darling. Only I think they enjoy it.' He leans in and kisses my earlobe, whispering, 'If we weren't standing in the middle of a crowded room, I swear to God I'd rip that dress off you and kiss your glorious curves and . . .'

'Calm down, Jack,' I say, enjoying the flutter of his breath against my neck. 'Otherwise I'll rip it off for you.'

51

We descend the grand stairway and the vast arrangement of tables pans out below us. People are milling around, like illuminated trails of ants, under the stunning art-deco crystal chandeliers, weaving between the round tables all laid to perfection, each adorned with a massive floral display on a tall gold stand, filled with pink and white blooms. Sprays of eucalyptus trail over the sides. Five pillar candles, perfectly placed, flicker beautifully, their flames captured in the crystal glassware, which sits to the right of the gold cutlery, alongside the gold-rimmed white china on crisp white tablecloths. The arrangement is topped off with a gold ice-bucket hugging a magnum of champagne.

'They don't do things by half in your country, do they?' I say.

'Stick with me, kiddo.'

'I intend to.'

We sit in our named places and I introduce myself to the man sitting next to me, who smiles politely and introduces me to his wife, who nods hello and smiles, with eyes that look as though they've seen it all a thousand times before.

Waiters open the magnums with immaculate coordination, the sound of popping corks reverberating around the room. Behind them, men with baskets of warm rolls, from which I can choose *seeded, plain or wholemeal, madam*? I tear off a piece of *seeded, please*, spreading it with a thick layer of the soft butter. I look around, to note that not one other woman at the table has taken a roll. I put it down.

Jack is talking animatedly to the couple next to him. I turn to see the couple next to me talking to the couple next to them. I stare ahead, wondering what to do, then think, What the heck? and pick up the roll, occupying myself with small nibbles. Jack puts his hand on my thigh and squeezes it. I wonder if he's proud that I'm the only woman at the table eating carbs.

Salmon and tuna sashimi is served. I watch Jack enjoy himself, engrossed, awed. He looks back at me from time to time.

'You okay?' he says.

'Yeah good,' I say. 'Sashimi is amazing.' I want to grab you by the hand and run away with you, I think. As far away from here as possible. You look so goddamn handsome.

'Hey, guys,' he says, like he's had an epiphany. 'I haven't introduced you. Daisy meet Jemima and Hugo. They breed racehorses. Travel the world.' He leans into me, cupping his hand over his mouth, as though he's starting a game of audible Chinese whispers. 'They have a private jet,' he says. 'We need to get in with them!'

Hugo smiles. 'Consider yourselves in.'

Jack does a sort of honk. 'High-five, man!'

I smile at Jemima. She is wearing a gold dress with organza sleeves, revealing long slender arms with enviably defined biceps, which obviously don't do carbs. Her face is lightly tanned, her hair a perfectly highlighted sharp blonde bob, the sides tucked behind her ears to show off her diamond studs. Three ever-smaller ones travel up her right lobe. She has perfectly glossed lips.

'Do you work, Daisy?' asks Hugo.

'Daisy's an interior designer,' says Jack, interjecting before I've had a chance to open my mouth. 'She designed most of our hotels.'

Hugo looks at his wife with a huge beam. 'Jemima does interior design, don't you, darling? She's done all four of our houses.'

'I'm hoping Daisy will design my new house.'

I look at him. 'What new house?'

He turns back to Jemima and Hugo. 'We've had a bit of a break. I'm trying to take it slowly. Whatever that means. I haven't told her about the house.'

I force a smile.

'So where is your new house, Jack?' says Jemima. 'Let me guess . . . Monte Carlo?'

He smiles, unsure. 'Actually, I'm happy to pay my taxes.'

'Pah! You say that now,' says Hugo.

'Shush, Hugo,' says Jemima. 'I want to hear about this house.' She tips me a wink, like she's asking especially for me.

'It's in Kew. Four acres. Eight thousand square feet. Six beds, seven baths. Tennis court. Swimming pool. Hot tub. It's already been subject to a massive renovation. The interior designer is a famous Argentinian – you ladies might have heard of him if I could only remember his name. Anyway, you'll have fun accessorizing, Daise.'

'Sounds amazing,' says Jemima, holding his gaze for what I consider to be two seconds too long.

'So tell me about your horses,' I say, trying to decode her behaviour. 'I'm not a horse person. Never even put a sugar cube into a horse's mouth. The closest I've ever got is Elizabeth Taylor in *Black Beauty*.'

Jemima snorts. 'I think you'll find it was *National Velvet*.'

'Yes, of course,' I say, thinking she's just proved my point.

291

Jack laughs like he's not quite sure where this is going, like he's hoping he won't lose access to their private jet.

Jemima looks to Hugo. 'You explain, darling.'

'I could tell you weren't a horse person,' he says. 'But don't worry, they're the last thing we like to talk about. Probably in the same way you don't like talking about paint.'

'Oh don't get her started,' interjects Jack. 'Daisy loves talking about paint, don't you, baby? She's an ampersand obsessive.'

'A what?' I say.

'You know – Farrow & Ball, Osborne & Little, Paint & Paper. The names are embedded in my consciousness.'

'You do talk nonsense,' I say, fiddling with my gilt napkin ring. 'Anyway, it was because we used to work together. You needed to know.'

'Looks like you might want to gloss over that one, Jack,' says Hugo, smirking.

'Are you suggesting I'm treading on eggshell,' honks Jack, and they give each other another high-five.

'Oh, Jack!' says Jemima, flapping her diamond-embellished hand. 'You're hilarious.'

A shiver runs down my spine.

The sea bass arrives. Or there's *filet mignon* served with a Jack Daniel's pepper sauce on the side. Both are accompanied by a mêlée of organic vegetables, *petits pois à la française*, fondant Yukon potatoes, a cauliflower timbale and wild rice. There's a vegetarian option, which is put in front of the woman to my right. Matching wines are poured; champagne continues on tap. I feel the urge to get drunk but know I mustn't. Jack has no such concerns.

'How's your fish?' he says, turning to me.

'Why didn't you mention the new house when I saw you at the weekend?' I say.

He stabs some potatoes with his fork. 'Because I thought it might scare you.'

'Have you sold the cottage?'

'I'm going to rent it out.' He looks at me as if he can't believe I've asked such a ridiculous question. 'It has scared you, hasn't it?'

'So, Jack,' says Hugo. 'What's your opinion on the Chase Manhattan . . .?'

Blah-blah-blah. In a nanosecond they're back talking money.

It's not the house that scares me, I think, as I push around my food. What scares me is that not so long ago I would have moved happily into that house in Kew, designed by some renowned Argentinian whose name he can't even remember. I'd have happily 'accessorized' it, made it a beautiful space for us, unaware of Polly, or the next Polly whenever he felt bored or under pressure. I would have filled the bedrooms with children, or at least a child. If we were lucky, it might have happened naturally. Or, if we weren't, I might have had to undergo the ordeal of IVF, which we could have afforded no matter how many attempts it took, and I'd have put myself through that hell while Jack went out shagging to cope with the annoying stress of my unpredictable moods thanks to the hormone treatment which was taking the gloss off his gilded life. What scares me is I'd have thought my life was blessed, ignorant of the fact that Jack was having his cake and eating it, several times over. And maybe that would have been okay. I'd have been happy in my ignorance. But what if one day I woke up and saw my life for exactly what I'd allowed it to become?

I look around me. Suddenly all I can see is the fakery and the fawning and the ostentation and Jemima's lingering stare. Then a voice inside my head screams, SHUT UP!

You are here! You are with Jack again, which is what you want, what he wants, what everyone wants, because it will make you happy. Do not self-sabotage!

Desserts are served. Most of the women are eating delicately from a rather magnificent fruit plate. I eat a deconstructed tiramisu for the sheer hell of it.

The man next to me, whose name I now know is Florian because his wife, the veggie, repeats it all the time, asks if I wouldn't mind passing the water. 'Fizzy or still, Florian?' I say.

I pass him the bottle of still and he asks if I'd like some too, which feels like the most considerate thing anyone's said to me all evening.

'Thank you,' I say. He fills my glass and turns back to his wife, who hasn't even glanced at Jack, making me grateful even though she's barely glanced at anyone.

'Ladies and gentlemen,' says the master of ceremonies, 'may I have your attention, please?' The noise in the room moves, like a slowly breaking wave, into silence. 'Can I ask you to take a moment's pause and put your hands together – before you dig deep into your pockets – for tonight's host and auctioneer extraordinaire, Mr Justin . . .' he escalates the name up the scale until he reaches his limit and shouts a resounding '. . . BOY DOYLLLY!'

Lots of feet stamping, like rolling thunder, accompany the banging of hands and the wild clatter of cutlery marks the moment. I watch as the well-groomed celebrity strides through the tables, bathed in the confidence of popularity, checking his bow-tie, undoing his jacket button, as he walks up the six steps to the stage before doing it up again. He shakes hands with the MC, walks towards the podium, fiddles with the mic, pitching it up then down, until he's comfortable it's in precisely the right position. Everything is effortless.

'Good evening, ladies and gentlemen,' he says, and the mic lets out a piercing squeal. He makes a sign for someone to adjust the volume while people cheer and boo, like we've landed in a pantomime. His eyes scour the room and he laughs, playing up to his character, encouraging the noise, obviously happy for any form of recognition, because it's all adulation to him. The mic stops squealing and he starts his set, teasing everyone for being rich bastards, then praising them in advance for their massive donations to tonight's three charities, announcing the first lot.

'A first-class spa weekend at the Chewton Glen Hotel . . .'

I listen, thinking how much I'd love a spa day let alone a weekend, but when the bidding starts at ten thousand pounds, I switch off. People are offering crazy sums, goading one another from across their tables, the great and the good no more sophisticated than kids in a food fight, only they're throwing money, huge great wads of it, because it's fun. Meaningless. Not even worthy of a flinch or a twinge in their back pocket.

Around table six, we all clap appropriately when the hammer comes down. Jack whistles between his fingers at the winning bid and Jemima smiles, which somehow bothers me more than it should.

The stage busies with activity as a cute little Vespa in a beautiful soft blue appears. Justin Doyle is handed a matching helmet, which he duly puts on, climbs on the bike, making like he's about to go for a quick getaway, attracting the requisite laughs. The flash of cameras, everyone recording the moment proudly for their Twitter followers, for Instagram, for the charity newsletters, to show off to their friends, because no matter how rich you are, fame trumps everything. He jumps off, removes the helmet, hangs it over the handlebars, smoothes his hair and returns to the mic.

'Want it?' says Jack. 'If you want it, it's yours.'

'Jack!' I say, confused. 'Isn't that what your friend is going after?'

'He's not my friend. His company bought my company.'

'Even so. No, thanks.'

'Shame. I'd have enjoyed the tussle. Where is he?' He stands up, scanning the room. 'There!' He makes a loud whistle, his fingers to his lips again and does big arrow signs towards the bike. 'Go, Nick!' I wish he'd sit down. I wish he'd stop drinking. I wish I didn't care so much.

The bidding commences, quickly reaching ten thousand pounds. Then twenty. TWENTY THOUSAND POUNDS!

'How much is one of those worth?' I say.

'Who cares?' says Jack, shushing me with his hand. 'It's for charity.'

I tell the devil on my shoulder to go away. He didn't mean to be dismissive. He's in the moment. I must be in the moment too. I'm going to enjoy this. I am! I am!

Along with Nick, Hugo turns out to be one of many bidders and Jack's eyes flit from our table to the other side of the room where Nick keeps outbidding everyone.

'Wow! He's really going for it,' says Jack.

'He's certainly minced me,' says Hugo.

Numbers abound. Shouting, braying, stamping of feet. Justin Doyle asks for some decorum so that he can catch the interested parties. He slams down his hammer on £56,500.

'Woohoo!' says Jack. 'He could have bought a garage full at that price.'

What happened to charity? I think, as 'in the moment' slips through my hands.

He jumps out of his chair and runs around the table, working his way through the throng, heading to Nick's table, his swagger that of a man who thinks he owns the room.

'Aren't you glad I came?' I say to nobody.

I sip my water, occupying myself by watching the presenter, who seems totally in control of his role, examining the next lot, which is being brought on by two stage hands. It's a huge, rather unappealing painting of a dark modern landscape.

I'm wondering how he'll make it sound attractive enough for people to bid some massive sum.

I'm wondering whether, when he goads these people about their wealth, it's because he doesn't care or because he cares more than he should.

I'm wondering which of those I am.

I'm wondering when this will all be over.

Jack slips back into his seat. 'Want it?' he says, nodding towards the painting.

'No, thanks.' I want to say. 'Please don't ask again. I don't want anything.' But I don't think he'll even hear me.

'I need to bid on something. I'm getting bored.'

'So bid on it.'

'I'll wait for the holiday. We could do with a holiday.' He takes my hand. 'You okay?'

'I'm good.' I flash my eyes to hide the lie.

He nods slowly. 'Good is good! Where's the champagne guy?' He looks around the table. 'Anyone for more champagne?'

'I'm going to powder my nose,' I say. I pick up my bag and start to make my way through the labyrinth of tables. As the bidding starts, I hear a voice shout, sending a shudder through me. I turn round, hoping I'm wrong. Jack has his hand up. He's just bid ten thousand pounds for that horrible painting. I shrug off my growing disenchantment, thinking he's merely playing at it because he's bored. I stand on the stairs watching the sport. The champagne has been brought to our table and is being poured. Jack knocks back his glass in one gulp. Instantly holding it up for a refill. Bids again. The numbers edge up in steps of five thousand. He's now bidding thirty thousand. He's loving it. Jemima stands up and shifts elegantly past Hugo, standing behind Jack, placing her hands on his shoulders, like she's spurring him on.

I turn away, swallowing my pride. I can't watch any more.

In the refuge of the Ladies I fiddle with the feathers and the sequins, trying to drag them up around my hips so I can sit down on the loo.

I really don't want to let the negative feelings win. I want to make this work. But there's no ignoring them. I'm so uncomfortable. So out of place. I wish I could be more like the other women here and immerse myself in deep gratitude for being among such privilege. I wish I could simply enjoy my good luck, enjoy Jack, enjoy his success because life would be so much easier if I could. But I can't. I know that now with every passing second, with every interjection, every swagger, every put-down. I know it every time I catch a woman's lingering gaze.

These are Jack's people. He's different with them. I hate the way he talks for me in front of them, like I'm his possession. Like I don't have a voice. I hate myself for wearing this beautiful dress because I'm colluding with him, allowing him to believe he owns me. *This is my girlfriend, Daisy.* He thinks he's won me back. And he very nearly did.

I hate Jemima because now every woman is guilty for Polly. And I hate myself for being jealous of a woman who's done nothing to deserve it other than own a flirtatious stare. And I hate me. Because over the course of six years I abandoned who I was for a man and in so doing I lost everything, including myself.

But I've found myself now and I need Jack to see who I am. Six months on, everything is different. I'm different. I know I can survive intense sorrow and loneliness and loss and disappointment and be okay. I can create beautiful homes and people remember my name and I can be proud of my work. I have friends who love me. Real friends. Not people I befriend for their private jets. And somewhere deep down, something is telling me I don't want this life, the life that Jack thought would impress me. The life that impresses my parents, that makes them happy for me. And even though I really want them to be happy, it can't be at my expense.

I hear the sound of thunderous applause. The painting has obviously sold. But who won it?

As I go to leave the Ladies, Jemima approaches. She smiles sweetly. 'You'll be pleased to hear he didn't get it. Ghastly painting, right?'

I force myself to look her in the eye. 'Ghastly,' I say.

52

We're following the trail of people to the cloakroom, barely speaking. Jack is holding both of our tickets, checking his phone, his bow-tie undone, hanging loose from under his collar. His hair is slightly dishevelled. He looks so sexy. I wish he didn't.

'Right!' he says. 'Text from Nick. We're off to the casino.'

'I'm exhausted, Jack,' I say.

'You're coming, baby. You're my lucky charm. You'll rally! I'll line up some tequila shots.'

'I can't. I'm going home.'

He pulls me away from the queue to the side of the room, ushering me up against a wall. 'What's wrong with you, Daise? You've been acting strangely all night.'

I'm slightly thrown by the unexpected insight. I hadn't thought he'd noticed. And I definitely don't want to talk about it tonight. 'I'm tired. That's all.'

'No,' he says. 'That's not all.' He scratches his head.

I take his hands and look into his dark, dilated pupils. 'Maybe I shouldn't have come.'

He pulls away from me, his arms flailing, not knowing where they're meant to be, then running his fingers through his hair, then pushing his hands deep into his pockets. 'I don't understand what's with you. You act as though you're ashamed that I've got money.' He looks at me with those probing blue eyes. 'Is that it? Does my money offend you?'

'Don't be ridiculous.'

'It's true, though, isn't it?' His voice falters. 'You're not comfortable with my success.'

I shake my head, feeling misunderstood, wishing I could just leave and go home. Work out how to articulate my feelings. Discuss this in the sober light of day. 'You're totally wrong. You're more than entitled to your success. You should be very proud of yourself.'

'I am,' he says. 'But you're not proud of me, are you?'

I swallow hard. 'I am, Jack,' I say. 'But not in the way you want me to be. I don't think this works for me.'

There it is. I've said it.

We lock eyes. He's hurting. I'm hurting.

'That's ridiculous,' he says.

'I'm sorry, Jack. I really am. I wanted us to work. But this is not the life I want.' He stares at me, in shock. 'I'd like to want it,' I say. 'I see the pleasure it brings you. But . . . I don't know. It's just not me.'

He leans back against the wall, deflated. 'I don't understand,' he says. 'What bit about this life could you possibly not want? We can have everything our hearts desire.'

I read the incomprehension in his eyes. 'But our hearts desire different things.'

He scoffs. 'Like what?'

I hesitate, wondering whether it's worth putting it out there. Grabbing for that last fine, imperceptible thread of happiness. 'A baby,' I say.

'Oh, God!' He sighs. 'Here she goes.'

My jaw clenches. 'What are you saying?' I stare into his eyes. 'You wanted a baby too. We were about to start a family!'

'Who knows any more? Look around you. There's more to life than kids.'

I put my arm out to steady myself. 'How could you?' I say. 'How could you be so callous? How dare you belittle my dream?'

His face reddens. He lets out an angry snarl. 'Because you just belittled mine!'

He looks away, then moves towards me, cornering me, resting his warm forehead on my cold bare shoulder. 'I'm so sorry,' he says. 'I'm drunk. I'm so drunk. I didn't mean that. I didn't mean any of it. It was kneejerk.'

I feel my bottom lip tremble. 'That wasn't kneejerk,' I say. 'I think we sometimes say what we really mean when we're drunk. And you were right. I did belittle your dream. I didn't mean to. But I hear you and I'm sorry.' I place my hand on the back of his neck. 'But I'm so sorry you don't want babies.' I play with the soft ends of his hair.

He lets out a long, low sigh. 'Oh, God, Daise. Don't do that. Only you do that.' He lifts his head and looks at me. I take my hand away. 'I'm just not sure any more. I wish I could be. For you. But I can't.'

I swallow the disappointment and it burns my insides. 'Thank you,' I say. 'For being honest.'

We stare at each other, our deepest truths unearthed.

'I'm going to miss you. I miss your touch.'

'You'll forget about me.'

'I've tried. Trust me,' he says. 'You're not that easy to forget.'

And neither is Polly, I want to say. But I don't want to tell him that for me she's still here, in every other woman in the room. I don't want to tell him I'm terrified of spending the rest of my life wondering who's looking at him, who he's looking at and why. I don't want him to know I've become that kind of woman because I don't want him to tell me I'm being ridiculous. And he would.

302

'I can't believe we're having this conversation,' he says. He looks so vulnerable. I wish he could always be this person instead of the wild, drunken, swaggering show-off who emerged in that room. But that's like only loving a child when they're asleep. And that's not fair.

'You're going to be okay, Jack,' I say. 'Look at you in your Dior suit. You fit in perfectly here. I'm in a rental.' I laugh at myself.

He rolls his eyes. 'You're beautiful in everything. I can't even do up my own bow-tie without you.'

'There will be someone else to do up your tie. You were the one who said there were loads of available women out there.'

'And I didn't care about them.'

'You've slipped into this world so seamlessly. It's where you belong. But it's not where I fit.'

He looks at me, puzzled. 'You haven't even tried.'

I hesitate. 'That's the problem,' I say. 'I'll always be trying.'

He's downcast, then looks me in the eye, like he's trying to work out what's going on inside my head. He holds his stare, then shrugs his shoulders and straightens. I watch him transform into some kind of Marvel hero as crumpled, vulnerable Jack leaves and winner Jack reappears. 'So I guess you're not coming? Not even for the craic?'

'No,' I say.

His finger traces a line down my fake-tan arm making the goosebumps appear. He smiles briefly, knowing he still has that effect on me. Because, for good or bad, he will always have that effect on me. I want to tell him I hate him for that. But most of all I hate him for Polly.

We hug each other and I breathe him in one final time, the smell of him, feeling the once-so-familiar warmth of his body against mine, the shape of him, knowing the alchemy of us has already left.

'Here's your coat ticket,' he says. 'You go on ahead. Good luck, baby!' He turns to walk away then adds, with a disenchanted shrug, 'Oh, right! You're not my baby.' He does not look back.

I return to the queue, clutching the numbered card in my hand and give an ironic smile. This single ticket no longer fills me with dread. It's a symbol of my authenticity, my self-reliance and courage. It says there is hope. That I can fly solo. And I will soar.

PART THREE

PART THREE

53

'It's better you found out sooner rather than later,' Benedict says. 'Painful though that may be.'

'Actually,' I sob, 'it's not that painful. I've learnt that I'm stronger than I imagined.'

'So I see,' he says, handing me a Kleenex. 'This is what I call a good show of strength.'

I cry-laugh into the tissue. 'To be honest, I think my parents are the most disappointed.'

'I don't think this is about your parents, though, is it?'

'They seem to think it is.'

He retracts his chin, trying to stifle his amusement. 'I think they'll get over it.'

We walk further along the towpath. 'The thing is,' I sniffle, 'I'm not crying for me or for Jack. I'm grieving for the babies I'll never have.'

He puts his hand on my shoulder and pulls me into his body as my leg kicks out to the side, trying to maintain my balance.

'Never say never,' he says. 'With apologies for the cliché.'

I look up at him, knowing that half my mascara is streaking down my cheeks. 'Actually, I made an appointment with the fertility clinic today.'

He looks at me, surprised in a delighted way, and we stop in front of a graffiti-covered wall that says 'Fucking Cool'.

'Oh, wow, Daisy,' he says. 'I know the strength it must have taken for you to do that. Good for you.'

'Then I called back and cancelled.' I feel the warm tears trickle out of the inner corners of my eyes and down my nose and blot them.

He fiddles in his pocket and fishes out another Kleenex and takes away my wet disintegrating one, which he puts in his opposite pocket.

'Don't forget to take that out,' I sob, 'before you take your jacket to the dry cleaner.'

His body shakes with contained laughter. 'I love that you can be both sad and practical,' he says, and I'm grateful that he sees it that way. 'So why did you cancel?'

I puff out my breath. 'I can't do it, Benedict,' I say, wiping my nose. 'I needed to book the appointment. Like a test. To prove something to myself. To see if I could move forward with it. And I can't. I failed. And now I'll never be a mother.'

I sob into his jacket and he lets me, even though I know I'm going to leave horrible black marks, which I feel bad about because I'm sad and practical. 'Why am I always ugly-crying when I'm with you?' I say, pulling back.

He laughs. 'Is there pretty-crying?'

'Meg Ryan pretty-cries.'

That laugh again. I like it when he laughs. 'She has better lighting. Anyway, you're not always ugly-crying. In fact most of the time I'd say you're smiling. Or laughing.'

'You're just being nice.'

'You're just being sad.'

We start to walk again and I feel better for being with him, better for being outside in the fresh air, better for talking. 'Thanks for agreeing to see me,' I say.

'You make it sound like an appointment.'

'I don't mean to.' I pause. 'It's just . . . I like talking to you. I know that what we say to each other stays with each other.'

'Chatham House rules.'

'Is that what it means?' He nods. I laugh, which comes out like a hiccup. 'Yeah. We're so Chatham House.'

He slips my arm through his and I lock myself to him. 'I enjoy talking to you too, Daisy. I'm not the greatest talker but you somehow manage to bring me out of myself. And that's a good thing.'

I turn to look at him. 'Even with the crying?'

'Even with the crying.'

'When I've stained the lapel of your jacket?'

He looks down at his jacket and brushes it, then rubs a bit harder but the black mark doesn't shift.

'I have my limits,' he says, and scowls at me theatrically, then switches to a broad grin because he can be both pissed off and happy. 'Fancy an ice cream?'

'That would be nice.'

He goes for his reliable stracciatella and mint. This time I choose quickly. Pistachio and salted caramel.

'Well done!' he says. 'That was no mean feat.'

We continue along the towpath and I tell him about how Jack seemed to be two different people. So charming and lovely when he was trying to woo me in Whitstable, so arrogant and smug once he'd assumed he'd won me back. 'He had this obnoxious swagger about him. He was so self-aggrandizing. He wouldn't even let me speak for myself.'

'Success. Power. Money. They're a potent mix. Maybe he's just finding his way around them.'

A young man passes wearing a baby carrier. We can see the baby's head peeping out of the top. I sense Benedict's tension. 'It's okay,' I say. 'I can't afford to be that sensitive.'

'So you weren't in the least bit tempted?' he asks. 'To hang on in there for the sake of a baby?'

My jaw drops at his suggestion. 'Sure I want a family but I want it to be with the right person.'

'Don't act so surprised. A lot of women might have gone for the financial security, and who could blame them?'

'You don't mean that?'

'It's true, though, isn't it?'

I exhale at the flash of memory. 'I was surrounded by those women. Not my tribe at all. I don't need gazillions. I'm happy with enough.'

He smiles. 'And how much is enough?'

I lick around the cornet catching the melting drips of *gelato*. 'I don't know if there's a number to put on it,' I say. 'I just want to be able to have a nice life, be self-sufficient, buy myself choice. You know . . . be able to afford a better apartment at some point, go on nice holidays, enjoy dinners with friends and, if I get lucky, have a baby.' My heart jolts with the weight of hopelessness. 'What about you? Are you aiming for trillions?'

'Bit late for that.' He finishes his ice cream, right to the end, not throwing away the soggy bottom. 'No, I'm like you. As long as I can be comfortable, as long as I can keep a roof over my head, help others in greater need keep a roof over theirs, that'll be just fine.'

'Yes, of course. Helping others is a good intention.' There he goes, impressing me again.

Further along he says, 'But what if Jack's idea of enough is gazillions? Why are we any better than him?'

I stop and look at him as he waits for my riposte. 'We're not better. We just have different values. And I prefer ours!' I laugh at how that sounds. 'You should have been there. Seen those people. I don't think anything would be enough for them. When you get to that stage, what else is there to aim for except more?'

'But at least they give it away too.'

'Pah! Giving it away is easy. I watched them at the

auction. It was all about showing off under the pretence of charity.'

'But don't you see?' he says, 'For them that's not showing off. They're among their own, their tribe as you say. For them it's standard practice. You just see it differently—'

'Because I don't fit, right?'

He nods. 'Maybe.'

'And I'll never fit. When I said that to Jack he was shocked. Didn't believe me. But I just knew.' I take in a staggered breath. 'I wanted not to know. I wanted so badly for us to work, but it was visceral.'

I bite the bottom of the cornet and tip my head back, sucking out the ice cream, making a gurgling-drain noise.

'Am I now in the privileged position of being allowed to enjoy all your disgusting habits?'

I put my hand over my mouth and chuckle. 'Sorry. I forgot myself.'

'My work is done,' he says.

54

The apartment on Mount Street is on the third floor of an old red-brick building above some high-end boutiques. There was a time when living over the shops was frowned upon. I don't think anyone would be frowning on these.

The black-and-white marble chequered floor runs through the entrance hall leading to the lift, which dates back to the early twentieth century. The car sits within a bronze cage shaft that rises through the centre of the building. You can see the pulley ropes and antique weights in action as they crank the car up and down. It's a wonder they keep going but they do.

Oscar Tudor Moss greets me at the second floor, drawing back the manual gate of the lift. 'So good to see you, we're very excited about the progress.' We walk through into the hall, the reliable musky smell of the Le Labo candle they always leave burning masking the smell of paint and dust.

Oscar is tall and sophisticated, carrying himself with a languorous ease. He is immaculately presented, as always, today in taupe linen trousers, a subtly striped shirt and monogrammed velvet slippers. Thick ebony hair sits glossily just above his shoulders, falling into curtains in a kind of man bob, his chin sporting a permanent five o'clock shadow even though I imagine he's as clean-shaven as he ever can be.

His wife, Portia, is beautiful. She used to be a model.

You'd know that because of the way she glides through rooms. Both Oscar and Portia wear the same floral perfume and it glides with them. The flat is filled with layer upon layer of scent. They are quite bohemian in their taste, sending me into new territory, challenging my thinking, which, at a time when I need to be diverted from my own personal woes, has been extremely helpful.

'Daisy! Our lovely Daisy!' Portia wanders in, her long wavy mid-brown hair tied up in a silk scarf, wearing a light flesh-coloured silk kimono dress with pink detailing, a loosely tied pink belt. 'Latte?'

I smile. 'That would be great, thanks.'

We go into the kitchen, which is practically finished, its dark units set against arabescato marble worktops. It looks stunning. Portia busies herself around the swanky Italian coffee machine, which puffs and spits and gurgles out the smoothest coffee imaginable. She puts a metal jug of milk under the steam spout and zhuzhes, like a professional, then sets down an oversized delicately painted china cup in front of me, full to the brim of thick, creamy froth.

'I don't know how you do this,' I say, 'but I'm very glad you do.' I think of the coffee machine I was so keen to reclaim from Jack, which sits in my kitchen, redundant, the point-scoring once so important now so trivial.

She laughs.

They wanted this vast kitchen completed first so that they had a haven to relax in while the rest of the refurbishment continued. It started out as a poky parlour with sixties units, doors hanging off hinges; the entire place had been unloved for a very long time. Fortunately their architect had got planning permission to knock through into what was once a massive formal dining room. The space is now unrecognizable.

We sit at the island on temporary stools. The new ones, kilim-covered seats on ebony legs, are being made bespoke and won't be delivered until the work is finished to avoid gathering dust and being damaged by workmen passing through. They have a lot of beautiful inherited pieces in storage, which I've seen in order to know how to accommodate them, to know what to build around, but in the meantime, an old sofa sits under the window, covered with embroidered silk throws. I'd almost be tempted for them to keep it but they say it's seen better days and they're ready for something different. For the purpose, I have sourced a huge L-shaped sofa, which is being upholstered in a beautiful wine-red velvet, with cushions covered in different fabrics, including vintage silks and more kilim, some with trims. It will all come together to create something sophisticated, boho and fabulous. Exactly like them.

Portia passes Oscar his coffee and he sits down beside me. She joins us with a green tea. I wish I could love green tea – she makes it look like it must do wonders. I pull out all the new swatches for the flooring. They originally wanted reclaimed parquet throughout, matching the existing parquet that is restorable and worth keeping, until Oscar saw some leather flooring at a club somewhere, thought it looked beautiful, took a photo and asked me to source similar for his office.

'This is the full range of skins and colours,' I say. 'It's cork-backed so it's pretty waterproof – although you wouldn't want to drench it – and it can be laid anywhere.' I hand over the eight swatches.

'So it could go in the bathroom?' says Oscar, with a delighted smile.

I nod. 'If that's what you want, unless you're heavy splashers.'

'Great, eh, Porsh? What do you think?'

'Lovely,' she says. 'But, thinking of the splashing, you know . . .'

'Tell Daisy,' he says.

She blushes and her face breaks into a massive grin. 'We have good news.'

'Oh?' I say. They leave me hanging, looking from one to the other. I push my face forward as a kind of nudge.

'We're pregnant,' she says.

My stomach does a somersault. I take a beat. 'Congratulations!' I say, sounding slightly strangulated, the news of another pregnancy like a slap in the face with a wet towel. I smile excitedly, clapping my hands, like a drunken seal. They look at each other, glowing, and I know they're too immersed in their own joy to care about my artlessly hidden angst.

'It's totally unexpected,' says Oscar. He reaches towards Portia and envelops her elegant hand in his. 'We didn't think we could get pregnant.'

My ears prick up.

'I've had several failed attempts at IVF,' she says, her eyes turning wistful. 'Too many miscarriages. No way did I think it would ever happen naturally.'

'I'm so thrilled for you,' I say. 'A miracle baby. How have you been?'

'So sick,' she says, and they grimace, as though Oscar has been sick too.

It occurs to me that 'we are pregnant' is an odd expression. The woman is pregnant. The woman gives birth. I'm not sure 'we' are pregnant. I mean, what does the man do other than participate in the pleasure of conception? When he gets to share the pain, then we should say 'we are pregnant'.

'I'm amazed you've never noticed,' says Portia. 'I think I've looked like the living dead for months.'

'You could never look like the living dead,' I say, enthused by their success, trying to temper my kneejerk envy, which seems so hard to control.

'I'm twenty-five weeks,' she says, before I've dared ask.

'So you're on the home run?' I smile.

'Who knows? I can't take anything for granted.'

'I'm sure it's not easy.'

She looks at me like she's weighing up her next move. 'We're only telling you now because . . .' she turns to Oscar '. . . even while being cautious, we'd like to take the leap and ask you to redesign the third bedroom as a nursery.' Her face switches between a grin and a frown as she tries to keep her excitement in check. 'We want to keep it quiet from everybody else for as long as possible. It's just they constantly ask how you are, thinking they're being kind and then it's so awful telling everyone if you lose it.'

I swallow hard. 'I understand,' I say, wishing I didn't. 'I'd be delighted to design your nursery.' I would. I would. I would.

55

I'm in team Blondie. There are six tables of six. The others are Fleetwood Mac, Roxy Music, ELO, the Bee Gees and Talking Heads. I'm not sure why I'm here – I'm terrible at pub quizzes – but Bee thought it was a good idea. The other people on our table are Rob, Victoria and Gina. Gina has dragged along some young single guy from her office and I'm starting to believe he's the real reason why I'm here. No one has actually said anything but it becomes pretty obvious that he has been placed deliberately next to me. And Gina keeps winking at me.

'George has just bought a new flat,' she says. 'You should get Daisy round.' WINK. 'She's a genius. Everyone should have her clever eye.'

'Great,' says George, sounding underwhelmed. I get the feeling he's already regretting accepting the invitation.

We eat before the quiz and George, who looks about twelve with a neat shaggy haircut and perfectly pressed white shirt, with black buttons, top button done up, tells me about his new flat. He's a first-time buyer and relieved to have got on the ladder. His parents helped.

'That's amazing,' I say, wondering how Gina could even imagine he was appropriate. As I watch him scoop up his peas, I want to say, 'It's a fork, not a shovel.'

When he goes to the loo, Gina says, 'George is lovely, isn't he?'

'Lovely,' I say. 'Does his mother know he's out?'

Rob and Bee burst into hysterics.

'What were you thinking?' says Victoria.

Gina scowls. 'I just thought it was worth a try,' she says, somewhat disgruntled. 'You should give him a chance, Daisy. Honestly, he's a really nice guy.'

George returns to the table and we sit drinking, waiting for the first round of questions.

'Have you heard of Blondie, George?' I say. 'Bee's mother was obsessed with her, which is the only reason I know her music.'

'My mother thought she looked like her,' says Bee.

'Your mother was a looker then,' says Rob.

'Still is,' says Bee, meaningfully.

'Sure I've heard of her,' says George. 'Lascaux covered "One Way Or Another". Epic!' he says.

I glance back at Bee, who gives me her boss-eyed look. Victoria nudges me. 'Be nice.'

When the questions start, we behave like we're on *University Challenge*, all desperate to prove our proficiency, including me. We forget ourselves and as soon as one of us gets the right answer we stand up and do a kind of punch-the-air jig. By contrast, when George gets a correct answer, and he seems to get more correct answers than the rest of us put together, he stays calmly in his seat. What is it about young people, these days? They're so adult.

George turns out to be very useful if you want to win a pub quiz. We stare proudly at our prize pens and winner coasters.

'Well, George, what would we have done without you?' says Gina.

'Glad I could help,' he says. He coughs awkwardly. 'Do you mind if I . . .?'

'Sure. See you tomorrow,' she says.

When he's gone, she says, 'Sorry, Daise. Probably not for you.'

'Yeah, well,' I say. 'Thanks for trying. You may choose not to believe this but actually I'm okay on my own.'

'For now,' says Bee.

'For as long as I'm happy to be,' I reply.

56

Several silver-and-pink helium balloons float over the metal bedstead shouting, 'It's a Girl!'. There are fresh flowers and cards everywhere. The air is heavy with scent.

'A girl! A girl! Can you believe it?' says Doug, as if we need any more notification.

Eve looks exhausted, despite the glow of the balloons, sitting up in her hospital bed, wearing too much blusher, too hastily applied, a hint at her state of mind. I'm not sure having our entire family occupying the room is helping. It's warm and muggy. All of our cheeks are colouring.

'We're so thrilled,' my mother says. 'She's beautiful.' She's taken immediate possession of her new granddaughter, rocking her in her arms. 'Coo coo,' she says. 'Coo coo, darling.'

'She's not a bird, Grandma,' says Monty, who's sitting on my father's lap.

'Fancy a cuddle?' says my brother, looking at me.

'Yes, please!' I hold my arms open and my mother passes me the tiny pink bundle, letting go cautiously. 'I've got her,' I say.

She smells of newborn, like biscuity powder. Doug grabs his iPhone. 'Smile!' he says.

I sense my mother watching me. I know she can tell my smile is forced, that she can feel the ache in my heart as though it's hers.

My brother shows me the photo. 'I'll send it to you.'

'Thanks.'

'Show me,' says my mother. 'Lovely.' She smiles. 'Send it to me too.'

My father plays with Monty, who giggles as he produces a penny from behind his ear. 'How do you do that, Grandpa?'

'It's magic,' he says.

Eddie tugs my arm. 'I want to hold her again.'

'It's Auntie Daisy's turn,' says Doug.

'It's fine,' I say. 'Perhaps you should sit down on the bed, Eddie, and I'll pass her to you.'

He climbs onto the bed and crosses his legs. Eve's face betrays a moment's discomfort. 'Sit still, Eddie,' she says. 'No bouncing.'

'Sorry, Eve,' I say. 'Wasn't thinking.'

I place the baby gently in his lap and he looks on with total adoration. 'Will she break if I drop her?'

'Try not to drop her,' says Doug, and Monty says, 'You're so stupid, Eddie.'

Monty jumps off my father's lap and comes over to inspect. 'She's boring,' he says. 'She'll never play football.'

'Yes, she will,' says Eddie. 'She'll be even better than you.'

'Hear, hear,' says Eve. She looks at Doug. 'See! We've produced a feminist.'

I sit down on the arm of my father's chair. I prod at his lip. 'Where did it go?'

'Went to the barber,' he says. 'Fancied a change. I'll see how I feel about it.'

'It suits you,' I say. 'I've never seen your top lip before.'

'Looks odd to me,' says my mother. 'When are you coming home, Eve?'

'Tomorrow, I think.'

'I want you to come home now,' says Eddie.

'I don't!' says Monty. 'We'll stop having pizza and McDonald's!'

'Oh,' says Eddie, his face registering the mistake.

'Doug!' says Eve.

'Thanks, guys,' says Doug. 'I told you that was our secret.'

'We don't have secrets,' says Eve. 'Do we, boys?'

'It would seem not,' says Doug.

'Do you have a name?' I ask.

'Not yet,' says Eve. 'We want to see what she looks like once her newborn face settles down.'

'I want to call her Elsa,' says Eddie. 'Then I can dress her up in my Elsa outfit.'

Monty laughs. 'I want to call her Messi.'

'That's not nice,' says Eve.

'He means the footballer,' says Doug.

'We're not calling her that,' says my mother.

Monty, hands on his hips, looks back at her. 'We'll be the ones to decide, Grandma!'

I try to contain my amusement, as Eve sinks slowly under the covers.

57

For once recording my melancholy thoughts in my journal is not helping. I can't shift this sadness.

I pick up the phone and he answers. 'You know the couple I'm working with in Mayfair.'

'Oscar and Portia?'

'Right. I didn't mention it before but they're pregnant. Kind of unexpected although they've been trying for quite some time.'

'I see.'

'And my brother had his baby the other day. A girl,' I say.

'Congratulations!'

'Thank you.'

The moment is heavy with an ominous silence.

'Daisy?' he says. 'Are you okay?'

'Are you busy?'

I hear Benedict shut down his computer. 'I'm on my way,' he says.

* * *

I attempt to organize my face so that it's not too puffy. Put cold spoons against my eyes, look at myself and give up.

The doorbell rings. He's standing there with flowers and a bottle of wine.

'My favourite garage,' I say. 'You shouldn't have.' I sob into his shoulder. 'Sorry.'

'I came prepared. It's the same jacket.'

'I'm not wearing make-up,' I say.

'But you're very, very snotty.'

I laugh through a snivel.

He hangs up his linen jacket and we walk into the sitting room. I put the flowers into a jug of water, not bothering to cut the stems, emitting the occasional uncontrollable whimper and he pours the wine. We sit down side by side.

'Fuck it!' I say, holding up my glass.

'Fuck it!' he says, and we clink. He puts his arm around me and I curl into him, swinging my bare feet up onto the sofa.

As we drink the wine, I fill him in on Oscar and Portia.

'Well, that should give you hope,' he says.

'It does. And it doesn't.'

I tell him about my visit to the hospital, that I'm genuinely thrilled for Doug and Eve but that it doesn't stop the morose feelings that strangulate my throat as soon as I leave. He takes my hand and nods, like he understands. I tell him about holding the baby, about the photographs, and my mother looking at me with concern, which makes me feel worse, about the boys and their thoughts on names and he laughs as he listens.

'Why won't you start dating again?' he says. 'Surely that's some kind of solution.'

'Is it, though? By the time I find "the one", supposing he exists, it will be too late for babies. I don't need to date for the sake of it.'

'And yet you told me I had to!'

'Did you?'

'No!' he says, affronted.

'Oh, God!' I sigh. 'What am I going to do? I can't be miserable for the rest of my life. I have to find a way forward.'

He refills our glasses. 'All right,' he says. 'If you're that set against dating, I may have a possible solution.' He lays his arm across the back of the sofa and taps the cushion. 'I've been thinking about you. But this is merely a suggestion. Something for you to consider. I don't want to frighten you off.'

I hold him in my gaze, intrigued. 'Is it that scary?'

'Maybe.' He clears his throat, raises his left eyebrow. 'I wondered whether you would entertain the idea of allowing me to be your donor.'

I practically drop my glass.

'Quite scary, then,' he says, with a snort.

I ask him if I heard correctly and he repeats it. 'Is this . . . like a pity thing?' I say. 'Because, if it is, I'm sorry. I've been wrong to burden you with my misery.'

He smiles benignly. 'No, Daisy. Absolutely not,' he says. 'You've never burdened me. We share our sadness. That takes trust. I want to do something to help you out of your sadness, the way you've helped me.'

'I wasn't expecting you to do anything in return, Benedict.'

'I know.'

'We just talk. That helps me. For me that's already huge.'

'We don't need to pursue this,' he says, 'if it makes you feel uncomfortable.'

'I don't feel uncomfortable.' He looks at me as if he's not convinced. 'But I don't want you to feel uncomfortable either.'

'I wouldn't have mentioned it.'

'Oh, gosh,' I say, and put down my wine. 'This is a very big gesture.'

He sits forward, turning into the room, scratching the

side of his neck, clasping his hands, his long fingers interlaced. 'Do you want to discuss it? Is it worth my explaining my thinking?'

'Please.'

He inhales, then releases his breath. 'Okay . . . As I understand it, and forgive me if I'm wrong, the thing that has been holding you back from the IVF process is not just the fear of it going wrong . . . but equally the fear of going through it on your own.' He looks back at me.

'Maybe,' I say.

'I thought if I could be your emotional support then perhaps it wouldn't be so daunting. And . . . and this is random, of course, because I'm no scientist . . . I wondered if using a different method might produce a different result.'

I find myself sitting cross-legged, held by the natural flow of his words, his sense of clarity, the fact he's genuinely thought this through.

'So you become my emotional support and my donor?'

'Yes.'

We stare at one another and I look at him with newfound wonder. I like him. I trust him. I lean on him. But this?

Would I? Why would I? Could I? Why couldn't I?

'Do you want a baby?' I say.

He scoffs in a way that says he's asked himself the same question a thousand times. 'No,' he says. 'Not in the conventional sense. Not in the everyday, longing way that you want a baby.'

'In what way, then?'

He raises his shoulders. 'In whatever way works between us. I think for me, wanting a baby was an expectation that disappeared when I met Lisa. Now, though, being around you, there's a part of me that's been renewed.' He takes a sip of wine. 'I've revisited my original thoughts on children but from the perspective of an older man. Being candid, I have neither the time nor the inclination, let alone the years, to be a hands-on father. My thinking is, if you agree and it works, my involvement would be purely from the sidelines. I'm there for you if you need me. But it would make me immensely happy to make you happy. Win-win.'

'My anonymous donor with benefits.'

He chuckles but his eyes remain serious. 'That's one way of putting it. It allows you to be a solo mother, the mother you want to be, without any outside influence, least of all from someone entirely unqualified.'

'We're none of us qualified, Benedict.'

He nods, cogitating. 'True.'

I tuck myself into the corner of the sofa, grabbing my knees into my chest, bewildered, excited, finding myself drawn into this possibility, bizarre and unexpected though it is. 'So what if I do get pregnant? You genuinely don't want to be involved at all other than if called upon? You don't want to be known as the baby's father? I mean, I know this is all hypothetical but we would need to work it out, right? And you're my friend. I want you in my life. Won't it be odd being a mere spectator?'

'Possibly. But I have huge self-discipline. It's how I've survived the turbulence of my life.' He leans forward and looks me in the eye. 'Honestly . . .' He pauses. 'I've dug deep into my soul because I need to be candid with myself as well as you. For me this is Chatham House. Entirely between us. It reflects the very nature of our relationship. I don't need anyone to know I'm the father. I don't want people questioning your judgement. Asking what my intentions are. Why him? He's twenty years older. Casting aspersions. Worrying you because, no matter how defiant you may feel,

I know you worry about other people's opinions. This way, if it works, when it works, what could be more important than our understanding of what exists between us? And you having that longed-for baby.'

I smile. 'Chatham House rules, then?'

He gestures for me to place my hand in his. 'This is about our rules. Yours and mine. It's about trust and respect. You can tell people however you want to tell them, whenever. But I think it's healthier, better, that I remain anonymous.'

I move towards him, looking directly into his open face. 'This is the most beautiful gift anyone's ever offered me.'

'I hope that's not true, Daisy.'

It is, I think.

We sit in silence.

'Listen,' he says. 'It's not totally altruistic. There is one thing that appeals to me . . . for me.'

'And what is that?' My mind rushes around wondering what might appeal to him. The materialization of his genes? The sense of heroism?

He plays with my fingers. 'I'm too old for full-time fatherhood. Too tied to my work. Is that awful?'

'It never put Rod Stewart off.'

'But I'd like to leave a bigger legacy other than a few interesting buildings. There's something rather reassuring in knowing your genes won't die with you.'

I smile, nodding. 'I hear you,' I say. 'It's beginning to make a sort of sense.' I'm captivated, revved up. 'But what if it doesn't work?'

'Then we've given it our best shot.'

'Yes, but maybe I'll become even more morose?'

He takes a gulp of wine. 'That's up to you, Daisy. You're the only one in charge of your emotions. But may I remind you that you were the one who pushed me out of my grief. I could have sleepwalked through the rest of my days, merely existing, if you hadn't nudged and cajoled me to wake up. So you might have to nudge and cajole yourself. With a little bit of help from your friends. I include myself in that. And you have to move on. To re-engage in life the way you made me re-engage. You've changed my world, Daisy. I was concreted in sadness and you made me break free. Now I want to help you.'

I practically throw myself at him. He swiftly holds his glass out, avoiding my impact. 'Fuck, Benedict. Fuck! You are the best friend a woman could ever hope for.' I pull back, gripping his arms. 'What if I say yes? You're really sure? You're not going to change your mind? I mean, tell me this really isn't just a pity moment?' I'm shaking him by the shoulders. 'Tell me!'

He smiles calmly. 'This is not about pity, Daisy. This is about looking forward, walking towards hope. I don't think it's the most straightforward arrangement in the world but I have faith that you and I will navigate through it. And come out the other side even stronger.'

'With or without a baby.'

'Exactly.' He smiles. 'That's the best way to look at it.'

58

I'm sitting in the office, listening to Marcus, my mind replaying the conversation between Benedict and me over and over. I'm almost giddy with excitement at the prospect of hope. At the possibility of another chance, one that feels so much less lonely. I can't believe this man has come into my life and taken on such a significant role. I'm becoming more and more certain that I want to commit.

'What do you think about this for carpet?' continues Marcus. 'I mean, I hate carpet but the client is determined. They don't want pattern, just plain. So, under the circs, I think this is the best carpet non-carpet I can find.'

He hands me the swatch.

'And they don't want coir or sisal?'

He screws up his face. 'It has to be carpet. To be fair, it's only for the bedrooms.'

'I had to put carpets in the bedrooms in Peckham. They looked good. I mean it wouldn't have been my choice but, you know . . .' I feel the pile, stroke it in every direction. Hold it up to the light. 'Is it expensive? It feels quite luxurious.'

'It's a good price.'

'Then I think you've done amazingly well.' I hand it back to him and he checks the reference on the back, making a note on his computer.

'They're putting leather flooring in the main bedroom

and en suite at Mayfair. It started as an idea for the office but it's grown.' I wave my arms in a huge circle.

'Seriously?'

I smile. 'Yeah. It's going to be beautiful!'

He pushes back his chair, places his hands behind his neck. There are tiny half-moon patches of sweat under his armpits. 'I'm dead jealous you're working there. I could fancy a bit of Mayfair.'

'You'll have to come and see it when it's done.'

'I'd love that. I never saw Peckham. I have to check our Instagram account to see what you're up to.'

'Likewise!'

'It's not the same seeing it in photos. Although it looked FAB-U-LOUS.'

I laugh. 'Thanks, Craig. A rare ten?'

'Nope. It's a nine.'

'Damn. And I thought I'd done a perfect cha-cha-cha.'

'I think you excelled when you were solo. Not so good in hold.'

I laugh. 'Oh, yeah? And who was I in hold with?'

'Shaw, of course.'

I laugh awkwardly. 'Of course. Although by the end we were dancing a lot better together.'

'I've noticed,' he says, with a sly smirk.

'I like him,' I say dismissively. 'He's become a good friend.'

'That's fortunate. Because he's an excellent architect. He may be useful.'

I try not to react.

59

*I swear that everywhere I look there are pregnant
women. Everywhere! It makes me edgy with
excitement. I want to go up to them and ask how
they did it. Naturally? In a Petri dish? With a
donor? Anonymous? A friend? I'll say I'm carrying
out a survey. 'I hope you don't mind my asking
but . . .'*

*I'm not going to discuss what I'm about to do with
anyone, not even my closest friends, least of all my
family, which is probably what prompts this desire to
intrude on other people's intimate lives. Obviously if I
get to twelve weeks I'll be singing from the rooftops,
or maybe fourteen weeks, to be safe, but the name
Benedict will not be mentioned. Our rules. Maybe
this is how things will work for a lot of people in
the future. Women who want to have babies but
don't necessarily need to be with a full-time partner.
Who's to say we'll be any less a parent for not being
two? I read an article the other day which quoted
a maternity nurse who said that children need two
things: 'Discipline and love.' She never said they
needed two parents.*

*Tomorrow is the beginning of the middle of my
cycle. That's prime time. Benedict and I have agreed
to go for three attempts in a row. It makes sense. If*

we were having sex, doing it a few times mid-cycle
allegedly increases the odds so why not the same with
a syringe?

I put down my journal and look around my bedroom. How ironic. I thought I'd be here for a short time, say six months, and look at me. I'm still here. I'm part of the fabric of this building. Mr Henderson and I speak regularly in the hallway for longer than ten seconds. We don't just talk about the weather. We go as far as telling each other when we're going out and when we think we'll be back. He's actually rather lovely. I wonder why he's alone. Is he a widower? Was he always a bachelor? We're not so close I can ask that kind of question yet.

I pick up my phone and log into the pregnancy calendar. Again. As though it might have changed since the last time I looked but somehow I need to peer at the dates to believe I'm doing this. Okay, so if it works, and let's think positive, the baby would be due at the end of January. Aquarius. A water sign. According to a Google site Aquarians are advanced, self-reliant, clever, exceptional and optimistic. I think these are all wonderful attributes to have in this constantly changing world, which, should I get pregnant, may be run by robots when my child reaches eighteen. I write that down.

I want it to be tomorrow night now. To be honest
I want to get the first try out of the way. There's
no doubt it's going to be awkward. But the second
night will be easier and the third should be a breeze.
Benedict asked if I wanted to stay over but I told him
I'd prefer to come home. I might want to spend the
evening with my legs in the air.

333

I laugh to myself. I look at the pages. I'm deep into my third book. I have never looked back over what I've written. When I've finished this one, I'll put the set away somewhere safe, hopefully not in this bedside table, and write where exactly I've put them in the next book, for fear of forgetting. Then, say in five years' time, I'll take them all out and either burn them or read about myself, to rediscover who I was when I turned forty, when I thought my life was over.

60

'You'll be wanting these.' Benedict passes me an envelope. I make a questioning face. 'Copies of my test results,' he says. 'You should keep them somewhere safe.'

I smile, relieved. Not quite sure what I was expecting. 'Thanks,' I say. 'For doing that. Sounded like a lot of faff.'

He tops up my glass of filtered water. 'Had to be done . . . So? Are you sure you're ready for this? Do you want to talk about it any more? Any concerns, any doubts?'

'No, thanks. I'm all talked out. I'm completely committed. What about you?'

'Committed.'

'And it's the perfect moment in my cycle. Talk for too long and we could miss it.'

'Let's not miss it.'

He leads the way upstairs. I feel odd. Awkward. As though I'm trespassing on Lisa's territory. As we pass the window on the landing, there's a framed wedding photo and there she is. She's tall, and slender, long blonde hair. I don't know why I'd imagined her to be a brunette. She's wearing a full-length frothy white gown with big puff sleeves, very much the fashion in the eighties. Benedict is in a grey morning suit. They make a very handsome couple. I wonder whether to say anything, like *You were a handsome couple*, but decide that now is not necessarily the time.

'Right!' he says. 'This is your bedroom. There's an

en-suite so you can do . . . erm whatever you need to do. I've left a towel on the bed with the syringe.' He coughs, cupping his hand in front of his mouth.

'Thank you,' I say.

'I'll be in there.' He points to a door: the master bedroom and en-suite.

'Good luck,' I say. 'With whatever you need to do.' I'm trying desperately hard not to look embarrassed.

'Let's not . . .' He ahems. 'I'll knock when it's ready.'

'Yes, please.'

'This is really awkward,' he says.

'I don't know what you mean.'

Once he's shut the door, I wander round the room, checking out the asymmetrical print that hangs above the bed in a large matt-black frame. I like his taste even though he's not that keen on mine. I throw myself onto the mattress and make a snow angel then push myself up with my elbows to the wooden headboard. The pillows are soft as anything. Goose down, for certain. They're all-enveloping. Part of me would simply like to fall asleep, woken by a prince's kiss and handed a baby.

'Oh, my God, oh, my God, oh, my God.' I giggle nervously. I don't know where to start. What I'm meant to do. I stare at the syringe, then break it free from the blister packet. Practise moving the plunger up and down.

I wriggle out of my knickers, placing them neatly to one side. No knickers while still fully dressed feels strangely sexy. But this couldn't be further from sexy.

I sit up and wait, drumming my fingers on my thigh, then the bedside table. Looking around. Wondering what they used this room for. Guests, I suppose. His parents. Her parents. I wonder if any of them are still alive.

There's a tentative knock.

I straighten my skirt, covering my knees. 'Ready.'

A disembodied hand appears, clutching a cup.

'I'll just pass it round the door. I can't look at you!'

I jump up and take it from him, trying not to fumble, trying not to laugh for his sake, he's so embarrassed. I'm embarrassed.

'Thanks,' I say.

'Good luck,' says the disembodied voice, as the disembodied hand quickly disappears.

I look at the cup now safely sitting on the bedside table trying not to think about its contents. My heart is in overdrive. My hand shakes as I put in the syringe and draw up the viscous fluid, watching it rise through the barrel to just over half full. Just past three millilitres. Is that good? Does Benedict know he's a three-millilitre man? Oh, my God! What am I thinking? I waggle my tongue in disgust.

I lie back, faff around trying to find my vagina, wet my fingers hoping saliva doesn't interfere. I should have brought my Rabbit. Tomorrow night. I could have brought lube but something in it might have messed with the process. I'm not taking any chances. I slip in the syringe, meeting a bit of resistance, then give it more of a push, getting it as deep as seems possible and push the plunger. I try to think positively, not to cringe at the indignity. If all goes well, there are a lot worse indignities to come.

I wait for a few moments, letting my heartbeat settle, and pull out the syringe. I have no idea if this is apocryphal or proven but I swing my legs up in the air, keeping my hips steady with my hands and hold myself there for as long as possible.

* * *

When I go downstairs, Benedict is making tea in the kitchen.

'Please, sir,' I say, holding out the cup and the syringe, 'may I have some more?'

I look at him. His trembling mouth gives way.

We know we have no choice.

The two of us break into fits of laughter, me holding onto my stomach, Benedict holding onto the kitchen worktop.

'Stop,' I say. 'I'll lose it all.'

'I can't,' he says, laughing-crying. 'It's the weirdest, oddest, funniest thing that's happened to me in my entire life.'

'And we're going to do it all over again tomorrow! And the next day.'

'It won't be so funny by then,' he says.

61

Bee walks into the office. 'Evening, all!' she says.

'Evening!'

Marcus and I start to tidy our desks, getting ready to leave.

'Before we go out,' says Bee, 'can I just play with your books and swatches for a bit? I love wading through this stuff and dreaming about the home I'm never going to have.'

'Go ahead,' I say. 'Dream as long as you like. You've got five minutes!'

Sometimes it's useful seeing your world through other people's eyes. What has become quotidian and mundane gleams again when someone else shines their excitement over it. It's the same sometimes with work projects. You work on them for so long you forget what the space used to look like and can no longer see the incredible transformation you've created. Then the client walks in, gasps and gets excited, wows and sometimes even punches the air, and you see it through their eyes and know you've done a good job.

Marcus puts a file into his briefcase.

'Working from home tonight?' I say.

'No. Early site visit tomorrow morning.'

'Oooh. No hangover for you, then.'

'I'd rather not.'

'Me neither,' I say, knowing I won't be drinking at all.

'Spoilsports,' says Bee. 'Oh, my God! This wallpaper is fabulous!'

I look at the book she's flipping through. She's gazing at a huge floral on a black background. 'Yeah, they've done a really great job this year,' I say. 'They've upped their game. They had to. They'd stagnated for a while.'

Marcus agrees. 'Ready when you are,' he says, and throws on his jacket.

At the pub, we find a table and Marcus says it's his round. 'What can I get you?'

'G-and-T,' says Bee.

'What are you on tonight, Daise. Wine? Negroni?' he asks.

'Lime soda, please. I've got an early start tomorrow as well.'

He does a double-take. 'Come on. Just one real drink before you move onto the lime sodas? I'm having a G-and-T too. Have one!'

'Honestly, I'm good,' I say.

When he goes to the bar, Bee says, 'Is there something you don't want to tell us?'

I raise my eyebrows suggestively. 'I am going to tell you, actually, but only you two. Strictly between us.' I tap my nose.

Her eyes are on stalks. She grabs my hand. 'Tell me!'

'When Marcus comes back.'

Marcus puts our drinks in front of us. 'Crisps, snacks?'

'Not for me,' says Bee. 'Sit down. Daisy has something to tell us. Strictly *entre nous*. It's killing me.'

'It's been two minutes,' I say.

'What?' says Marcus.

'You have to swear on your mothers' lives you will not tell a living soul until I grant you dispensation.'

'Who are you? The Pope?'

'You're pregnant,' says Bee.

340

I smile. 'Not quite. I wasn't going to tell anyone but I feel I should tell you guys. I'm trying again.'

Their faces light up. 'Well, good for you!' says Marcus. 'We've all been hoping you'd say that for a very long time.'

'Have I been that miserable?'

'On and off,' he says, and Bee nods. 'But that's not the point. We know how important this is to you.'

Bee throws me a hug across the table. 'Well done. I know how scared you were to try again. This is big. This is brave. When do you go back to the clinic?'

I flip my hair over my shoulder and fiddle with the ends. 'I'm doing it differently this time. A different sperm donor.'

'Oh, wow!' says Bee. 'Please tell me it's not Facebook Man.'

'I'm saying nothing.'

'Oh, God, no! And you think it's going to work?' she says, trying hard not to look revolted.

'Who knows? Anyway, I think I've said enough. I don't want to feel like I'm jinxing it again. But I wanted you both to know. Because you're my besties. And Marcus would only guess anyway.'

Marcus grins at his witch-like senses. 'Thanks for sharing,' he says. 'I'm honoured to be your bestie.'

'Ditto,' says Bee. 'Be lucky, Daisy.'

* * *

Later, in bed, when Benedict and I are speaking on the phone, I let him know I've told them. 'They didn't even ask who. Bee assumes I'm using a guy on Facebook. It was easy.'

'Okay,' he says, and I hear an email ping on his computer. He genuinely never stops working. 'What about your parents?'

'That won't be so easy,' I say. 'I'll only tell them if I get pregnant. They'll definitely ask questions.'

'So how will you handle that?' he says.

'I don't know yet. I'll work it out when it happens.'

'Do you realize that's the first time you've said *when* not *if*?'

'I hope I'm not running away with myself.'

'Sweet dreams, Daisy.'

'Ditto,' I say. If you ever sleep.

62

I keep expecting my period. Checking myself all the time.
By the time I'm four days late, I'm practically apoplectic
with disbelief. Could it be possible? Can I really fall pregnant after a first attempt or three? Or am I someone who
falls pregnant easily but can't hold on to it?

Finally, I give myself permission to use one of the two
leftover pregnancy tests I've kept at the back of a shelf in
the bathroom cabinet.

I pee.

I catch it mid-stream.

I wait.

I look at the window on the stick and swallow hard.
Three glasses of water later I try the other test.

Same again. I have to sit down.

* * *

Benedict is sitting at a table by the window in the café,
wearing his thick-rimmed glasses. He looks very intellectual, reading his newspaper. I can see he's already had a
coffee.

'Hey!' I say, flapping the pages, so that he looks up. 'That
must be some very important news you're reading.'

He smiles and takes off his specs, placing them in the
glasses case that's lying next to the emptied coffee cup on

the table. 'Nothing really,' he says, 'Usual depressing non-sense.' He folds away the paper, slipping it behind him on the chair.

'You're looking very pleased with yourself,' he says.

I lean down and whisper into his ear. 'I'm pregnant,' I say, throwing him a look that says, 'Can you believe it?' By return, his look tells me he can't. 'Only just, though,' I add, as if he can't do the sums. I kiss the top of his head, his hair is softer than I expect, and sit down.

Benedict leans back in his seat. His face is still registering disbelief. 'You're sure?' he says. He rubs his chin.

'Yes,' I say. 'Seems I can get . . .' I mouth 'pregnant'. 'The worry is, can I stay . . .' I mouth it again.

He breathes out. Taps his fingers, one-two-three, on the table. 'You ready for a coffee? Or something stronger?'

'Benedict!'

'Sorry. Of course! Coffee, then?'

'Yes, please. Decaf. Thank you.'

He catches a waitress's eye, and orders for both of us. 'I really hope this one works out for you, Daisy. But I'm here for you. Whenever. You know that.'

'I do,' I say, feeling a rush of adrenaline fizzing through my body.

We stare at each other, both smiling, our eyes reflecting our amazement.

'How are you feeling?' he says.

'Honestly, no different but it's so early. I just thought you'd want to know. In case it's over in two minutes.'

He puts his hand over mine. 'Try not to think like that.'

I allow him to leave his hand there. I enjoy the fact that he's tactile. I never would have imagined it from the first Benedict I met. I never could have imagined any of this from that person. 'I'm trying not to but I need to be able to voice

344

everything to you. All my hopes and fears. You're the only person I can say everything to.'

He releases my hand with a little squeeze of acknowledgement. 'Noted.'

'It's a bit weird, isn't it?' I say.

We go silent as the coffees are put in front of us, then thank the waitress.

'Which bit?' he says, stirring his coffee.

'The fast bit.'

He plays with his spoon. 'Better that way surely.' He makes an awkward face. 'I mean, I would, of course, you know . . . again . . . but I'm glad not to have to.'

'For sure.' I smile, revisiting those awkward moments in his house, which, even though they became easier, were still awkward. 'I feel blessed. I mean, the emotional exhaustion that some women must go through every month, expecting, expecting, hoping and praying and being let down. I feel very lucky. I just don't want to be let down further along the line.'

His mouth puckers. 'It's a pretty huge emotional investment, isn't it?'

'You feel it too?'

He nods thoughtfully. 'Yes. I do. I'm as surprised about that as you. I wasn't expecting to feel like this. It's a bit like not caring about horseracing – I don't – and then you're taken to the races and you put money on a horse and suddenly you're entirely focused on it winning, and you're screaming as though your whole life depended on it.'

'Are you screaming like your whole life depended on it, then?'

'Probably not as loudly as you but in my own way, yes.'

'Would you put a bet on it?'

He scoops up some of the froth from his cappuccino with

his spoon and swallows it, looking at me across the table. 'I don't need to,' he says. 'I have faith.' He holds up his cup as though toasting me.

My body shivers. I can feel the goosebumps appear on my arms. 'Do you realize that when you say things like that, you make me want to cry?'

He looks over the rim of his cup, raising his eyebrows, his brown eyes staring back at me. 'Really? Why?'

'Because I can't believe how lucky I am to have met someone like you, that's why.'

'That's very sweet,' he says, and I feel like he's put me and my emotions back in their box.

63

The cloying summer heat isn't helping.

'You off again?' says Marcus, as I rush past him.

'Sorry, yes.'

Often it's just a feeling I'm going to be sick but nothing actually happens. I can't leave it to chance, though.

When I walk back in Marcus holds out a glass of ice-cold water.

'I don't think I dare,' I say.

'Oat cake?' he says. 'Digestive?'

'Please.'

He fetches me a plate with two oatcakes.

'You're my hero, thank you.'

Even though I obviously hate morning sickness, which sometimes has the temerity to go beyond morning, I appreciate what it represents. It makes me feel properly pregnant. Last time I had practically no symptoms other than tiredness. This time the pregnancy is quite different. I'm rigorously writing my journal, registering how I feel, good days, bad days. At the back, I jot down what I eat, to see if there's any correlation with the sickness. I listen to my body. The idea of an orange makes me want to heave. On the other hand, I have a real craving for anchovies – I must have had more anchovy pizzas in the last month than I've ever had in my entire life.

In Mayfair, I'm designing what is hopefully a truly

unique nursery for Oscar and Portia. Portia is starting to show but only just. She's so neat. I can tell by her demeanour she's relaxing into the belief that it's actually going to happen. But we don't discuss the pregnancy. When we talk through the plans, I watch her eyes brighten. That says it all.

One of the designs has a yellow-and-white-striped trompe-l'oeil tented ceiling, dropping down into wide yellow and white striped walls, a whimsical merry-go-round light, the most beautiful round white cot, which converts into a daybed for the toddler years, a lovely nursing chair covered with a tiny emerald-green-and-white spot, fun furry animal wall hangings and a carpet that looks like grass. The other designs are more traditional. Just in case they want to play it safe. She falls in love with the circus.

'I love the yellow and green,' she says. 'So good to steer away from the obvious blue and pink.'

'Let's go for it,' I say, knowing she must be approaching her due date in a matter of weeks. 'Better that it's ready.' She smiles as though she daren't allow herself to believe. Sometimes you have to let other people believe for you.

I've managed to keep my sickness at bay on site visits. Like my body knows it has to behave. Or maybe it's down to adrenaline. Or luck. I'm not ready to share this development with anyone other than the three people who already know. This time I feel less inclined to shout it from the rooftops. I don't have the same faith as Benedict. Not yet.

'I get a vicarious pleasure from hearing your stories about triple-glazed windows,' I tell him, in one of our night-time conversations.

'Oh, I know. Waiting for glass is riveting,' he says.

'It's better than stories of morning sickness.' I wipe my neck and arms with a hand towel. Then my stomach. Sweat seems to find its way into the folds of my skin. Whereas in winter the flat was freezing, now it retains the heat even with the windows wide open.

'You will tell me once you've had the scan, won't you? I'm aware it must be coming up and that it's a significant date for you so I won't ask anything. I'll wait for you to tell me.'

'But you're on standby, you know, just in case.'

'My whole life is on standby for you,' he says.

It's funny how he's picked up on what's about to happen without any mention from me. The twelve-week scan is tomorrow. I don't want to tell him yet because I don't want to think about it. I don't want to give my body the opportunity to revive the muscle memory. I want to get past this moment and tell Benedict I made it through.

Having reached peak intimacy with the exchange of sperm, having succeeded sooner than we could possibly have imagined, we had discussed what might lie ahead, going over and over the different scenarios, his involvement or lack of it, finally agreeing only to broach each stage of my pregnancy as it arrives, taking each step as it comes. The first significant one being the scan. We agreed he wouldn't come. Not to any of the scans if I get that far. I don't need him to see my jelly-covered belly. To see me lying there with a paper towel wedged in the top of my knickers.

Bee has that privilege, and Marcus. Dr Baldwin has referred me to Queen Charlotte's Hospital.

We're standing in one of the ultrasound rooms after what felt like the longest wait in the world. Particularly if you have a very full bladder – required.

We all three cry at the sound of the heartbeat. If it weren't inappropriate, I think the sonographer would be crying too, because the emotion in the room is contagious.

'I don't know what we're looking at,' says Marcus, 'but it's beautiful.'

We laugh and sob. 'Yes,' I say. 'It is a beautiful thing.'

'It's not a thing,' says the sonographer. 'It's your baby. Will you want to know the sex?'

'No!' we say as one, and we laugh.

'It's a cooperative baby,' I say. 'It's going to have a lot of parents, which is going to be interesting because, as you can tell, we all have very strong opinions. Fortunately, at the moment, we all agree.'

'Okay, good!' she says, smiling. 'I'll make a note of that for your next scan.'

Afterwards we sit at an outside table of a juice bar, enjoying the evening sunshine. Bee hands us the tube of sun cream she reliably carries in her bag for Will and we cover ourselves in what is best described as toothpaste. We have all ordered kale smoothies, an unspoken gesture of generosity towards me, like we're on some kind of nutrition trip together. We are pregnant, I think, beginning to understand.

'Are you allowed to be excited yet?' asks Bee, sipping through a straw.

'No,' I say. 'But I am. I can't help myself.'

'I like the idea of a cooperative,' she says. 'Can I include Will? Does it mean babysitters on tap? I think Rob will be relieved.'

'Is he getting bogged down with the commitment?' I ask.

'I think he's used to more freedom,' she says, 'but he's cool about it. It isn't like he's not free to do his own thing.'

'Everyone should be free to do their own thing,' says Marcus. 'That is the secret to a healthy relationship.'

'Oh, thanks for that,' I say. 'I've always wondered.'

'You're doing your own thing and you've never been happier.'

'She's in a healthy relationship with herself,' says Bee.

'Yes!' I say. 'I am. I'll take that.'

'When are you going to tell your parents?' says Marcus, who's taken the lid off his drink and is now guzzling it down in one. 'Thank God that's done,' he says, knocking his fist against his breast bone, looking like he might bring it all back up. He burps loudly. 'Pardon me,' he says, like he's six.

'I think I'll wait another couple of weeks before I tell my mum who can tell my dad. I'm not that brave!' I sip very slowly. I can taste the ginger. I convince myself this has to be doing me and my baby some good. Otherwise, what's the point? It's disgusting.

'What are you going to say when they ask the how-who questions?' says Marcus, wiping his lips ferociously, his nose turned up, still suffering on my behalf.

'I'm hoping they'll be well behaved like you guys and not ask.'

'That doesn't mean we don't want to ask,' says Bee. 'Unless it's Facebook Man.'

'I don't need to ask,' says Marcus, tapping his nose. 'I know.'

Bee looks affronted.

'He doesn't,' I say. 'He's just teasing.'

'I'm not teasing, I'm guessing. But I'm pretty certain.'

I'm intrigued to know who he's so certain about. 'Who, then?'

He hesitates. 'Do I win anything if I get it right?'

'Yeah. Another kale smoothie.'

'Let's hope I'm wrong then. It's . . .' his smirk is disconcerting '. . . Benedict Shaw.'

I feel myself jolt. I scoff, hopefully quickly enough to divert any attention away from my surprise, attempting to act revolted at the very thought. 'What on earth makes you say that?' I say, rolling my eyes.

He looks at Bee, then at me, like he hasn't fallen for my act. 'Because your eyes light up whenever you mention his name.' He winks at me.

'That's because I like him. I told you, he's become a good friend.' I'm not going to let on. Not for anything. Not even if he waterboards me. It wouldn't be fair to Benedict.

He snorts. 'We're good friends, Daise. We're your besties, and don't take this the wrong way, Bee, but . . .' he looks amused '. . . Daisy's eyes don't light up when she talks about you.'

Bee chuckles. 'Nah. Her eyes don't light up when she talks about you either.'

'I rest my case,' says Marcus.

I take a long slurp of my drink and try not to gag. 'You can rest your case wherever you like,' I say. 'But you're wrong. And I'm not participating in any more guessing games.' I take a deep breath. 'I'm just going to continue to enjoy this smoothie.'

Marcus laughs. 'Shame I'm wrong, then,' he says. 'I'd have gifted you my prize.'

64

Benedict has suggested we meet at the Love, Fame, Tragedy show, an exhibition of unseen Picasso paintings from 1932, his annus mirabilis. Most of the pictures focus on Picasso's affair, at forty-five, with the seventeen-year-old Marie-Thérèse Walter. It's incredibly erotic and colourful and exciting and we wander slowly, at our own pace, separating from time to time, then hooking up again. I love that Benedict is happy to linger. Jack would have raced around in thirty minutes.

When I spot him in the next room, he's engrossed in a painting called *The Dream*.

'How beautiful is this?' he says, as he becomes aware of my presence. 'Look at the depth of colours and texture. I never thought of Picasso in this way.'

'Beautiful,' I say. 'I'm not sure I really understood him until now.'

As we walk around the final room, I say, 'I have a surprise for you, when you're ready to sit down.'

He turns to look at me, smiling. 'Good,' he says. 'I can tell it's a happy surprise.'

'Don't spoil my moment,' I say, and he laughs.

He takes me to the members' bar and we find a table on the terrace and he goes to get us tea and water. I stare at the stunning skyline across the Thames, the majestic dome of St Paul's, set against a background of skyscrapers, the foreground of brutalist architecture, and allow myself to think that life is good.

He returns balancing a tray. 'I got us some cake too,' he says, and puts a slice of Victoria sponge in front of me. 'I couldn't resist.'

I feel my eyes light up. Not at him – aside to Marcus, if he were present. At the cake.

'I love this view,' he says, leaning against the balcony. 'It's worth the membership alone.'

'I've been taking it all in,' I say, taking my pot of Earl Grey. 'It's spectacular. This is such a treat.'

He sits down and cuts into some cake. 'So, now for your moment. What's the surprise?'

I lean down into my bag, fish out the envelope and hand it to him.

His brow gathers into two deep creases. 'What's this?'

'Open it!'

He puts down his fork and opens the envelope, peers in, then feels inside his jacket pocket and puts on his glasses. I've cut the strip of four photos from the scan into individual shots and he pulls them out.

He stares. And stares. Trying to make out the tiny shape of life, captured in the screenshots. The most beautiful screenshots I have ever seen.

'I don't know what to say,' he says, biting his lip. 'This is amazing, Daisy. Congratulations. Well done! It's kind of official now, isn't it? I mean your body gives nothing away. I never wanted to assume. I just knew I'd get the call if the worst happened. I've been on unexpected tenterhooks these last few weeks. I've had to tell myself off for being full of fear.'

'Fear for you or me?' I say.

'Good question,' he says. He rubs his forehead. 'If I'm honest, both.'

'So you can relax a bit now.'

'Are you more relaxed?'

'Not really. Happy that I've got this far but I know there's a long and tricky road ahead.'

He stirs the tea in his pot and pours, then adds some milk. 'Who did you go with in the end?'

'Bee and Marcus. I think you need to know that Marcus has kind of guessed.'

He scoffs. 'How could he possibly guess?'

I take a deep breath. I'm not going to tell him the criterion Marcus used for his deduction. Mainly because it's not true but also because, even if I say it in jest, he might wonder if it is true and it will terrify him. 'I think it was just random. Anyway, I put him off the scent. But you know what people are like when you withhold information, particularly something like this. Everyone is suddenly an armchair detective. They can't help but try to solve the conundrum.'

He slips his glasses back into his pocket. 'Well, I guess it would be naïve not to expect people to ask questions.'

The sun disappears behind a cloud, a momentary respite from the heat. 'And what if it gets out?' I say.

'We'll work that one out when it comes to it.' He hands the envelope back to me.

'You can take a photo,' I say.

'No,' he says abruptly. 'You keep them.'

I look at him curiously. 'Don't you want one?'

He shrugs. 'Not really.'

My heart starts to race. I take a deep breath. Somehow it feels like he's rejected his own child and I need to spring to its defence.

'Why not?' I say, and he looks at me like I'm being unreasonable. 'What is it you don't want, Benedict? It's a photo. Just a photo.' I look away, unsettled.

'What's the problem?' he says. 'It's exactly that. Just a photo.'

I take a deep breath, feeling confused. 'I'm not sure I understand what you want from this, Benedict.'

He stares into me, his face suddenly like stone, like the old Benedict. 'I don't need a photo. Is that so hard to understand?'

'Yes,' I say, and I stuff the envelope back into my bag. 'Enjoy the rest of the cake.'

* * *

I walk aimlessly, needing to go over everything in my mind. Was I right to react like that? What have I done? How could he be so cold? It was a photo. Just a photo. What did he think I was asking of him? Surely I wasn't crossing a boundary by offering a photo. In wanting him to show interest by taking one.

I wander into a corner shop and buy myself a bottle of water.

'Cheer up, love, it might never happen.'

I hand over my cash, shooting him a look. How fucking dare he?

I find a bench and sit down, sipping the water. How did that escalate so quickly? What triggered it? Him or me? Maybe hormones. But I felt so personally hurt. Hurt on behalf of my child. Our child. And maybe that's the problem. What does our child actually mean?

I carry on walking until I'm exhausted both mentally and physically. Until I can barely move my legs another step. My feet ache. I stand and wait at a bus stop, feeling lost and alone. You are pregnant, I tell myself. That's all that matters. My head runs away with all sorts of different narratives. Imagining the worst. Maybe Benedict has served his purpose. Maybe he knows that. Maybe that's what this is about. He's acting coldly so that I walk away because he doesn't know how to. I can't believe I didn't see that coming.

I check my phone to see if he's tried to call me. Nothing.

* * *

Nearing the house, under the glow of the streetlamp, I make out the shape of a hunched figure. I approach wearily, not in the mood for conversation with one of the drunks who occasionally take up position on our front steps. Fortunately they're never threatening. They always move on. But some of them can be annoying, holding you in some random exchange which barely makes sense and you just have to laugh and hope it's appropriate.

'Excuse me,' I say, politely.

He looks up. 'Daisy!'

'Benedict,' I say, swallowing hard.

He stands up. 'I'm so very sorry,' he says, his face struggling to hold it together. 'Can you ever forgive me?' He takes a deep breath. 'In being overly protective of my feelings, I trampled all over yours. I didn't mean to hurt you.' He swallows. 'I'm just scared.'

'I'm scared too, Benedict.'

'I know you are. And if you'll let me . . . I'd really like a photo.'

I look at him in a moment of unmitigated relief. All my fears, of rejection, of being misunderstood, all my second-guessing his behaviour to prepare myself for abandonment, melt in his presence, at his offer of genuine contrition, his courage at making himself vulnerable.

'I'm sorry too,' I say. 'I truly am.' I smile. 'Cup of tea?'

65

Doug is in charge of the barbecue, the boys play on the trampoline, Eve is cutting aubergines and courgettes into very neat slices on an outside table, and I'm preparing a huge salad. The remote for Violet's baby monitor is on the step next to where we're prepping. There's an occasional whoosh and crackle but otherwise it would seem Violet is done for the afternoon.

'So, are you thinking about trying again?' asks Eve.

'Are you a witch?' I say.

She looks up from slicing a courgette. 'Am I right, then?'

I feel weirdly coy. 'I was going to tell you guys but I was waiting for a quiet moment without little ears hovering. Do they ever get tired?'

Eve's eyes are on stalks. 'I can stick them in front of the TV,' she says, bouncing on the balls of her Gucci slide-clad feet. 'Are you by any chance at the stage where you might need your burger well cooked?'

'Yes,' I say. 'I've already told the chef. He didn't bother to question it.' I laugh.

'Daisy! He's a man.' She gives me a big smile. 'Oh, wow!' she says.

I love that we're bonding. That motherhood (potential in my case) has finally offered us a connection. I feel I may have wronged her, judged her according to my values.

Because what's to say my values are worth any more than hers? She happily buries herself in the lives of those kids in the way I bury myself in my clients. For her motherhood is enough. And yet I pitied her for it. For what I saw as her small life. But now I see I should have celebrated and admired her. The ones to be pitied are not the Eves of this world but those who never find their enough. For whom contentment will always be as elusive as a cloud. Never within their grasp. And that could still be me.

We eat massive burgers around the long wooden table, a vegan one for Eve, a well-done one for me, with cheese and raw onion slapped under the bun. Turns out grilled courgettes and aubergines are surprisingly delicious. By the time it gets to my salad, everyone is pretty well stuffed.

'Telly, boys?' says Eve, and they run into the house without even answering. 'I'll check on Violet,' she says. 'Do *not* start without me.'

'What's she talking about?' says Doug.

'That would be starting without her,' I say.

When Eve comes back to the table, I tell them my news.

'It's ironic, isn't it?' says Eve. 'This is the perfect moment to crack open the champagne but you can't drink it.'

'She can have a sip,' says Doug.

'I'm not risking even a sip,' I say, and Eve nods.

'Is this another of the embryos?' she asks.

I feel myself blush. 'No. Different method. Different Mr Anonymous.'

'I'm guessing you're already past the twelve weeks?' says Doug. 'Otherwise you wouldn't be saying.'

I go and fetch the envelope from my handbag and hand them the three remaining photos.

'Oh, Daisy,' says Eve, passing them to Doug. 'This is wonderful news.' She cross-checks the date in the small print at the bottom, as only a woman would. 'That was over two weeks ago? You're . . . what? Fourteen, fifteen weeks now?'

'Yes.' I smile. 'This time I'm hoping it's for keeps.'

'Wow! I'm so excited for you! Congratulations!'

Doug jumps up and comes round the table to hug me. 'Bravo, you brave woman. I'm so impressed.'

'Thank you!' I say, deeply moved by their reactions. 'I'm excited but I'm not letting myself believe it quite yet.'

'Have you told the folks?' says Doug, still smiling.

'Not yet.'

He looks back at me, surprised. 'They're going away soon. What are you waiting for?'

'I just wanted to be able to give them better news this time, not take them on that emotional rollercoaster again. I'll go over next weekend. Before they leave.'

'The annual golf pilgrimage to Portugal,' says Doug. 'Somehow it feels like it's come round quicker this year. I must be getting old.'

Eve tsks. 'You keep saying that. How do you think it makes Daisy feel?'

'Older!' I snigger. She still has her Eve moments but I let them bounce off me.

Doug laughs. 'I'm really thrilled for you, Daise.' He hands me back the envelope and takes my free hand. 'I just wish, and I know I shouldn't say this but I really wish you had a partner.'

'Shut up, Doug,' says Eve, rolling her eyes. 'Lots of women are doing this now. Stop being so twentieth-century.'

'I told you I was getting old,' he says.

* * *

360

My mother is in her bedroom, sorting out their holiday clothes. She always packs at least a week before their departure.

'Eventualities,' she says, because if there's one thing my mother hates it's being taken by surprise. She should have been a Boy Scout. Her motto is 'Be prepared.' I'm hoping this surprise will be received differently.

My parents go on the same golfing trip every year. My mother can sit by the pool and read while my father plays golf from early morning when it's cooler (even though in the Algarve there's a constant breeze throughout the day) with the same people he's played with for the last seven years.

I sit on the bed while my mother organizes neat piles around me.

'I was wondering if we'd get to see you before we went away. You've been quite the stranger.' She places a pile neatly in one of the open suitcases and turns it around, this way and that, looking at it like it's a piece of a jigsaw she's not sure she's placed correctly.

'I've been fairly busy what with one thing and another.'

'So you said. Doug said you saw Violet last week. Beautiful, isn't she?'

'Very,' I say. 'Although she was mainly asleep.'

'Such a good baby,' she says, with a proud smile.

'I have news,' I say, thinking this is a natural segue. 'Are you sitting down?'

She looks at me like I'm mad but then it registers. 'Are you?'

'Yes,' I grin.

My mother abandons my father's yellow polo shirt mid-fold. She comes and sits next to me. 'Are you really?' she says. 'Oh, Daisy!' She brushes my hair away from my face.

'Really,' I say.

'With one of the frozen embryos?'

'No,' I say. 'I've done it differently this time. It seems to have been more successful.'

I see her working out what precisely that means, her eyes boring into me. 'How successful?'

'I'm nearly sixteen weeks.'

'Oh! Congratulations,' she says, looking unsure.

'Is there a problem?'

'No,' she says. 'No. I'm just slightly surprised.'

'Happy surprised?'

'Did you tell Doug and Eve?'

'Yes. Do you think we should tell Dad this time?'

'It would be the kind thing to do.' Her expression is definitely troubled.

* * *

The three of us sit at the kitchen table, with tea freshly poured from the pot, whisky freshly poured from the decanter.

My father talks about his excitement for the forthcoming trip. 'Although Mike dropped dead last year,' he says. 'Heart attack apparently. At the sixteenth hole. Terrible. They tell me he was playing badly.'

I laugh. He frowns at me. 'Are you saying it would have been better to go out on a hole-in-one?' I say.

My father thinks for a moment, puffing. 'At least get to the nineteenth!' he says.

My mother broaches my news, and my father says, 'Is it going to work this time?' and carries on eating his sandwich.

'Who knows?' I say.

'So when are you due?' says my mother.

'Late January.'

'Midwinter,' says my father. 'That's an awful time.'

'I'm not sure I care about the time, Dad, so long as the baby's healthy. Would you like to see photos of the scan?'

They look at each other as if they need to make sure they're in agreement. 'Of course.'

'So who's the father?' says my father, glancing briefly at the photos. 'Do we know him?'

'He's anonymous.'

'Again?' He groans. 'I'm not sure I approve of all this anonymous malarkey.'

'Has he written letters?' says my mother.

'No.'

She looks up. 'So how did you choose him?'

'Differently,' I say.

She hands the photos back to me. 'Are we not allowed to know how?'

'What else do you need to know other than that I'm pregnant? I mean, that's a good thing, isn't it?'

'It is, darling,' says my mother. 'But—'

'Well, I'd like to know who the father is.'

'What difference does it make if you know who he is?' I say.

'It's normal,' he says.

'It might have been normal for you but things have changed.'

'Not necessarily for the better.'

'Can I please speak?' says my mother.

We both take a deep breath. 'Of course,' I say.

'I'm really happy for you,' she says. 'I'm so glad you're this advanced, I really am. I just wish I'd known earlier. I feel like I'm out of step with something truly major happening in my daughter's life.'

I let out a frustrated sigh. 'Honestly, Ma! I was merely trying to protect you. Last time was such a major disappointment. It was so traumatic and I know you felt hit hard by it too.'

'But I'm your mother. It comes with the territory. You shouldn't need to protect me. My job is to protect you.'

'I think that role ended when I moved out,' I say cavalierly.

'It never ends, Daisy,' she says. She takes a breath. 'I want to know . . . we want to know more about the father. And it's not because we're prying, not because we want to know exactly how you found him. It's just, and this may sound quaintly old-fashioned to you, but we need to feel he's a decent man from a decent family.'

I raise my eyebrows.

'Do you even know what he looks like?' she continues. 'What he does? Because having a baby is not just about you. It's about the baby too. And the father, whether you like it or not, has a significant part to play in this.'

'Well, this one doesn't.'

'His genes do.'

I take her point. 'That's true,' I say. 'But you'll just have to trust me.'

My father lets out a loud sigh. 'Sometimes you're impossible.'

I clear my throat. 'I'm really trying to accommodate your concerns but there are some things that just can't be known.'

'Oh, well,' says my mother. 'At least I asked.'

'How about you come to the next scan? The twenty-week,' I say, trying to brighten her up.

'I'd love that!'

It occurs to me it's booked during the two months they're away. 'Sorry,' I say. 'The one after.'

'If you'd told me sooner,' she says, 'I'd have curtailed our holiday.'

'Over my dead body,' says my father.

'I don't think you should say things like that,' I say. 'Not after what happened to Mike.'

66

The weeks seem to pass without drama. I attend the next scan on my own. Not through choice. At twenty weeks it's an important one that might bring up any potential problems. But with my mother in Portugal, and neither Bee nor Marcus available, there was no alternative. I thought of asking Eve but resisted. I'm not quite ready to invite that kind of involvement from her.

In a way going alone was empowering. Knowing I could cope. That I'm feeling stronger in myself.

As per the first sonographer's notes, I wasn't asked if I wanted to know the sex so I couldn't change my mind. Which might have been a temptation, with no one there to veto it. But better that way. I'm already so attached to my baby, so in love with this unknown being who's dependent on me for its very life force, that knowing the sex might make it feel more known and I don't want to push my luck. There's still a long way to go.

Fortunately, everything was fine. 'A strong heartbeat,' said the sonographer, as we heard the whoosh-whoosh sound. I watched my baby stretch and wave, floating inside its amniotic sac, like some creature in space with no pull of gravity. I gazed in awe. How did this even happen?

My belly continues to grow and, slowly, I find my energy again, feeling like a rounder version of my old self. I buy bigger clothes from charity shops because I'd like to lose my baby weight and not need them again, riffling excitedly along the rails, thrilled at my new purpose.

The morning of my birthday arrives and I marvel at what a difference a year makes. I lumber downstairs, still in my dressing-gown, hoping not to bump into Mr Henderson (literally) or either of the other tenants and check through the pile of post that sits on the mat. Cards from my parents, from Doug and Eve, Bee and Rob, Caro. Even a card from Jack. It has a foreign stamp. Monaco. And he wants me to know! I open the envelope, read his sentimental good wishes and check myself. How do I feel? The answer is okay.

I get back into bed with a cup of herbal tea. *I feel okay*, I note in my journal. *I don't even need to google him to find out what he's up to. I know enough. How wonderful to know I have moved on. To realize I have finally forgiven him. Forgiveness is so powerful.*

* * *

Benedict is the first to call. 'Happy birthday! How are you feeling? And don't say older.'

'Happy!' I laugh.

'Can I drop something round later?'

'Later-later?' I feel bad putting him off. 'Only I'm having a casual supper out with Marcus tonight.'

'I'll come tomorrow, then, if that works? I don't want to put pressure on your evening.'

'Perfect. Thank you.'

* * *

I feel it for the first time, in the office. The best birthday present ever. 'Marcus! Come over here. Quick, quick!'

Marcus runs towards me. 'What?'

'Feel my stomach.'

'Ew, what?'

I grab his hand. 'Just feel my stomach.'

We both stare at each other. Nothing. Nothing. Then there it is.

Marcus jumps back. 'Oh, my God!' he says. 'It's Alien! It's going to burst through your stomach. HELP!' He runs around the office, his hands flapping wildly.

'Fine,' I say. 'Very funny. You've just ruined it for me.'

* * *

We walk round the corner from the office to the cosy little Italian.

I hang my coat over a light blue bouclé coat exactly like one Bee owns. I look at Marcus. 'You haven't?' I say.

'Haven't what?'

'Are we in the private room?'

'Walk this way, please, madam,' he says, and I hold his hand as we squeeze through the bustling tables, with their red chequered cloths and red napkins, candles in old Chianti bottles with basket bottoms, thick with the tears of dripping wax, and I'm kind of laughing-crying as people make way for the obvious curve of my belly.

Marcus pushes aside the red velvet curtain and they all scream, 'SURPRISE!'

I stand rooted. Amazed. 'You are incorrigible,' I say, and I kiss him, because even though I wanted a low-key night, who can be a party pooper at their own party?

'Look at you, sis!' says Doug, as Eve hugs me.

'Happy birthday!' she says. 'You look fantastic. Over halfway now, right?'

'Yes,' I nod. 'Felt the first kick today! At last!'

'Woohoo!' she says. 'Now it's really real!'

I take in everyone. Bee and Rob, Victoria and Gina, Flynn, Caro, saying, 'How did you keep it so quiet?'

'You're not the only one who can keep a secret,' says Bee, pointedly.

Marcus is orchestrating everything, including the table placements.

'No, Rob!' he shouts. 'Partners are not allowed to sit next to partners, move along, mate! Opposite end from Bee but pole position next to the birthday girl.'

Rob folds himself into the chair next to mine, squeezing his long legs underneath the table. I shuffle along a bit and he apologizes for his bulk. 'How you feeling, birthday girl? Good surprise? Bad surprise?'

'Put it this way, it's a better surprise than the one I got last year.' I go to open a bottle of water and he takes it from me, opens it and pours me a glass.

'That's a low bar, Daise! But look how your life has moved on. Who'd have thought just a year later you'd be pregnant with someone-nobody-knows's baby?'

'Point taken,' I say, ignoring his prod. 'And who'd have thought you'd be with Bee? I'm so happy for you.'

I see him look down the table at Bee, who's talking to Victoria but immediately clocks his look and gives a little wave. 'How's my bestie?' she shouts.

'First kick!'

'Amazing! Freaky, right?' she says.

'Freaked Marcus.'

Marcus flaps his hands, re-enacting the moment.

Baskets of focaccia and ciabatta are put down in front of us, along with carafes of wine. The wood-panelled wall behind the table is a heady maze of black-and-white photographs of Italian celebrities. Caro is sitting under a shot of Sophia Loren. Above Sophia is Dean Martin, next to him Giorgio Armani, Valentino, Gina Lollobrigida kissing someone and so on. Others I can't put a name to but they're so deliciously Italian. So classically stylish. The photos are signed, not that you can decipher most of the signatures. If you wet the ink, would it run?

Marcus pours everyone wine, passing the bottle over my head.

Caro is sitting diagonally opposite us. She has super-long eyelashes, which are hard to ignore.

'What's with the eyes?' I say. 'Very sexy.'

'Thanks. I'm testing a new product. They're semi-permanent. Expensive. Whaddaya think? Bit too long?'

'They look great,' I say. 'I reckon they'll be a massive hit.'

'Miss you, girlfriend,' she says. 'Where does the time go? Glad Marcus thought to invite me.'

'Of course he'd invite you,' I say. 'You're family.'

She blows a red-lipped kiss.

We dive into arancini balls and deep-fried zucchini. Pizzas are brought out and we tear and share. If I was thinking the best way to celebrate my birthday was quietly, I'm quickly proven wrong. Tearing and sharing with friends should never be underestimated.

After we've polished off tiramisu, scoops of ice cream, panna cotta and some coffees, Marcus calls for quiet. The chatter and laughter abate at his command.

'A toast!' he says. 'To our remarkable friend!'

'And sister!' shouts Doug.

'No heckling,' says Marcus, to laughter. 'We all love you, admire you, want to be you! If we ever doubted you and, of course, we *never* doubted you, you have proved, without question, that sisters are *doing it for themselves*!'

There are loud whoops, accompanied by the banging of cutlery.

They stand to toast me. I tear up as my skin tingles and I want to cry with happiness and disbelief that so much can change in a mere twelve months. That hopes and dreams can be smashed, yet somehow you must never give up because there's always hope. And you must always dream. That life is tough but it's beautiful. That I may be flying solo but I'm surrounded by good wingmen and wingwomen. I am not alone.

'Happy birthday, Daisy!'

* * *

We leave the restaurant, kissing and hugging goodnight, forming a huge huddle blocking the pavement, hearing people tut as they pass by.

'You will tell me when it happens,' says Caro.

'It's next year, Caro. I'll see you before then.'

'I'll hold you to that,' she says. 'And if you need any help, any treatments, we've started offering acupuncture, pregnancy massages, and you may want a mani-pedi.'

'And semi-permanent eyelashes!'

She laughs. 'Whatever you want. My gift will be to you. The baby will get plenty.'

'Thank you! Love you!' I say, and she grabs my face between her hands.

'Love you too. And you,' she says, looking at my bump.

'You do know you've given me the strength to do this, don't you? To go solo,' I say.

'The strength is all yours, babe. Power to you!'

'To womankind,' I say and she smiles.

'Told you you'd get there.'

We go our separate ways as Doug sidles up next to me and we walk down the street with Eve. It's a mild October night. The shops along Oxford Street are just beginning to shut their doors.

'You getting a cab?' he says.

'Tube. You?'

'We're getting an Uber from the corner of Regent Street. It's going to be here in five minutes. We can drop you off on the way if you'd like.'

'Great,' I say, and we stand together as Doug monitors his phone screen. 'It's arriving . . . over there!' He points and holds up his phone arm as a big people-carrier slows down on the opposite side. It does a U-turn to where we're standing and we climb in.

'Doug Settle. I've added a stop. That okay?'

The driver nods. 'No worries!'

Doug sits on the hump in the middle. 'Nice night. Did you have any suspicions?'

'None! I only guessed when I recognised Bee's coat hanging up. Even then it didn't really dawn on me what it meant.'

'I gather no one knows who the father is,' Doug says. 'I thought he might be there.'

I turn to look at him. 'Really? Why?'

He puts his phone into his top pocket. 'I thought maybe it was just us who didn't know. That it was someone you didn't want Mum and Dad to find out about. They certainly think that.'

'It's not a conspiracy, Doug.'

'I think your parents feel a bit excluded,' says Eve.

I lean forward so that I can see her. 'Have they said that to you or are you just supposing?'

'Mum mentioned it the other day when we went over

with the kids,' says Doug. 'She says she worried about you the entire time they were away.'

I scoff, looking out of the window as we drive past the red-brick terraces that line the Bayswater Road. 'She's not mentioned that to me. She called me several times. She never said anything about being worried.'

Eve decides to elucidate. 'I think she thinks you're being secretive. You know, about the donor. That worries her. Katherine told her it might be someone from Facebook she's heard about. Who sounds a bit dodgy.'

'Well, it isn't. Anyway, that's ridiculous,' I say. 'I'd never do anything like that. Sometimes I think her friends enjoy stirring things up.'

'The thing is,' says Doug, 'they never thought you'd undergo sperm donation. So, as far as Mum's concerned, nothing's ridiculous and anything's possible.'

'I find that insulting.'

'I think she does too. She felt more involved last time, more in the loop,' says Doug. 'She thinks you have something to hide. You might want to have a word with her. Reassure her. She's building it up into something it obviously isn't.'

* * *

'Of course I'm worried,' my mother says, exasperation pulsating down the phone. 'I've told you why.'

'Remind me.'

'Oh, Daisy. It sounds so stupid when I say it out loud. I feel excluded. And I know you're going to deny it but I think you know the father and you're not saying.'

'What makes you think that?' I say, caught off guard.

Her voice ramps up. 'Mother's intuition. I can tell. Doug says nobody knows.'

'They don't.'

'But listen to you. I can tell by your voice that you know him personally.'

'How on earth can you tell from my voice?'

'You sound defensive. Is he not a popular man within your set?'

I squawk. 'You're being ridiculous.'

'Am I?'

'Yes. And even if you were right, am I not allowed to keep anything for myself? Can't I own anything without having to make it public knowledge? I'm forty-one. I'm not a teenager.'

'I am not public knowledge. I'm your mother. Anyway,' she says, 'if you want to keep it for yourself, then do. I won't ask again. Happy birthday, Daisy. I posted your present. You obviously haven't got it?'

'Not yet.'

'I hope you like it.'

'Thanks,' I say, feeling grubby. 'I'm sure I will.'

* * *

I take out my grubbiness on my journal, scribbling vehemently:

I'm angry that I can't do anything without everyone feeling they're entitled to a part of me. Why? Why can't they trust me that I know what I'm doing? In a way, if Ma and Dad knew Benedict, saw the kind of man he is, I know they'd stop worrying, that they might even understand. But why should I give in to them? They don't own me. No one does. Then again, they might find fault with him and that would be too

awful. 'He's sixty-one. He's a widower. What were you
thinking?' I can hear Dad railing against him now.
And he, no doubt, would influence Ma. No! I have
to stand firm. For myself and for Benedict. I have to
believe in my own intuition, which, in this instance,
trumps Ma's. I am the mother. I will be the mother.
I will be the best mother I can possibly be. And
Benedict will not be the traditional father because
that's our choice. Nobody else's opinion matters.

67

I open my door, letting in the stale smell of the hallway, listening to the sound of Benedict's feet climbing the stairs. He smiles when he sees I'm already there, waiting for him, and waves the bunch of flowers. In his other hand, I notice a small gift, wrapped in yellow paper and tied with a green bow.

'Happy birthday,' he says, kissing my cheek. 'Don't let me stay too long. I've got too much work on and an early start tomorrow but I wanted to see you.'

'I'm guessing this is for the baby,' I say, as he hands me the gift.

'Open it.'

He deals with the flowers, cutting the stems, arranging them in the jug and I notice how comfortable he is here now. He sits down next to me, huge grin. I take off the bow and unfold the wrapping.

I gasp. 'Baby's first booties! They're so cute,' I say. 'I love to think of you going into a baby shop and buying them.'

'What do you mean?' he exclaims, affronted. 'Knitted by my own fair hands.'

'Shut the front door!'

'I'm serious.'

'I don't believe you. You're knitting? The father who doesn't want to be known as the father.'

'That's a whole other thing.'

'I know!' I say. 'Anyway, I love them! Thank you.' I place them on the table. 'I'll put them away somewhere safe.'

'So how was your evening with Marcus?'

'Turns out it was a surprise party.'

'You really didn't know?'

'Not a clue. I'm surprised Marcus didn't try to invite you.'

He furrows his brow. 'Why would he?'

I shrug. 'Because he knows we're friends. He might have.'

His expression says he supposes so.

'Would you have come?'

'Were you expecting me to?'

'No. I wasn't expecting anyone, was I? I was just wondering in hindsight. I mean everyone's desperate to know who the father is. It might have put them off the scent because there's no way they would expect to see him at my party.'

'Is it causing you grief?' he says.

I pick up one of the booties and stroke it against my chin, sensing the softness. 'It's definitely becoming complicated. I had a really difficult conversation with my mother this morning. Her intuition has picked up on the fact that I must know the donor. She doesn't understand why I'm keeping it a secret. Unless he's "unpopular within your set".'

He chuckles. 'Maybe I am,' he says. 'How did you handle it?'

I tell him my line about being allowed to own it. He listens intently, looks at me and sucks his teeth. 'She's your mother, though. It must be tough for her.'

'Don't side with her,' I say.

He laughs. 'I'm not siding with anyone. I'm very firmly in your court.'

He stretches his arms in front of him, gyrating his shoulders. 'Listen. For me it's preferable that I remain an unknown. Just a good friend who occasionally helps out.'

'A good friend whom nobody seems to know.'

'I'm a work colleague. We became friends. Nothing unusual in that.'

'I guess.'

He sighs. 'I honestly think that if you can hang on in there, once the baby is born, no one will care about the father. Not in the way they do now. They'll care more about you and the baby. Probably the baby. Get in the queue!'

I chuckle. 'Yeah! Let's hope. Hang on in there, baby,' I say, gazing at my stomach. I look back at him to catch him staring at my bump too. I think he feels the same awe as I do. 'Anyway, I don't want to change anything we're doing. I like that this is ours. Between us. And I don't want to upset the path we're on.' I stroke my bump. 'So far, so good.'

I grab Benedict's hand. 'Feel that?'

He looks shocked by my unexpected action. 'Sorry. I probably shouldn't have done that,' I say, releasing his hand but he leaves it there.

'He's a footballer,' he says, unfazed.

'How do you know it's a he?'

He does a double-take. 'I don't obviously. But that's one hell of a kick. Your stomach must be bruised inside.'

'My heart feels a bit bruised too, if I'm honest.'

'Really?' His face drops. 'Did my reaction upset you?'

'Of course not. No. Ma's. She was quite cold. I hate knowing she's unhappy with me.'

'Daisy,' his tone says, 'Get a grip, she's living her life. She's made her choices. You must live yours.'

68

'Welcome, ladies!' says Miriam. 'Welcome to your first ante-natal class.'

Miriam is slim, or maybe she just looks slim because we can no longer recall what slim looks like. She has red corkscrew curls that sit in a halo around her pale, freckled face. There are ten of us, all in different styles of comfort wear, tracksuits, dungarees, sitting barefoot on large floor cushions that have seen better days. We are all shapes and sizes, some bumps more pronounced than others. I'm among the larger ones. My sweatshirt seems to want to cling to me conspicuously and I keep pulling it down, trying to get comfortable.

We have occupied a small primary school. During the day, I imagine, this is the assembly hall, with its Formica floor, scarred from the dragging of chairs, which are stacked at the back of the off-white-painted room, the cracks running through it badly filled, like varicose veins, which, so far, I have happily managed to avoid. On other nights, yoga classes and art classes are some of the activities that help cover the running costs of this sadly dilapidated building, whose radiators work hard at pumping out heat, as the windows fight with the condensation.

'Let's start by going round the circle and introducing ourselves, who we are and maybe giving details of how we're getting on with our pregnancies. You don't have to do this if you don't want to but it's a good way of bonding with one another. I think it's important to have ladies in your life who are going through the same, or pretty much the same, experience as you are. Now look around you. You see! You are not alone.'

We smile awkwardly at one another, obeying Miriam's enthusiasm. There's a shuffle of bottoms as we try to get more relaxed. I notice the soles of feet staring back at me, some pink, some raw red from pressure, others dusty. I check mine. At least they're clean, I think, but I could do with a pedicure. I make a mental note to call Caro.

'Amanda, would you like to start?' Miriam says.

We look, waiting to see Amanda reveal herself, and a young girl, with long blonde hair tied in plaits, pink sweats, dusty feet, announces herself.

'I'm Amanda. I'm twenty-four years old. I got married at the beginning of the year to my childhood sweetheart, John. People say we're two peas in a pod. I didn't expect to get pregnant this quickly but here I am. I was very sick for the first couple of months but I've been absolutely fine ever since. I'm hoping for a natural birth and I'd like to deliver in a birthing pool if possible and John—'

Miriam holds up her palm and smiles.

'Oh!' says Amanda. 'And I talk too much.' She makes a gurning face. We all laugh with her, appreciating her unfiltered charm, glad she was brave enough to kick off this process and break the ice.

'Thank you, Amanda,' says Miriam, turning her face to the woman on Amanda's left.

As we carry on round the circle, I start to worry about what I'm going to say, how I'm going to pitch myself. No one else is single. Everyone seems to be in their thirties, apart from Amanda. There is one gay woman called something like Cyrille or Sybille, I didn't quite catch it, but otherwise they all appear to be pretty average, all in solid relationships, including Cyrille or Sybille. Most of them already know the sex of their baby – approximately half girls, half boys. The universe is clever, I think, wondering which half I'm going to be in.

Miriam's eyes land on me. I cough, uncross my legs and fold them into my side, shifting my weight on the lumpy cushion. 'My name is Daisy. I'm forty-one years old. I'm not in a relationship but I knew I wanted a baby, so I'm doing it on my own.'

The atmosphere in the room changes. I can feel their faces leaning in towards me, like they're hanging on my every word. I stop for a moment, looking at Miriam, but she throws me an expression that urges me to continue.

'I had IVF using an anonymous donor, which didn't work out, but this time I know who my donor is. I'm still going to be a solo mum but in a different way. I really have no plans about the birth. I'm just happy to have a baby whichever way it comes out. Hopefully the right way,' I add hastily.

The room bursts into light applause.

'Thank you,' I say. 'I'm not sure I deserve that.'

'Thank you, Daisy,' says Miriam. 'Look at the support you have around you. You will not be doing this on your own.'

I feel the emotion building inside me and tip back my head to hold off the threat of tears. I had not expected this reception. Maxine, next to me, reaches out and puts her hand on mine, which makes it even harder. I'm overwhelmed with relief and gratitude. I no longer fear I might be the freak.

Miriam gives us a general overview of what is going to

happen over the next six weeks. Some type everything into their phones, some, including me, scribble everything down in a notebook. We finish with some gentle stretching exercises and Miriam ends the session with a quote. She makes us repeat it and together we say, 'I am the closest I will ever come to magic.'

'Beautiful,' says Maxine.

'Thank you so much for coming, ladies,' she says, looking at the clock. 'Please stack your cushions in a pile at the back, where you found them. I look forward to seeing you next week but do let me know if you can't make it. If ladies don't show up and I don't know why, I start to panic!' She starts a round of applause and we all join in.

Cyrille or Sybille approaches me as we walk outside. We wander down the front steps of the building in tandem.

'Daisy,' she says, 'so good to hear your story.'

Up close I notice her eyes are such a bright blue they look unreal. She has bleached-white hair tied tightly in a bun. 'Thanks,' I say.

She smiles, appraising me. 'Let me guess. Some kind of artist?'

'Interior designer. You?'

'Fitness trainer,' she says.

'Of course,' I say. She does look remarkably fit.

'I'm trying to be as cool about this as possible,' she says, 'but you can tell from some of the others, they're all about who's going to be teacher's pet.' She rolls her eyes. 'Who's got the best bump. Who's going to have the best birth. Fuck it! I just want a baby.'

I laugh. 'Me too,' I say. 'I'm grateful to have got this far.'

'I'm Cyrille, by the way, like the bloke's name only double-*l e*. Don't go giving your baby a name they have to spell out to everyone. Fucking pain! Gotta dash. Going to the gym. Make up for lost time. See you next week. Keep breathing!'

I laugh, watching as she hurries away.

From behind you'd never know she was pregnant.

69

I stare at myself naked, sideways on in the mirror. I'm starting to look very pregnant indeed. I can see the feathery signs of stretch marks but I don't care. I'm honoured to have them. I watch, in a kind of awe, the baby's movements under my skin. It's disconcerting yet simultaneously reassuring. Occasionally, if it goes quiet for what I think is too long, I poke it gently, anxious until it moves again, thrilled to feel the weird pushing against my ribs.

I'm lucky. It's head down. Two of the women in the antenatal class have been told their baby is breech.

'It can change overnight,' says Miriam, as positive as ever. 'You're not yet thirty-six weeks. If it gets to that time, your obstetrician might turn it. For now, just keep doing your exercises and your yoga.'

I climb over the side of the bath, holding on to the handrail that I always thought was for old people, and turn on the shower. As the water trickles over my body, as best it can from the ancient calcified shower head, I wash myself with a special gel for mothers-to-be that Caro gave me. I admire my feet, the beautiful pedicure. For someone who doesn't want babies, she's been incredibly caring.

I'm looking forward to a day of doing nothing. Of sitting at my laptop and ordering the Moses basket my mother has offered to buy for me. I think she's decided that retail therapy is her way of connecting. I phone her regularly to keep her happy and I can tell by her tone that things aren't entirely how she would like them to be, but that's how they are. My time. My choice. Thanks, Benedict.

As I climb out of the bath, my phone rings.

I answer immediately. 'Are you okay?' I say, because Bee never rings during the day.

'Can you come round?' she says, sounding distraught. 'I can't leave Will.'

'Of course,' I say, panicking. 'I've just got out the bath. Give me an hour.'

* * *

She opens the door in her dressing-gown, blowing loudly into a screwed-up tissue. 'Thanks for coming,' she says, through a sob.

'What the hell's wrong? Where's Will?'

'Watching CBeebies in my bedroom. Can't believe his luck.' She lets out a long sorrowful breath. 'Oh, Daise. It's terrible. I feel so awful. Patrick's getting married again.'

I bite my lip.

'Don't laugh,' she says. 'I know it's funny but please don't laugh.'

'I'm laughing with relief,' I say. 'I wondered what you were going to tell me.'

'I'll make us some tea.'

I sit down on her couch as she goes to check on Will.

'Fast asleep.' Her face tells me that seeing him sleeping is still deeply endearing to her. *I am the closest I will ever come to magic* pops up in my thoughts.

She sits on the sofa and draws her legs up beneath her. 'I shouldn't feel like this but I do. I feel weird.' She blows her nose. 'It's not like I'm on my own. I mean, Rob is just perfect. You know. Really loving and caring. It's just – it's kind of a shock he's getting married.' She shudders. 'And he'll probably have kids with her.'

'If she can.'

'She's twenty-eight. Of course she can.'

'Is that what hurts? Because I get that.'

'It all hurts.'

I wrap my arms around her. 'Aww, Bee. This isn't like you. But you know what? You're dealing with it. It's an emotional detox.'

She laughs and shrugs. 'I mean, what was I expecting? Of course he'd get married again. Of course he'd have more children. I just worry for Will.'

'Why? Do you think, if Patrick has more kids, he'll neglect Will?'

She looks at me from over the top of her mug. 'It happens. Without a doubt he'll move down Patrick's list of priorities.'

'But you don't know that. You don't even know if he wants more kids.'

She lets out a long sigh. 'Come on, Daise. He always wanted more kids. I wanted more kids. Just not with him.'

'With Rob?'

'Maybe.'

'Oooh. Soon?'

'Sooner rather than later, yes.'

I clap. 'I'm so pleased for you.'

She smiles weakly. 'Yeah. It's a good thing, right?'

'It's the best thing! Although they'll be very, very tall. Listen, whatever happens, Will will be fine. He's got you and now he has Rob.'

'You're right.'

We sit in the silence of our thoughts.

'I feel better now you're here,' she says. 'It's okay to feel ridiculous with you.'

'Thanks,' I say, not quite sure if that's a compliment.

'You're really growing,' she says, tipping her chin downwards. 'That's a proper bump you've got there.'

'Tell me about it. Starting to weigh me down. Can I tell you something ridiculous too?'

'I insist.'

I put my hands on my stomach. There's a gentle hint of movement. Enough to relax me. 'So, last antenatal class. Everyone was encouraged to bring their partner. I never gave it a second thought until the actual evening when I was the only one sitting there on my own. I felt awful. Sticking out like a sore thumb. Miriam used me as her demo for all the exercises.' Bee's expression says she's imagining the indignity. 'It's the first time I felt alone in all this.'

'Why didn't you ask me? I'd have come along.'

'You've done enough for me, Bee.'

'What about the father? He's really not interested in anything?'

'It's too intimate,' I say.

'You've had his sperm!'

'That was different. It's not like we had sex. Anyway, all the partners were holding the women's shoulders, rubbing backs, breathing in sync with them, listening to what's going to happen. I don't have that kind of relationship with him.'

'What kind of relationship do you have with him?'

'A good one,' I say. 'We respect each other's boundaries.'

She nods, like she's humouring me, but I'm inured to that now.

'One good thing came of it. There's a really nice woman there called Cyrille. More of a girl, really, who I seem to

387

have bonded with. She was there with her wife. Both super-cool. Super-kind. Cyrille knows I'm comfortable being a solo mum but I think she spotted that I was feeling a bit vulnerable. She offered to be my doula.'

Bee looks momentarily miffed. She rubs her nose with her palm.

'You're top of the list, of course. But if it happens at a time when you can't get away I have back-up. She's due a few weeks after me so, fingers crossed, she'll still be around.'

'I'll drop everything. Except Will! I really want to be your doula!'

'And I want you to be my doula. But this gives me some comfort.'

'Yeah. Of course.'

I tap the back of her hand. 'So how did Patrick tell you?'

She puffs. 'He emailed me a copy of the wedding invitation. Titled "FYI". Can you believe that?'

I practically choke. 'You're kidding me.'

'Said he'd discuss it next weekend when he collects Will. Didn't want me to hear from someone else. Like who, for fuck's sake? I don't know anyone he mixes with any more.'

I pat at the tears rolling down her cheeks. 'If you're waiting till next weekend, how do you know so much about her?'

She snorts. 'Checked out his Facebook page. He's "in a relationship!" So I looked at her page. Didn't want to but couldn't help myself.' She lets out a long, ponderous sigh. 'I should probably have looked before but never suspected there was anyone else.'

I cringe, knowing how she feels. 'What would we do without Facebook, eh?'

She grabs my arm tightly. 'I know you know him now. It's obvious from the way you just talked about him so don't fob me off with Facebook Man!'

'Maybe Facebook Man took a particular shine to me.'

'And maybe I'm the Queen of Outer Mongolia.'

'Your Majesty!' I say with a wave of my hand.

We giggle contagiously because sometimes you have to laugh at life's absurdities.

70

Christmas, as always, will be spent at my parents'. Benedict and I have agreed to see each other on Boxing Day. He is spending Christmas Day alone. He assures me he's done it for the last couple of years and it feels okay. He likes to listen to music and watch bad movies.

'Are we doing presents?' I ask.

'Why not?' he says. 'I always liked the presents bit.'

'How about we do a Secret Santa and have to guess who it's from.'

'Very funny,' he says.

* * *

I see Doug clock my weary face. He jumps out of the car and picks up the bags of presents that are resting at my feet on the damp pavement and puts them into the boot, squeezing them in among the other bags overflowing with gifts. My wrapping is rather cobbled together this year: (a) I couldn't comfortably bend over to wrap, and (b) I couldn't be bothered even if it was possible.

I climb into the front of the car and grapple with the seatbelt, eventually managing to strap myself in without strangulating my stomach. 'Merry Christmas, everyone!' I say.

'Merry Christmas!' they repeat in unison.

Eve is in the back squidged between Eddie and Violet's cot-cum-car-seat with Monty on the other side.

'Have you bought us presents?' says Eddie.

'You don't ask questions like that,' scolds Doug.

'Santa is in charge of presents,' I say.

'Not this year,' says Doug, putting on his seatbelt. 'I'm afraid his secret is out.' He leans towards me and whispers, 'Monty has a rather precocious friend.'

'Oh dear,' I say. 'Then I guess they're in the boot, darling.'

'You're very big,' says Monty. 'Bigger than Mummy was. Are you going to have twins?' He sniggers. Then Eddie sniggers.

'Hope not,' I say. 'But thanks for the compliment.'

'You don't tell someone they look big,' says Eve. 'Honestly, Monty. It's a very sensitive time for Auntie Daisy.'

'But she's huge!' he mutters.

'Can't argue with that,' I say. 'You should see my ankles!'

The boys and my brother make vomit noises.

Doug starts the car and we drive off, slowly at first, mindful of the endless road bumps, pleased to get onto the motorway, which is practically empty. The trees look sad and naked, the landscape grey and gloomy. When we hit the village, it's good to see a bit of Christmas jollity: the streets lit with fairy lights, which swirl down tree trunks and along branches, the shop frontages along West Street adorned with wreaths, holly and more fairy lights. There's a house in my parents' lane, fortunately at quite a distance from them, which looks like it's entered some form of Christmas competition, with sequenced flashing lights and a Santa on the roof.

'Look! There is a Santa after all,' I say, and the boys shout, 'Where?'

'He's trying to get down that house's chimney. Didn't you see?'

'Auntie Daisy's being funny,' says Doug, and they groan.

I remember when I first realized Father Christmas was Dad. I caught him in the early hours, filling the pillowcase at the end of my bed.

'Father Christmas is so busy he asked me to help out this year,' he said, through guilty lips. We both knew the game was up.

When we pull into the drive, I let out a loud involuntary burp and the boys burst into hysterical laughter.

'Apologies, everyone. That was the baby.'

'That was you,' says Eddie.

'You're no fun any more,' I say.

We all get out of the car. Monty jumps off the footboard, Eve helps Eddie, then leans in to release Violet's car seat.

'Do you need a hand?' I ask.

'Not from you,' she says. 'You do know you shouldn't be lifting anything heavy now?'

'I do. With the exception of Christmas presents.' I hover in the cold, damp air, enjoying the scent of burning logs from the chimney, signalling the fire has already been lit.

'Mum and Dad are okay, aren't they? They're still a bit weird with me,' I say to Doug. 'I really don't want the Spanish Inquisition.'

'They'll be fine,' he says. 'It's Christmas. They'll be as chilled as normal.'

'They're never chilled at Christmas.'

'Precisely,' he says, giving me a big good-luck grin.

The boys are running around, chasing each other, on the wide driveway, screaming happily. Doug starts shifting the bags from the boot to the front step. 'Ring the bell, Daisy. They're probably in the kitchen. They can't hear we've arrived.'

'They must be deaf if they can't hear this screeching,' I say.

'They're not getting any younger,' says Doug.

I ring the bell, taking a deep breath, exhaling and rubbing my chest. I can feel the threat of heartburn before I've cracked a single walnut. Brewster starts barking. He must be going deaf, too, because he normally reacts as soon as we're out of the car.

My father finally opens the door. I'm getting used to his lack of moustache. 'Hey, Dad!' I say. 'Merry Christmas!'

'Daisy,' he says, manoeuvring his massive stomach around mine, kissing me lightly on the top of my head. 'Getting bigger by the minute. Want a hand, Doug?'

'Don't need to lift a finger, Dad,' says Doug. 'I'll bring everything in.'

Eve brushes past me.

'Am I really that big?' I say, to the woman who only ever looked perfect in pregnancy.

'You're pregnant,' she says. 'And you look great.' She walks into the house and I gaze at her slim, belted waist. Oh, how I long to wear a belt again. Then I scold myself for being ungrateful.

'Monty! Eddie!' my father shouts and they scramble around him, trying to tussle with one another. 'There you are, my little elves. Do you want to see the tree?' he shouts at their backs as they run through to the house.

'Yes,' they scream.

'And where's the tiniest elf of all?'

'She's already inside,' I say. I slip my hand through his arm and walk through with him.

I can hear my mother in the sitting room telling the boys to calm down.

'Hi, Mum,' I say. 'Merry Christmas.'

'Daisy,' she says, with an exhausted smile. 'Look at you! You're even bigger.'

'Why is everyone so keen on telling me I look big?' I say.

'She's like an elephant,' says Monty, and Eddie giggles behind his hand, looking at me, waiting for me to get angry. I wave my arm like a trunk, making trumpeting sounds around them, and they squeal, bending away from me. I can feel my mother looking on in dismay, managing to make me feel even more cumbersome. She goes back into the kitchen and I follow her, still trumpeting as if it might actually make her crack a smile.

'Need help?' I say, through my trumpet arm. 'Give me the potatoes to peel. Or I'll happily do the sprouts.'

'Already done,' she says. 'I got up very early this morning. I'm completely prepared.'

I feel strangely robbed. 'Can I lay the table?'

'Done,' she says, flapping a hand at me, waving me away. 'I've made you some non-alcoholic mulled wine. It's on a hotplate on the buffet. Go and help yourself.' I feel rebuffed with a side of kindness.

'Thank you! Can I get you anything?'

'No,' she says bluntly.

Doug is organizing the piling of gifts under the tree.

'Where are the boys?' I ask him.

'Eve's doing the toilet run.'

'I'm telling you. Mum is acting weird.'

'Mum is always weird at Christmas.' He checks the label on a gift. 'Oooh, for me,' he says and places it on the floor.

Doug makes eggnog for Ma and Eve, Dad drinks whisky and I drink the non-alcoholic mulled wine.

Dad and I are instructed to sit at the table. 'You're off the hook this year,' says Ma pointing at me.

Dad looks at me triumphantly. 'There are some advantages to being fat,' he says.

'I'm not fat,' I say. 'I'm pregnant. In case you haven't noticed.'

'Hard to miss,' he says.

We open the crackers. My mother moans at the quality of the gifts. 'I told you,' says my father. 'Doesn't matter how expensive they are, you're always going to be disappointed.'

'It *is* disappointing,' says my mother.

'It's a Christmas cracker, Ma!' says Doug.

Violet cries and Eve jumps up, picking her up from her car seat and pacing the room with her.

'You shouldn't pander to her,' says my mother. 'She probably would have settled. She'll expect to be picked up every time, if you do that.'

'We've had three kids, Mum,' says Doug. 'Eve knows what she's doing.'

'If you don't want my advice, that's fine,' says my mother. 'I'm just trying to help.'

'Can we eat, please?' says my father.

Lunch is served. The normal smoked mackerel pâté with melba toast. Then Doug brings in the turkey and the boys bring in the dishes of vegetables. Eve, who has settled Violet, despite her apparently poor parenting skills, brings in the gravy.

'How's your work going, Daisy?' asks my father, as my mother hands around the warmed plates and Doug serves.

'Good, thanks, Dad,' I say. 'A few new projects already in the roster for new year. Keeping going for as long as I can.'

'You're very big,' says my mother, as if I might momentarily have forgotten the last time she told me. 'Are you sure you're going to be able to keep working?'

'You're way bigger than I was expecting,' says my father.

'Do you have to keep repeating that?' I say. 'It's actually quite hurtful.'

'Hmm,' says my mother.

'What does that mean?'

'Sally,' says my father. 'Please don't. We agreed.'

'What did you agree?' I ask.

Doug shakes his head agitatedly. 'Don't!' he mouths.

I feel a slight kick from Eve under the table. I wish the baby would kick. Except it's so big there's probably no room.

We eat for a while, just the clatter of knives and forks and little-boy chatter, my mind churning. I know I shouldn't poke the bear but I can't resist.

'Can we get rid of the elephant in this room?' I say. 'I'd like to enjoy a normal Christmas.'

'Do you want to go home, Auntie Daisy?' says Eddie, innocently.

'I am not the elephant in this particular instance, Eddie,' I say, with unintended impatience.

'Who wants more turkey?' says Doug.

'Just put some on their plates,' says Eve. Doug stands up and starts serving more turkey to everyone.

'I'll go and get the pudding ready,' says Ma.

'I'll come with you,' I say.

'Sit down!' says Doug, issuing an order.

I ignore him and follow my mother into the kitchen.

'So go on, tell me what's wrong?'

'Okay,' she says. 'I will.' She shuts the kitchen door. 'And let me tell you, this brings me no pleasure. I really wanted to have a normal Christmas, but when you said we were being hurtful, I think you should know we feel the same about you.'

'So you have a problem with my pregnancy?'

'No. That's not it. I'm pleased for you. Excited even. First time round I was scared but then, well, this time is harder for me.'

I lean against the island. I want to say, 'It's not about you,' but I don't think that will go down well. 'Harder than when I had the miscarriage?'

'Of course not,' she says.

'Why are you so desperate to know the baby's father?'

Her eyes flash at me. 'Because you know him. I don't understand why you won't tell us who he is. It makes me nervous. What type of man is he? Why won't you say?'

I hesitate for a moment. 'He's a good man,' I say, in the hope it might shut down the conversation yet knowing it won't.

'Oh, my God,' she says, collapsing onto a bar stool. 'You do know him! That makes it worse. I can't believe you're keeping it from us.'

'I haven't told anyone.'

'We are not anyone!' she shouts, which shocks us both. She takes a deep breath, trying to calm herself. 'We are your parents. Your family. We want to know who's in your life.' She grabs a tissue from the box and blows her nose, unusually indelicately. 'You've pushed us away,' she says, snivelling. 'We used to be as close as anything . . . and now I feel you're not even allowing me to be your mother.'

'You will always be my mother. I'm sorry you feel that way.'

'We all feel that way. You're secretive. You're distant. I mean, you go ahead with something so major without even a mention—'

'I told you why. A thousand times.'

She wipes her forehead with the back of her hand. 'Don't you think you're taking solo motherhood a bit too literally, Daisy? Don't you realize that actually, in the real world, you cannot do everything on your own? You will need your family.'

'I want you!' I say, gasping. 'I know I'm going to need you.'

'So why are you pushing us away?'

'I'm not.'

'Then why won't you let us know the name of the father?'

'And the Son and the Holy Ghost. It's not that kind of deal.' I feel light-headed. Strange. Like this is happening in a different dimension. I can feel the blood pumping inside my head.

'You see? That's what I hate. The way you bat off a perfectly legitimate question. It's not funny!'

I'm tired. I feel weird. I'm ready to give in, to spout his name, when the door opens and in strides my father. 'What's happened to the Christmas pudding?'

'She knows the father,' my mother says. 'I told you, Ted. I always knew he was not anonymous.'

'It's Christmas, Sally. Can we just go back inside, please?'

'Tell her how much she's hurt us, Ted. She needs to hear it from you!'

He looks resigned, although probably more annoyed at having his pudding delayed.

'We're just concerned for you, Daisy,' he says, remaining calm. 'You've made it very difficult for us.'

I take a deep breath. 'How have I made it difficult for you?' I puff. My back aches. 'Listen,' I say, rubbing the base of my spine. 'I don't understand why you need to know his name. It won't make any difference. He'd still be anonymous to you. Isn't it more important that I know who he is? Doesn't that reassure you?'

'It would if you didn't behave like it's some sort of government secret,' says my mother.

My heart starts pumping wildly, my head is pounding.

My father's face contorts. 'Ooof,' he says.

'Honestly, Daisy, I love you,' says my mother, 'but you've made me feel useless and excluded.' She casts a teary-eyed look at my father, who moves to put his arm around her.

'Look,' he says, visibly stricken. 'Look how upset she is.' He rubs his chest. I rub my back.

'I'm sorry,' I say, feeling queasy, wondering if I'm having a reaction to the smoked mackerel pâté. 'I never ever intended to upset you.'

'I have a pain in my chest,' says my father.

My mother swings round to look at him. He's suddenly grabbing for breath. 'For goodness' sake, Ted, sit down! Breathe!' She swings back to glare at me. 'See what you've done now!' Her face is etched with terror.

'What have I done?'

Doug wanders in. 'What's happening to the pudding?' he says.

'Your father's having a heart attack. Call an ambulance.'

'No, Sally! I just feel tightness across my chest.'

'Call an ambulance, Doug!'

Doug rushes to fill a glass with water. 'Here, Dad,' he says. 'Drink this.' He goes to pick up the phone.

I hold on grimly to the island, supporting my weight against it with both hands. I feel strange. My stomach feels tight. Then *boof*! It's like I'm being held in a vice. 'Ohhhhh,' I sigh, letting out a loud groan. 'Oh, my God, that's massive.'

'What?' says my brother. 'Not you,' he says, into the phone. 'Ambulance, please!'

'Braxton Hicks. It's just a weird one. I've been having them lately.'

'She's just trying to draw attention to herself. It's probably indigestion,' says my mother, staring at my father.

'Oh dear,' he says, gripping his chest. 'It's not good.'

'Ohhhhhhhh,' I say, unable to contain the pain ripping through me.

'For goodness' sake, Daisy. Please! Stop catastrophizing! This is not about you! Are they doing anything, Doug? What's happening?'

'I'm on hold.'

At that moment, my father lets rip the most enormous fart.

'TED!' says my mother, flapping her hand in front of her nose. 'That is dis*gus*ting.' Brewster comes over and starts sniffing the air.

My brother is bent double, laughing hysterically.

'I'm afraid it might have been the sprouts,' says my father. 'But I do feel a lot better.'

'Emergency over. Apologies,' says Doug, replacing the receiver.

I'm huffing, leaning my forehead against the cool surface of the worktop. 'I might be having an allergic reaction. Or food poisoning,' I say. 'My indigestion is not going away.'

'Here,' says Doug, his shoulders still shaking with laughter, handing me a glass of water. 'Drink. Slowly. You'll be fine. Got any Gaviscon, Mum?'

I try to stand upright when there's a sudden whoosh beneath me. My legs feel warm and wet. My feet are standing in a pool of water that looks like weak wee. Doug looks from my face to the floor to my face again. 'Did you just wet yourself?'

'I didn't,' I say, feeling sick with fear. 'Oh, Doug,' I say. 'I've jinxed it. It's too early. I'm not due for weeks.'

He steps around the water and rushes to rub my back. 'About five weeks to go, right?'

I can't think. 'More. No, less. I can't think straight. Something like that.'

'Their lungs should be okay. That's the important bit.' He looks at our parents, slumped against one another, too emotionally exhausted to care what's happening on my side of the island. 'Daisy's waters have broken.'

Ma immediately springs to life. 'Oh, my goodness,' she says, suddenly at my side. 'Are you okay? Have the contractions started? Should we phone for an ambulance?'

'No,' I insist, my gaze firmly fixed on the worktop. 'They'll take me to the local hospital. I want to give birth in my hospital, with my midwives. Can you drive me back, Doug?'

'Of course,' he says. 'Let me just gather my things.' He looks left then right, not knowing which way to move first. 'Have you got a bag ready?'

'Not really. I've got a drawer. Ohhhh,' I yell, feeling a clenching around my stomach. So different from a Braxton Hicks. My back feels like it's burning. 'Ohhhh.'

'Breathe, Daisy,' says my mother. 'Breathe through it.'

'We need to time between contractions. If they're close together, I'm afraid we'll need to call an ambulance,' says Doug. 'I'm good at making babies, not so skilled at delivering.'

'You time them. I can't think straight, let alone count.'

'Breathe,' says my mother on repeat, and I throw her a dark look.

We stand waiting for the next contraction, all eyes on me. My eyes on my stomach, waiting for that hit of pain. Doug is staring at his watch. I think of Bee. Of Cyrille. It's Christmas Day. Neither of them will be available. Best-laid plans and all that. I'm seriously going it alone.

'What are we waiting for?' says my father.

'The next contraction,' says my mother.

'I think I'll go and check on the kids,' he says.

'Fine,' says my mother, his health no longer her concern, her focus entirely on me.

'Oh, God, here it comes!' I yell. 'And don't tell me to breathe.'

'You need to!'

'Eight minutes,' says Doug. 'There's still time. The roads will be empty. Let's just get you to the hospital. I'll collect what you need from your flat afterwards. '

Doug places my coat around my shoulders and I heave it off. 'Too hot,' I say. 'Just throw it in the car.'

'Sure, sure,' he says, sounding wrong-footed. 'Let's go,' he says.

'Are you going to tell the father?' asks my mother.

'You don't get it, do you?'

'Obviously not. In which case, I'm coming with you,' she says.

Doug and I stop in our tracks to stare at her.

'Well, someone needs to be with her. She can't do everything on her own.'

As we're leaving to an audience of observers, Eve holding Violet, Monty and Eddie in stunned silence, my father says, 'What about the Christmas pudding?'

'Nobody likes Christmas pudding,' says my mother.

'I do,' says my father.

'You are the last person who needs it,' she says.

Doug squeezes my hand.

Nothing makes sense any more. Nothing.

71

'Phone as soon as you've got news,' Doug says, as he leaves us in the hospital reception area. 'It doesn't matter what time of night it is, just phone. We'll stay with Dad until you're home, Ma.'

I'm taken in a wheelchair to a delivery room, relieved to have my mother by my side, no longer caring about her earlier assault.

'You're five centimetres dilated,' says the midwife. 'You're doing really well.'

'Thank you,' I say, pleased someone approves of my activity.

I walk around the room. I crouch. I lie on the bed. I walk around the room again. I lean against the wall. I squat. I rub my back fiercely. I rant and rave against the world. Against the injustice of it all. I rip at my hospital gown, then take it off, throwing myself around the room totally naked, without a care that my mother or anyone else is there.

'Do your breathing,' my mother says, at various heightened moments.

'I'm doing my fucking breathing,' I say, in between huffing and puffing.

'Please mind your language,' she implores.

'Fuck off!' I say.

But she doesn't. She stays right there by my side.

'Do you want an epidural?' she says, as she's rubbing the base of my spine.

'Anything,' I say. 'Anything!'

'It's too late,' says the midwife. 'She's nearly fully dilated. You can do this, Daisy!' she encourages.

'I don't want to,' I say. 'I want to go home.'

*　*　*

I'm sweating. Exhausted. It's long past the point of remembering my breathing.

'One last big push,' says the midwife. 'You're nearly there.'

My mother looks like she's the one doing the pushing and the breathing. 'Push, darling,' she says.

'I can see the head,' says the midwife.

My mother moves towards the end of the bed. No, I think, but I no longer have the reserves to stop her.

'I can see the head, Daisy!' she exclaims, with excitement. 'Oh, my goodness. What a lot of black hair. Oh, my goodness. Push! Come on! One last push.'

'I'm trying,' I exclaim.

'Okay,' says the midwife. 'We're going to have to wait for the next contraction but as soon as you feel it, I want you to push it out like a big poo.'

'I think I might do a poo.'

'You might,' says my mother. 'I did with Doug. Thank God your father wasn't in the room.'

'Maaaaa—' I can't finish the sentence. I feel the contraction and, with all my might, I give one massive guttural yell and push as hard as I can. It's a weird sensation. It rips through my insides.

'Here it comes,' says the midwife.

I yell. There's a tug, a sense of something slipping and suddenly all sensation subsides and there's a huge cry, a yell, even louder than mine and so much more welcome.

'Nothing wrong with this baby's lungs,' says the midwife, holding it up for me to see. 'It's a girl,' she says. 'Well done, Mother!' She puts the baby on my chest. My daughter! My daughter. I have a daughter. I stare at her through watery eyes, in total awe. She smells of sweetness and life and love.

'Would you like to cut the cord, Grandma?'

To my amazement, I hear my mother say, 'Yes.' I watch as she calmly cuts the cord and the midwife clamps it.

I cuddle and gaze. 'So that's who you are,' I say. 'I've been wondering for what feels like for ever. Welcome to the world, Baby Settle.'

All too soon, she is taken from my arms by the attending nurse to be weighed.

'Well, that was quite something,' says my mother.

'Two point four kilos!' they announce.

'What's that in pounds, please?' says my mother.

'Oh, my God!' I shout. 'There's another one coming!'

The midwife rushes to my side. 'It's only the placenta.'

'Breathe!' says my mother.

'If you say that one more time . . .'

'It's out!' says the midwife, and I breathe.

'I don't want to see it and I definitely don't want to eat it,' I say, and my mother looks at me in disgust. Finally, for the first time in what feels like days, I actually laugh.

The nurse approaches. 'Would you like to hold her again before we take her to the neonatal unit?'

I sit up, wince, my arms open, as she passes me this light-weight bundle wrapped in a cotton blanket printed with balloons, and rests her on my chest. My smile is so wide it aches.

'Are you planning on breastfeeding?'

'If I can.'

'Okay. We'll come and help you express some milk. She won't be ready to feed from you yet.'

It all sounds so clinical. So impersonal. 'I'm guessing that's normal?'

'Absolutely. But I don't think this little one will be in neonatal for long so please don't worry.'

'Can we see her later?' I ask, as they take her from me.

'Of course. The unit is just at the end of this corridor. But first you both deserve a cup of tea. I'll make sure someone brings one.'

I watch the baby leave the room, feeling this inexplicable anxiety in the pit of my stomach.

'You were amazing, Daisy,' says my mother. 'I'm so proud of you.'

'Do you mean that?' I say.

'I wouldn't have said it otherwise. You were magnificent.' She sits down at my side. 'Your language could have been better but I don't think anyone was shocked.'

'Except you!'

She laughs. 'I'm allowed.'

'Do you think she'll be okay?'

'I have no doubt she's going to thrive.'

I realize that my mother couldn't have played a bigger part in this. Fate has intervened and re-established our bond in a way we could never have planned. She has rightfully claimed back her role.

* * *

We drink our tea, the best I've ever tasted.

'I'm so tired,' I say.

406

'Me too. We should call Doug,' says my mother.

'It's five in the morning. Let him have some sleep.'

* * *

We've moved into a small anteroom where my mother is now sleeping on a camp bed at my side, fully dressed, lying on top of the sheet, purring.

I reach for my phone. It's nearly seven in the morning. I imagine Benedict's is still on silent. *The bad news is that I can't make lunch today. The good news is I gave birth to a baby girl. Merry Christmas! And congratulations. See you as soon as I'm out of here xx*

I put my phone down and finally manage to drift off to sleep.

72

'She's a very determined little girl,' says the young nurse. 'You can go and see her if you want.'

'Go,' says my mother, curling up on her sheet.

'Come with me.'

The neonatal unit is decorated with cut-out paper balloons, tinsel and glitter stars dotted on the window. I press my nose against the screen, trying to make out which cot she's in.

'You can come in,' says the nurse on duty, opening the door and beckoning us through.

I spot her mass of black hair. She's wearing a little pink bracelet, which says Baby Settle and her weight.

'Do you want to hold her?'

'She looks so peaceful, I don't want to disturb her.' I gently stroke her palm through one of the round vents at the side of her Perspex cot, avoiding the wires and tubes, and watch her perfect little fingers react.

'Let me know if you'd like to hold her. Skin-on-skin contact is good for premmies.'

'Can I, then?'

Turns out skin-on-skin contact is good for mothers too. The warmth of her, the smell of her, the living, breathing presence of her. I am at peace with myself. I am a mother. My mother stands over us and I see her eyes fill with tears.

* * *

Doug arrives with a bag full of my things. 'Congratulations, Mummy!' he says, kissing me. His face is puffy with tiredness. 'There wasn't much in that drawer, apart from a lot of notebooks, which I didn't think you'd want. A pair of booties, no vests or sleepsuits, so Eve is sorting some out for you,' he says. 'And I managed to find some toiletries you might need and the pair of pyjamas that were under your pillow. Oh, and your bathrobe.'

'Thanks, Doug,' I say. 'You're a hero. I'm desperate to get into my own stuff. And to clean my teeth.'

'She was amazing,' says my mother, hugging Doug. 'Is Dad okay?'

'He's fine. The kids loved staying over. Eve is making everyone breakfast.'

'Do you want to come and see her?' I ask, tying my bathrobe around my bump.

'Am I allowed?'

'I think so. Just a peek.'

* * *

'This is my brother,' I tell the nurse. We stand over the cot and I put my hand through the vent to stroke her again.

'Oh, Daise, she's so sweet,' he says. 'Well done! You're amazing. To think it could merely have been another sprout fart.'

* * *

My mother stands up as soon as we come back into the room. 'Well, I think we should make a move,' she says, stifling a yawn. She starts to arrange the sheets on her camp bed. 'Now are you going to be okay here on your own?'

'It's how it's got to be. I'll manage.'

There's a knock on the door.

I organize my bathrobe. 'Come in,' I say.

A face peers into the room. 'I'm so sorry. Am I interrupting family time?'

'Come in, Doctor,' says my mother, touching her hair, looking weirdly awestruck.

Benedict and I exchange awkward grins.

'This is Benedict,' I say. 'A friend.'

'Oh,' says my mother, thrown off course. 'We were just leaving.'

I can see Doug registering immediately.

'Doug,' he says, holding up his hand. 'Good to meet you.'

'And you,' says Benedict. 'Congratulations.' He goes to shake my mother's hand, then my brother's.

'Thank you!' says my mother, who is starting to register what is happening.

'I'm taking you home,' says Doug.

My mother's tired eyes are sparkling. 'Nice to meet you, Benedict.' She smirks. She thinks she knows but she's not sure. Either way, she's okay with it. I know she is. I can read her. After all, she's my mother (again!).

Benedict shifts back to let them move past him to get to the door.

My mother looks round at me. 'Him?' she mouths.

I shuffle my eyebrows. 'Thank you for everything,' I say, blowing her a kiss.

73

Benedict comes over to the bed and kisses my cheek. 'Congratulations,' he says. 'How are you? How is she?'

'I'm kind of blindsided,' I say. 'I mean, you just showed up. That was brave.'

'What choice? You weren't answering your phone. I needed to know everything was okay.'

'Damn! It's on silent. I forgot. Sorry!' I grab his hand. 'She's good. She's going to be okay.'

He almost collapses with relief. 'Thank goodness. I mean, she's a baby in a hurry, isn't she?'

I smile at him. 'Ready to meet her?'

* * *

I hear Benedict inhale deeply. He leans down and strokes her hand with his little finger. 'I can't believe this,' he says. 'I'm simply overwhelmed. She's so tiny yet so perfect. Do you think she'll be all right?'

'She'll be just fine,' says the nurse. 'Would you like to hold her?'

Benedict looks at me.

I nod.

'Yes, if that's okay?' he says. 'I mean, she looks so small.'

'She'll fit into your palms.' I smile.

Benedict sits down next to the cot and the nurse passes

him the baby. She goes to yell and he looks on in shock, then jiggles her lightly and she settles immediately.

'You're a natural,' I say.

'She weighs nothing!' he says, exhaling deeply.

'I'll have you know she weighs two kilos four.'

'Is that good?'

'It is for a little premmie,' says the nurse.

'I think I might have microwaved her for the final weeks. She looks pretty cooked.'

'She's perfect,' says Benedict.

*　*　*

We go back to my room and I climb onto the bed. My mother's camp bed sits there reminding me of her being at my side. Never in my wildest dreams! None of this. If it's a dream, please don't wake me.

Benedict sits on the chair next to the bed, clearly dazzled by it all.

I tell him about the events of Christmas Day and he listens in disbelief and tells me I was lucky. That I might have been on my own when it happened but I was with the right people, precisely the ones who needed to be with me.

'And now you're here,' I say. 'How do you feel?'

'Speechless,' he says. 'Taking it all in. The reality of it.'

'Is that what made you decide to "come out of the closet"?'

He laughs. 'I didn't make that decision. It was made for me.'

I ponder on how strange life is. How Fate has yet again intervened, realigning the balance of my universe.

'Listen,' I say. 'There's something I feel I have to tell you, something I've been wanting to say for a very long time.'

He looks at me, his face regaining its colour, wondering.

I start my unrehearsed speech. 'This has been the most extraordinary thing that could ever have happened to me. You are the most extraordinary thing that's ever happened to me. Knowing you're here has made me strong. I know I can be a solo mother and yet not be alone. That if I reach out, you're there to catch me and sometimes I don't even need to reach out.'

He smiles, as though agreeing.

'I'm so glad we risked going down this route together. I feel so lucky. I have you and I have family and I have friends. And you are the greatest friend of all. And I need to say this too . . .' I swallow hard, knowing I'm about to make myself vulnerable but feeling strangely invincible. 'I really love you, Benedict. I love what we have. I love that we don't need to be with one another twenty-four seven. That we have enough. And now we have a daughter. Who could ask for anything more?'

He presses at the inner corners of his eyes and lets out a deep sigh. 'Oh, Daisy Settle,' he says, puffing his cheeks, taking my hand. 'You've rocked my world. I knew when I sat waiting for you in that damned taxi, on that horrible rainy night, that something massive was going to happen. That Fate was opening a door, daring me to walk through it. And on the other side there you were, rattling my cage. Telling me I had to get out there and start to live again. And now look at us! We risked a shot at something with no guarantees, agreeing an arrangement that smashes through convention.' I'm not sure if he's laughing or crying or both but I'm definitely crying. 'And she's arrived! The best Christmas present of all time.' He plays with my fingers, absently stroking them. 'Look what's happened to us, Daisy. Out of our shared grief has come new life.' I see him feel for his wedding ring and touch it for a moment, like he's telling Lisa it's okay.

'New life!' I say, through tears. 'How beautiful is that?'

'And I love you too, Daisy. Thank you for being brave enough to say it. I've wanted to say it for a long time but there was never the right moment.'

I smile. 'There's no such thing as the right moment. You should just think "fuck it!" and do it!'

He laughs. 'I'm not sure that's quite my style.'

'Oh, it is,' I say.

He scoffs. 'In what way?'

'I never told you, but I wrote a Fuck It list.'

'You mean a Bucket list.'

'No, really. A Fuck It list. I wrote it when I was at a crossroads; not knowing whether I was brave enough to start IVF. Or if I was even capable of being a solo mother. But then I thought . . . fuck it! I've always wanted to be a mother, and I may be terrified but who wouldn't be? So I'm going to do it.'

'And you did.'

'Exactly. But I failed.'

He dips his chin.

'No, I did. But you . . . you set this in motion. And even though we were both scared of what might lie ahead, we stared down the fear and we did it! You see! It is your style.'

'And it worked.'

I press my fingers into the corners of my eyes. 'Yeah,' I say.

He smiles, his head nodding from side to side. 'And we'll continue making it work,' he says. 'We'll prove that we can be a different kind of parent. We'll fumble our way forward together apart. And you and the baby will dictate my role.'

'Holly,' I say. 'I think I'd like to call her Holly.'

He beams a smile. 'Holly Settle,' he says. 'Who knew?'

'The universe,' I say. 'The universe knew all along.'

Acknowledgements

Huge thanks to Zita West, who introduced me to the solo mother community via Becky Kearns (@definingmum), who in turn introduced me to Jocelyn Bull (@motheringsolo) and Mel Johnson (@the_stork_and_i). And to Francesca Cavallerio. Thank you all for sharing your incredible stories with me. I am in awe of your courage, determination and fortitude. Although Daisy's story is her own, you are very much a part of it.

Sophie Wilson. Thank you for pummelling me into discovering precisely what I wanted to achieve with this book and giving me the confidence to do it.

To my wise agent Felicity Blunt. Thank you for your faith in me and for saying, 'You've done it before, you can do it again,' which left me wondering what the hell I'd done before. The truth is you can't put your finger on it, but I think I've done it again. To Rosie Pierce and Sharika Teelwah, your appreciation of my work and your resilience in reading endless (sometimes appalling) manuscripts meant so much. Thank you! And Susanna Wadeson. Big heads up to my lovely, patient, impatient, brutal, kind editor. I know I frustrated you along the way, but we made it to the end of the marathon, and I couldn't be more grateful to you for allowing me my pace and getting me over the finishing line.

To my copy editor Hazel Orme, thank you for laughing so hard you had to stop reading for ten minutes! And my cover designer Marianne Issa-El-Khoury for brilliantly encapsulating Daisy's drive and determination. A special thanks to my publicist Chloe Rose and marketing supremo Sophie MacVeigh.

To my readers: Basi Akpabio, Mandy Ayres, Sue Barnes, Genevieve Nikolopulos and Mary Weaver. Thank you for bravely wading through early drafts which would never see the light of day! A special thanks to Victoria Dry for your wry observations and input. Mwah! To Neil Masters of CantorMasters (the Cantor was me for five minutes!) for checking my interior design authenticity. And to Claire Ewings who read the closest to a final draft and cried at the end. Who could ask for anything more? As always grazie to Federico Andornino for your constant support and advice, despite becoming incredibly important!

To my family for allowing me to disappear into a manuscript fog and for not noticing! My sons, Alexander (who won't read this book) and Joseph (who will). The new additions to the gang, Talia and Rosie, and the newest addition, my first granddaughter, Noa Rae. I may never get to see the woman you become but I hope you will be confident, kind and tall!

Finally, Mabel. Yes, the dog gets a credit again. Trust me, she deserves it.

About the Author

Melanie Cantor worked for many years in PR and as a celebrity talent agent. She also dabbled in interior renovations, which led to her hosting the Channel 4 series *Making Space*, in which she tidied up people's messy houses. She has since concentrated on writing. Her first novel, *Life & Other Happy Endings*, was published in 2019. She has two grown-up sons and lives in Dorset and London with her dog, Mabel.

If you have enjoyed *The F**k It! List*, you'll love this too . . .

'Brilliantly funny and thought-provoking – an absolute joy'
Rosie Walsh, author of *The Man Who Didn't Call*

Three letters. Two mistakes. One last chance.

When Jennifer Cole is told she has three months to live she decides to write three letters sharing the desires, fears and frustrations she has always kept to herself. And, at first, she finds that telling the truth makes her feel free and liberated.

But three months later, Jennifer's secrets are alive and out in the world . . . and so is she. As she discovers, sometimes the truth has a way of surprising you . . .